ABOUT THE AUTHOR

DOROTHY EDEN was born in New Zealand and for many years has lived in London. A versatile and prolific author, she is known for her period and historical fiction, as well as for her suspense and modern Gothic novels. Among her many bestselling books are *WAITING FOR WILLA, MELBURY SQUARE, AN AFTERNOON WALK,* and *SPEAK TO ME OF LOVE.*

Sleep in the Woods

Dorothy Eden

A FAWCETT CREST BOOK

Fawcett Publications, Inc., Greenwich, Conn.

SLEEP IN THE WOODS

THIS BOOK CONTAINS THE COMPLETE TEXT OF THE
ORIGINAL HARDCOVER EDITION.

A Fawcett Crest Book reprinted by arrangement with Coward-
McCann & Geoghegan, Inc.

Library of Congress Catalog Card Number: 61-6835

Printed in the United States of America
October 1972

I will make with them a covenant of peace, and
will call the evil beast to cease out of the land:
and they shall dwell safely in the wilderness,
and sleep in the woods.

EZEKIEL XXXIV. 24

Author's Note

For the purposes of the story the author has en-
larged the area of Te Kooti's campaign in the
North Island of New Zealand. The episode re-
lated concerning his famous flag, the Whip, is
fictitious.

CHAPTER 1

Just after midday the wind dropped. Briar, at last, was able to proceed with the packing and fastening of the trunks unaccompanied by the sickening pitch and sway that made her head spin dizzily, but which did much more devastating things to Sophia and Mrs. Crewe.

Although they were in sight of land, Mrs. Crewe had to take to her bunk for the twentieth time during the voyage. Sophia, however, threw off her malaise and went for a last walk on the deck.

"When you've finished packing, see what Prudence is doing," Mrs. Crewe instructed Briar weakly. "Goodness knows, she can't come to much harm now, within an hour of arriving, and in broad daylight, but never will I undertake to chaperone two young ladies on a long voyage again. Never!"

Briar looked at the plump prostrate ineffectual woman with guarded contempt. All the way from England she had fussed like a hen with a hatching of ducklings who constantly escaped her into the water, and Prudence and Sophia had giggled behind her back and gone their flirtatious way. At least, Sophia had bestowed her attentions on all and sundry with a careless gregariousness, but Prudence had fallen in love with the handsome second officer, and was already in anguish at the thought of parting. She was probably regarding Mrs. Crewe's indisposition as heaven-sent, Briar reflected.

But nothing much could happen now except a prolonged farewell. For they were within hours of landing.

Briar folded the last of the girls' voluminous muslin and silk gowns with her meticulous care. The ship tipped a little, and through the porthole she caught a glimpse of wooded hillside. Suddenly uncontrollable excitement seized her. Casting a quick look at Mrs. Crewe's humped back, she crushed the billowing materials heedlessly into the trunk, banged the lid, and ran from the cabin on to the deck.

A sharp cool breeze and brilliant sunshine struck her. Across the blue bay the hills, as bare as a plucked chicken on the summits and with the green bush running like water down

7

the hollows and crevices, rose in an encircling wall. In the distance, at the foot of the hills and rising thinly up their sides, lay the scattered buildings of the township. No, not a township. A town. An aspiring city. Wellington, the capital of New Zealand.

That little cluster of buildings towered over by the hills and the windy sky! The place they had all spoken of so optimistically during the long voyage, where Mrs. Crewe was to join her son and daughter-in-law, and where Prudence and Sophia were to find husbands.

No one had said much about what Briar was to find, but then what was she looking for, poor little thing? She wouldn't expect much after what she had come from, a good position as housekeeper, or perhaps marriage to an honest, sober type of immigrant who wouldn't enquire too closely into her antecedents.

"Aunt Charity will find you a husband," Sophia had said blithely. "She just loves marrying off people. That's why she's sent for Prudence and me. She says she's always longed for daughters, and the colony needs gentlewomen, but really she's only looking for the fun of arranging weddings. She promised Mamma she'd see we got well-bred husbands, so I haven't a doubt that when Prue and I are settled she'll find someone for you, too. Though you're such a prickly little thing, aren't you? I don't know who'll marry you."

Briar's chin went in the air, but she forced herself to reply meekly, "I don't expect your aunt to find me a husband, Miss Sophia." "There you are, you see!" said Sophia. "You mustn't be so hoity toity. It's out of place for someone in your position. I don't expect Prue and I would keep you a day if we were back in England. But here we are in the back of beyond where goodness knows if we'd ever find another maid—" she shrugged her pretty plump shoulders— "and now we've been so much together we're really quite fond of you. I'll speak to Aunt Charity myself. She'll know of some suitable young man."

"No! Don't you dare!" cried Briar, then bit her tongue. "Please, Miss Sophia. I don't really want a husband. At least, not one that's found for me."

"Oh well, if you're going to be too proud! Silly little creature! You'd be quite pretty if you had more colour and more flesh on your bones. Did your family starve you as a child?"

"No!" said Briar fiercely.

"Well, don't get angry about it. I'm just giving you advice. And I'm sure Prue and I won't scorn Aunt Charity's help to find husbands. I long to have one. Goodness me, I'm twenty! I'm getting old!"

But Prudence had fallen in love with Second Officer Edmund Wheeler, and her face, less round and jolly than Sophia's, was already getting wan and strained as the inevitable farewells drew near. For Edmund was a penniless younger son with only his career as a sailor, and it wasn't likely that Aunt Charity would permit such a marriage. That was, if Edmund was serious. Everyone said never trust a sailor . . .

Marriage! The girls and Mrs. Crewe talked of nothing else. Briar was weary of the subject. Was there nothing else in life? And if that were so, what was her life to be? A servant and an orphan who did not even know who her parents had been, who had been rescued out of the dead arms of her mother in a ditch by a passing farmer who heard her feeble cries.

The farmer had been a rustic with a poetic turn of mind, and had said, as from her dirty bundle of clothes she gave him her fleeting tremulous smile. "A liddle briar rose, that's what she be. Growing in a ditch."

He had taken her home to his wife, and the police had buried the unknown girl who had been, one presumed, her mother. She had grown up with the farmer's own brood of children until she was old enough to be sent out to her first position. The farmer's wife had been kind enough, but had never really cared for the thin little changeling, and was relieved to see her go. She had been rescued from death, and was now given a good start in the world. Neither the farmer nor his wife had anything on their consciences. And Briar, aged nine years, was taken into the home of a schoolmaster and his wife to be fed and clothed and educated a little (because Andrew Gaunt was a born teacher and could as little tolerate illiteracy as starvation), in return for multitudinous household duties.

The next seven years were Briar's first and only taste of happiness. She had a quick eager mind, and Andrew Gaunt, somewhat to his own astonishment, had found himself not only acquainting her with the English classics, but with the French, and also with a little Latin and Greek. He corrected her rustic accent and encouraged her instinctive good taste.

His lean scholarly face was the only one she had ever grown to love. When he died she was desolate.

Another position had to be found, because his widow was left too poor even to be able to feed an extra mouth. That was when, hiding her intellectual ability (for no one required a maid with a knowledge of the classics and a love, of all things, for the works of Montaigne), she obtained employment with a clergyman's widow, and later with a Mrs. Carruthers, the mother of Sophia and Prudence.

Here, there was a household of five girls, a Jane Austen Mrs. Bennet's household, Briar had told herself, all of them to be married, and none of them beautiful or witty enough to compensate for her lack of dowry. So that when the suggestion came from their mother's sister-in-law in New Zealand that she longed for one or perhaps two of the dear girls to come out to her—she had a large house, the climate was ideal, and marriageable young men abounded—poor distracted Mrs. Carruthers leapt at the opportunity and arranged to send the two eldest, Sophia and Prudence, in the care, of course, of a suitable chaperon and accompanied by a maid.

Briar had been judged to be about three months old when she had been discovered in her dying mother's arms. Her rescuers had subsequently been able to tell her nothing about her mother beyond the fact that the young woman had had a fine silk petticoat, strangely enough, beneath her ragged cloak, and had been very young. This had been material enough for Briar's inventive and lonely mind to feed on. Her mother had been a lady forsaken by her lover, or perhaps a young widow with no one to whom to turn. But she had fiercely loved her baby. That was one thing Briar always insisted to herself. She, whom her foster parents had merely tolerated as a stray kitten, and then whose quick sharp mind Andrew Gaunt, the schoolmaster, had played on . . . But her mother had loved her. That she knew. And some day, some day . . .

Her incoherent longings ended in genuine deceit. She lied to the Carruthers about her family. She said she had parents in Devon who were too poor to keep her at home. But they wrote her letters, of course, and were deeply interested in her well-being.

Before this deceit could be found out the tremendous excitement of the voyage to New Zealand had come up.

Briar would never forget that interview with Mrs. Carruthers.

"Briar, if I asked you to go to New Zealand with Sophia and Prudence, would your parents agree?"

Briar's heart leaped in awful excitement. She felt as if a clean cold wind from the ends of the earth were blowing in her face. A new country, a new start, the chance to be somebody, a person who sloughed off all her memories except those of dear Mr. Gaunt and the slim young girl in the silk petticoat who had closed her loving arms round her baby even as she died . . .

Confused and terribly excited, Briar could not define her emotions. And before she could speak Mrs. Carruthers was going on, "Of course, you would have to want to go yourself. I wouldn't ask you to do such a tremendous thing against your will. But it seems to me a young thing like you might well have better prospects out there than here—they say a great many honest labouring men are immigrating, and wanting wives. You would have to promise, of course, to perform your duties with my daughters as long as they needed you. And to behave correctly. But you seem to be a quiet intelligent girl who knows her place. Now supposing I write to your parents—"

"No, let me, let me!" Briar cried. Then remembering herself she added, "Please let me, ma'am. I can persuade them to almost anything if I try. They don't like to refuse me, you see." Her lashes were downcast, hiding her brilliant eyes, dilated with excitement. "I'd dearly like to go, ma'am. And I do promise you I'd look after Miss Sophia and Miss Prudence."

Mrs. Carruthers smiled tolerantly. "You're younger than either of them, but I believe you have a lot of sense in that little head. Very well, write your letter yourself, and let me know when you receive an answer. By the way, who taught you to write?"

Briar lifted demure eyes. "My father, ma'am."

A few days later Briar, with the deliberately mis-spelt letter purporting to be from her mother, went to Mrs. Carruthers and gasped, "I can go, ma'am. Oh, ma'am, I'm so happy!"

"What do you think *you're* going to find in this strange country?" Mrs. Carruthers said dryly. "Very well, child, you must have the true pioneering spirit. Now remember, I trust you to behave as befits your position in life, in all situations. Do you understand?"

Long ago, twelve whole weeks ago in England, she had

11

nodded gravely and said yes, she understood. But already, with the clean cold wind in her face, and the dark hills looming nearer, she felt an uncontrollable reaching out to something that awaited her, something that would make her a real person, an individual, someone of whom voices would say tenderly and lovingly, "Here's Briar come!"

Mrs. Carruthers and her bouncing unmarried daughters were suddenly the people who were unreal . . .

It had been a long long voyage with patches of tedium, humour and tragedy. There had been gales, and periods of hot airless calm, fights had broken out in the steerage, and flirtations had progressed on the upper deck. Two babies had been born, one to die almost at once and the other to be kept alive with milk from the unhappy Devonshire cow, Daisy, incarcerated below, the property of an optimistic young settler who prayed that he would get her to her destination alive. There had been an outbreak of measles, that most dreaded of shipboard complaints, and seven of the children had died.

The woman, Jemima Potter, who had the fragile new baby, lost two of her four other children, and it was Briar who stood at her side when the two small bodies, almost too weightless to sink, were slid into the curling waves. Jemima recognised an instinctive sympathy in the slim, soberly dressed girl with the shut face, and a bond sprang up between them. Jemima was only twenty-six, and had already borne her phlegmatic husband, Fred Potter, five children. Now three survived, and Briar saw deep apprehension in her face as to what the new country would do to the remaining children. But Fred had wanted to go somewhere where he could have his own little patch of ground to grow potatoes, so they had come. It seemed as if his freedom had been purchased at very great cost.

These were the only friends whom Briar had made on the voyage, and it was to them she turned when at last the anchor ran down into the blue depths of the bay.

She slipped below to find them in the mêlée of trunks, bags and milling people.

"We're here, Jemima!" she cried. "Just imagine! We're here."

"Why, Briar, you look downright pretty when you're excited. All flushed, like a rose."

Briar laughed. "Don't waste time paying me compliments. Let's get up on deck. Here, I'll take the baby."

"What about your mistresses?"

"Oh, they can take care of themselves for once."

"That's no way to talk, Briar," said Fred Potter, in his ponderous way. "You may be in a new country, but you're still in the same station in life."

"Yes, you're still a servant, love," said Jemima anxiously. "You're dependent on them."

Behave as befits your position in life . . . came the echo of Mrs. Carruthers' voice.

Briar tossed her head, spinning her dark curls. Her eyes were a brilliant green, her cheeks glowing. She could not understand the excitement that possessed her, as of some strange unexpressed dream about to come true.

"I won't be a servant for long. You'll see!"

On the top deck, Sophia looked impatiently about her. Where was Prudence? Where was Briar? Where was Mrs. Crewe—though one didn't want her clickety-clacking in one's ears any more. More important still, where was Captain Bower, who had been so flattering to her, always complimenting her, and Geoffrey Standish, the owner of that absurd cow, Daisy? Geoffrey had probably disappeared to see to Daisy's welfare over the last stage of the journey, and Prue, the scamp, was hidden somewhere behind the lifeboats with her Edmund. She'd have to get over that infatuation, Sophia reflected practically. Aunt Charity wouldn't stand any nonsense about penniless sailors. She would have the most eligible young men lined up. After all, she was the Governor's cousin, and virtually the leader of society.

Really, what did it matter that one stood alone at the rail at this last moment? Everyone on this mortally dull ship would matter less than nothing in a few days. She, Sophie, was much prettier than Prue, and anyway Prue would be looking pale and sulky, as she always did when she was unhappy. She would be the one to sweep the young men of Wellington off their feet and be the belle of the city.

Aunt Charity had written about Government House balls, and week-end parties at country houses, and all kinds of sophisticated festivities. With those new gowns, the latest fashions from London and Paris that Briar was packing, everyone would gasp with admiration. "There goes Miss Sophia Carruthers, niece of the Governor, catch of the season . . ."

Oh, yes, one would do very well in this new country.

But it was rather unbecoming to be standing here alone, as if one were the most unpopular young woman on board ship. Sophia stamped her foot pettishly. Where *was* Prudence?

In the cabin, becoming conscious of the diminished motion of the ship, Mrs. Crewe stirred and sighed, then heaved her bulk off the bunk. One would have to pull oneself together. One would be going ashore presently, and would have to present the young ladies in good order, and no fault of hers if they were not still virgins.

Relations of the Governor. Well, perhaps. But who was the Governor of a small new country like this? Miss Sophia and Miss Prudence might find they gave themselves airs in vain. They'd end up marrying hobbledehoy farmers or bank clerks, and doing their own housework, most likely. And that wouldn't do them any harm. Indeed, it might be that that snippet of a maid with her secret face and her deceptive meekness might do as well. It was a free country, they said. Conventions went by the board. Even barmaids married the gentry. And as for those dark-skinned Maoris with their war cries and their tattooed faces . . . Mrs. Crewe shuddered violently and thought she was going to be ill again. She wished she were back in England. Chaperon to the Governor's kinswomen or not. And was that sly Prudence still a virgin?

Mrs. Crewe need not have given serious thought to the latter possibility. Prudence had been far too strictly brought up to behave without decorum. Besides, she had the vaguest notion as to what constituted marriage, and thought that the faint trembling and dizziness that seized her when Edmund looked deeply into her eyes was due to some odd infirmity peculiar to herself. Once indeed, when only the light from the mizzenmast shone and phosphorescence eerily lighted up the sea, he had dared to snatch a kiss, but she had sprung away, shocked and confused. *That* sort of thing, at least, waited until after marriage.

But would he ever be able to marry her? Did he truly want to? She admitted to herself honestly that she and Sophie were the prettiest girls on board. Sophie, with her fair skin and round ingenuous pale blue eyes, was really the prettier, but at the time Edmund had become aware of them Sophie had been daringly flirting with the captain himself.

So Edmund had declared that he had eyes for no one but Prudence, and one had believed him because one had so longed to. And certainly his conversation had retained its ardent quality even up until this last day, even if now and then his eyes had seemed to wander. Once Prudence had realised he was staring at Briar, who had just come up the companionway and was ruffling her hair in the wind in a rather bold and languorous way. Briar, a maidservant! A little plain thing in her grey dress.

She must have imagined the flash of interest in Edmund's eyes on that occasion.

Certainly now, as the encircling hills grew closer, one could not complain about his undivided attention.

"Prue, my love! I may call on you at your aunt's?"

Prudence hesitated, then burst out boldly as Sophie would have done, "I'm afraid that will depend on your intentions. Aunt Charity is, I believe, very strict. At least, Mamma said—"

A strong hand came over hers, sending delightful tremors through her. "But, my dear Prue! You must know what I would like my intentions to be. The devil of it is, I have no money. I shall have to do several more voyages until I can save enough to buy land. Once one can buy land, fortunes are to be made."

"Fortunes!"

"Of course. All pioneers make their fortunes. Especially if they're lucky enough to buy land with gold on it."

"Oh, Edmund! If only you could!"

"Why shouldn't I?" His bright eyes rested on her. "Prue —I know I should speak to your aunt or your uncle first, but will you wait for me?"

"How old are you?" she asked, the enormous significance of his question suddenly reducing her to a strange calm.

"I'm nineteen. Old enough, goodness knows."

"So am I. Sophie's twenty, and no one has asked her yet to be his wife. So I'm the first," she finished breathlessly. "Oh, I don't mean I'm just gloating over Sophie. Edmund, we wouldn't be too old if we had to wait three years, say. Or even four. You'd have saved enough money by then, wouldn't you? And the time would go by. I could be making my trousseau, twelve of everything. Oh, Edmund, do you really mean it?"

"At the moment," he said recklessly, "there's nothing I want more than to kiss you. Oh, the devil!"

"Here's Sophie," said Prudence, trying to compose her face. "Sophie, Edmund and I are just saying goodbye."

"So I can see," returned her sister tartly. "Do you need to take quite so long about it? I should think Edmund had

15

other duties. Briar's disappeared, and Mrs. Crewe is putting on her cloak and bonnet. She says we must do the same. We're going ashore at any moment, thank heaven for that. I, for one, shan't be sorry to see the last of this ship. Indeed," she added, her habitual good humour returning, "when I get on dry land I shall kick up my heels just as poor old Daisy will when she gets to pasture. If Aunt Charity hasn't made plans for our amusement, we shall make our own!"

CHAPTER 2

The lace curtains billowed inwards in a sudden gust of wind, and Aunt Charity's large, fretted face appeared at the window.

"Drat this wind! Will it never stop!" She looked across the bay, and suddenly cried in great excitement, "Hubert! The *Mary Louise* is in! Hubert, come at once!"

When no voice answered her, she lumbered with more speed than grace to the door. She was small in stature, but definitely plump. Indeed, she strangely resembled the furnishings in her large draughty wood-framed house, where all the chairs were solidly padded and curved in shape, and all the cushions stuffed to bursting point. She was an animated cushion herself, tucked in at the waist, and swelling in rich curves above and below. Her little puffed hands were ornamented with several heavy gold rings, and her feet encased in elegant high-heeled boots, seldom visible beneath her flowing skirts. She wore a white lace cap threaded with black velvet ribbon which tied under her chin. Her mouth was too small in her large face, and tucked in in a self-willed manner, her eyes darted busily all the time, and her forehead was constantly knitted into anxiety of some kind.

It was obvious from the way she moved, and the restlessness of her face, that her tongue, too, was seldom still.

"Hubert, where are you? Don't you hear me? The *Mary Louise* is in. The dear girls will be here any moment."

She clattered down the stairs, not fast because of her bulk, but noisily, causing her husband at his desk to brace himself slightly.

"Oh, there you are, Hubert. Didn't you hear me telling

16

you the ship's in. She's dropped anchor already. Oh, how can you be so unmoved?"

In comparison with her restlessness, her husband was ponderously calm. He was also almost always preoccupied with affairs of the country, and even now, with the broad windows of his study framing the blue bay, and the little ship lying at anchor, his manner remained tolerantly withdrawn.

"They're your nieces, my love. As I told you at the beginning, they're entirely your affair. I can see weddings in your face already," unconsciously he sagged a little, "and all this endless feminine fuss and flurry."

"Now, Hubert, you're not to look so far ahead. There'll be plenty of parties and fun before there are weddings. We have to show the dear girls what colonial life can be. I expect they think they've come to the wilds!"

"So they have," said Hubert gloomily. "I've just had word from up north. The Maoris mean serious trouble again. They've embarked on a religious war now, and you know what that can mean." He looked briefly at his wife's face and added, "Or perhaps you don't."

"All I know is they can be a lot of howling savages, but that's in the bush country and doesn't need to concern us. We're perfectly safe."

"We're in New Zealand, my love. We've made it our country. We've got to be concerned about its troubles whether they're on our own doorstep or not. This Te Kooti is a fanatic. He's reverted to cannibalism, you know. I've a description here of a white soldier, one of your boys, my dear, being prepared for cooking."

"Cooking!" Aunt Charity echoed faintly.

Hubert Carruthers shot a glance at his wife's outraged face. Suddenly he was filled with anger that she should be so stupid, and have her head filled with nothing but frivolous parties and match-makings, when such terrible things were going on in this country which already he loved. He was no match for her domineering nature. He would dearly have liked children of his own, sons to give to this wild fertile country teeming with opportunities, and that Charity, despite her abundant body, had not been able to do this for him disappointed him deeply. But that she could derive such satisfaction from the arrival of two unknown nieces, and the opportunity to give vent to her match-making talents, filled him with obscure resentment.

He indulged in one of his few small revenges. "Listen to

this," he said, almost with relish. " 'I watched the preparation of the body of the white soldier for the warrior's feast. The head was first cut off with a tomahawk, and then the body was cut open and prepared as a butcher prepares a beast he has killed. The body was laid on red-hot stones in the bottom of the earth-oven so that the outer skin could be scraped off easily—' "

"Hubert, stop! This is barbarous. You're making me ill."

"Listen!" he commanded. "This is your country. You must be concerned with what goes on in it. 'Water was then poured over the hot stones to create the steam which was to cook the meal, and green leaves were spread on top of the stones. The body was cut up into convenient portions so as to cook thoroughly. The thickest pieces of meat were cut from the thighs. The hands were laid with the palms uppermost, because when they were cooked they curled up, and the hollow palm was full of gravy, which was a great delicacy to the Maori . . .' "

Aunt Charity's face, by now, was filled with a terrible fascination. Her mouth had fallen open a little, and her eyes at last were still.

" 'The body of the *pakeha* or white man took between two and three hours to cook. Then the oven was uncovered and the contents carried in small flax baskets, with kumara and fernroot. It was usual also to cook some of the young curly fronds of ground fern with the meat. It added to its flavour.' "

"Hubert! I must sit down."

Hubert, a little remorseful now, sprang to lead her to a chair.

"I'm sorry, my love. But these things are going on now, perhaps at this very moment, while you have your head full of nothing but social activities."

Aunt Charity, although still pretending faintness, for a gently-bred woman should never never have to listen to, much less witness such ghastly happenings, was possessed of a secretly tough nature. It would be unwomanly not to faint at such descriptions, but had she been brought face to face with these savages she would have showed a commendable amount of courage and resilience.

Besides, she hadn't an acute imagination. Her mind was still almost fully occupied with the bedroom upstairs awaiting her guests, with the anxiety as to whether the girls would be attractive and vivacious and worthy of her efforts on their

18

behalf, and what new fashions from London they would have brought to this sadly benighted and isolated country.

"Hubert, I forbid you to talk to Prudence and Sophia like this, and scare them out of their wits."

"They must know what to expect."

"But nothing like that will happen to them! They're going to live safely here with us."

"You're determined to find husbands for these young ladies, my dear. Isn't it conceivable they may marry young settlers who are moving into the bush country?"

"Oh, no, Hubert, that isn't at all likely." Aunt Charity, embarked on her favourite subject, became garrulous. "I've already decided that Peter Fanshawe will be ideally suitable for one of them. Such a nice boy, and of very good family. And he is settling down nicely in your bank, isn't he?"

"He hasn't a brain in his pretty head," Hubert grumbled. "Oh, yes, he'll make a good enough bank clerk. Nothing more."

"He's a very handsome young man!" Aunt Charity declared indignantly. "And if he isn't too devoted to his work—well, what young man is at his age? Besides, it isn't too important, is it? He has a very nice inheritance, I understand. I thought if he were to build on that piece of land overlooking the harbour, when it has been cleared of flax and tussocks —I predict it will be one of the best areas."

Hubert's heavy brows were raised in their tolerant whimsical line. His account of the cannibal feast had temporarily eased him of his vague resentment and dissatisfaction with his wife. "And having built Fanshawe's house for him, and installed in it Prudence or Sophia, what do you propose doing with Sophia or Prudence?"

"Well, do you know, I can't make up my mind about Desmond Burke or Allan Greaves, or perhaps Gabriel Brown."

"I'm surprised you haven't mentioned Saul Whitmore."

"I almost don't dare to," Aunt Charity declared, with sudden vivacity. "He's so elusive. Martha Burke declares he will never marry, he's too much of the lone wolf type. And then there's his mother who terrifies young girls. Susan Chittaway was reduced to tears after only five minutes' conversation. But I must say Susan is a mouse if ever there was one. One must admit, however," her eyes grew dreamy, "that Saul is a tremendous catch. First cousin to an earl, and only second in the line of succession. Mrs. Cooper would give her diamonds to see her daughter married to him, but then she'd

19

not hesitate to throw poor Amanda to the wolves. And I never did think much of her diamonds, anyway. They're out of place in this simple community."

"Saul," said Hubert mildly, "is, I understand, only a single wolf, not a whole pack. And he might, at that, be preferable to Te Kooti and his Hauhaus. Besides, my dear, didn't I see you wearing your diamond and ruby brooch last evening?"

"That was for dinner at Government House. One has to wear something! One isn't entirely reduced to savagery, as we will show these two dear creatures arriving today."

"And Saul Whitmore, I might point out, has bought land in the Taranaki district."

"I know. He's built a very fine house, I'm told. That does seem to give the lie to his intended bachelorhood, doesn't it?"

"Oh, indeed, indeed. Young Saul doesn't look the celibate type to me. But if you're planning to marry Prudence or Sophia to him, let's hope they're not timid creatures, scared of mice."

"Oh, I never thought Saul was that terrifying," Aunt Charity said comfortably.

"I wasn't referring to Saul, my love. I was pointing out that he has built his house in the Taranaki district. If I'm not wrong in my predictions it will be right in the heart of the Hauhau country. So let's hope your little nieces, or one of them, can stand up against a Hauhau attack. It's quite blood-chilling, I believe. Their war cry is like the bark of a savage dog, and their bare brown bodies and tattooed faces—"

"Hubert! Stop that indecency at once! I won't listen to another word. If Saul Whitmore takes a bride into the Taranaki country he will be well able to look after her. Anyway, I haven't time to stand here gossiping. I must go up and see that the girls' room is quite ready. That new girl, Polly, she's lazy Irish if ever there was one. I wonder if Prudence and Sophia would have preferred a room each? I did think they might be happier together at first. And that best bedroom really is a large airy one. Besides, there's the maid to be accommodated, too. That's if she stays. From what I know of girls nowadays she'll leave the moment she sets foot ashore. She'll have her eyes open for the nearest man. Marriage! That's all they think of."

"But aren't you planning her marriage, my dear?" her husband asked suavely.

Aunt Charity glared at him. "Don't be ridiculous, Hubert!

She's a servant. Although I'll do my best to see she doesn't get into trouble. One has that duty at least."

"Don't let it fret you, Charity. New Zealand needs sons and daughters."

"But not outside matrimony!" his wife snapped.

"Which room are you allotting?"

"I've told you, the big north bedroom. It gets all the sun, and has a beautiful view."

"I was speaking of the maid."

"Oh, her! Really, why do you ask? She'll go in the servant's quarters, of course. The little room next the kitchen. She'll have it entirely to herself. Surely you can't accuse me of not treating my servants well!"

Before ordering the carriage (the Carruthers were one of the few families in Wellington who could boast a carriage), Aunt Charity had time to go upstairs and cast a last critical eye over the bedroom in which presently her nieces would be installed.

Away from her husband's irritating determination to spoil her pleasure, she allowed her excitement to rise in her again. She was so full of plans for the next few weeks, tennis parties, excursions to the beach for picnics, balls, and, if they were fortunate, invitations to week-end parties in one or more of the sparsely situated country houses. That, of course, was if the girls rode horseback. If they didn't they would have to learn.

But that was a minor detail. Their mother would have brought them up properly in every other way, and they would be able to dance well, to talk gracefully, to be gay and vivacious, to play the piano and sing a little, to embroider, of course, and perhaps to paint. They would be ornaments to society. That was what this raw little community, bursting with life but sadly lacking in the more important refinements of life, needed.

Bringing out these two gently-bred girls was her contribution to the community. Hubert, in his coarser moments, had said it was equivalent to introducing a good strain of horseflesh or a pedigree cow. Hubert sometimes was quite intolerable, but when dear Sophia and Prudence were married and producing attractive babies, he could drop his sarcastic attitude and be as delighted as she.

Though that was leaping ahead. One had all the excitement of the courtship and wedding first. Perhaps a double wedding.

No, that would be swallowing her cake all in one mouthful. Sophia, as the eldest, must come first. One could decorate the church with arum lilies that grew wild on the hillside.

But they simply must be pretty. If their mother had lied to her about that she would never forgive her.

Yes, the room looked very clean and attractive. Polly had done her best here. Opossum and sheepskin rugs, much washed and whitened and fluffed out, lay on the bare scrubbed floor. The wide iron bedstead with brass knobs and high pillows was covered with a snowy cotton bedspread, and surrounded with a starched lace-trimmed valance. The dressing-table, also draped in starched runners and frills, held sundry articles of toilet, a gay pincushion, a hair tidy, and two floral china candlesticks, complete with tall white candles and match-boxes, ready for use. The washstand was occupied by Aunt Charity's best set of basin and jug, soap dish and other necessary bedroom equipment all in a delightful pattern of leaves and pink blossom. The high windows which rattled slightly in the wind and emitted faint eddies of cool air (for no one had yet been able to build an entirely draught-proof house in this windy town) were attractively curtained in white Nottingham lace as snowy as the bedspread. The room was high-ceilinged and light, and looked over the hillside and the bay.

Soon, Aunt Charity reflected ecstatically, the girls' trunks would stand on this floor, and the little strange maid, whom one hoped would be reliable and sober, as good maids really were at a premium, would be hanging away the fashionable English dresses in the enormous wardrobe. There was even a long gilt-framed mirror, sacrificed from her own room, hanging on the wall so that the girls would be able to look at themselves in their ball gowns.

She was so sure they would be happy at once. How could they be anything else, with herself, like a fairy godmother, ready to wave her wand and produce out of this crisp bright air their future happiness?

Yes, the bedroom couldn't be more ready to receive her guests. Now for a final look in the kitchen to see that her orders for dinner that evening had been completely understood, as cook was scarcely more trustworthy than the slow, lazy Polly.

On the way to the large kitchen situated at the back of the house on the ground floor, Aunt Charity paused to look into the maid's room.

That, too, was spruce and clean. It was small, certainly, but it had everything a girl could require, even a bright rag mat at the bedside, and washbasin and jug in plain white china. The window looked out into the wilder part of the garden, and the flax bushes crackled like flicked whips, but after three months at sea a young woman wasn't going to be nervous of a few noises outdoors. She could lock her window if she were. But one did hope she was the old-fashioned type of maid who put her work and her mistress first, and wouldn't get these flighty ideas of independence that almost all immigrants seemed to get. Because, with parties and balls, there would be a great deal of sewing and laundering and ironing to do, and even perhaps waiting on table. Let's hope the girl was adaptable, and knew her place.

On the whole, Aunt Charity was well pleased with her plotting and planning. She lived in one of the finest houses in Wellington, her husband was a respected bank manager, she herself stood in the coveted position of cousin to the Governor, and therefore an acknowledged leader of society. For a comparatively new community she had contrived a surprisingly comfortable and civilised standard of living. Soon, one didn't doubt, the social amenities would bear happy comparison with those belonging to a similar standard of life in England. It was really enormously exciting pioneering such a worthwhile cause.

There was no reason at all, simply none at all, to let one's mind dwell for one shocking second on that horrid description of Hubert's, that poor white hand slowly crisping and curling with heat and filling with dreadful gravy . . .

CHAPTER 3

The man on the black horse drew rein for a minute to look at the new ship anchored in the bay. Boats were on their way out of it. Shortly, another batch of bewildered homesick immigrants would stand on dry land wondering what roof would shelter their alien heads, and what they were to do with their conglomeration of possessions, pianos, kitchenware, family portraits, bedsteads and crinolines transported sentimentally from their homeland.

Saul Whitmore was able to feel superior to this far-off scene. He had sailed several years ago in a cargo ship along with his first consignment of sheep and cattle, and, in company with a tough hard-working crew, had escaped the emotionalism and confusion of a shipload of immigrants.

Now this beautiful wild country was his home. He had hacked out his farmlands from the bush, turned loose his livestock, and, over the last five years, built his ambitious house. It was the finest for many miles.

He did not particularly want to boast of owning the finest home in the district, but he was accustomed to a certain standard of living, which it seemed only sensible, if possible, to maintain even in the bush.

Besides, one did not take a bride to a mere labourer's hut. One offered the best one could—even to an as yet unknown woman.

Saul's horse, sensing his master's mood, fidgeted restlessly on the dusty track. Saul cast another look downwards at the midget boats toiling across the wrinkled blue water, and spoke to his horse, "Come on then, old fellow. Home now."

But his brow was dark as he turned down the track towards the town and his mother's house. It was a pity, he was reflecting, that women were so necessary.

His mother, a toweringly tall old woman, thin as the *niu* poles which the Maoris hoisted at their incantation ceremonies, with yellow-tinged skin and enormous high-bridged nose, looked at him comprehendingly.

"Well, my boy, you've come."

"Yes, mother." He kissed her cheek. He did not need to stoop. She was as tall as he. They were good friends, these two. She knew why he had come and what he was thinking. Even if they had not been friends she would have known, for she had strange powers of intuition. The people who were afraid of her she scorned. Some of those silly giggling girls, for instance, one of whom this black-browed son of hers would have to make his wife.

"How are things? Do you want tea? Or whisky?"

"Whisky, please. Things are so so. The house is finished. I've called the place Lucknow."

His mother's face softened. "Thank you, Saul. That's a nice tribute. But why are things only so so?"

"It's the old trouble." Saul flung down his pack. "The Maoris. Oh, they're friendly enough on the surface, but now Te Kooti has escaped from the Chatham Island his myth is

24

spreading. He's bad, but he's a devastatingly clever war leader, and he uses these horrible pseudo-religious initiation ceremonies to get recruits."

"They're savages, of course. In spite of the poor optimistic missionaries."

"Poor missionaries is right," Saul agreed. "Have you heard what happened to that poor devil, the Reverend Volkner? He was beheaded with a tomahawk, and they put his head in church on the pulpit. There the chief gouged out the eyes and swallowed them, one by one. That's his way of defeating the enemy, apparently, though I believe the last eye nearly choked him. Sometimes I think these Maoris are not human. If you've heard one of their attacks when they yell like wild dogs, or wolves, *hau hau, hau hau,* you'd believe they're fiends. They take their initiation ceremony round the severed head of a British officer, stroking or even licking the decaying flesh. They'd drink its blood, if there were any left!"

"This is only a disease they have temporarily," Mrs. Whitmore said.

"But it's spreading. Especially with a fanatic like Te Kooti. He's a handsome devil, you know, with that curly black hair and arrogant tattooed face. He's young, too, and strong and very brave. He wears a cloak of black and white feathers, and one of his men always carries his own particular flag into battle. *Te Wepu,* the Whip. Oh, he knows all the tricks."

"Why did they let him escape from the Chathams after he was imprisoned there?"

Saul shrugged. "He's another Bonaparte, perhaps. At least, he has the same pattern of megalomania. His return has set some fires alight. There'll be guerilla warfare until he's caught again, or killed. One never knows where he'll strike. The bad thing is, one can't trust one's own natives any more. They disappear overnight or steal one's horses."

Then he smiled reassuringly at his mother. "Perhaps it's not as bad as that. We've had no attacks close at hand. They've been in Hawkes Bay and the Urewera country. But nobody listens to me when I tell them this trouble is spreading, and the army—I'm sorry, mother, but I've yet to find a more stupid commanding officer than Major Braby in our district."

"Something's happened to upset you recently, Saul?"

The old lady's eyes penetrated her son's sombre face. He didn't try to deceive her. He never had been able to, and he knew it was useless to attempt to do so now.

"I found young David Bowden's body in the forest. The heart had been cut out, and—" His face grew dark. "There's no use in talking about it. But all in all, it might be better if you don't come up until this trouble blows over."

"Don't talk nonsense. Haven't I always gone everywhere with your father?"

This was true enough. Mrs. Whitmore had been at uncomfortably close proximity to several battles, and had lived through the siege of Lucknow during which her husband, Colonel Whitmore, had died. It was true that she was not to be frightened by a couple of hundred yelling brown men, tattooed and almost naked. She had seen that kind of thing before. There was a limit to the horrors one's mind could assimilate, or the fear one could feel. There was even a limit to the various methods of frightfulness.

"I shall come later, Saul. That's definite. I'll shut up this house, if one can call it a house." There was a flash of humour in her extraordinary dark eyes as she looked round the tiny room, small-windowed and claustrophobic. "I'll be glad to get away from that smoky chimney. It's the strange currents of wind, I think. I hope you've managed better in Taranaki. But what about the girl?"

"The girl?"

"Don't pretend to be stupid. Your wife."

"Oh, that. Well—what do you suggest, mother?"

"Frankly, I don't know. Anyone would have you. Jump at the chance. Heaven knows why! You'll frighten the life out of them."

Saul grinned suddenly, his heavy brows lifting. "I won't put up with the vapours, if that's what you mean."

"There's Susan Chittaway, who weeps if you so much as look at her. Or Janet Reid. She'd give you healthy children, but what she would do in a Hauhau attack, I'd hate to think. Or that bold creature, Sarah Jane Maxwell. In some ways, she might be the better choice."

"There was a ship in the harbour as I came along," Saul commented.

His mother looked up with sharp interest. "That'll be the *Mary Louise*. Charity Carruthers has done nothing but talk of her for the last three months. She has two nieces on board. Coming out to find husbands. Perhaps you'd better look them over. Though what a niece of Charity Carruthers might have to commend her, I can't imagine."

"I'll take a trip to England," said Saul suddenly, with a hint of desperation.

"No, you won't. You'll stay right here and marry the first healthy girl who'll have you and start a family."

"Mother! Marriage isn't that important."

"It is for you, Saul," said the old woman, fixing him with her intense eyes which made no secret now of her obsession. "You're the last of your line. I want you to have children. Your father longed for that. For his sake and my own, I want my first grandchild. You're thirty. You've waited too long already. I won't have you taking any more risks until you've made sure of this. Life's too uncertain anywhere, and particularly here, with this madman Te Kooti on the warpath again. You're not to wait any longer, Saul. I ask you not to."

Saul's brows were lifted arrogantly to face her. "And what am I expected to feel for one of these silly young virgins who'll be scared of her own shadow. Love?"

"Call it what you like," his mother said impatiently. "But find a healthy girl and get her into bed. Don't go on dallying. You need a wife, and I want a grandchild. I haven't super-human patience, even if you have. What's wrong with you, may I ask?"

"Nothing at all," Saul grinned. He pressed his mother's shoulder affectionately. "Very well, you old tyrant. I'll show you. But she ought to be able to cook, don't you think?"

"Certainly. And sew, and run a household efficiently. If her face is pretty, so much the better. I'm sorry, Saul. If you were in England I'd be content for you to go to every ball in the country. But you're not in England. You're in a new country where the simple facts of existence are the ones that count. I shouldn't have to tell you what they are."

"Mother, be assured you don't."

"Then what about starting by going to Charity Carruthers' welcome party for the two nieces. She'll be overjoyed if you walk in."

Saul sighed with distaste and boredom. "Must I?"

"It's a beginning. And when you're married, if you don't want to take the girl to the country until things are quieter, you can leave her here with me." The old lady's eyes twinkled with macabre humour. "I, at least, won't eat her."

Saul swallowed his whisky and went out to unsaddle his horse. The wind was cool now, and carried the tang of the sea, although here a shoulder of the hill hid the bay from sight. The little ship riding at anchor was hidden. Yet, for some reason, she was vividly in his mind. Perhaps she carried on board the woman he wanted, the single one in the whole world whom he could imagine permanently at his side. Because there was such a woman, he knew. Or was that just one of the foolish fancies he had caught from his mother? His mother was a very dominating woman, but since he had outgrown childhood she had not dominated him. If he did not wish to marry he would not.

Yet in this instance he secretly agreed with his mother. He already loved this country and wanted to do more than his best for it. One necessary thing was to populate it with its own true sons, not this miscellany of people who drifted out on immigrant ships in search of some El Dorado that never existed. He would like to give it several sons, to create green fertile lands out of the wild bush country, and to turn the Maori back into the fine, intelligent, handsome native he was.

Besides these lofty ambitions, it came back to the simple fact his mother had pointed out. He needed a wife.

Suddenly, standing there in the cool wind, he thought of a woman's white hand on his flesh, and he tensed and trembled. It had been a long time. Abruptly he turned to re-saddle his horse.

"Sorry, old fellow. But we're going into town."

A wife, yes. A soft-skinned girl who spoke the Queen's English, and would become an efficient mistress of his new home.

But not tonight . . .

CHAPTER 4

Aunt Charity stood back from the three girls, biting her lips with disappointment.

What had she got here? Really, what had she got here?

Sophia, the eldest, was untidy. Already she had lost her reticule twice, her bonnet was askew on her head, and her light-coloured fine hair, the kind that needed the most careful and secure arrangement, was slipping loose. Also, she talked too much. Her tongue hadn't been still since that moment of meeting on the wharf. Didn't she know that a too busy tongue could drive away a prospective husband? Surely her mother must have taught her better manners. No doubt, indeed, she had, but the long voyage with little supervision from that stupid Mrs. Crewe had taught her undesirable habits.

As for Prudence, she had performed the incredible folly of falling in love with a penniless ship's officer, and her face was unattractively blotched from crying. One would have to talk to her about the impossibility of that love-affair. But not yet. Tears were still too incipient, and Aunt Charity loathed a damp and sniffing young woman.

There remained the maid, Briar—was that her impossible name? She stood in the background meekly enough, her eyes downcast, her pale face telling nothing. But already one sensed a wildness about her, and too much arrogance in that slim figure.

Perhaps it was only that she made Sophia and Prudence look too plump and heavy. Though that was absurd, for as long as a girl had a slim waist a man preferred curves, a swelling bosom and rounded hips.

Aunt Charity, complacent about her own very firm and ample curves, decided that perhaps she was judging too hastily. She had looked forward so eagerly to the arrival of the dear girls, and built so many hopes on their English milk-and-roses complexions, not yet tanned and dried by the vigorous antipodean sun and wind, that she had forgotten one must arrive dishevelled and travel-stained after such a long journey, living out of trunks for weeks, and in a state of emotional upheaval.

Aunt Charity could be very kind when she deemed it necessary. Her tight mouth relaxed into a warm smile, and she leaned forward to kiss each of her nieces affectionately.

"Well, here we are, home. Now I wonder what you will think of my house at the end of the world."

"It's very nice, Aunt Charity," said Sophia, remembering her manners, but looking doubtfully at the wide hall, the wooden staircase, and the bowl of unfamiliar *raupo* reeds, arranged like sheathed swords in a tall vase. "Is it always as windy as this?"

"Mostly, I'm afraid. We're on a bluff that catches the wind. But you'll get used to it. It's a little difficult for large hats, and one's skirts need to be weighted down. I do hope you dear girls have brought some new fashions from London. We *hunger* for new fashions. Anyone just arrived is the centre of attention."

Sophia's eyes began to sparkle pleasurably. Prudence sniffed and fumbled for her handkerchief.

"But come along upstairs and see your room and freshen up. Tom will bring your bags up later. And then you must meet your uncle."

Aunt Charity sailed towards the stairs. Halfway up she paused to look down at the silent girl left standing in the hall. There was something in that erect figure, the aloof gaze, that made her uneasy. Really, the girl had only been ashore an hour, and already she seemed to have acquired that haughty independent look that was so to be deplored among the working classes here. A look, if one could believe it, of deliberate equality!

"Just wait, will you," she called. "I'll be down presently to show you your room. And then your mistresses will require your help to dress for dinner."

So it was that Briar met Uncle Hubert.

He came pottering out of his study at the other end of the long passage and saw her standing there obediently, her composed face giving no clue as to her feelings.

"Hullo," he said genially. "I thought I heard voices." He held out his hand. "Which one of my nieces are you?"

"Neither, sir. I'm the maid."

"Oh! Oh, I see. Well, welcome just the same. I'm Hubert Carruthers. You'll be seeing me around a good deal. Did you have a pleasant voyage?"

"Quite pleasant, thank you," Briar answered, with her impeccable accent.

It caused Uncle Hubert to look at her more closely. H'mm! If his wife's two nieces also looked like this there was going to be quite a stir in town. The local young ladies were going to seem definitely gauche and colonial.

"How long did it take? Twelve weeks?"

"Just over, sir."

"Captain all right? Good type? Nice passengers? Not your business to comment, I imagine, though you have got two eyes in your head."

And very fine ones, too, Uncle Hubert noted. He was a friendly person who had been away from the rigid caste system of Victorian England long enough to see people as they were. They were all worth knowing, he had discovered. As bank manager, he had set many a rough-voiced honest young man on his feet, and one or two of them now had finer houses and better bank accounts than his own. If it hadn't been for his wife, with her social ambitions and conventions, combined with her strong personality, he would have lived a very simple life, choosing his friends for their qualities, not their birth.

It was rather important to Hubert Carruthers at this moment to make this stray composed girl, with just that hint of lostness behind her composure, feel at home.

"You'll like this country," he said. "It's full of opportunities for young people like you. As soon as this Maori question is settled—"

"Maori?"

"The natives. We've had land troubles for years, of course. But they've been settled, fairly or unfairly one can't be sure. The ignorant human who can't use modern tools because he hasn't worked them before is always the loser. But even the Waikatos and those wild Urewera chiefs finally agreed to the settlement. Then a fanatic called Te Kooti decides to stir up a religious war based on the old Maori grievances. It's a potent mixture of Judaism, paganism, and a little elementary Christianity which has stirred the natives up so much that they've reverted to cannibalism. Pretty horrible, eh? Even the Waikatos have gone back on their word. Now they say *Ka Whawhai tonu! Ake, ake, ake!* which translated is 'This is the word of the Maori. We will fight on for ever and ever and ever.'"

The girl's huge brilliant eyes were fixed on him. "What a musical language!" she exclaimed.

"The Maori? Yes, they're a musical people. And poetic. Full of lovely old legends and superstitions. But when their fighting spirit is roused and they dance their battle dance, the *haka*, you can wait for trouble. Well, I mustn't frighten you."

"I'm not frightened, sir."

The girl's head had gone up, and her eyes were glinting. By jove, she wasn't frightened, either. She was challenged, as every good pioneer should be. No little suppressed shrieks, no attacks of the vapours.

"Where do you come from, my dear?"

"My family comes from Devon."

"And they were willing for you to come to this strange country?"

"Oh, yes sir. They thought it would be for my good."

"That's the way. Fine unselfish parents." He leaned nearer, his long face dolorous. "They didn't send you out here just to find a husband?"

31

"No, sir."

"Oh, well, perhaps you're not one of five girls. That must be quite a problem to any mother. One should sympathise, I suppose. I warn you, we're to be plunged into some social festivities here. Oh, we're not behind the times. We have race meetings and hunts and balls. Certainly, one might be reduced to wearing last year's ball gown. But one can camouflage, and be a little ingenious even about that sort of contretemps."

"Hubert!"

Aunt Charity advanced down the stairs, concealing, with a visible effort, her annoyance.

"Yes, my dear!"

"The girls are just freshening up. We might take a little light wine with our dinner to celebrate their arrival. Will you see to it? Briar, come this way. I'll take you to your room."

Briar picked up her modest bag and followed Aunt Charity. Her short encounter with Uncle Hubert had done a great deal to restore her cheerfulness. He was kind. He didn't look through people like her, he actually saw them. He was even interested in what they felt. But his wife, this large definite woman ahead of her, would not approve. Already Aunt Charity's disapproval challenged Briar as much as the strange and distant threat of an encounter with the warlike Maori. She was not afraid. She refused to be afraid.

Aunt Charity opened a door at the end of a dark passage that ran past the kitchen. "I think you'll be very comfortable here. You have the room all to yourself, you see. Now I'd like you to go upstairs as quickly as possible and see what you can do for Miss Sophia and Miss Prudence. You will have your dinner in the kitchen with cook after we've had ours. Is there anything you would like to ask?"

Briar's challenging unafraid eyes diplomatically dropped. "No, ma'am."

"Very well, then. Do as I have told you."

Upstairs, Sophie was running from one window to another, making exclamations of mingled excitement and disappointment.

"It's so much smaller than I thought it would be. You can almost count the number of houses. And they're all built of wood. They look shabby already. Even Government House is only built of wood. I wonder if they're poor. I thought this was a wealthy country. I can't imagine living in a house

32

like this. Listen to how it creaks! And the windows rattle." Sophia dropped her voice. "What do you think of Aunt Charity, Prue?"

Prudence, who was sitting forlornly on the bed, not even having taken off her bonnet, muttered that she didn't care for her particularly.

"Yes, I think she's rather alarming, too. But I'll manage her. You'll see. Oh, Prue, for goodness' sake stop looking so miserable. You'll see Edmund again. This isn't the end of the world. Though it almost is, isn't it?" Sophia giggled. "I do think it's all rather exciting. And Aunt Charity has promised us a luncheon party at the end of the week. I'm going to wear my Swiss muslin with blue ribbons. Or should I wear the pink silk which is really more sophisticated? Do you really think it's true that we'll be leaders of fashion? Oh, Prue, do cheer up and take some interest!"

"Do you think I need go down to dinner?" Prudence asked. "I've a headache."

"Of course you must go down to dinner! Briar will rub your temples with eau de Cologne. Here is Briar! Prue has a headache and wants her temples rubbed, and I want you to hurry and unpack something that we can wear this evening."

Briar, looking at her autocratic young mistress, thought fleetingly of her own bag, untouched in her room.

"Which dress, Miss Sophia?"

"Oh, I don't know. It's only Uncle Hubert, isn't it? No need to dazzle him. Just my grey bombazine, but with a fresh fichu. You did launder them on the ship, didn't you? And the same for Prue, I should think, if only she'd take some interest."

Briar, looking at Prudence's forlorn face, had a feeling of sympathy. It must be dreadful to be in love so hopelessly. She would take care that such a thing never happened to her!

"Here's the eau de Cologne, Miss Prue. I'll just dab your temples. There! Isn't that better? It's fresh and cool. And I imagine your aunt will excuse you to go to bed early tonight."

Her calm voice caused fresh tears to well in Prudence's eyes. "You're so kind, Briar. Are you going to be happy here? Has Aunt Charity given you a nice room?"

"Very nice, thank you. And all to myself."

"Of course Briar's going to be happy here," Sophia said in her confident voice. "I expect we'll lose her soon enough to some young man. But mind, not until you've dressed both of us for our weddings, miss!"

"I hope to do that, Miss Sophia," Briar answered meekly.

But did she? Busy with the girls' billowing dresses, brushing their fair young heads and neatly pinning up their hair, tidying away their discarded petticoats and travelling dresses, the seething untamable excitement was within her. Sophia's chatter scarcely reached her ears.

She was reliving that moment when she had stood on the wharf, firm land under her feet at last, and breathing in the smell of earth and green trees, the smell of the new land which was to be hers.

Nothing, she had declared to herself then, would alarm or depress her, nothing would defeat her. The Almighty, who had let her defenceless young mother die in a ditch, had set her own feet on a strange path full of opportunity. She would seize every experience that came her way, she would become the real and vital person that already she felt hidden within herself. And she would find love. . . .

"Briar!" She had scarcely heard Jemima Potter's voice at her side. "Briar, what are you staring at in that funny way?"

"The town. Just the town. It's so new. Climbing up the hillside like birds' nests on a ledge. Oh, I'm so excited, Jemima."

"Are you, love?" The little woman clutched her baby and looked over the calm waters of the bay. Her eyes were full of sadness. There was no need to ask what she was looking at or thinking. The sea that had swallowed two of her children had temporarily stolen her courage. But it would come back.

She gave the quick smile that lighted her thin face. "Briar, Fred and me want to call the baby Rose, after you."

Briar coloured with pleasure. "Really, Jemima?"

"Because you're a briar rose. Not even scratchy when anyone gets to know you."

"Oh, Jemima, your head's full of nonsense. You'll have to come down to earth if you're to get on in this country. Look, there's Fred and the children waiting for you. And I'll be seeing you as soon as I can get time off. They must give me an hour one day soon. Oh dear, and I think that's Mrs. Carruthers coming. She looks very grand."

"She won't get the better of you," said Jemima confidently.

That first look at Mrs. Carruthers had been a bit alarming, but Briar, remembering Jemima's confidence in her, and her own undefeated feeling of optimism, had not allowed herself to be intimidated. She had kept her head up and behaved in a quiet unflustered way. It had not been so bad, after all, for the talk with Uncle Hubert had immensely cheered her; and then trying to put some courage into Prudence had made her forget her own strangeness.

That had not come back until at last she had gone to bed in the narrow little room off the kitchen. Then she had had to confess that the night sounds were alarming. The window opened directly into the dark garden, and there were strange rustlings and sighings. Sometimes a bush clapped together with a dry sound, like castanets, and there was the constant sigh of the wind running up through the grass and rattling the windows. The stars, too, were still unfamiliar, although she had looked at them often enough on board ship after crossing the line. Once, long after midnight, there had been a mournful crying that sounded like a small owl, and later she had almost leapt out of bed with fright as there was a sharp rustling in the grass just outside her window, followed by a harsh screaming cry.

But morning came, with dazzling sunlight streaming in, and a fresh clean smell to the air that was irresistible. She sprang up, full of happiness. What did it matter who or what had cried in the night? The night was over, and there was the garden, rather wild and untended, with the cause of the castanets, an untidy coarse-leaved flax bush, and beyond it the silver-plumed *toe toe* grass that rustled with a silken sound in the wind.

The cries she had heard, cook explained, would have been made by the small native owl called morepork, and perhaps a kiwi had blundered by, giving its harsh call. They were great birds, the kiwis, unable to fly, and no use for anything. But she would soon get used to strange sounds at night, and there was nothing to be afraid of.

"You don't need to lock your window," cook sniggered. "There's not likely to be anything prowling but birds and opossums. Too bad, isn't it?"

But Briar was to remember those words when cook had forgotten them.

They went driving in the town that afternoon. Aunt Charity said there was room in the carriage for Briar, too, as she would have to learn her way about the town.

Prudence had cheered up considerably, partly because she was young and could not remain indifferent to new surround-

35

ings, and partly because Edmund had called on Aunt Charity and had found that lady unexpectedly kind.

Actually, Aunt Charity had been very shrewd. She had summed up the situation at once, seeing in Edmund a likeable enough but not too strong character, and guessing that with the roving life he was leading he would tire soon enough of his vows of faithfulness to Prudence. Prudence, too, would eventually recover from her shipboard romance, but in an effort to make the recovery as painless as possible, and to prevent more of those detested tears and melancholy looks which would surely drive every other eligible young man away, Aunt Charity had decreed that the young man might be permitted to present himself again when he returned to New Zealand, and thus prove the seriousness of his intentions.

Prudence had flung her arms gratefully round her aunt, and at last there were smiles instead of tears. So it was in a general atmosphere of good temper that the carriage set off.

The roads were steep, dusty and made uneven by rocks embedded in the hillside. The horse proceeded at a walk, and Aunt Charity was able to point out the houses of friends, the Morleys, the Maxwells, the Reids, all of whom had daughters, the Fanshawes whose only son Peter would be coming to the luncheon party, the Browns and the Pattersons. Not the least, the wide-verandahed Government House set in a flat space of lawns and gardens, where the girls would duly be presented to the Governor and his lady. Up a steeper narrow road Aunt Charity pointed to a small cottage which she said belonged to old Mrs. Whitmore.

"She lives alone. She's a little odd, people say, but she went through the siege of Lucknow where her husband was killed. Enough to turn anyone's head, poor thing. She has a son, Saul."

"That's an unusual name," said Sophia interestedly.

"And an unusual person," returned Aunt Charity, rather grimly. "He's quite a recluse. He spends most of his time on his land in the Taranaki district, and when he comes home he's the most elusive person imaginable. One would think he hated women."

"Then he isn't married?" Sophia enquired eagerly.

"No, not yet."

"Is he eligible?"

"Oh, very. I should say he's the most sought-after young man in the province. He's first cousin to the Earl of Marsham. His father was a colonel in the Indian Army, and I believe was decorated several times. Saul himself has taken part in the earlier Maori wars. But all that dreadful business is over."

"Uncle Hubert says it isn't," Prudence put in.

"Oh, dear, has he been frightening you girls? I particularly forbade him to do that. He has an obsession about this business. We're perfectly safe here in Wellington. It's only a small outbreak here and there in the forest and bush country. Actually, I think the Maoris are quite harmless. You'll see some presently, and realise what I mean."

"Aunt Charity," said Sophia, with her single-minded persistence, "is Saul Whitmore coming to our parties?"

Aunt Charity pursed her little mouth. "If he's in town he'll be invited, certainly. But that's no assurance that he will come. He's the rudest person I've ever met."

"You adore him, Aunt Charity!" Sophia said daringly.

"Well!" Aunt Charity tossed her head, and fretted her brow into innumerable lines. She puffed her chest and looked, thought Briar, self-important and absurd. And she didn't like Saul Whitmore. He outraged her. But he was first cousin to an earl. Aunt Charity had not left her class-consciousness behind in England. She had very definitely brought it to this new country.

Briar decided that she, too, would dislike Saul Whitmore. If she ever met him, which was unlikely.

The first group of Maoris they saw on the roadside looked harmless enough. A woman in a blanket, carrying a brown-faced baby, another in an absurd, large straw hat trimmed with ribbons and flowers which was obviously treasured finery received from some white woman, and a man also in a blanket, with a tattooed face, and a feather in his tightly curled black hair. They all looked up, smiling in the most friendly way.

"They're lazy and they have very *native* habits," said Aunt Charity, not very explicitly. "But I still can't believe your uncle's accounts of their dreadful nature in wartime. I sometimes think he just likes to shock me. There's a *pa* or Maori village just a little way out of town, so you'll see plenty of these strollers. The children run wild. Now here we come to the shopping area," she went on more brightly. "Prices can be quite exorbitant, you know. Eggs are fourpence each, and milk fivepence a quart, butter one and six or even two shillings a pound, and a two pound loaf of bread is ninepence, which is scandalous. I paid sixpence for a cabbage the other day. As for good china, or good quality silks, they're almost unobtainable. But I suppose one must expect that, living at the ends of the earth as we do. Somehow one manages. You'll be surprised at how the ladies can turn themselves out when they really try. I've found a treasure of a dressmaker, a Miss Matthews who came out last year to set up business. She makes the smartest bonnets, too. I've already whispered to her about the probability of wedding gowns." Aunt Charity tapped Sophia playfully. "You first, my dear, as the eldest. And then dear Prue."

Sophia gave her jolly, good-natured laugh, tilting her bonnet crooked, gazing about her with interest. "That Saul Whitmore sounds fascinating. Do you think he'll be rude to *me?*"

"No one will be rude to you, my darling child," said Aunt Charity with finality.

She sat back in the comfortable seat of the carriage, feeling much more contented than she had done last night when her first impressions had not been particularly accurate. For Sophia, if not a raving beauty, was very vivacious, and that was always a great attraction. Prudence, now she had lost her doleful look, was really quite pretty, her skin was charming, and clever Miss Matthews might make her a bonnet that would modify the longness of her face. Even Briar seemed a discreet, quiet little thing, minding her own business even if she was not as biddable-looking as one would have liked. But she would realise that society existed here, too, and keep her place.

"You dear girls must write letters home this afternoon," she said comfortably. "The *Mary Louise* will take them when she sails. We have to take care to catch every ship, as sometimes there are very long intervals without news. Briar, you may also wish to write to your family."

"Yes, thank you, ma'am," replied Briar, thinking of her dear Andrew Gaunt who had taught her to correspond not only in perfect English, but in French. She would compose a letter to him in heaven, telling him of this new remarkable turn in her life. He would be deeply interested. Wouldn't he? For if he would not, who in the whole wide world would?

"Then don't look glum, child. You may have an hour off to write your letter."

But Briar, sitting in her narrow room alone, was suddenly violently unhappy at the pretence. Was it not unendurable that she alone should have no one who cared to receive a letter from her, or was concerned for her health and happiness? Inventing a loving family who waited to hear from her made her able to hold up her head in front of others, such as smug, overbearing Aunt Charity, but it did not ease the lonely ache in her heart. For the first time since her arrival her confidence left her, and she felt the orphan she was, alone and destitute.

But someday, she told herself fiercely, she, too, would have things. People and things.

On an impulse she left her room and began to steal softly through the silent house. There was no one about. The girls were in their room writing their letters home, Aunt Charity was resting, cook was out marketing, and Tom digging in the lower part of the garden. Uncle Hubert would be at his bank.

She was able to go through the rooms lingeringly, looking at everything, the furniture and carpets brought from England, the crystal and china, the Chinese lacquer cabinet picked up perhaps on the voyage out, or brought by some trading schooner, the rich blue Bristol glass goblets in their own glass-fronted cupboard, the piano draped with a long-fringed shawl. She stopped to touch the thick pile of the red plush table-cloth, then stared up at the portraits of Aunt Charity's parents, one on either side of the fireplace. They were badly-painted, and showed over-weight people, heavy-jowled with small piercing eyes, strangely alike, but perhaps the painter had been able to paint features in one shape only. They were not at all attractive people, yet Briar yearned towards them, thinking of their solid flesh and blood, their realness.

In the dining-room there were twelve mahogany chairs set round the long shining table. The heavy oak sideboard, which Briar inquisitively opened and looked into, was crammed with china and glass. There was a dinner service with enormous meat platters and vegetable dishes—Briar turned over a plate to study the Royal Worcester imprint—and a Rockingham teaset arranged carefully on a shelf to itself. These were valuable possessions, doubly treasured in a country as yet empty of the treasures of civilised life. How did Aunt Charity, that stout, ordinary, unimaginative person, come to have so much?

In the top draw of the sideboard was the silver, wrapped in baize. This, Briar could not resist handling. She was balancing a Georgian soup ladle in the palm of her hand, delighting in its cool roundness, thinking that some day, and before long, she, too, would have things like that, when there was a sound behind her.

"Har-rumph!" said Uncle Hubert. "That's a nice thing, isn't it? George the Third. Interested in silver?"

Briar started violently. For a moment she gazed speechless into the long, dolorous face, trying to read the expression in the heavy-lidded eyes.

"I—like pretty things," she said at last. "I—was just looking."

"Of course, my dear. If you really like pretty things come into my study and I'll show you something."

Trembling, she laid down the soup ladle, closed the drawer, and followed him.

In the study, a small dark room with leather-covered chairs, and book-lined walls, Uncle Hubert picked up an object made out of a smooth green substance and handed it to her. It was a curiously shaped little figure, made in whorls, and with a devilishly mischievous face, eyes aslant and a tongue poked impudently out of the grinning mouth.

"It's a greenstone *tiki*," Uncle Hubert explained. "A Maori good luck charm. The Maori is a very superstitious fellow, you know. He always likes to have one of these. But he can't always get one in greenstone. It's the most valuable mineral in this country. He makes axeheads and other weapons out of it. It's very hard. Feel."

The strange little ornament lay in Briar's palm. She lifted entranced eyes.

"I like it, sir. It makes me feel—" she shivered slightly, the delicious unexplanable excitement filling her again.

"If it makes you feel lucky, you'd better keep it."

"Keep it!"

"Of course. If you'd like it."

"But—" Briar tried again to read the sardonic face. He had caught her prowling through his house, handling the silver. How did he know she wasn't planning to steal it? She was an unknown servant girl just off a ship. Would he ever believe her if she tried to explain that she merely loved and longed to own beautiful things?

"You'll need luck, most likely," the extraordinary man was saying. "You haven't been endowed with the power of my wife's blessing, as have those two pink and white misses upstairs. But you'll do as well, maybe." He stared at her broodingly. "You like books?"

"How did you know, sir?"

"I saw you looking at them. What have you read?"

"Samuel Richardson, Sir Walter Scott, Shakespeare, of course, Donne—" she hesitated, "Montaigne."

"In the original?"

"Yes, sir."

"The devil! You don't tell me your father taught you all that?"

"N-no, sir."

"Well, none of my business. But if you ever have time from the needle, or the flat iron, or whatever you're kept busy with, you have my permission to come in here."

Briar's lip trembled. "You are very kind."

"Not at all, not at all."

"And—not surprised."

"Surprised?"

"To find this out about me—that no one else has found out."

"This is a very young country, my dear. All kinds come, under various guises. No, nothing surprises me. But some things," he added kindly, "please me. I hope you will find whatever it is that you have come to New Zealand for."

Briar, clutching the smooth strange little charm in her hand, could only nod vehemently.

In bed that night Aunt Charity, clad in a voluminous linen lace-trimmed nightgown, and with her daytime cap replaced by a more substantial night one, sat up and prodded the recumbent figure of her husband.

"Hubert! You can't be asleep yet!"

"I am, you know."

"Hubert, you must listen. Saul Whitmore's in town."

"So I heard."

"You heard and didn't tell me!"

"My dear, I didn't think your grapevine would have failed you."

"Oh, tush! You just like to be secretive. Did you hear the rest of it?"

"I heard a little. What did you hear, in far greater detail?"

"Why, that he's been in and out of Cooper's public house for twenty-four hours, and that most of the time he's been in the company of—well, not the kind of women we know."

"Speak for yourself," Hubert murmured, and was rewarded with a sharp slap across his shoulders.

"Hubert! Will you never be serious!"

"I'm very serious, my love. I'm just wondering what it's to do with me, or you, whose company Saul, after months in the bush, chooses to keep."

"Of course it's to do with us, since I planned asking him to the luncheon on Friday. But is he the kind of person one introduces innocent young girls to? Am I doing the right thing?"

"Right or wrong, my love, you'll ask him. He's Saul Whitmore, the cousin of an earl. You're only the cousin of the Governor. Really," Hubert humped the blankets irritably over his shoulders, "I don't know why you wake me to ask me something you've already made up your mind about. Now blow out the candle and let's get some sleep."

Aunt Charity sat a moment in the flickering candlelight looking at the humped back of her already deeply breathing husband. Her small mouth pouted discontentedly, her forehead creased in rebellion. Really, if this was where marriage led one, to share the same bed forever with a man who jibed at her in a gentle facetious voice, and whom she didn't know one bit better today than she had twenty years ago, was it so all-important?

If it came to that, she didn't even care much about sharing the same bed. She never had. If one were to add up the time she had spent dressing and undressing with tortuous efficiency, concealing her body beneath petticoats and corsets, and then the all-enveloping nightgowns, so that what eventually happened at least happened unseen, it would come to days and weeks and months.

Were her ardent, ambitious plans for her nieces to come to this dreary anti-climax?

"Put that light out, Charity!" came her husband's impatient voice.

Automatically she obeyed, leaning over to blow out the candle, and then to lie down on the plump pillows, smelling the faint acrid smell of the smoke from the candle wick.

But marriage to Saul Whitmore would not be like that. Whatever it was, it would not be dull. And one had always heard that there was no better citizen than a reformed rake. Dear Sophia, who was not timid or afraid, would manage him. Yes, of course he must come to the party. It was foolish of her even to have mentioned the matter to Hubert.

CHAPTER 5

At last, just as the first carriage rolled up, the girls went downstairs, holding up their voluminous petticoats, Sophia chattering at the top of her voice.

Briar was left in the bedroom that was like a flower garden through which a gale had swept, petticoats tossed on the floor, lace fichus and flowery bonnets on the bed, discarded morning dresses over a chair.

Sophia had changed her mind three times as to what she would wear. It had turned out to be so fine a day, for once both still and sunny, that Aunt Charity had suddenly decided to have the luncheon party in the garden; and everyone had been working frantically carrying out tables and chairs and linen tablecloths and china and glass.

So that finally there had not been a great deal of time to dress. Then Sophie's intention of wearing her white Swiss muslin sprinkled with pale blue flowers had had to be changed, because the flowers in her bonnet did not match the flowers in her dress. She had tried her striped foulard, and torn that off in exasperation, and had finally decided on her pink silk with that stiffened bodice and wide crackling skirts which Prudence had said was much too grand for what was virtually only a picnic.

Prudence herself wore a much more demure gown, and looked nervous and unhappy. She had no wish to sweep impressively into Wellington society, as had Sophia. She had followed her elder sister downstairs reluctantly, sure that she would burst into tears when the first young man (because he was not Edmund) spoke to her.

This was going to be Sophia's day, there was no doubt about that.

Briar, alone in the bedroom, began to tidy up. But she kept dropping a garment to dart to the window to watch new arrivals.

Not many people could arrive grandly by carriage, for few of them yet owned carriages. Most of them had to walk up the narrow steep road, holding their skirts fastidiously out of the dust. The older women carried parasols, and were importantly enough dressed in flowery hats and rich silks. The girls did not appear to have any great style, mostly their dresses were simple and of last year's fashion. They looked gauche, Briar decided critically, and as for the young men, they seemed ordinary enough. Moustaches were much in evidence, and even one or two vigorous beards which belied the youth of the faces above them.

Which one of these polite strangers would marry Sophia? For one of them would, surely enough. And which was for Prudence, if her heart mended?

And which one for me, Briar wondered irrepressibly, and suddenly pictured herself downstairs, curtseying to the young men, looking at them demurely beneath her lashes.

Then she caught sight of herself in reality in the mirror, a slender, unexciting figure, extinguished by her apron and her dove-gray gown.

"Why, Miss Briar, haven't you a more fetching dress than that?" she demanded, and on an impulse unbuttoned the sober garment, stripping it off and standing in her petticoat before slipping Sophia's rejected Swiss muslin over her head.

She tossed off her cap, pulled the pins out of her hair and let it fall in ringlets on her shoulders.

The gown was too big. It slipped off her shoulders, but if she held it at the back, like that, ah, she was pretty! Her eyes sparkled, and her cheeks flushed the colour of her own namesake, the wild briar rose.

She curtseyed to an imaginary stranger, and said in a meek voice, "I'm Miss Briar Rose Johnson. Good-day, Mr. Fanshawe, good-day, Mr. Whitmore, good-day, Mr. Carruthers. I'm Briar Rose Johnson. I'm Briar." Her voice rose in delirious excitement. "I'm me, me, me!"

"Briar!" came Aunt Charity's voice up the stairs.

She stood a moment, petrified. She didn't covet Sophia's dress, just as she hadn't coveted the silver Uncle Hubert had found her admiring. She just knew that one day she would have similar things. Or better.

She felt so vivid and alive inside Sophia's dainty dress, as if it had been the delicate flame to set her alight. This was how she was meant to feel. She would show people she was not a grey-clad meek shadow.

But not yet, she reflected ruefully, as Aunt Charity called again on a rising note, "Briar!"

The muslin dress slid off. Briar opened the door and stuck her head cautiously round. "Yes, ma'am."

"What are you doing up there?"

"Tidying up, ma'am."

"Then leave that at present. I need you down here."

"Yes, ma'am."

Briar had grasped her own dress and was feverishly dragging it on.

"Come at once. Mary has had an accident. She's scalded her hand. You'll have to help wait at table."

"Yes, ma'am."

Her hair was unpinned and her apron crooked. She was sticking in hairpins as she ran downstairs.

But this is still *me*, even fetching and carrying dishes, she told herself. This gay vivid person is only just hidden under my working dress. And anyway, this was a chance to share in the gaiety and to look at the guests.

"Just do as cook says," Aunt Charity hissed. "Put your cap straight. Briar, have you been using *rouge*?"

"No, ma'am."

"I should hope not. But you look very flushed. Now don't get nervous. And don't spill things."

The sun was shining with the clear brilliance peculiar to antipodean sunshine. Fantails swooped and flirted, spreading their fan-shaped tails like miniature peacocks, the young gum trees at the bottom of the garden rustled, and cast thin shadows over the laden tables. The women in their full-skirted dresses moved about in a stately fashion, giving cries of admiration for the garden, the sunshine (presumably specially arranged by Aunt Charity) and the two nieces, so newly arrived, so fashionably dressed, so impressively connected.

Mrs. Hunt was giving a dinner party, it was dear Sarah Jane's coming-out ball next week, there was a seaside picnic on Saturday. Dear Sophia and Prudence must come to everything, it was so refreshing to see new faces, one was so hungry for news of the home country. The young men bowed and made stiff conversation. Prudence was trapped by a dowager with a lorgnette and a monstrous hat. Sophia had, with surprising skill, extricated herself from a group of talkative young ladies and was annexing for herself the most handsome young man.

It was clearly Sophia's day. Briar, carrying a bowl of fruit punch, heard her saying, "I'm such a silly, I didn't catch your name."

"Fanshawe. Peter Fanshawe, Miss Carruthers."

He was tall and sandy-haired, with a fair skin that flushed easily and bright blue eyes.

"I would like to be talking to him," thought Briar, and this wasn't quite the same as the silver and Sophia's borrowed dress. She was conscious, for the first time, of a sharp resentment.

"The cut-glass tumblers!" Aunt Charity was hissing in her ear.

"Yes, ma'am."

"And the silver ladle!"

She scurried to the house. In the dining-room she loaded up her tray and began the careful journey back to the garden, across the hall, down the passage.

Someone hurrying in jolted her elbow. The tray tipped and the glasses crashed to the floor. She gave a cry of dismay.

The person who had caused the damage, a very tall man, paused briefly to look down at her. She saw a lean sunburnt face with narrowed dark impatient eyes and very black brows.

"I'm sorry! My fault. I'll apologise to your mistress."

And he was gone, leaving her sitting among the broken fragments of Aunt Charity's precious cut-glass tumblers.

The thoughtless clumsy beast! she thought wrathfully. This she would not tolerate, being *walked* over the moment she arrived in a new country. Who did he think he was, anyway? The Governor himself?

"Saul!" came Aunt Charity's rich cooing voice from the garden. "I'm *so* glad you could come. You're such a *busy* person. Let me introduce you to—"

Saul! The name had a curious harsh sound that somehow rasped her nerves. Or was it just that she had cut her finger on a broken tumbler.

"What's happened here? You've had an accident?"

Briar looked up sharply to see the sandy-haired Peter Fanshawe, with the startlingly blue eyes, bending over her. His face was full of concern.

"Can I help you? Let's pick this débris up. Look, it's not too bad, there isn't much broken. Don't cry."

"I'm not crying!" Briar snapped indignantly.

He looked at her with slight surprise. "No, I can see you're not." His gaze lingered. No doubt he hadn't previously met a young woman who would not, in these circumstances, have dissolved into floods of tears. "Your hair's coming down," he said, with sudden interest.

Briar fumbled at her insecure hair. She hadn't had time to pin it up properly when Aunt Charity had called her down from upstairs. Now, although not in tears, she was embarrassed. Because a few moments ago she had longed to talk to Peter Fanshawe, and now she was doing so, but in a state of dishevelment, with her hair falling down and blood dripping from her cut finger.

"Oh, I say! You've cut yourself! Here, you must wrap it. Take my handkerchief."

Before she could protest he had wrapped her hand in a snowy linen handkerchief. "There! Is that better? You must get it bandaged properly."

Briar scrambled to her feet. "Cook will do it for me. I'll take the tray. Thank you so much!" And she fled.

The cut was not serious, and presently she was able to appear again, bandaged and generally tidied up by a disapproving and contemptuous cook.

"Can see you're only fit to have a needle in your hand. Now don't drop that lot. And hurry, or mistress will be screeching her head off."

The party in the sunshine went on serenely. The guests were relaxing and mingling more freely. There were scraps of conversation about the price of wool, the rumour of gold discoveries in the South Island, the Governor's planned measures against the latest Maori atrocities, the difficulty of transporting building material into the bush country, over mountainous country and unbridged rivers, the expected arrival of the next ship, and, as a running background to this more serious talk, the frothy feminine chatter about new clothes and hair styles, the whispered news of someone's pregnancy, someone else's flirtation, the rumour of some new eligible young man come to town.

Out of the corner of her now discreetly downcast eyes Briar saw that Sophia was talking to the tall dark man who had so casually brushed past her. Sophia's face was flushed and animated. She was glad she had worn the pink silk, one could see, although the heat was wilting it a little. She talked all the time, and the young man with the strange harsh name seemed merely to listen. Aunt Charity had turned her head to watch them with a small benevolent smile.

Prudence at last was in conversation with an earnest, rather stout, young man. Uncle Hubert was walking about drinking quantities of fruit punch and dropping an occasional dry remark here and there.

Peter Fanshawe came to take a cup of coffee from Briar's tray, and gave her his bright personal glance. "All right now?" he whispered.

She nodded. She looked steadily into his face for a moment. The day, brilliant enough already, seemed to explode around her. She had made a decision. She would marry Peter Fanshawe. Not only was he good-looking, young and eligible but he would be able to give her the position she desired. And with his gentle manner he would be easy to manage, an important point for someone as ambitious as she. Yes, she had made up her mind. Impossible as it seemed to achieve, she would marry Peter Fanshawe.

Afterwards, there was talk, talk, talk.

Briar was forgiven the dropped tray and the broken glasses.

"Mr. Whitmore explained to me what happened," Aunt Charity said in the benevolent manner she used only when she was pleased with life in general. "He took all the blame. He was worried about arriving a little late. Oh, and my dears," her attention so briefly and casually on Briar had gone back to her nieces, the vehicles through which she could enjoy her present social popularity, "Saul's mother is coming to call one day next week. In the past she has cared nothing for the conventions, but she wants to meet you girls. There can be only one reason for that," she added significantly.

"Is Saul—Mr. Whitmore—very eligible?" Sophia asked.

"My dear, I've told you. He's one of the most promising young settlers we have had, so your uncle says, and moreover he's first cousin to the Earl of Marsham."

"He terrifies me," Prudence murmured. "He looks so dark and aloof and scornful."

"Oh, that's just a pose," said Sophia. "He doesn't terrify me. He doesn't even have much to say, except about his property called Lucknow, and of course the Maoris. Something about a Major von Tempsky who is the cleverest at fighting them in the forest. I begin to find the Maoris very boring as a subject."

"Then what did you say to him?" Prudence asked.

"Oh, this and that. I asked him if he liked my gown."

"Sophie!"

"Why not? He obviously wasn't going to tell me without being asked. Do you know, I'm not sure that I didn't like Peter Fanshawe better than Saul Whitmore. He was much more amusing. He hasn't an earl in his family, has he, Aunt Charity?"

"Not an earl, but his family's very good, nevertheless. He's working in your uncle's bank at present, but I believe he means to take up land."

"Wouldn't it be fun," Sophie cried irrepressibly, "if you married him, Prue, and I married Saul, and we both lived in the same district. Or if I married Peter and you married Saul?"

"I told you, he terrifies me," Prudence said unhappily. "And anyway how can you talk of my marrying anyone but Edmund?"

"It does no harm at all to meet other young men," Aunt Charity said firmly. "It's a healthy attitude. You must neither of you make hasty decisions. But I do think we have begun very nicely. Now let me see, we go to Mrs. Hunt's dinner party tomorrow. And on Friday there's the ball at Government House. You will make a grand toilette for that, my dears. And next week there's Sarah Jane Maxwell's coming-out ball, which won't be on the same scale as Government House, but very nice, nevertheless. Her father owns several cargo ships, that carry stock and supplies to the different ports. By the way, I must tell you that there's always a shortage of young women at these balls. So it's expected that you dance all the time. You mustn't refuse anybody, or go wandering in the garden, for instance. It really becomes quite strenuous, I can assure you, but you're young. I expect you'll survive."

"Aunt Charity, if we're to go to all these balls we simply haven't enough gowns!"

"Then we must call on my clever Miss Matthews. And Briar sews very neatly, I've noticed. I'm sure she can be of great assistance."

"I'll wear my white brocade to Government House," Sophia decided.

"Oh, you think of nothing but clothes!" Prudence cried in sudden exasperation. "Clothes and men!"

Sophia opened her pale blue eyes wide. "But what else is there to think of?"

In the small house at the top of the steep track, with its ineffective screening of *manuka* trees, Mrs. Whitmore looked at her son.

"But wasn't there anyone there at all of any interest?" she insisted.

"No, I told you so. They're all too soft and silly. I want a woman who can live hard."

"That would come."

"What! You believe that when all the clothes and silly chatter are stripped off there's still something there?"

"It depends whom you're contemplating stripping," his mother said flatly. "Come now, tell me what the nieces from England were like."

"One hadn't a word to say for herself, and the other talked all the time."

"Could be nerves in both cases. But they were attractive young women?"

"Fair enough. Over-dressed."

The old lady's eyelids fell and lifted again, with a slow movement like a parrot's. She had a hooded secret look today. She was trying to control her impatience with her dark-browed son, and to move cautiously and with tact. He had the quick flaring nature that could make him saddle his horse and set off for Lucknow in the next hour if he so pleased.

"Perhaps you're making unfair comparisons, Saul."

He flung round, his face suddenly alight with humour and appreciation. "How right you are, mother." For those care-fully tended doll-like faces of today's party had had none of the lively vitality and warmth and unashamed tenderness of the company he had recently kept. Bawdy and not too young and not always over-clean, but alive, alive!

"Though there was one," he began, then stopped. Where had he caught a glimpse of a flushed angry brilliant face, with tumbled hair and a bitten back imprecation on her lips. Not at Charity Carruthers, that was certain. It must have been at Cooper's last night.

He sensed his mother's carefully concealed disappointment, and his very great and unselfish love for this strong, wise, courageous woman who had borne him, her only child, when she was nearly forty years of age, and was now growing old, uncomplainingly but with hunger for grandchildren gnawing at her, made him say, "I'm not much good at these social things, mother. I'd rather talk to Hubert Carruthers about my wool clip, or Te Kooti's latest move, but I'll stick it. Actually, the older one, Sophia, was attractive enough. And she didn't behave as if she was scared I'd seduce her on the spot. I'd like you to meet her."

"I will. I plan to call on Charity Carruthers next week."

In the long wooden barracks situated at the foot of the hill near the wharf, where immigrant families newly arrived were temporarily accommodated, Briar at last was able to visit Jemima and Fred Potter.

Jemima ran forward to hug her and exclaim delightedly, and Fred, who was almost inarticulate, said with pleasure, "Here's a face we know at last!"

The two thin children, Jimmy aged seven and Lucy, five, grinned shyly. Always silent children, they had grown preternaturally silent as a consequence of the long ship journey, and the deaths of their two younger brothers.

"How's the baby?" Briar demanded.

"Oh, she's thriving now. We can get good milk for her, and you'd hardly know her. Look."

Jemima led the way to the wicker basket, and turned back the shawl from the tiny face.

Briar felt her heart stir at the sight of the miniature creature. "Why, she's bonny. She has colour in her cheeks. You'll be glad now that you've come, Jemima?"

Jemima's lips twisted. But she nodded vigorously. "Aye. It will be all right, as soon as Fred gets work and a place to live."

"Hasn't Fred got work yet?"

Jemima looked towards her silent husband. "He could get a job as a baker's help, but he doesn't fancy the flour all the time. He wants the land, Briar, and that's the truth." She was very loyal to the small, rather stout, not particularly intelligent man who was her husband. He had simple desires, and she loved him enough to want him to achieve them. She didn't mind this uncomfortable and uprooted way of living for a little while.

"He's waiting to get a place on a farm," she went on. "Then we'll all be moving into the country. It'll be fine for the children. And now, Briar, tell us what you've been doing. Have there been all kinds of exciting goings on? You've changed, somehow. You've got a look about you. You haven't fallen in love?"

Briar shook her head. "No, and I don't mean to. It's silly. But I've found the man I'm going to marry." She laughed a little. "He only spoke to me once. I'd cut my finger and he wrapped it up. But he was kind and gentle. As if he cared what happened to me." In spite of herself, wonder was in her

51

voice. It was still so intoxicating a sensation to know that someone, even fleetingly, cared about her pain. "He'd make a very good husband, and give me what I want," she added more practically.

"But who is he, Briar dear?" Jemima asked anxiously.

"His name is Peter Fanshawe. He came to the party the other day."

"You mean your young ladies' party? But then he's—"

"One of the gentry," Briar flashed scornfully. "Why not?"

"But Briar dear, even in this new country there'll be conventions."

"Oh yes, there are plenty of them, More, perhaps. But they're made by silly snobbish women like Mrs. Carruthers, and one can fight her sort." Briar's head went up with its familiar proud lift. "I don't intend to be a servant all my life. And you'll see, I won't be."

"No, of course you won't. You're not the sort. You'll marry some nice man with his own little business, perhaps."

"I'll marry the man I want," Briar declared. "And then maybe I'll have—" her gaze went to the cradle. She touched the baby's soft cheek. "I feel she's part mine, Jemima. I did help to keep her alive, didn't I? Look after her for me."

"We will, lovey. And you look after yourself. Don't get too high-flown. We understand, Fred and me, but other people might not."

"I'm not high-flown, Jemima dear," Briar said simply. "I just know what I want, and I intend to get it."

So Jemima and Fred thought she was getting ideas above herself. What would they have thought had they known the wild idea that came into her head later, which she meant to carry out?

It had been a week of social activities for Sophia and Prudence. There had been dinner parties, picnics, and then the ball at Government House to which they had gone dressed in their very best finery, Sophia in white brocade, Prudence in pink, and Aunt Charity looking enormously impressive in black satin trimmed with a great many jet beads.

As usual, Briar had to sit up until they came home, to unbutton the young ladies, help them out of their stiff dresses and into night attire.

Sitting in the lamplight sewing (Sophie was always ripping flounces or splitting seams), she wondered how much longer she would be able to bring herself to do this task meekly, saying, "Yes, ma'am," and, "No, ma'am," fetching and carrying, laundering and ironing, always looking cheerful and obedient, crushing down her own personality until it was not noticed. At the very beginning she had not minded. She had listened with slightly amused contempt to Sophia's endless chatter about marriage, and to Aunt Charity's snobbish plotting.

But now everything had changed. For everywhere the girls went they met Peter Fanshawe, Saul Whitmore and others. One could not help meeting the same people all the time in such a small community. Sophia chattered freely about them all, but obviously her favour wavered between Peter and Saul.

And she, Briar, had to sit at home and mend gowns, and help to make Sophia beautiful for these occasions! Every day the fury inside herself grew.

Was she herself never to meet Peter again? Or never on his own ground. Always, just as the rather pitiable figure of a parlour maid in trouble, to whom he extended his careless comfort.

Before she knew what had happened one of those stupid, simpering but socially elect young women would have got him, and he would never know that she existed as a woman, warm-hearted, tender and loving.

She had to make a plan that would give her the opportunity of seeing him again. And this time not in a maid's cap and apron, but as a well-dressed and attractive young woman.

It seemed impossible. Even to within ten minutes of her mistresses arriving home from the Government House ball it seemed impossible. But suddenly the opportunity was tossed to her by the prattling Sophie. And her mind was made up.

As usual Sophie arrived home hot and dishevelled, her gown trodden on, her gloves rumpled and dirty, her hair tumbling askew. "But it was a wonderful ball! Wasn't it, Prue? Oh, don't say you didn't enjoy it. I noticed James French never took his eyes off you."

"I wish he'd kept his feet off mine, too," Prudence retorted.

"He was too enraptured with you, I dare say. We really were by far the best dressed there, Briar. Everyone looked at us. Even Saul Whitmore brought himself to compliment me, without my prodding him into it. And dearest Peter was full of admiration. He says the most extravagant things."

"I expect he's been saying them for years," Prue said waspishly.

"Don't be absurd! *I* haven't been here for years. I must say even Saul looked a little put out tonight. He wanted me for the supper dance, but I'd already given it to Peter. Though I must say there's something ruthless and dangerous about Saul that I find very exciting. The way he looks at me with those deep eyes. I don't think I'd ever dare to deceive him. Briar, must you be so clumsy?"

"Sorry, Miss Sophie," Briar murmured automatically.

"Have we kept you up too late? It's only two o'clock. You wouldn't think it was late if you'd been at the ball. Saul asked me to walk in the garden. I refused, of course. Do you know, that pretty little Mrs. Morgan has eight children. And all living! She's only twenty-seven. No chance for me to do that, but I vow I'll have three at least by the time I'm twenty-seven. And *what* do you think about that Sarah Jane Maxwell?"

"What?" Prudence asked indifferently. She was already in her nightgown and brushing her own hair, since Sophia monopolised the attentions of Briar.

"She's going to have the marriage dance at her ball next week."

"The marriage dance?"

"But didn't you hear? Really, Prue, you must live with your head in the clouds. Or in the *Mary Louise*. All the ladies are blindfolded, and when the music stops the man they're in front of is their chosen mate."

"You mean truly?"

"Well, I suppose you don't *have* go stick to it. But Sarah Jane says most people do. Certainly I'm sure people like Saul and Peter would because of their honour. You see, there are far more young men than young women in this country, and that's sometimes the fairest way of getting a wife. Of course Sarah Jane's only having the dance because she hasn't been asked yet. She's driven to it, poor creature. She's twenty-two! I should think she's planning to get Saul Whitmore."

"But how can she plan to get anyone if she can't see?"

Even Sophia had to look baffled at that. "Yes, they say there's no cheating. You really can't see. But I expect the men, if they recognise one, can do a little plotting. They're not supposed to recognise us, of course. The masks cover our faces. Don't you think it's terribly exciting?"

"I don't think I shall do it," said Prudence nervously.

"Oh, Prue, you are a little fool, falling in love with that penniless Edmund and spoiling all your fun. Don't you agree, Briar? Wouldn't you like to dance in the marriage dance?"

Briar drew a deep breath. "Yes, Miss Sophia," she said coolly. "I would."

CHAPTER 6

Oriane Whitmore sat on one of Aunt Charity's upright chairs, clasping her black umbrella. She looked like a thin, elderly, alert crane nursing a broken wing. Her skin was yellowed and dried from years spent in the parching Indian sun, and her tall body seemed fleshless. But her magnificent eyes, hooded and brilliant, missed nothing.

Aunt Charity fluttered about as nervously as a schoolgirl, fussing as to whether her visitor would take tea, or perhaps a cool drink after her long walk. Perhaps she would like to sit in the garden in the shade, although it was rather windy.

"I always hope that in summer the winds will stop, but they never do," Aunt Charity chattered. "I wonder if the Taranaki district is less disturbed in this way. Though my husband talks a great deal about the Maori problem there. They're such fearsome fighters when aroused, one hears. It seems hard to believe when one sees them sitting about their villages so lazily, selling fruit and kumaras. Do you care for the kumara, Mrs. Whitmore?"

"I prefer the potato unsweetened." The old lady shifted her position and stated in her definite voice, "The Maori trouble in the north will blow over. No woman with any spirit would be afraid to live there."

"Of course you lived through that dreadful siege in India," Aunt Charity murmured admiringly.

"One acquires the necessary courage when the emergency arises. Well, Mrs. Carruthers, where are these two nieces I've heard so much about?"

Aunt Charity's face was a mixture of excitement, apprehension and nervousness. So it really was true that Saul Whitmore was interested in Sophia. It must be Sophia, because Prudence in her present lovelorn state wouldn't interest the merest mouse.

What a triumph it would be to write home to England to report that Sophia had annexed the most eligible *parti* in the whole of the island. She had had her hopes, to be sure, but she privately hadn't thought even Sophia, let alone that silly moping Prudence, would interest a man of Saul's distinction and dash. And experience, one had to add to oneself, regrettably.

"I'll call the girls," she fluttered. "They're resting. Such a gay life they're leading."

Oriane Whitmore sat erect to observe the girls as they came in.

They curtseyed gracefully enough, eyes downcast, cheeks prettily flushed. But they were what she had expected, plump, healthy-looking creatures reduced to gaucheness by her deliberate stare. And young. So young!

The younger one could be dismissed at once. She had a meek, long-suffering look that would drive a man like Saul to fury. But it was Sophia, the elder, in whom he had expressed interest, so it was Sophia on whom she bent her intense regard. Not beautiful, but pretty enough with those flushed youthful cheeks and wide blue eyes. Good-tempered, one would imagine. Vain, obviously, because of the fussiness of her toilette, but a little vanity did a woman no harm. It helped to keep her pride under difficult conditions. Garrulous, indeed (one could see her chafing already under her enforced silence) but there again Saul was sometimes too silent, and a little frothy chatter would be good for him.

Intellectual? A man did not need intellectuality in a wife. He wanted a healthy attractive body, good temper, and the ability to keep a comfortable well-run house.

Mrs. Whitmore nodded ever so slightly to herself.

"Now perhaps," she said, looking at Aunt Charity, "if I may accept your very kind offer of tea. It was hot walking today."

"Indeed, yes," cried Aunt Charity. "If you will excuse me a moment. Polly—Briar—" In an uncharacteristic twitter, because of all days Polly should choose this one to beg for an hour to visit her mother, and once again there was only Briar who was so much better with her sewing needle than with tea trays, Aunt Charity vanished.

Mrs. Whitmore turned her undivided attention to Sophia.

But afterwards she walked home more slowly than usual. The hot summer sun had taken the springiness out of her step. Was she right in forcing this decision on Saul? No, not forcing it because he would never be forced, but presenting it as not only an emotional obligation, but a necessity.

The girl had been right enough. At least she hadn't fidgeted and threatened to burst into tears. She had looked back at Mrs. Whitmore fearlessly enough and answered all her questions in a pleasant if naïve manner. But she was far from adult. Those eyes had been the clear blue eyes of a romping schoolgirl. How would she be, living the lonely isolated life of a pioneer's wife? How would she behave in a Hauhau attack?

Mrs. Whitmore stamped impatiently up the dusty road. One could be over-critical. And Saul must marry. She would be enthusiastic in her report of Sophia. And if one wished those round blue eyes had been less empty, and more steady, like the darker ones of—whose had they been, those bright dark green eyes which had stared at her with cool assessment?

Good heavens, they had belonged to the maid who had brought in the tea. How extraordinary!

After Mrs. Whitmore's departure Sophia was in a whirl of excitement. "Aunt Charity, what shall I do? I believe Saul means to propose!"

"That's how it looks, my love," Aunt Charity said complacently.

"But what shall I do? Oh, I like him well enough. He's got that dark dangerous look that's really too exciting. But I like Peter, too. He says nice things, and a girl likes to be flattered. Oh, dear, what shall I do?"

"Pull yourself together!" Aunt Charity's voice was tart. She was mistress of herself and her home again now that strange disturbing woman, Oriane Whitmore, had gone. "Act sensibly. Saul's much the better match."

"But I'd have to live in the wilds!"

"He's second in line to the earldom," said Aunt Charity. "You may be a countess one day."

"I'd be so bored in the country. No parties. And I might not even have enough servants. I might have to do my own housework!" Sophia was deliciously torn between this embarrassing plentitude of prospective husbands. "But to be a countess," she murmured, and suddenly her face was as speculative as Aunt Charity's.

"That wouldn't be much use to you if you're tomahawked," said Prudence, whose own uncertain chance of happiness was already making her grow acid. "Or if you're baking your own bread. Pioneer women have to work."

"Even as Peter Fanshawe's wife you might have to do that," Aunt Charity told her. "You girls have been spoilt so far. I wanted you to be, until you had settled down. But you'll find most of the women who come to the balls and parties have come from their kitchens. They're not all as fortunately situated as I am. And scarcely one of them has a personal maid. You won't be able to keep Briar for ever, either of you."

"One hardly expects to," Sophia said cheerfully. "She's sure to marry, anyway. Haven't you noticed how the gardener's boy looks at her already? All the same I can't imagine what Prue or I will do without her. I want her to sew some new ribbons on my bonnet. I bought them this morning. I must show you."

She went bouncing upstairs, and burst into the bedroom. "Briar! What are you doing with that dress?"

Briar flushed crimson. Sophia had come so suddenly that she had not had time to put the dress back in the wardrobe. But in a moment she had regained her composure.

"I noticed it needs a stitch at the hem, Miss Sophia. You must have torn it at the ball the other night." She gathered a fold of the gleaming brocade in her hand, carefully not displaying the imaginary tear.

"Oh, how tiresome! One of those clumsy young men must have stood on it."

"What gown do you wish to wear to Miss Maxwell's ball?" Briar enquired softly.

"Oh, that isn't a very grand affair, and the first dance is to be this quite terrifying marriage one. It has to be the first before the young men recognise us by the dresses we're wearing. We're all ushered in very secretly. It's really awfully daring. Perhaps it will help me to make up my mind, too. Though one doesn't have to take it seriously, of course. I think all it does is prompt the bashful young men into proposals they've been too shy to make. Oh, I'll just wear my blue muslin for that, Briar."

"Very well, Miss Sophia," Briar replied sedately. "I'll take the brocade to my room to mend. I'll do it this evening."

"That's very good of you, Briar. What would we do without you? I'd turn into a frump, I'm sure. And Prue is practically one already. She's been in floods of tears because the *Mary Louise* has sailed with her precious Edmund. Well, perhaps the marriage dance will solve her problem, too."

Very few of the Wellington residents had yet been able to build houses large enough in which to hold balls. As a general rule the local hall was hired for the occasion, and decorated lavishly with bunting, ferns and the long plumy *toe toe* grass to hide its deficiencies. The pianist and a pair of fiddlers sat on a raised platform at the end, and chairs were provided round the walls for chaperons, and any young lady who might inconceivably be sitting out a dance. Though this was such a rarity that she would almost have had to be physically deformed. The youthful male population was very much in the majority.

Sometimes during the festivities an inquisitive dark tattooed face might appear at the window, gazing with naïve pleasure and bewilderment at the strange behaviour of the *pakeha*. Shellfish, in plaited green baskets, or kumaras, cooked and smoking hot, might be brought to the door for sale. But these were seldom necessary, for the hostess, as a matter of pride, would have seen that there was an abundance of food.

This was the setting for Sarah Jane Maxwell's ball.

Briar, arriving on foot and alone, was able to make her carefully planned entrance just as the other girls were being shepherded, blindfolded and giggling, from the adjoining building which served as dressing-rooms to the main hall.

She had had to lay her plans like a military manœuvre, reconnoitring the previous day to see how long it would take her to walk from Aunt Charity's, how the hall was situated, and whether she could, at the last minute, mingle unnoticed with the legitimate guests.

Everything had gone amazingly well. She had finished Sophia's and Prudence's toilettes well ahead of time, to the accompaniment of Sophia's grumbles that Briar was being very clumsy that evening, pulling her hair and dragging at her gown.

"Anyone would think you were going to the ball yourself, you're in such a tizzy," she said good-naturedly. And then, with unexpected perceptiveness, had added, "I suppose you would like to go to a ball one day. Well, perhaps you will. Goodness knows, some of the people one meets have had little enough background. But they've made money, or been clever in some way, so all seems to be well. Even the Governor meets them. Who knows? one day even you might curtsey to His Excellency."

"Yes, Miss Sophia," said Briar composedly. "Is that all you require now?"

"I think so. But you're in an awful hurry tonight. What are

you going to do while we're away? You're not planning a clandestine meeting with some man, are you?"

"I was going to finish mending your white brocade, Miss Sophia."

"I scarcely believe you, you know. You look as if you have a secret. Anyway, you don't need to sew all the evening. Read a book for some of the time."

Briar didn't, as it happened, need to sew at all, for the dress was ready, taken in at the waist and shoulders where it had been too big, so that now it fitted her as if it had been made for her. She had tried it on in her room late last night when she was unlikely to be disturbed. In the small cloudy mirror, by the wavering light of her candle, she had seemed to hover like a white ghost. She had nearly wept with exasperation because she could not see herself clearly.

When everyone had gone tonight and the other servants were in the kitchen, she had planned to slip up and look at herself in the long mirror in Aunt Charity's room.

But she hadn't been able to do that either, for Polly had been walking about, and once cook had called to her. It was too risky to go through the house in the shining dress. She had had to climb out of her window at last, and slip across the garden, holding her skirts up from the dewy grass.

She had covered herself with her dark cloak, and when she was on the road leading to town she had wrapped it round herself and prayed she would not meet anyone who recognised her, or who thought it strange that a young woman in a ball dress should be walking alone.

She wasn't nervous, for she was on fire with excitement. The beautiful dress had brought back confidence in her own physical beauty, and she knew that her slender body and high proud head were the equal, if not the superior, of any she would see tonight.

When Peter Fanshawe stripped off her mask and saw her glowing face, her narrow white shoulders, her body embellished with the clothes that were its due, he must fall in love with her, or at least be intriguingly aware of her beauty. If he did not, he would surely be far too courteous to ignore the implication of this particular dance.

A young man who did not do so, it was reputed, was labelled a cad. For the very fact of joining in it meant that he was more than half serious.

Nor was there any cheating possible, for the blindfolding of the girls was strictly supervised, and they held hands as they walked in their slow dark circle. Almost all the candles in the hall were put out. It was, they said, almost like an incantation, a spell, with the slowly moving girls, the thin sound of the fiddles, and the tense waiting young men.

But Briar was not going to be blindfolded by any hands but her own, and she meant to leave herself a generous peephole. She would drop her cloak in the bushes as she arrived at the ball, tie the scarf round her eyes, and then, as the giggling girls fumbled their way to the door, unobtrusively join them.

She was tense with anticipation. At last something was happening to her, and she was making it happen. She was, as she had always meant to do, creating her own destiny.

It never occurred to her for one moment that it could go wrong.

CHAPTER 7

Saul hadn't meant to take part in this foolish game. But before presenting himself at the ball he had drunk fairly liberally at Cooper's, and his mood now was one of recklessness.

He needed a wife, he must take a wife. Sophia Carruthers, who pleasantly stirred his senses though she did not, unfortunately, touch his heart, was the obvious choice. Sophia, who was garrulous and gay and almost as reckless as himself, would certainly not be left out of the fun of this childish and daring game. If she should be claimed by some other man, in the excitement of the moment who knew that she would not accept him on the spot?

So that if one were to make sure of possessing her, one had to stand in that uneasy circle in the smoky darkened room and watch the long string of whispering giggling stumbling girls come in.

No one should have been able to be identified by her gown because they had not yet displayed them this evening. But Saul not only saw extremely well, even in the almost pitch dark, but had a good memory for women's clothes. He recognised at once the white brocade Sophia had worn to the Government House ball the previous week. It shone faintly in the dark, and was unmistakable. Sophia, the devious little wretch, had planned this so as to be recognised, and claimed by the man who most wanted her. She was taking no chances after all.

Saul chuckled softly to himself. This was a game at which two could play. He fixed his eyes on the moving glimmer of the dress, and as the tension grew unbearable and one of the girls screamed, "Stop! Stop!" his acute ear warned him that the fiddles were drawing to a wailing stop. He moved swiftly, stuck out a deft foot, caught the young woman as she was passing him, and as the music ceased pulled her into his arms.

The noise was chaotic. Someone began to relight the lamps and candles. The light grew. Saul whipped off the silk scarf hiding his captive's face, then gave an exclamation and both hands fell to his sides.

He was looking into a completely strange face. A young, brilliant-eyed, furious face.

"You!" the girl cried, on a note of disbelief. She turned her head like a caught hare. Her glance fell on Sophia, giggling hysterically in Peter Fanshawe's arms, she suddenly clapped her hand to her mouth as if in acute pain and consternation. Then, before he could say anything at all, she turned and fled.

It was a very long way down the hall and out at the open door. Everything, to Briar's dazed eyes, was a blur, a sea of faces lost in the yellow candlelight. She only knew she had to get out of here, away, away, where she could not see that dark, startled, lean and sardonic face looking down at her.

She heard Prudence's intensely shocked voice, "It's *Briar!*" And then she was out in the blessed cool dark night, running down the road, heedless now as to whether or not she dirtied the hem of Sophia's gown.

She had nowhere to go except back to her own room, the only haven she knew. Down the dusty road she hurried, tripping on boulders, her hair tumbling down, tears of shock and dismay and intense humiliation already staining her cheeks. Through the front gates, standing open for the return of the carriage, round the house, across the garden where the smell of roses and gum leaves mingled, smearing the dusty hem of the gown with dew so that it would be beyond wearing again. Tumbling through her open window, and then breathlessly dragging at the dress so that she could tear it off and forget it. Forget the whole nightmare had happened.

For it wasn't only looking into Saul Whitmore's strangely

expectant face that had dismayed her. It was seeing Sophia so willingly in Peter Fanshawe's arms.

She had gambled and she had lost. The odds against a girl with no name, no family, no background, had been too much, even in this country. Her life was over!

She was still crouched on the floor in her petticoat when there was a curious noise at her window, a tapping and then a swift lifting of the bottom frame.

In the darkness she saw a man silhouetted. He had already swung one leg over the sill.

She should have screamed. But even that, on this disastrous night, was not possible. Her dry throat gave no sound, and she crouched back against the bed staring helplessly.

"Let's have some light," said Saul Whitmore's voice.

He swung the other leg over the sill, and was right in the room. He closed the window behind him, with the most complete assurance, and then struck a match and lit the candle on her bedside table.

The frail yellow circle of light showed him her face, up-turned to him defencelessly. All he could see was the pallor of her cheeks, her tumbled hair and the enormous dark pools of her eyes.

"Well," he said easily, "I believe you look better in your own petticoat than you do in your mistress's dress. Don't borrow other people's plumes again. You don't need to."

"Get out of here!" she hissed. Her voice still had no volume, but it was full of fury. Her momentary appearance of defencelessness had been an illusion. This girl, he saw now, would never be defenceless.

And suddenly, although this was what he had come intending to do, he now did it with twice as much vigour.

"Not yet," he said. "Not until I've said what I came to say."

"You have no right to say anything to me! It's nothing to do with you if I chose to dance tonight. It's to do with my mistress only. And if I've ruined her dress, that's nothing to do with you either. So please go back the way you came. This minute!"

"Now wait," said Saul, laughing with amusement. "I haven't come to chastise you. I've come to ask you to be my wife."

"Your—your *wife*!"

Her incredulity made him look at her with even greater interest. Perhaps he had startled her. But even so he had not expected a reception even remotely like this the first time he spoke those momentous words.

He had pondered on speaking them for some years now, but he had never thought they would be said in such strange surroundings, by candlelight in a narrow servant's bedroom to a girl with a paper white face who stood with a curious instinctive pride in her petticoat.

"But that's utterly impossible!" she said, and had even the effrontery to speak haughtily, like an outraged gentlewoman.

"Why is it impossible? You danced in that ridiculous dance tonight. You must have done it because you wanted a husband. So why do you look at me with such contempt?"

"In the first place," she said, "are you in the habit of climbing through the windows of ladies' bedrooms at night?"

In spite of the cutting quality of her voice, her enunciation pleased him. She spoke with a better accent than her mistresses did. And at this moment the fury in her eyes might have quelled even the warlike Te Kooti himself.

"I apologise for that," said Saul, enjoying himself enormously. "But you asked for it. And I couldn't scare the other servants out of their wits by bursting through the house. Besides, you look very fetching in that petticoat. Why haven't I seen you before?"

"You have!" she retorted furiously. "You knocked a tray out of my hands one day. But it was another man who picked it up."

"Oh!" he said slowly, his eyes narrowed with amusement. "I see it all now. That little episode made you think you fell in love with this man. And so you planned to smuggle yourself into this affair tonight. A brilliant idea, of course, but not infallible."

"Someone tripped me!" she said in a muffled voice. "It spoilt the whole thing."

"And so you have ended up with me." His voice was sardonic. "And I with you."

She backed away from him, her slim figure taut. "Nothing of the kind! I haven't the slightest intention of marrying you, even if you meant your absurd proposal."

"I meant it," said Saul. "And what's more, it shall happen. And you'll find me a much more interesting husband than the one you planned to get, I assure you."

"You're quite abominable!"

He smiled, enjoying again her fury. Then he reached out and pulled her into his arms.

64

Before she could scream he had kissed her.

He didn't know whether she would have screamed, anyway, for when he let her go she made no sound at all. She cowered back again the wall, looking at him with those enormous eyes. Suddenly he had an almost overmastering impulse to take her in his arms again and throw her on the bed and strip off even that scarcely modest petticoat.

But no. He could wait. She was to be his wife. She would be worth waiting for.

CHAPTER 8

By the time she heard the carriage returning and voices outside, the loud decisive tones of Aunt Charity followed by Uncle Hubert's soothing mumble, Briar had packed her box and was dressed in her outdoor clothes.

She was very pale, shadows of exhaustion and distress beneath her eyes, and her lips still throbbing slightly from Saul Whitmore's kiss. She had never been kissed before, and she had not known the angry confusion of feelings such an experience would bring.

When her door was flung open by Aunt Charity, monumental and overpowering in her black satin, she was still biting her lips to cool their burning. But she had enough presence of mind to speak first. For she did not intend to pretend a humility she did not feel.

"I've packed my box, ma'am, and I'm just leaving."

"Leaving! And where do you propose to go at this hour?"

"To the barracks where Fred and Jemima Potter are. But I didn't think you'd care where I went, ma'am."

Aunt Charity was obviously struggling to control her feelings. Her mouth worked and her small eyes blazed furiously. But from the background Uncle Hubert's calm voice came.

"Bring her out here, Charity. We can't all talk to her in her bedroom. Bring her into the drawing-room where she belongs."

"Belongs!" whispered his wife incredulously.

"From now on," said Uncle Hubert. There seemed to be an undercurrent of amusement in his voice. "You can't entertain Saul Whitmore's wife in a servant's room. After all, she may be a countess one day."

"It's monstrous!" Aunt Charity got out in a strangled voice. She opened and closed her hands helplessly. Then she managed to say, "Come into the drawing-room, Briar. We want to talk to you. And take off your cloak. You're not going anywhere. Not tonight, anyway. Because we have a great deal to discuss."

Sheer surprise made Briar follow Aunt Charity's large doomlike figure meekly. Uncle Hubert stood aside to let her pass. "I see you're wearing the greenstone *tiki*," he whispered. "You'll need it."

The good luck charm which she had kept on under Sophie's dress that evening. Much good it *had* done her, Briar thought ruefully. She had been tempted to throw it out of her window, but a strange superstition as to the power of this little, grinning, irreverent god had stopped her.

"Sit down, Briar," Aunt Charity commanded austerely.

Both hanging lamps had been lit, and the room looked grand and forbidding. Briar had never before sat down in it, and now perched nervously on the edge of one of the mahogany chairs.

Uncle Hubert, indeed, was the only one of the three at ease. He took a leisurely time lighting his pipe, and said conversationally, as if Briar were a guest who must be entertained, "Sophie and Prudence have stayed on at the ball. Mrs. Brown has taken on chaperoning duties. Sophie's having the time of her life, but Prue wouldn't dance in that damn fool dance. I don't blame her. That's for the adventurous, not the meek."

Briar looked from his unmistakably twinkling eyes to Aunt Charity's, still blazing with their baffled fury. "I'm sorry if I've made you very angry, ma'am," she said stiffly.

"Angry!" burst out Aunt Charity. "Why, I'd like you out of the house this minute, no matter where you went. I'm quite shocked and disgusted at the way the moment you girls reach this country your heads get full of grand ideas and you're no use any more as decent obedient servants. I knew this would happen to you the moment I set eyes on you."

"Now, my love! That's not what we planned to say to Briar.'"

Aunt Charity gasped and puffed out her chest, and subsided. "Very well, Hubert. But that I had to say, or die. Now Briar, Saul Whitmore has come to us and told us he wants to make you his wife. Why he has reached this decision is not for me to guess at, but I'd point out that it's a very great honour he is doing you, and I only hope you will be able to prove yourself worthy of it. So you see," she smiled wryly, "whatever you planned to do tonight, you succeeded."

"But I didn't!" Briar gasped.

"I have explained to Saul, and he knows it himself, that this wretched dance, which, of course, must be forbidden in future, was not to be taken seriously. But he is very strangely obstinate. He says he's determined to marry you. So my husband and I, since your parents are not here—" Aunt Charity could not resist shooting an angry glance at her blandly smiling husband—"have agreed that you should remain in this house, temporarily at least, until further plans are made. No one wants a scandal. And one must, after all, be broadminded in a new community. Social values have to be reappraised quite frequently. I'm sure—" her stiff reluctant voice stopped, and Uncle Hubert finished easily: "What my wife is trying to say, Briar, is that you are of the stuff of which pioneers are made, and we're quite sure you'll make Saul a very successful wife."

Briar sprang up, her cheeks crimson. "But I haven't the slightest intention of marrying Saul! You're all making the most enormous mistake. It wasn't Saul I meant to marry! But now everything is ruined!"

And abruptly she ran sobbing from the room.

The girls were home and Sophia was demanding, "Where's Briar? What has she to say for herself? Has she apologised for wearing my dress? My best one, too. I'll never be able to wear it again."

"My dear Sophia," said Uncle Hubert, "one day, say in a hundred years, a facsimile of you will stand in a glass case in a museum bearing a card, 'Type of gown worn by young woman in later Victorian period' and no one will see your face or your eyes or your lips or your soul. Because that's all you will represent, the fashions of your day. And that, heaven help you, is all you seem to represent at this moment."

Sophia looked at him uncomprehendingly. "Uncle, don't tease. I've had such a wonderful evening, in spite of Briar. I believe Peter's on the very point of proposing. I shall accept him, of course. Actually, Briar's behaviour has helped me to make up my mind, so perhaps she has done me a good turn. Where is she?"

"She has gone to bed," said Aunt Charity repressively.

"She's hysterical and quite tiresome. But she'll see reason in the morning. Personally, I'd be glad never to have to set eyes on her again. Now I must go to bed or I shall collapse. Prudence, would you bring me some sal volatile?"

"Of course, Aunt Charity. And a hot drink? Something soothing when you are in bed?"

"Well—some hot chocolate, perhaps. That makes me sleep, if ever I shall sleep again."

When she was in bed, ensconced in her nightcap and all-enveloping nightgown, she gave an enormous sigh. Prudence was tiresomely without spirit and vivacity, constantly mooning over that wretched sailor, but at this moment she was quiet and comforting. Aunt Charity sipped her hot chocolate and began to revive.

"I wanted to dismiss that impudent chit instantly, but your uncle forbade it. He said that I could be a laughing stock, or I could be the admiration of all intelligent people for my tolerant attitude. After all, one does have to be tolerant in a small community with such a mixed population. And if this girl is to be Saul Whitmore's wife, one simply can't quarrel with the Whitmores, as your uncle sensibly pointed out. But if New Zealand is to be ruled by these impudent little baggages, I tremble for its future. Besides, I had so counted on Sophia—" she sniffed weepily—"Saul had seemed greatly taken with her. But there! Your uncle says all isn't lost. Although I do wish he wouldn't *enjoy* this impossible situation!"

Prudence patted her hand. "Don't worry, Aunt Charity. Get some sleep. You're tired."

"I'm utterly exhausted! You're so kind, my love. You're a dear child. I'm very fond of you."

"Thank you, Aunt Charity,"

"Sometimes I wonder—I mean, one tries so hard, and finally captures one—but is it really worth the effort?"

"What are you saying, Aunt Charity?"

Aunt Charity's face was crumpled and bleak. "What am I saying? Merely how peaceful a bedroom is without a man in it."

Then she sighed again, resignedly. "Run along, child. Your uncle will be wanting to come to bed."

The next day Briar sat again on the edge of one of the mahogany chairs in the drawing-room.

Perhaps it had been the whisky he had drunk the previous night, Saul reflected. What else had made him think this girl was such a creature of mystery and fire? Or perhaps it had been that she was in her petticoat, her hair tumbled, her shoulders naked, her slim waist blooming into the lovely curve of her breasts.

For now, in her neat grey gown with her hair smoothly pinned back and her face closed, she was a stranger. He didn't know her at all. Much less did he want to make her his wife.

Unless he were to discover again that other identity of hers, the furious person whose eyes blazed green fire, and whose taut hostile body suggested such rich promise.

If he had not dreamed her, of course. Looking at the chilly person opposite him he was afraid he had. But he was a man of honour, and he meant to stick to his word.

"Thank you for allowing me to see you again," he began. It was not possible for him to speak humbly. The aloof politeness of his voice was his nearest approach to humility.

"I understood you wished it," she answered, with equal courtesy.

"I did. Perhaps I was too abrupt last night—"

"I'm only seeing you because they insisted that I do so," she broke in, and he realised all at once how hard it was for her to retain her attitude of dignified aloofness. She was still seething with anger, and she was not normally inarticulate.

He was right about her, by heavens! Exultantly he wanted to laugh out loud. She would be won, but after a fight. One owed it to her to allow her to salve her pride in this way.

"It's very generous of you to see me. I acknowledge I behaved badly. But I also meant what I said last night. I want you to be my wife."

She raised her eyes then. As green and cold as that Maori charm she was wearing round her neck, they gazed at him. "Thank you, Mr. Whitmore, for your courtesy, but it isn't possible for me to accept your offer."

"Why not?" he asked bluntly.

"I suppose, among other things, because I don't love you."

"I shall make you do that, I promise."

Her chin tilted. "Shall you indeed, Mr. Whitmore? But I fear you won't have the opportunity."

She was only sitting across the room from him. But the carpet might have been the width of a raging flooded river, or the snow-capped range of the Rimutaka mountains.

If he had her in his arms again . . . Damn it, that one kiss was not all he was ever to have! He flung his riding crop down and exclaimed, "This isn't a thing I make a habit of doing, nor do I do it lightly. You're the first woman I've asked to marry me. I have a house ready for you. From the upstairs windows you can see over the top of the forest to the peak of Mount Edmont. The rooms are large, and there's adequate furniture. You can find a maid and take her with you. We'll sail to New Plymouth, and then ride across country. The country is beautiful, wild and green and full of birds." He paused in his enthusiasm. "Is it because you are afraid of the Hauhaus?"

"I'm not afraid of anything."

But her voice trembled slightly, and he knew that she was afraid of something. The hostile Maoris? Himself? He remembered his heated defence of her to his mother, and his voice came as near to gentleness as it ever would.

"I promise I would take the greatest care of you always."

But this again was the wrong thing to say, for where she countered arrogance with arrogance, now his momentary softness roused her to hysteria.

"I don't want you to take care of me, Saul Whitmore! I'm perfectly well able to take care of myself. I thank you for calling, and for your kind offer but—" she had risen and was wringing her hands agitatedly. Her face was brilliant in her distress. "Now will you please go. The whole thing is impossible. I can't marry you."

He made a movement towards her, but she backed away.

"I'm asking you to go," she begged. "You have done this out of courtesy, and I'm refusing your offer. So your honour is satisfied. There's nothing more to be said."

"There's a great deal more to be said!"

"No. Nothing at all. I dislike you, and I never want you to touch me. So please go."

He stared at her a moment in disbelief. Then he looked absently at his empty hands. So she never wanted him to touch her again. Had she minded his touch so much? Had she shuddered from it just now?

A wave of heat swept over him. Suddenly as angry as she, he picked up his riding crop and strode out of the room.

Briar realised that she could not stay on at Aunt Charity's. Already she was in the uneasy position of being between two worlds, with cook grumpily bringing her meals to her room, and Sophia apologising for requiring her services.

"But if you're really not going to marry Saul you'll have

to go on being a lady's maid, won't you?" Sophia pointed out. "I think you're mad. I'd jump at the chance, especially in your position. Why, you'll have your own house!"

"Aren't you angry with me?" Briar asked.

"I am, for ruining my dress. But otherwise, no," said the good-natured Sophia. "I'm very happy. Peter's going to propose any day now. He's just being a little bashful."

Is he? Briar wondered, and refused to believe that this would happen. She was not in love with Peter. She didn't love anybody. But she was bitterly resentful that her plans had been frustrated. She couldn't tolerate failure, and it would be doubly infuriating if Sophia should succeed where she had failed.

On an impulse she went to see Miss Matthews, the clever dressmaker of whom Aunt Charity had spoken, and suggested sewing for her. She sewed very neatly, she explained, and would not mind long hours, or the endless seams of crinolines and flounces.

Miss Matthews, a small, sharp-eyed monkeyish woman, looked at her with deep interest.

"So you're Saul Whitmore's latest fancy?"

Latest fancy! Briar's chin went up haughtily. "He wants to marry me."

"So I hear." The shrewd eyes went over her. "I believe I can see why. You don't look a namby pamby, at least. Why don't you have him?"

"Because I don't love him."

"That's a reason, but not a practical one. Yes, my dear, I'll give you a job if you need one. But you'll sew here for twelve hours a day and ruin those pretty eyes. It's stuffy in summer and cold in winter and dusty and windy all the time. And no matter how irritating and stupid your customer is, you must always be polite. You might find it easier than being mistress of Saul Whitmore's fine house. Certainly it will be less exciting. But I'll wager I'm making your wedding dress before the summer is over."

Jemima Potter didn't talk in that crisp sardonic way, She merely looked at Briar in incredulous astonishment. "Do you mean you refused him!" And abruptly began to cry.

Briar threw her arms round the thin shaking body. "Jemima, what's it to you whether I marry Saul Whitmore or not?"

"It's nothing, really. Yes, it is. I was so proud for you when I heard. And then Fred—well, he's finding it hard to get the kind of work he wants. He's had one disappointment after another, never the sort of job he's set his heart on. And he thought—" Jemima gazed at Briar with pleading eyes— "he thought you might persuade Mr. Whitmore to give him a job on his farm. They say he's got such a big place, and there might have been an acre or so where Fred could grow his own potatoes. It would be so good for the children, too," she added wistfully.

"It's hostile Maori country," Briar managed to say. "Wouldn't you be afraid?"

"Not if you and Fred were there. We'd all be together."

Briar took her hands. "Oh, Jemima, I can't, I can't! Don't ask me to. I'm so muddled and unhappy, I wish I were dead. But I can't marry Saul. I hate him!"

"Not even for a house and all those things a woman likes to have? Things that are the due of someone like you? And little Rose," she added slyly. "Wouldn't you like a baby like that?"

A baby with Saul Whitmore to father it! A dark tide of revulsion ran through her. She remembered his savage and hurting kiss, and pressed her hands to her face.

"Jemima, don't ask me to!" she begged.

But what she had refused to believe did happen. Peter Fanshawe proposed to Sophia and was accepted with promptitude. Aunt Charity, immensely relieved by this one piece of good fortune, was restored to her bustling managing ways, and immediately began making elaborate plans for the wedding.

"Now, Briar," she said, determinedly overcoming her dislike for this strange, silent, difficult girl, "you'd better be just as sensible and put that poor man out of his misery."

For it occurred to Aunt Charity that it might be an amusing and piquant situation to have two weddings from her house, Sophia's first, of course, and later this odd beggarmaid–King Cophetua wedding. After twenty years of marriage, some of her husband's dry humour and philosophy seemed to have rubbed off on to her after all.

And one had to look at things in a practical way. If Briar married Saul, the Governor and his lady would receive her, so how could Aunt Charity stand by?

The next day old Mrs. Whitmore came to call again.

"I want to see this young woman my son has lost his head about," she stated uncompromisingly.

So for the third time Briar was permitted to sit in the drawing room.

This time she stared with unconcealed hostility at the yellow-faced old woman with her long, thin, unbending body. Did this autocratic person think she could bludgeon her into marrying her precious son?

But no, she didn't, Briar perceived with surprise. "She hates me," she thought, "and hopes to frighten me away. She's daring me to marry Saul. She thinks I'm not good enough. I'd like to show her . . ."

The idea began to grow. Why, after all, shouldn't she show Oriane Whitmore that she could do as well and a great deal better than any society miss? There was nothing more to lose. Peter, who would have been infinitely preferable as a husband, was Sophia's. Being a lady's maid all her life would be even worse than sewing for twelve hours a day with Miss Matthews. Besides it would be wonderful to make Jemima and Fred Potter happy.

Briar's face softened at that thought, then hardened again. She returned the old woman's gaze steadily, stare for stare, and made deliberately untrue replies to questions about her family. She believed she would marry Saul, after all, just to prove—To prove what? In her room that afternoon, with the sheet of letter paper in front of her, Briar wondered bleakly what there was worth proving.

That she could be a good wife and perhaps a mother, that she could cook and sew and manage servants, that no one would ever need to be ashamed of her . . . Were those things so important?

But she would possess things. She would have beautiful silver and china, polished furniture, rugs on the floor, a garden in which grew the brilliant New Zealand rata blossom, and English roses. She would be a person of importance. She would curtsey to the Governor.

She remembered old Mrs. Whitmore's hostile haughty voice, "The wife of my son would need to be equal to any situation . . ." and bit her lip angrily and began to write,

Dear Mr. Whitmore,

I realise I have been very rude and ungrateful to you. Please forgive me, but I have not been myself, and was scarcely appreciative of the great honour you were paying me in asking me to be your wife. If you still want me—she hesitated, remembering again that out-

73

rageous kiss. Determinedly she went on—*I would be happy to see you again*—

Then abruptly she flung down her pen. This was cowardly, writing this humble letter. She thought of Mrs. Whitmore's intense scathing gaze, and her jaw tightened.

If she was to do this, she would do it in person. She was not afraid to face Saul and his mother and admit she had been wrong.

Rapidly she began to put on her outdoor clothes. The sun was blazing, and the dust blowing in little eddies down the hillside. The tussocks shone silver, and the tawny *toe toe* plumes waved. In Aunt Charity's garden the grass was burnt dry, the roses had shed their petals, and the gum leaves crackled on the ground. Briar would like to have gone without a cloak, but she had only her working gown and her best dark grey wool, which one could not wear on such a hot day. She must wear her cloak over her working dress, and dream of the day when she would have as many gowns as Sophia and Prudence.

Looking out of the window she saw Sophia and Peter walking in the garden, his head bent attentively to hers.

Briar's resolve stiffened. If it was not Peter's bright head, but Saul's dark one that bent to her like that, what of it? The loving attention was the thing.

She slipped out quietly, telling no one of her errand. She had to walk through the town, down the long street of shops and trading offices with verandahed fronts and nothing but the merest lean-to at the back. People looked at her curiously. Everyone knew of her fame, or ill-fame, by now. Her cheeks burned, she was too hot in the heavy cloak, but she continued quickly on her way. There were horses tethered outside Cooper's public house, and a great deal of noise came from within. As she passed, a man strode out towards the big black horse tethered at the hitching rail.

He almost knocked her over, caught her arm to hold her upright, and said, "Sorry, ma'am!" Then, "Briar!"

"Saul!"

It was the first time she had called him by his name. It came to her lips spontaneously, and she saw how his dark face gleamed. But whether it were with pleasure or triumph, she could not guess. Suddenly it was impossible to tell him why she had come, impossible to think that she could marry this arrogant, insolent stranger.

"Where are you going?" he asked. "To take a glass of ale at Cooper's?"

The angry sparkle in her eye made him chuckle. "Come now, Miss Briar. Going to a ball unescorted and unchaperoned didn't worry you. Nothing would surprise me about you."

"You're making fun of me."

"I'm admiring your practical attitude. You wanted a husband so you went out to look for one. It was just bad luck you happened to encounter someone so distasteful to you as myself." He was walking over to his horse. "Can I escort you somewhere, or would you prefer to be without my company?"

"N—no." Her tongue tripped over the word. How could he make this so difficult for her? And how could she tell him, standing in the dusty road watched by who knew how many eyes behind curtains, that she had made a mistake?

"Saul," she said rapidly, "I have had second thoughts."

His hand paused on the bridle. He turned to look at her, his eyes narrowed.

"About what?" he asked infuriatingly. For he must have known what she meant. Yet he refused to help her. Was he now going to say that his offer was withdrawn?

Briar was suddenly paralysingly afraid that this was so. And it was as if the bottom had fallen out of her life. It had been all very well to toy fastidiously with his offer, wondering how she could endure being his wife, but the thought of losing all the material things he offered because of her own sentimental foolishness made her aghast. Now it was no longer just a matter of spiting his mother. It was a matter of coming to her senses and grasping the opportunity so fortuitously offered her.

She stood very erect, looking at him levelly and willing her voice to be steady.

"I did not mean to tell you here, in the road. I was coming to call on you. I—" *Would* he not help her? She believed that behind his brilliant gaze he was laughing at her. "Does your offer still stand?" she finished in despair.

"Of marriage?"

"What else?" she asked icily.

"Well, now," he said, his gaze running over her from head to foot, "am I to infer that you have fallen in love with me overnight?"

"I do not imagine you fell in love with me at the dance," she retorted.

"On the contrary. I admired you immensely. But since then you've shown me clearly enough that you find me distasteful."

"And you're not used to being scorned," she said involuntarily.

"Why did you scorn me last week and come to me now?"

"I have had second thoughts, as I told you."

"And now you think it would not be too distasteful to be Mrs. Saul Whitmore?"

"I would be a good wife." She made her voice prim. She could not now meet his hard insolent gaze.

Suddenly he burst out laughing. "You amaze me. So you will be a good wife. You will not just try. You will be so. You are certain enough of yourself to know that. Well, that remains to be seen."

"Then it is settled?"

He laughed again at the quick eagerness in her voice. But there was no mirth in his laughter, nor was there tenderness in his eyes. He seemed to be measuring her as an opponent.

"You are a strange young woman. I think we'll have no illusions about this. You have decided you need a husband—"

"Not just a husband, Saul Whitmore," she had enough wit to interrupt. "You."

He smiled crookedly. "Let's leave the play-acting out. You need a husband, and I need a wife. I will not say I need you particularly. But it happens I want you. As a woman. So, since it's more comfortable to observe the conventions—" His unnerving gaze held her—"my offer still stands."

Anger at his insolence seethed within her. But she, too, had made a decision, and would not draw back.

"You are honest, anyway," she murmured.

"More than you, I suspect. And I, at least, don't hate you."

"Do you imagine I hate you?"

He grinned, his face mocking. "You'll get over it, my love."

CHAPTER 9

Charity Carruthers was certainly able to preen herself on her popularity nowadays. For everyone admired her broadminded and generous attitude towards the young nobody, the lady's maid, Briar Johnson, who was walking off with the country's most eligible bachelor.

There were inevitably the spiteful who said, "What else can she do? She can't risk not being on speaking terms with someone who may one day be a countess." But these were in the minority, and generally it was agreed that Charity, in offering to give Briar her wedding dress and a trousseau, was behaving admirably.

The wedding was planned to take place in the early autumn, for Saul had had to go back to Taranaki to attend to matters on his farm and to prepare the house for his bride.

His mother remained bitterly opposed to his choice. She was convinced that Briar was a devious, clever little upstart who had schemed to get Saul and had succeeded.

"She hasn't even the grace to be ashamed of herself. She stared me in the face as if she's my equal."

"Perhaps she is," Saul said, amused.

"What! A servant!"

"That might be Charity Carruthers speaking."

"If you mean I'm just being snobbish, you're wrong. I don't trust the girl. Why is she so aggressive when one asks perfectly straightforward questions about her family? If her father is merely a working man of the lower classes, why doesn't she say so? She has no need to be ashamed of that. I won't despise her for it. But I won't endure deceit."

"She wants to be somebody, mother. One can't blame her for ambition."

"And you will let her use you like that! I thought you would have had more pride."

"Perhaps I'm using her, too."

"How can you be? Any girl would jump at the chance of marrying you. You know that. I just don't know why you had to choose this one. I think she has you bewitched."

Saul gave his amused, derisive laugh. "Perhaps she has. I never meant to marry her after she refused me once. But she's got a toughness I like. The woman I take up to that wilderness has to be tough. Briar and I will do very well."

His mother eyed him shrewdly. "I grant you she has looks. I hope you haven't been taken in by them alone."

Saul remembered Briar as she had been that night in her bedroom, flushed and vivid, with tumbling curls. He could have had her then, and sought later for a well-bred wife. But instinct told him that everyone else would be unendurably insipid after this fiery creature's hostility. She had so hated being humble the other day. It was strange and intriguing that a young woman born to her circumstances had no humility. At least, she was honest in that, even though she was devious in other ways.

It would be amusing to tame her—if one wanted her tamed.

Briar herself lived through those summer days in a state of unreality from which she did not want to be awakened lest she should be too aghast at what she had done. She was glad that Saul had gone back to Taranaki, so that she need not have any more of those uneasy meetings with him until the wedding. Even the fact that to please her he had taken Fred Potter with him did not rouse her greatly, although her first opportunity to distribute largesse had been undeniably pleasant.

Jemima was full of delighted plans for the future, when they would live in one of the small cottages in the tiny township adjoining Saul's property. Saul had told them about it. There was a church, with a minister who went long journeys on horseback to christen and bury, and a doctor who was likely to be twenty miles away when required. There was a store stocked with almost every practical requirement, from lengths of cotton print to cough mixtures, a public house, a main street which for four or five months of the year was almost impassable because of its winter mud, and a small flour mill which ground wheat for the making of bread. The rest of the handful of dwellings belonged to labourers who worked on the adjoining farms, felling trees and clearing away the interminable ferns and manuka scrub.

This small settlement was reached after a thirty-mile trip on horseback or by dray from the seaport of New Plymouth. The whole of the province was towered over by Mount Edmont, that strange isolated mountain lifting its eight-thousand-foot height out of the surrounding plain, and whose cone-shaped peak enclosed its extinct volcano.

Saul had told Briar all of this, enthusiasm lighting his face. The house at Lucknow was sparsely furnished as yet. The furniture had to be transported the thirty miles from New Plymouth by dray or bullock waggon. The piano, indeed, had been slung on poles and carried on foot by a team of friendly Maoris. The rest of the stuff they would take up on their wedding journey. It would be wise if Briar were to learn to ride a horse, as well as making her trousseau, hemming sheets and pillow-cases and nightgowns and petticoats, while he was away.

And also she had better look for a housemaid. At present the only help he had in the house was a half-caste Maori, Mabel Kingi, willing, but untrained in white ways, and with some outlandish ideas. Briar would feel happier with another white woman in the house. The next ship from England would bring the usual quota of immigrants. No doubt she could find someone who would be suitable.

She, so recently a maid herself, to engage one! To give orders, to be the mistress! This, at least, was real.

And Saul Whitmore, soon to be her husband, was more than real. Indeed, his dark triumphant face had a disconcerting habit of haunting her sleep and making her wake as from a nightmare.

The excited expectancy she had felt as she had sailed up the harbour in the *Mary Louise* only a month ago had been fulfilled, indeed, but not in the way she had hoped. She, who had thought she could be mistress of her destiny, had found that she was merely the victim of it.

At the end of that month a new ship sailed up the harbour, the *Lady Sally* direct from the London docks. As well as new settlers, their goods and chattels and such livestock as had survived the long voyage, some stud sheep and cattle destined for the larger sheep and cattle stations, she brought the eagerly awaited mail. There were letters from home at last. Prudence and Sophia pounced hungrily on theirs. Then Prudence suddenly gasped and went pale, and clutching a single letter to her bosom fled to her room.

Later she emerged shyly to say that of all miracles the *Mary Louise* and the *Lady Sally* had passed in mid-ocean, and exchanged letters for their separate destinations. So that months sooner than she had expected it, Prudence received a letter from Edmund.

"He still loves me," she said raptly.

Sophia looked at her with tolerance. She could afford to be understanding now, for weren't they all in the same position, even Briar.

"We're all lovesick," she said. "What a trio. But listen to what Mamma says. Everyone is well, and Sarah has a beau. Mamma hopes we've settled down happily, but won't be in too great haste to marry! She's sending us some materials and some pictures of the latest fashions, but they'll arrive too late for my wedding. Still, who cares? Peter says he would love me in rags. Briar! Where are your letters? Didn't you get any?"

Briar murmured, "No, they must have missed this ship. I must go out, if you please. I'm to look for a maid to take to the country, and if I go down to the barracks where the newly arrived people are I might find someone."

At least she had successfully changed the subject, for Sophia looked up with interest and amusement.

"*You* choosing a maid! That's really funny. You'd better let Aunt Charity do it. She'll know what sort of girl looks capable and trustworthy."

Briar tied on her bonnet decisively. "I think I'm quite capable of knowing that myself."

"There's no need to be so hoity toity. It just seems so odd—but I'm sure you'll manage very well. I don't think we ever knew you before. You hid behind that meek face, and we thought you were so good. But you're not good at all, are you?"

No, she wasn't good. She was lying and deceiving and scheming. She lied about a non-existent family, and she let Saul think she wanted to marry him. This latter thing was the biggest deception, for she still awoke shuddering from his image in the night. Like Prudence and Sophia, she had the vaguest notion as to what actually happened when one was married. But whatever else might happen, marriage certainly consisted of sharing the same bed, of lying sleepless while that dark head and strange gleaming unknowable face of her husband lay on the pillow beside her. It meant more of those disturbing kisses, and perhaps Saul's hands on her body.

At that point in her imaginings Briar always stopped, and added firmly to herself that marriage was not spent entirely in bed, that a great deal of it she would be able to accomplish very well. She must do this, for there was nothing else for her in life but this lonely battle to prove that she could be somebody loved and desired.

How could there be letters for her on the *Lady Sally* when there was no one to write them?

Briar felt tears stinging in her eyes as she hurried down the street towards the wharf. She remembered Mrs. Whitmore's persistent enquiries about her family, and realised that explaining away the absence of letters today was another hurdle to overcome. She thought wistfully of Andrew Gaunt. He would have written to her had he been alive, long intellectual letters full of quotations from the classics which would have impressed everybody. But as it was she had nothing visible to prove her relationship with anybody, only an accent that would have been rare indeed among the lower classes.

There was a knot of people on the wharf, and a great deal of bustle and shouting. Briar recognised the looks of bewilderment and lostness on many of the faces. There were women clasping children, and others still pallid from prolonged seasickness. Baggage was strewn everywhere, and little was being done about organisation. Someone was yelling in a stentorian voice. "All those requiring food and shelter or assistance, come this way."

A young woman near Briar got up to obey. She was carrying a baby, and also attempting to lift the wickerwork travelling bag on which she had been sitting. To this bag had been strapped what seemed to be two pictures in gilt frames, but as the bag was moved the strap broke and the pictures fell with a clatter.

Briar sprang to help. She found herself looking at the painted faces, very pink and white and blue-eyed, of a middle-aged man and woman.

"Oh, thanks," said the woman. "Those wretched portraits. Dan said to bring them and I did, but he's never here to carry them, and what we're to do with all this stuff if we go straight off to California is more than I can guess."

"California?" said Briar.

"Dan's heard about the goldfields. You'd think now we've come so far he'd want to stay a little while, wouldn't you? For mine and baby's sake at least. But no. As soon as he can get a passage on a ship we're off to California, he says, and I drag these pictures round the world again. They're not even my parents, they're his."

"They're nice," Briar said slowly.

The stranger looked at her curiously. "Do you like paintings? Oh, yes, they're nice people, though you'd never think they were the kind to have a son who was so footloose. I hardly knew them, to be truthful, and if my husband can't look after his own mother and father, why should I have to?"

The girl was scarcely Briar's age. Her indignant weary face looked at Briar helplessly. The baby in her arms was whimpering and she herself was near to tears.

"It's all so strange," she said, "and I don't know where we'll sleep tonight."

"Would you sell me those portraits for a guinea?" Briar asked.

"You mean you'd like to have them!"

"Yes, I would, very much. If you're really going to California, and don't want too much luggage. A guinea is all I have with me." (It was her entire wages to date, and all she had in the world.)

"Oh, my!" whispered the girl. Tears did spill over on to her cheeks then. "I don't know why you want them, but a whole guinea—I won't tell my husband. I'll keep it for baby, if we're in trouble." With youthful resilience she began to twinkle through her tears. "I'll tell him the pictures fell in the sea."

She waved with jauntiness as she walked away, and Briar picked up the portraits slowly, then clasped them to her bosom, avariciously. She had a family at last. Her parents were not any longer two imaginary people. For they were here, with faces and names.

"Mr. and Mrs. Johnson," she whispered. "Meet your daughter!"

But she did not feel she knew them well enough yet to take them to Aunt Charity's. Besides, how would she explain her sudden possession of them? She decided to leave them with Jemima Potter who loyally would ask no questions. But now, she thought exultantly, I can show that snobbish old woman, Saul's mother!

Later she remembered her original errand, and found, among the newly arrived immigrants, a half dozen girls who wanted positions as housemaids or cooks.

She didn't ask a lot of questions. She felt, all at once, that she herself was one of this forlorn group, hoping eagerly for a kind mistress and a good home, and praying that no searching questions would be asked about background and family. She became shy and inept, and pointed almost at random to the youngest, a red-headed freckle-nosed creature, little more than a child, who looked as if she had an irrepressible cheerfulness, and who said her name was Katie O'Toole.

She'd be glad to take a position anywhere, especially with such a pretty lady. "Begging your pardon, ma'am," she said, blushing violently and endearingly. She could cook and scrub and bake bread, and when Briar warned her about the possibility of attacks by the Maoris, she said optimistically that she didn't think she'd be afraid of murdering heathens like that.

All in all, the acquisition of the portraits and Katie O'Toole cheered Briar immensely. She felt much older and more confident, and Katie had thought she was a lady.

Perhaps she would make Saul a good enough wife after all.

CHAPTER 10

Except for the sound of birds, it was very quiet in the forest. Every footstep Saul took seemed to crash echoingly. The brown kaka flew screeching from his approach, and a bell-bird sent out its lovely delicate cry, its miniature chime of bells, before flitting away. Wood pigeons gave their comforting gurgle, and the friendly black fantail slipped coquettishly from bough to bough, spreading its tail and chirping irrepressibly.

If the birds had been silent he might have been able to detect other sounds. The ferns were broken, as if someone or several persons had passed this way not long ago.

Saul had his rifle cocked, and Fred Potter, sweating behind him, was in a deplorable state of nerves. But Saul had deliberately taken him on this scouting venture. If he was to be of any use in this country while hostile bands of Maori still roamed, he had to go through his baptism of fire, or at least this nerve-racking absence of a visible enemy.

The reason for the lonely foray was that a Maori, naked except for the traditional flax skirt, had been seen lurking suspiciously on the edge of the bush within sight of Lucknow, but when challenged had disappeared silently into the screen of tree ferns and scrub.

He might not have been alone, Saul knew. Even now the forest might be full of brown men lurking behind the massive kauri trees and screening ferns, ready to fire or spring on him with upraised hatchet.

But he was as experienced a fighter as they, and his only sign of tension was his narrowed eyes and the taut muscles of his cheeks. Every few steps he motioned to Fred to stop, and in the stillness listened.

There was no sound but that of the everlastingly talkative birds. When finally he decided they had gone far enough to ascertain that the single intruder must have been alone, he turned back. Fred's relief was so palpable that it was almost humorous. He mopped his face and muttered, "Sorry, boss. This is new to me."

"You're living on a frontier up here," Saul said crisply. "If you don't like it, say so, and I'll take you back to Wellington when I go. But if you stay, you'll have to be prepared to do not only this but defend your home in an attack."

Fred nodded. His face was red with exertion and a multitude of emotions. But his eyes were steady.

"I'll stay, boss. Jemmie's depending on it. I look at it this way, she risks her life every time she has one of my brats, so I can risk mine doing what she wants."

"Good man," said Saul approvingly. "Then let's go and see what Mabel has thought up for supper."

Half an hour later they came into the clearing where the buildings of Lucknow, the large new house and the shearing sheds and outhouses, lay in the green hollow.

One of Saul's shepherds saw them emerge from the bush and ran towards them shouting excitedly. "Boss, those devils have stolen the horses!"

"Damnation!" exclaimed Saul.

So it had been a trick. The lone Maori had lured him into the forest, and the rest of his band had stolen round the other side, and with only Mabel Kingi, probably fast asleep in her afternoon stupor, and this elderly shepherd about, had had no trouble at all in catching the three horses.

"How many of them?" he demanded.

"I'm not sure. I just caught sight of them riding off. About five or six."

Saul narrowed his eyes against the forest-bound horizon. Everything was peaceful. The cattle grazed on the cleared land, and a blue drift of smoke rose from the kitchen chimney.

Part of the Maori tactics was this marauding. It kept the settlers nervous and ready to jump at their own shadow. By the time a planned attack was launched the morale of the women, anyway, was at its lowest. Often, however, the thieving that went on was done by lazy natives of peaceful tribes, and this particular theft may have had no more significance than that.

Saul reported the matter to Captain Maltby of the local militia, and kept an all-night watch that night, and for several nights after. But nothing more happened to disturb the peace.

Nevertheless, Saul was deeply uneasy both about leaving

Lucknow at this time and bringing a wife up here. Was it right to bring women into this atmosphere of false peace? For there was no doubt that there would be a flare-up of hostilities, if not here at least in the surrounding country. He shuddered at the thought of exposing women to that frightfulness. He had seen too much himself. The unleashed savagery of the fighting native knew no limits, and after every indecency had been inflicted on the dead body of his enemy, it was often prepared for the feast.

Saul had once witnessed a horrible ceremony when eyeless heads, stuck on poles, had been carried in a ghastly procession. And worse than that, when the curious revolting smell of roasting human flesh had seeped through the forest.

A week before he was due to leave, he called on the Reverend Peabody, that gallant man known to everybody simply as 'the Reverend'. He was in his habitual shabby black clothes, his white hair flying, his round pink face as calm as if he talked in an English vicarage about a delinquent child.

He was a wonderful man, the Reverend Peabody, and his wife Martha was a fit mate for him. She seemed to know no fear, and quoted constantly her favourite text, *Thou shalt not be afraid of the terror by night, nor for the arrow that flieth by day* . . . Indeed, she had been known to include it in a recipe for baking bread. It was one of her weapons. Her others were her calm-faced husband and her own tolerant, serene outlook that accepted every phase of human behaviour.

The Peabodys lived in a cottage next to the tiny wooden church. One room was overflowing with books, and the other was the bedroom. Behind that was a kitchen, and in front a verandah. A loft above provided a spare room for the not infrequent guest. It was a working man's cottage, but the Peabodys behaved as if they lived in luxury, and no one was more fortunate than they. They could, if circumstances demanded it, fire a gun with deadly accuracy, but the Reverend was happier with a Bible in his hand, and his wife with her wooden mixing spoon.

They listened seriously to Saul's problem.

"What's the little lassie like?" the Reverend asked.

"She's not one to be afraid of her own shadow."

"She's bonny, of course," said Martha Peabody. "Bring her here as soon as you can, Saul. You need her, and we'll take care of her."

"But supposing—"

"Now, look," said the Reverend philosophically, "this fiend Te Kooti, when he escaped from the Chathams, had his boat becalmed. Have you heard this story? So he pushed an old man overboard to placate the gods, and at once a wind sprang up, and carried him to these shores. Now how far can a man who behaves like that succeed? He'll be stricken down at any moment by a just God who abhors human sacrifice."

"What is to happen will happen," came Martha's calm voice. "If your wife is to die, she will die, no matter where she is. But why should she die? You bring her here, Saul. We'll give her courage."

"She has that already," said Saul, smiling ironically. "That, at least, I know about her."

Martha looked puzzled and a little anxious. "You do love her, Saul?"

Saul lifted his black brows. "Love? I need a wife. That's the long and short of it. To be truthful, I scarcely know her."

"But you're concerned for her safety," Martha pointed out shrewdly.

"No one wants to see a woman scalped. Besides, she has pretty hair. Oh, she's pretty, Martha, if that's what you're wondering."

"And you'll love her and make her happy!" Martha said severely.

Saul grinned. "The books say love comes after marriage."

"It should come before, you foolish boy! Otherwise, think of the ordeal for a woman, coming up here to this strange lonely country with a stranger. You know as well as I do how some women have gone, for lack of companionship or understanding. Oh, you men!" Martha's broad face was full of impatience. "As long as your wife cooks your food and has your children you think you've done your duty by her. But you listen to me, Saul Whitmore! You set to work and be a loving husband."

"Yes, ma'am," said Saul, his eyes gleaming. "But Briar has to be tamed before she can be loved, and I'm not sure that I want her tamed. So there's a pretty problem."

He shrugged and turned to the Reverend Peabody. "Then, sir, you think this winter will be fairly safe?"

"Oh, there'll be trouble in patches, you can be sure of that. Mind you, the Maori has a certain right to a grievance. He's parted with his lands ignorantly, for sometimes less than two shillings an acre, and he's resentful and angry about being deceived. Everything wasn't settled at the Treaty of Waitangi when those fine old chiefs laid down their arms. But this devilish kind of warfare must be stamped out. Te Kooti is simply deliberately stirring the Maori's wild fighting blood. There's one of his kind bred every generation or so, whether it be here or in Europe or the Americas, and we can only cope with the trouble he causes as best we can."

"I've heard," said Saul, "that some of the soldiers don't care to fight the Maori. They say their ancestors might merely be men who escaped from Cromwell's persecution and now are browned by two or three generations of sun."

The Reverend nodded in approval. "I agree. The Maori will be a fine fellow when he loses his savagery. He might even be fighting side by side with us for the British Empire one day. But that's looking a long way ahead, and we've got this winter to get through. We're going to build a stockade in the village, and the militia is never far away. We'll come through safely. Don't worry, my boy. Your wife will be needed here, most likely. . . And whether you love her or not," his eyes twinkled, "as I can see my wife is going to argue ad infinitum, I can't see you being foolish enough to choose either a spoilt beauty or a timid mouse. So bring her to Lucknow as soon as you can."

CHAPTER 11

Peter Fanshawe made an extremely dashing and handsome bridegroom. After the ceremony, he went boldly kissing all the girls, who shrieked and giggled, his bride giggling most of all, as if getting married were a tremendous romp.

But Briar evaded his amorous advance. She ran from the room like any shy schoolgirl, and heads nodded approvingly. She was, after all, to be married herself in a few weeks, and this fastidiousness proved her devotion to Saul. No one could know that she was still bitterly resenting the fact that her plans had gone so awry. Peter would have been such a suitable and tractable husband. She could have shaped him to her wishes. Saul, she knew, would never be shaped.

She looked at the assembled guests scornfully, despising

them for their lack of perception. But then she caught old Mrs. Whitmore brooding on her behaviour and she realised that there was one who was not deceived. "She knows my true feelings!" Briar thought in a panic, and suddenly she was afraid she was never going to be able to go on with her own wildly improbably marriage.

But Sophia and Peter had at last departed, Sophia possessively and triumphantly taking Peter's arm as he led her to the carriage. The last glimpse Briar had of her was her triumphant face, and Peter leaning tenderly towards her. She clenched her fists and muttered, "I will marry Saul. I'll show them."

A fortnight later, on their return from their honeymoon spent in a cottage in one of the more sheltered bays, Sophia came to call. She had blossomed into a confident young matron. Already she was house-proud and was planning her first dinner party. Not that she could take too much interest in the very modest house Peter had found for them, for Peter was restless and dissatisfied with his banking career. He wanted to buy land and make money quickly as the more enterprising settlers did. He planned to go north looking for a suitable property, and talked of settling in the Taranaki district where Saul was doing so well.

"So we may be living near you, Briar," Sophie said. "Wouldn't that be wonderful? Oh, Briar, do come upstairs and help me with my hair. I've never been able to do it as cleverly as you did."

In the large bedroom occupied now only by Prudence, who missed her sister sadly and grew quiet and peaked, Sophie untied her bonnet, plumped herself on the stool in front of the dressing-table, and said, "I really do want you to do my hair, but I wanted to see you alone, too."

"Why?" Briar asked, with a beating heart. Had Peter found he didn't love his wife, after all?

"Because I thought you ought to be told something about marriage. I mean, you're to marry Saul in less than a month, aren't you? And somehow—" she had flushed scarlet and seemed overcome with embarrassment—"I don't think Saul will have quite the nature to be as thoughtful as Peter. I admit he would terrify me."

"You mean in bed?" Briar asked flatly.

Sophia nodded. "You see, Briar dear, no one had told me anything about what happens, and I must warn you that it is a great shock. Indeed," she went on, rapidly regaining her confidence and beginning to enjoy her role of experienced woman, "if one were not in love, I don't think one could endure it. But if one is, of course, it's an entirely different matter. But I do think a new bride should be prepared a little."

"What does happen?" Briar asked bluntly.

"There, I know you'd know as little as me. So I really do think it's my duty to tell you. I should do the same for Prue."

Briar had picked up the hair-brush and begun to tumble the pins out of Sophia's hair. It was better to be doing something. All at once her legs were trembling. She wanted to hear, and yet so desperately didn't want to. For whatever it was, it had been Peter's gentle face on Sophia's pillow, and on hers it would be that dark burning one.

"Then hurry and tell me," she said crisply.

"Oh, Briar, you're so downright. Very well, then. If I can find words."

And Sophia promptly found words, boggled over them a little, and imparted the vital information.

"Oh, dear, do you think I'm being very immodest? But it's nature, isn't it? And, really, after the first night—I know one isn't supposed to take pleasure in it—Ouch, Briar, you're brushing far too hard!"

"Sorry," said Briar automatically. She wanted to run away and hide. She couldn't endure this. For although instinctively she had known, she had never begun to visualize such an act, and now she could not listen to Sophia boasting of her superior experience, much less could she think of Sophia in Peter's arms. And as for Saul with his iron hard arms pinning her down, a prisoner . . .

"And now," said Sophia smugly, "I expect I shall have a baby."

"Oh, stop boasting!" Briar said, between her teeth. "That's really all you're doing."

Sophia's round ingenuous face looked deeply hurt. "Am I? Oh, I didn't mean to do that. It was just that you being a bride so soon—" her eyes swam with tears. "Well, who else can I talk to but you? Only don't be frightened—"

"I'm not frightened!"

"You look so fierce and angry. I know it is a shock. But you'll be glad I told you. And don't let it spoil your wedding day. Think of other things."

Aunt Charity, with her incurable desire to take command of every situation, said that Katie O'Toole was far too young and irresponsible and ignorant. Whatever had Briar been thinking of to engage a servant without making a great many enquiries as to her ability and honesty? And preferably she should not have been such a child.

However, said Aunt Charity candidly, Briar was little more than a child herself, and only just graduated from the servant class. So perhaps she had been wise to employ a girl whom she could dominate. But Katie needed intensive training in everything, and there was less than a month in which to do it. Aunt Charity shook her head, flung up her hands despairingly, and proceeded with the greatest zest to deal with the situation.

Katie was installed in the house, sharing cook's room, and started on a nerve-racking course of cleaning silver, waiting at table, washing and laundering, and the elements of cooking. Her little untidy red head spun, and her eyes got a wild look, and she was inclined to burst into tears every time Aunt Charity came into the room.

But for Briar's sake she would endure this purgatory, and even learn a little, if so be the baker's boy did not catch her eye too often and distract her from her work.

Aunt Charity, with one wedding just accomplished and another on her hands, was a whirlwind of energy. She caused more disturbance in the house than had all the windows been flung open to the battering nor'-wester. She was enjoying her very unlikely role of fairy godmother to the full, and each day came home with bolts of linen for Briar and Prudence to hem into sheets and pillowcases, and with fine lawn for Briar's nightgowns and cambric for her petticoats.

Miss Matthews, that dried-up philosophical little dressmaker, who had come to rest so unexpectedly in this far off country, like a storm-battered swallow blown on to an unfamiliar roof, was busily engaged in making the wedding dress, to be sure not as grand as Sophia's, but very fine nevertheless, and real silk.

With her mouth full of pins she hissed her pungent comments. "I knew as soon as I saw you that you'd never be wielding a needle all your life. That young lady's got sauce, I said to myself. She'll get what she wants."

"You've made the waist too tight," Briar said coldly.

Her haughty attitude was not lost on the perceptive Miss Matthews. But that lady was not going to be intimidated by someone of her own class, though she did speak with a good accent, and gave herself all the airs of a lady.

"Sorry, love. We can't have you fainting on the important day, can we? I'll just ease it there. After all, your waist is small enough not to need pinching. Yes, I said, she'll get what she wants, that one. And you did, too, didn't you, dear?"

"I'd be obliged, Miss Matthews, if you'd just attend to your task, and not talk."

Miss Matthews took an unperturbed look at the averted face of her customer. "Sorry, dear. My tongue runs away with me. I can't help it. You mustn't mind. I'm just so pleased that instead of ruining your eyes sewing for me you're getting such a fine husband. I've always said what opportunities there are in the colonies, and you see how true it is. I've lost one seamstress after another. Even Molly Perkins who had a squint. She married a young man almost as homely in looks, and they went off to the gold diggings in the South Island. Most likely they've made their fortune by now. Yes, it's an exciting country. You'll never regret coming here. Now, turn round slowly, please. Walk to the door and back. Slowly. Ah, yes. Ah, yes." The little yellowish dried-up face with its imperturbable cheerfulness was rapt. "You'll make a beautiful bride, my dear. Much more beautiful, if I may say so, than the new Mrs. Peter Fanshawe. What she lacked was poise. Oh, yes, just a hoyden. But you—my, one would think you'd been born to the part."

But more than beauty was required. Mrs. Whitmore made that very plain to Briar, who was summoned to the draughty, small-roomed cottage high on the hillside, and put through another intensive examination, this time not about her antecedents but about her practical ability as a housewife.

"My son, I am sure, hasn't even begun to tell you what's expected of you," she said in her harsh voice, her eyes full of their dark contempt fixed on Briar unnervingly. "You will require to be able to cook not only for yourselves but for hired men, shearers in the shearing season and harvesters in the summer."

"But Saul said there was a cook," Briar pointed out.

"That Maori woman? Well—that remains to be seen." Mrs. Whitmore dismissed Mabel Kingi, and went on, "You will also have to make soap and candles from muttonfat, preserve fruit, make butter and bread, attend to all emergencies such as babies being born without medical help, and other illnesses or accidents. You will be virtually the lady of the manor, you understand?" Her eyes flicked over the slight erect figure opposite her. "You may even like to teach children to read and write. There'll be no school within miles, and I believe you read and write competently."

"Yes, ma'am. But what happens if I'm ill myself, if I—" the steady regard faltered for the merest second—"have a baby?"

"You will be expected to do the best you can in the circumstances."

"I believe you're trying to frighten me!" Briar burst out.

"No, my dear, not to frighten you. Just to warn you—while there's still time."

"I don't understand what you mean," Briar said stiffly.

"I'm merely pointing out that marriage to a pioneer in this country is not just a light-hearted prank."

Briar began to smile, with a twist to her lips. "I never imagined it to be light-hearted, Mrs. Whitmore. But thank you for your advice. It may please you to hear that I can cook and sew, and scrub floors, if necessary, and I'll soon learn to make candles and even to deliver babies. I'm not afraid."

"That we'll see, my dear. That we'll see."

The horrible old woman who sat tall and proud in her smoky little cottage had not believed that she was not afraid, Briar reflected indignantly.

And the worst of it was that she was entirely right. Because she was afraid. Of the lonely house on the edge of the forest, of the strange birds calling, and lurking shadows in the bush that might be silent-footed hostile Maoris, of sudden illnesses and emergencies, and most of all, of her unknown husband . . .

But she'd never show that she was afraid.

At last, by one of the tiny coastal trading ships, a letter arrived from Saul.

It was the first letter Briar had received in her life. She could not help gazing with fascination at her name written on the envelope, and if anyone wondered at her raptness they must think it was because the letter was from Saul, not that receiving it was so strange a thing.

She took it to her room to read, for, her first fascination over, she was filled with a curious dread. It seemed as if Saul's black intent eyes were looking at her, ready to catch her slightest expression.

Dear Briar,

  At last the Seagull *has arrived and we sail on Monday, but I am sending this letter ahead by Captain Browne, as his ship sails today. With fair winds and luck, I should arrive at the promised time.*

We will be forced to re-embark immediately after the wedding, as the Seagull *stays in port only two days, and, truth to tell, I do not care to be away from Lucknow any longer than can be helped. Please have everything ready, including what servants you may wish to bring, for our immediate sailing. And advise Jemima Potter also, as Fred remains here awaiting her.*

The last of my wool clip has been safely despatched to London, and everything looks well here, except that I have had three of my horses stolen. I wish you to learn to load and fire a gun when you arrive.

I am not, as you can see, fluent with a pen, nor indeed with my tongue. But there are other ways to compensate for these deficiencies, as I will prove to you.

       Your intended husband, Saul.

So that was the first letter she had ever received, that cold business-like communication. Get your bags packed, be ready to sail, learn to fire a gun! Where, in those autocratic commands, did he earn the right to hold her body in his arms?

Briar tore the letter in shreds. She would not cry. She would not let herself reflect even for a moment how she had longed for one line of tenderness. *I long for you . . .* words that would have melted her heart and given her strength. But in what foolish daydream had she ever imagined Saul Whitmore would say words like that to her? Neither of them had any illusions about this marriage. He understood her reasons, and she knew very well that she was merely to become another possession of this black-browed stranger, along with his horses and sheep, his house, his servants. And what were his other ways to compensate? Guessing at them, from her newly-acquired knowledge, Briar wrapped her arms round her slender body to stop her sudden shivering.

Yet one must be fair. If Saul felt little but physical love for her, she already hated him. Yet she was prepared to stand at his side in church and promise to honour and obey him.

So what right had she to criticise?

The small figure of Miss Matthews, struggling indomitably against the wind, was to be perceived coming up the road carrying her long dressmaker's box, almost at the precise moment that Aunt Charity screamed from upstairs that the *Seagull* had appeared in the bay.

So the silk wedding dress, white and virginal, was spread on Briar's bed and helping to give her courage when Saul's knock came at the door. She touched the silk swiftly. Once, she reflected, her baby fingers had clung to silk and perhaps at that moment a last prayer had been on her mother's lips that one day such a thing as this would happen to her little daughter. A fine wedding dress, a church wedding, a respectable husband, all the things denied to her herself. And if her mother had denied herself that other thing, that secret act between lovers, Briar thought with sudden wonder, then there would be no Briar standing here, feeling the stuff of her wedding gown, listening to the knock on the front door, and conscious of her body alive and beautiful beneath her grey working dress.

A thread of excitement ran through her, and with her head held high she answered Aunt Charity's call and went to greet Saul.

That was a stiff formal and brief meeting, for Aunt Charity remained in the room, and Briar could only think confusedly that Saul was taller than she had remembered, and his skin was burnt an even darker brown with the wind and sun.

He made a few polite comments about the weather, the passage he had had on the *Seagull,* the arrangements for the wedding, and then said that since he had just arrived and had a great deal to do he must go. His lips twitched a little, and he said that the next time they met it would be in front of the altar. If Briar had any regrets she must think of them quickly.

"Regrets!" echoed Aunt Charity unbelievingly. "Why, she's the luckiest girl in New Zealand."

Saul's eyes, blacker and more intense, bored into her. She repressed a shiver and said gaily, "I have the most beautiful wedding dress. Wait until you see it." And thought to herself that she might have been Sophie speaking.

But he gave his sudden grin that might have been of amusement or contempt, and took his leave. And he was still a stranger.

It was not Briar but Prudence who wept the next morning.

She helped Briar to dress, and the tears slipped down her pale forlorn face.

"It seems so strange, my doing this for you, Briar. But Sophie and I always knew you would get what you wanted. I, I wish I could be as lucky."

"You'll be lucky, Prue dear."

"Do you think so? Do you think Edmund will ever come back? After all, on board ship one can do foolish things, for boredom almost, and I'm not really as gay and attractive as he thought me."

Briar looked at the woebegone face and said briskly, "Certainly you're not when you cry. Please don't spoil my wedding day by weeping. As soon as I'm settled in the country I'll write for you to come up and visit. It seems so topsy turvy me being the mistress and inviting guests. I'll have to make preserves first, and candles, and I don't know yet how many bedrooms there are." She was talking too much, partly to cheer up Prudence, and partly to stop herself from thinking.

"Will you ask Sophie and Peter, too?"

"I think the country would bore Sophie."

"But she'll have to learn to like it, for Peter seems determined to buy land. He seems to change his mind a great deal about his profession, but he's so charming. Sophie's very happy."

This brought back the desolate look to Prudence's face, and Briar exclaimed quickly, "Don't cry again, or you'll be no use to me! Oh, dear, Miss Matthews has made this waist too tight after all. I can't breathe. I'm quite sure if I faint at the altar Saul will refuse to marry me. He wouldn't have the patience or understanding for things like that."

She had been so calm, but now, all at once, she was in a panic. The dress was painfully tight, she felt suffocated, too hot and a little sick. The colour had vanished from her cheeks and her lips were dry. Worse than that, her legs had lost the power to carry her. She couldn't go to the church. She just couldn't totter up the aisle like a feeble old woman to meet Saul's raking gaze.

But all this turmoil could not have shown in her face, for Prudence said, "How do you know Saul won't be very understanding and patient when it comes to the test?"

A fresh wave of sickness passed over her. "I hate him!" she whispered involuntarily.

"What did you say?"

"Just—undo that hook. It's too tight. That's better. For a moment I couldn't breathe."

Prudence, noticing nothing, had stepped back to look at her.

"Briar, you look beautiful! Really you do. If only your mother could see you now!"

Her mother who would have so loved this triumph for her daughter! Suddenly, as if by magic, her legs stopped trembling and her breath fluttering. She felt immensely calm and almost happy.

"Thank you for saying that, Prue. Thank you."

In the church only trivial things caught her attention. A fantail, inquisitively trespassing and flirting about the rafters, the scrubbed wooden floor, and the plain glass in the windows. And the hats of the guests. Miniature flower gardens perched on matronly heads or tied with satin ribbons round young chins. I'll make an English flower garden at Lucknow, she thought to herself busily, and all the beds of candytuft and thrift and petunias will look like the nodding hats at my wedding.

Fiercely she concentrated on their pools of brightness, whether they framed young envious faces or old wrinkled ones like the gnarled root from which the prolific blossom sprang.

Then they were behind her, and she was conscious instead of hands. Uncle Hubert's long thin bony one that surreptitiously patted hers as he left her to stand alone beside Saul; the minister's, calm and holy, white and fragile; her own which trembled ever so slightly in spite of the way she gripped Sophia's ivory-bound prayer book, lent for the occasion; and Saul's as he slid the gold band on her finger. Broad, strong, brown hands, these, the skin roughened from hard work, the nails cut square and very clean. A tremor ran over her at their touch. She looked at them and not into Saul's face. She did not look up at all.

With a shock of surprise she realised that Saul was taking her arm. The service was over and she hadn't heard a word, nor did she remember making the necessary responses. So it had been easy enough after all becoming Mrs. Saul Whitmore, by name at least. As for the rest—the triumph that flooded her at the thought of her audacious success shut out any thought of what was to follow.

CHAPTER 12

There was a brisk wind blowing as they headed for the open sea. Briar had been so busy getting Jemima and the children and Katie O'Toole settled in the cabin opposite the one she and Saul were to share, that she scarcely noticed when the anchor was pulled in and the encircling cliffs began slowly to move away.

It was not possible any longer to see the little knot of people on the wharf, for dusk had fallen, and all objects on land were merging into blackness.

Anyway, Aunt Charity and Uncle Hubert would have driven off in their carriage long since, the tears perhaps still flowing down Aunt Charity's plump cheeks, for it had been such a fairytale wedding, with a handsome bridegroom and a beautiful bride. Dear little Briar, at the end like one of her own nieces, or even her own daughter.

Weddings intoxicated Aunt Charity more effectively than strong liquor. But when exercised to display magnanimity, she did it wholeheartedly, and Briar had finally embraced her with almost as much affection as she had done Uncle Hubert and Prudence.

Uncle Hubert had murmured, "Have you still got that little green devil?" And when she had nodded he had given his significant smile. "Don't lose him. You see how he's working for you already. Be happy, my child. It's up to you now."

So he, too, had known that she didn't love Saul. She had suspected as much when he had given her that magnificent wedding present of Georgian table silver. "Some my wife and I had put by for just such an occasion," he had murmured deprecatingly. But obviously he had guessed her ambition, and also her lack of love. He was not a man to be deceived, but neither was he one to judge.

Prudence had wept again, clinging to Briar forlornly, until Sophie had come along saying briskly. "Whatever are you crying for? It's your turn next. I'll warrant you'll persuade Aunt Charity to let you marry Edmund the moment he sets foot in this country again."

Then she had enclosed Briar in a cheerful embrace, and

whispered, "Aren't you glad I told you what to expect to-night? Now you'll be prepared!" and had gone to cling possessively to Peter's arm.

Peter himself had at last got his long-delayed opportunity to kiss Briar, and had done so with an expertness that had made her sway a little before she could angrily push him away. It was as if he were seeing her for the first time, Briar realised. And of course this was so. His careless courtesy in the past had been only for a maidservant to whom one was kind, but did not particularly notice.

The hot blood swept into her face, and for the first time she took Saul's arm with some willingness. Saul, at least, had noticed a maidservant. One owed that acknowledgement to him.

The last farewell had been to Saul's mother, that tall thin broomstick of a woman standing a little apart, with her look of unalterable hostility.

"I'll be coming to visit later," she said in her dry grudging voice. "I'll expect candles to light me to bed."

"Where do you think we're living, mother?" Saul demanded. "In the dark ages? Of course there'll be candles. My wife will see to it."

As in the church when Saul's touch had sent that shivering tremor through her, now Briar felt another. "My wife will see to it." So, if not love she had responsibility, a place in the world, a use. She straightened her narrow young shoulders and said calmly, "They'll be very good candles, Mrs. Whitmore."

Her sudden stimulating sense of responsibility had enabled her to see to the comfort of Jemima and Katie, as, being the mistress, she must do. But now that was done, and with the increased pitching of the ship she was glad to seek her own cabin. There was nothing left to do but unpack the articles necessary for the brief voyage, and be alone with her husband . . .

The captain, a jovial, loud-voiced sailor, had invited Briar and Saul to dine with him that evening. The *Seagull* was a small schooner which plied up and down the two islands, carrying, apart from a handful of passengers, sheep and cattle, grain, wool and other cargo, sometimes a screeching cockerel and half a dozen Black Orpington hens, or a pair of goats, or a pedigree bull for some ambitious farmer's herd.

It was rarely, the captain said in his jovial voice, that he carried a newly married couple.

Briar smiled valiantly, and said she and Saul would be glad to dine with him.

In the tiny cabin, where there was barely room to stand upright, and the narrow bunks, one above the other, surely could never, never be shared, she looked doubtfully at her baggage and wondered whether she could change for dinner. Would it be expected on such a small ship? She was wearing a neat grey merino travelling dress made by Miss Matthews, who had said, "In the country this will serve almost any purpose." But this was not the country, this was on board a ship, and it was her wedding night.

Would a little festivity in her appearance help? But really, those narrow bunks—could what Sophia had told her about happen *here*?

She was afraid it could, for she had seen the way Saul had looked at her as he had brought her into this tiny cabin. He had said, "I'll leave you to get straight. I'll be back later."

She had stayed with Jemima and Katie as long as she could, but now she was back to struggle with the straps of her baggage and decide what to do about her appearance.

If she were to change her dress, she must do so quickly before Saul returned. She would not, could not, undress with his frank unabashed gaze on her. She had yet to be kissed by him again as he had that terrible night in her bedroom.

If only the ship would be steady for a little while . . . If only the bunks were a decent wide double bed, like Aunt Charity's, with high pillows and enveloping sheets and blankets. If only, discreetly attired in one of the high-necked lawn nightgowns she had spent so many hours sewing, she could tuck herself in such a bed and wait with fortitude.

But this place was impossible! A sideways pitch of the ship sent Briar stumbling across the opened bag, and anger and dizziness brought sudden tears to her eyes. She was, she realised, overpoweringly weary, and she wanted nothing so much as to creep into the bunk and turn her face to the wall.

The ship pitched again, and a faint feeling of nausea possessed her. Surely she was not going to be seasick! She had survived the twelve-weeks' voyage from England with scarcely a qualm. But now there was a darkness in front of her eyes, and the walls of the tiny cabin swayed dizzily.

Dragging at the things in her bag, she got out a nightgown, a wrap and slippers, her brushes and toilet articles and smelling salts. Really, she thought indignantly, Katie should be doing this for her. She was the mistress now, not the maid. She should not have to pack and unpack bags any more. She would be lying on the bunk, as Mrs. Crewe used to do, and giving commands in a faint voice. Now, at last, she sympathised with Mrs. Crewe who had always been a victim of seasickness.

There! She had found the buff-coloured dress with the flounces which was intended for informal dinner parties (if there were such things in the bush), and musical afternoons or evenings. If she could change into that, and then throw a cape over her shoulders and go up on deck she would quickly recover from this hot unpleasant faintness.

She managed to unbutton her travelling gown and step out of it, but it lay in a heap on the floor as the ship swayed again, and she fell against the bunk, bumping her forehead painfully. She was trying to steady herself when the door opened and Saul came in.

"It's getting rough," he said. "I hope you're a good sailor."

"I am," Briar answered, gritting her teeth.

"That's fine. I hoped you wouldn't be one of those sick complaining females. What are you doing? Changing your gown?"

He made no apology for having burst in to find her in this state of undress. But he had no need to, for he was her husband. Now he had the right to look at her in her petticoats.

"I thought for dinner with the captain—" Briar bit her lips, hoping that her cheeks were not as white as they seemed to be—"this gown?"

"It looks very well."

He stood within the doorway, immensely tall, adjusting himself easily to the tilting floor, looking at her with his unashamedly assessing gaze.

"This isn't a particularly elegant bridal chamber," he went on. "I'm sorry it's so cramped. "But," his thin dark face, his eyes smouldering with anticipation, seemed too near to her, as if already it were leaning over her on the pillow, stopping her breath, "we shall contrive very well. My love, what is it? Are you ill?"

The astonished disappointment and contempt in his voice was unendurable. Briar clutched at the bunk. "I'm a little tired. If I could lie down—oh, go away, will you, please!"

He did not go away. He swiftly and expertly unbuttoned her petticoats and slipped them off, then lifted her on to the

100

bunk and matter-of-factly announced that he was going to fetch a basin.

Briar shivered miserably, and felt the tears of humiliation on her cheeks. Of all the things she had imagined on her wedding night, to be seasick was the worst. She would not allow it to happen. She would somehow overcome it, and get up to put on the buff-coloured gown and dine with the captain.

Or if she could not do that, at least she must insist that Saul leave her alone to endure her humiliation privately.

He did not, of course. He was back almost immediately with an enamel basin and a damp cloth to wipe her face.

He had even hidden his momentary and overpowering disappointment, and said politely, "I'm afraid I was too optimistic. All the other ladies are in their bunks, too. In this choppy sea, one couldn't expect you to be a good sailor."

"I am a good sailor!" Briar insisted weakly. "Never before—"

Then, after all, she was glad to have him to support her, and when she lay back again she gasped indignantly, "It's this ship. It's nothing but a tub. I'd like you to tell the captain—when you apologise for me—" she looked up to see him grinning at her, that impudent grin that seemed to take pleasure in her discomfort. "And don't stand there gloating over me," she said tartly. "You don't have a wife tonight, that's certain."

"Don't fret! There are other nights."

Don't fret! He had the impudence to say that, as if she were longing for this ordeal! Did he have no imagination, no knowledge of a woman's sensitive feelings? Didn't he realise that she could scarcely endure the sight of him? Briar lay miserably on the hard bunk, enduring the sickening pitching of the ship, and thinking that perhaps she had been mistaken in wanting to live, and that this would be a welcome time to die.

She had hoped her indisposition would be only temporary, since it was true that she had never felt like this before, but either the *Seagull* was too uncomfortable and erratic a vessel, or else her tense state of mind had induced physical sickness. For two days went by before she could do more than raise her head from the pillow, and by that time they were in sight of the coast and their destination.

Jemima and her children were in similar case, but young Katie O'Toole had quickly recovered from her seasickness, and, when not flirting with the deckhands, had performed some haphazard nursing. She was clumsy and thoughtless and inexpert, but her cheerful freckled face and wide grin Briar found immensely comforting. Katie would have to be kept in hand, but she had the free enterprising spirit that Briar recognised as similar to her own, and she was very happy to have the girl with her.

When at last she could put on her clothes again, it was Katie who helped her, and she was standing, weak and wan but erect, when Saul came down to tell her that they were presently to disembark.

"Come up on the deck, my love. I must warn you that there's a heavy swell and it isn't going to be as easy as I had hoped to get into the surf-boat. One has to choose the right moment to jump."

"To jump!"

"It's really quite simple. Come and I'll show you."

The fresh wind and the sunshine were wonderfully stimulating, putting life and energy back into her after her long imprisonment in the stuffy cabin. But what she was next expected to do was horrifying.

The surf-boat, absurdly small as it lifted and dropped on the glassy billows, was surely impossible to jump into. Briar looked at it in complete dismay.

"But I am not a circus performer!" she exclaimed. "I do not dive into tanks, or anything like that."

"Quite simple, Mrs. Whitmore. Quite simple," boomed the captain behind her. "Just jump when we say so. I trust you are quite recovered," he added belatedly.

"I was, until now." Briar took another horrified glance at the boat heaving up and down. "Saul, I just can't do this. You will have to take me back to Wellington."

Saul's fingers were on her arm, iron-hard. "You can do it, my love. You must, because none of the other women will until you do."

His implacable voice reminded her. She was the mistress now. She might have all menial tasks done for her, but hers was always to be the example, the leadership. And if she failed he would despise her more than he did already.

"I'm going first," he said calmly. "Then the sailors will help you, and I'll be in the boat to catch you. There's nothing to it. See!"

He left her to climb down the swaying rope ladder to the

water-line, then clung poised, waiting his moment to spring into the restless boat.

The sailors, it was true, were very skillful. They gave the signal at the precise moment, and Saul's spring was as light and easy as a cat leaping on to a bough.

"Now, Mrs. Whitmore," said the captain. "Your husband's waiting for you."

Jemima, holding the baby, and with the two older children clinging to her, was gazing round-eyed. "Oh, Miss Briar, I can't do that!" she gasped. And Katie behind her was screeching, "Save us, I didn't come all this way to drown!"

Briar felt her back stiffening. She turned with haughtiness to the little group. "What nonsense! It's a simple as can be. Jemima, I'm ashamed of you, with Fred waiting over there for you, most likely watching now. And Katie, if you won't save yourself, then you must drown. Now I'm going."

Halfway down the slippery swaying ladder she had to close her eyes a moment, nausea sweeping over her again. One of the sailors gripped her, and the long black moment was over. She turned to the bobbing boat, and called in her clear voice, "I'm coming now. Are you ready?"

A moment later, wet and trembling, and consumed with hysterical laughter, she was supported by Saul and he was saying briskly, as if it were an everyday happening, "Sit there. Make room for the others. Now, who's next?"

In the distance, over the stretch of turbulent water, stood a horse harnessed to a dray, and up to its stomach in water. It stood very steadily and solidly, not heaving dizzily up and down, a large dapple grey draught horse born and bred on the banks of the Clyde in Scotland.

"This is where we change carriages again," Saul said as the surf-boat, rowed vigorously by the sailors, approached the stout little equipage. "Into the dray with you, and you'll all be ashore in less than ten minutes."

Katie began to giggle, and Jemima's children, Jimmy and Lucy, lost a little of their peaked look and timidly began to sparkle. Jemima, clutching the baby, had her eyes fixed on the shore, trying to pick out among the handful of people waiting the stout form of her husband.

Briar, sitting in the stern of the boat beside Saul, had a moment of proud ownership. She, who had had nothing, suddenly had all these people dependent on her. It was almost like creation, the beginning of a race. She looked inland to the cloud-scattered sky that arched above the green of the bush and forest. Then she encountered Saul's hard intent gaze.

"*Ao-tea-roa*," he said softly. "The land of the long white cloud. Well, there it is, my love. Our country."

CHAPTER 13

This time the floor was steady, the walls did not lurch, and she did not even have to unpack her bags, for Katie had done that for her. Katie had brushed her hair, too, twisting it into glossy ringlets and tying them back with red ribbon.

After that, it was obvious that Katie was eager to be gone, for although it was after ten o'clock and time she retired discreetly to her room, she was determined to slip into the bar where she had already made friends with the barmaid. On the pretense of helping to wash glasses she would listen to the men talking as they drank their ale, and be shaken to the core with fear and excitement for what was ahead. For Katie didn't think there was much to life unless there were men about, and if, in the bush, there were few white men, there were those magnificent, handsome savage Maoris who were reputed to cover their bodies with nothing at all! But her guilty stirring of interest in this particular type of male she kept as a deep and rather shameful secret.

In contrast to Katie, Briar, upstairs in the largest and best bedroom the Ship Inn possessed, had only one man in her thoughts, and him only because of his imminent arrival. She would have forgotten him if she could.

She had undressed because at least that spared her the embarrassment of doing so beneath Saul's inquisitive gaze. Now she had on one of the voluminous lawn nightgowns, with the high frill round the neck, and sleeves neatly gathered in at the wrists. She had even climbed into the bed and bounced tentatively on the feather mattress, but it was impossible to stay there calmly. She was so wrought up from the events of the day—landing on the beach and walking up into the little straggling town of New Plymouth to talk to people who were eager to meet Saul Whitmore's bride, then to take this room at the Ship Inn and eat dinner with Saul in the dingy brown dining-room, where her appetite for the roast mutton and potatoes failed her, later still to go up to the bedroom while Saul went out on the business of arranging transport for the morning.

It was impossible to relax. She thought of Jemima's meeting with Fred, and the happy way they had gone off, a child on either side and the baby in Jemima's arms. Her eyes had followed them enviously, noticing their intertwined arms. She had felt very lonely when they had gone, for Saul was already deep in discussions with men he knew, and Katie's restless eyes wandered this way and that.

However, she had never had an intimate friend in whom to confide. She told herself stoutly that being alone in this big room with its bare floor and austere furniture was no worse than many another time in her life had been. At least she need not be entirely alone, Briar realised suddenly, for she had the portraits in the bottom of her wicker bag. She had kept them hidden there, showing them to no one, preferring to keep them as a surprise when she arrived at Lucknow.

But now was the time to bring them out and range them on her side against the man who was presently to exact his price for her new respectable name.

Excitedly she leapt out of bed, and pattering on bare feet bundled all the articles out of the bag until she came to the two gilt-framed portraits packed flat at the bottom.

She lifted them out and stood them side by side on the mantelpiece. The two pairs of eyes staring at her were completely unfamiliar.

In a moment of panic Briar thought that it was like having invited the landlord of the Ship Inn and his wife up to witness her wedding night.

But that was nonsense. She had only to grow to know these two faces. They were kind, really. There, if she placed the candle between them the strange eyes were softened and less staring, the woman's mouth had a gentle curve, and the man looked almost intellectual. Certainly, they were respectable people. One knew that not only from their prim expressions, but their clothes, the woman's neat fichu clasped with a plain gold brooch, and the man very erect in his stiff collar and cravat.

"Good evening, Mrs. Johnson, Mr. Johnson." Briar bobbed a curtsey to each, then suddenly she heard Saul's step on the stairs, and she had to make a flying leap into bed and pull the blankets up to her chin.

She was sitting like that, out of breath, the red ribbons in her hair scarcely redder than her cheeks, when Saul opened the door.

He stood a moment looking at her. Then, with deliberation, he closed the door behind him.

"So here we are," he murmured, and crossing over to the rickety chair sat down and began taking off his boots. He fumbled at the laces, for his eyes never left Briar's face. The boots thudded on the floor, the chair creaked raucously as he stood again to divest himself of his jacket and cravat. The wavering candlelight made his face all shadows, a lean, elated, frightening face that was shortly to bend over hers, suffocating her.

"You haven't noticed," she said breathlessly.

"What am I to notice but you?"

"The portraits on the mantelpiece. My parents. You wanted to know them."

"My God, not tonight!" He didn't even turn to look, but with a practised flip he had thrown back the blankets. "Now, my love. Off with this."

"Not my nightgown!" she screeched.

"I want to see you."

"You'll do nothing of the kind!"

"For heaven's sake, I have no patience with false modesty. You're my wife. And I was never deceived into thinking that modesty was your strongest characteristic."

It was no use to struggle, for his strong hands would soon have wrenched the garment off. And there was no sense in having it torn, after all those hours of hemming that had gone into it, one part of Briar's mind told her prudently.

Rigid and trembling, with rage more than apprehension, her slender body exposed to his gaze, she lay while he lifted the candle from the mantelpiece and held it over her. He looked for a long moment. She couldn't see his expression. Then he put the candle down and pinched it out with his fingers. In the darkness she could hear him throwing off the remainder of his clothes. Just before he got into bed he gave a sudden snort of impatience, and went and turned the portraits, so carefully acquired and proudly displayed, face to the wall.

Afterwards, Briar lay stiffly by his side trying to control her tears. She was furious with herself for crying. For what use now were tears? She had gone into this marriage with her eyes open. Even after Saul had humiliated her so, in the road, outside Cooper's public house, a stubbornness had risen in her that made her determined to go on with her plan.

But she had not thought it would be like this, with Saul behaving like a victor with his spoils. If one were to endure this intimacy night after night—how many nights were there in a lifetime—there must be love, or tenderness, at least.

"Why are you crying?" came his hated voice out of the darkness, invading her privacy once more.

"I am not!"

His arm came across her, heavily. "Don't worry my love. Women usually do—I believe." His voice had been kind enough, but the belated end to his remark was the final humiliation. His arm pressing against her was the bar of her prison.

But she had entered it voluntarily, so there would not, if she could prevent it, be any more tears.

Surprisingly enough she slept and did not wake until dawn was lightening the big bare bedroom, full of the smell and sound of the sea. She sat up cautiously to see how she felt, and to take a surreptitious look at the sleeping face of her husband.

Her nightgown, she saw, lay on the floor yards away, and the blankets fell off her shoulders exposing them to the chilly morning air. Also, her husband was not sleeping. She was aware, all at once, of his eyes, narrowed and gleaming, watching her.

"Saul!" she said imperiously. "Get me my nightgown."

He made no move. His eyes were on her uncovered shoulders. Furiously she jerked the blankets round them, but it was no use.

Just as last night coming into the room and seeing her face brilliant in the candlelight, her eyes like dark green glass, and the red ribbons in her hair, he had been excited beyond bearing, now her shoulders and the glimpse of an uncovered breast worked the same spell.

She was his wife, after all, and she had not been forced into marrying him. Perhaps this time she would not be stiff and unresponsive, and he would find the passion he expected.

She did not cry afterwards. That was the only difference. She lay biting her lips, her eyes dilated and black with some unreadable emotion. It was not love, that was certain enough.

He tried to stifle his anger and disappointment. "Come, Briar. You're not aboard the *Seagull* now. At least this is better than seasickness."

107

He began to believe, as she gave him that brilliant unwavering stare, that her seasickness had been deliberate. Suddenly he was disproportionately amused. Small laughing matter that it was, wry amusement shook him.

"If that is how you feel about being Mrs. Whitmore," he said softly, but not without anticipation, "then we have some stormy times ahead."

CHAPTER 14

It was while they were having breakfast that there was the sound of a horse galloping down the road. It stopped outside the hotel, and excited voices outside made Saul spring up.

"Excuse me. I'll be back in a minute."

Briar waited impatiently for a few minutes, then, when Saul did not return, she, too, went out into the road to see a group of men collected round a young man in a soldier's redcoat. His horse, foam-flecked and exhausted, was being led away, and he himself was talking rapidly and excitedly.

Briar saw Saul and ran forward. "What's happened?"

"There's been a skirmish—nothing for you to worry about —miles from here."

But his face was grim. She did not yet know him very well, but well enough to guess when he was disturbed.

The young man, in a high voice that indicated hysteria and the limit of endurance, was saying, "They didn't eat him, thank God! There was just this enormous bonfire, and the *tohunga* with his wrinkled cheeks and his face black from tattooing, poking at it with a long pole and chanting his savage elegy to the dead. And then, just at the last, while the smoke was still pouring out, that crafty old chief Tito-kowaru stalking forward, and making his farewell speech."

"Saul!" hissed Briar. "Who is he talking about? Who has been killed?"

"Major von Tempsky."

"The man Uncle Hubert told me about, who led the forest rangers."

"The Maoris called him *Manu-rau*, Many birds," said Saul absently, "because they said he was as nimble as the birds of the forest."

Briar saw the tight line of his mouth. "You knew him?"

"Yes, I knew him. He was a brave man. He and his rangers have saved more white settlements than I care to think."

"And now he's—burnt to death?"

"No, he fell in the battle. The ensign has been telling us about the funeral pyre they built for him. He was respected by his enemies. The Maori admires a brave fighter. The old chief made an oration over his dead body."

"What did he say?"

Saul looked down at her tense face. He showed an uncharacteristic thoughtfulness. "You shouldn't be listening to these things."

"But I must. One should know one's enemy."

"I hope you will never meet this enemy."

For Saul, in his mind, could see very vividly the scene that had taken place—the battle over, the strewn dead, and the victors in their forest stockade mad with excitement. All the birds would have screeched away in alarm from the fury of the dancing savages who, naked, with blackened faces, would be yelling war songs and dancing the earth-shaking *haka*.

And the dead would not have lain undisturbed, for the women had their part in the dreadful celebration, doing their gruesome work of slashing the blood-drained faces with tomahawks. There were twenty white men lying there, the ensign had said, and all of them mutilated. He himself had escaped hours later from his crouching haven in a tall ngaio tree, the smoke of the funeral pyre blackening his face and the flames well-nigh scorching him.

But at least he could say that there had not, on this occasion, been any cannibalism. The body of the brave major and his men had been granted a grand and terrible farewell.

For, in his immensely dignified voice, the old chief Titokowaru had spoken to his fallen enemy: "In the days of the past you fought here and you fought there, and you boasted that you would always emerge safely from your battles into the bright world of life. But when you encountered me your eyes were closed in their last sleep. It could not be helped. You sought your death at my hands. And now you sleep forever. *Ka moe koe*."

At the end, the ensign said, his cheeks blanching again as he relived the experience, the tall green trees were scorched and the forest filled with the unspeakable odour of burning flesh.

Yet the dreadful grandeur of the scene had not been an unfitting way for the fallen men to depart.

Briar clutched Saul's arm. "How far away did this happen?"

"Oh, too far to trouble us. And Te Kooti's reported to be following the old battle trail in the Ureweras. That's a wild and savage part that is the other side of the mountain range."

Briar studied his face. "But there's something else, isn't there, besides the death of this brave major?"

"How do you know?"

"I can tell by your face."

"I didn't know you knew my face so well."

"Not with that expression, no. What is it, Saul?"

"There's been a man and his wife and two children murdered not twenty miles from here. They had a farm just off the road to Lucknow. It's a lonely place. They didn't have any near neighbours. The dog must have given the alarm because it was found with its throat cut. I'm sorry, I didn't want to tell you this."

"You've brought me here to live, so I must know. Go on." Her face was blanched, but her voice perfectly steady. Even if she had wept last night, she would not now let him see that she was afraid of a very different ordeal.

"There's nothing more to tell. Whoever did this—a roaming band of Hauhaus, one imagines—had apparently come on the pretence of selling potatoes, because there was one of those native flax baskets upside down, and potatoes lying about. John and Martha and the children had died very quickly," he added, giving her at least that uneasy comfort.

Briar pressed her hands together and straightened her shoulders. "We haven't finished breakfast, and we had planned to start at eight. Would you bring the bags down while I see if Katie's ready. And I'd suggest we don't mention this to Katie or Jemima. It's bad enough having to face it ourselves."

"Now wait a minute," Saul said sharply, "I don't intend to take women into this danger. I thought things had quietened down. There hasn't been a settler murdered for a long time in this district. But as it is now you'd better stay here for a while. I don't think you'll find the Ship Inn too bad. I'll arrange for Jemima and the children to move in, too. Fred, I'll need with me. But we'll come back for you as soon as possible."

"And when will that be?" Briar enquired politely.

"Oh, by the spring, I hope."

"The spring! And I'm to sit here and look at the sea for

four months! I never heard such nonsense! Just go upstairs and bring down our bags and pay the bill, and we can start."

He looked at her implacable face. Good heavens, last night she had trembled and wept in his arms, today she behaved as if facing a band of murdering Hauhaus were of little moment.

His crooked smile held admiration but not amusement.

"And see that we have muskets and ammunition," she added. "Each time we stop we must have some firing practice.

She hadn't shown him she was afraid, had she? Her voice had remained calm and her clenched hands hadn't trembled. But inside her grey travelling dress and her several petticoats her body was stiff with apprehension. The bruises at the base of her throat which Saul had inflicted last night were no longer such an outrage. *That*, at least, belonged to the world of living, and as such must be endured. One only hoped to reach the bedroom Saul had promised her at Lucknow with no worse wounds.

They were to travel over a road that was, in places, no more than a track across the scrub and tussocks, she and Saul and Katie to ride in the first bullock waggon, and the Potter family, accompanied by their baggage and various pieces of furniture, in the second. They would have to sleep one night by the roadside, creeping under the waggon for protection, for although the weather was still mild and humid it rained frequently.

Katie and the two children, Jimmy and Lucy, regarded this as a tremendous adventure. Jemima looked more anxious, as she worried about the problem of feeding the baby. That was such a small problem in comparison, Briar thought, knowing that she and Saul and Fred would not sleep at all, or if they did, in snatches, while one or the other kept watch. Besides, solely for the small Rose's benefit they were taking a cow, hitching her to the back of the second waggon. She was a two-year-old Jersey in full milk, and Saul said that if she arrived safely she would be Fred's own, along with the two ewes he had already promised. It was the small beginning of a farm, and Briar had a feeling of triumphant pleasure at the light in Jemima's face. Without her, Jemima and Fred could not have achieved this so soon.

And without Saul she could not have played the satisfying part of Lady Bountiful. She had to be fair and give him his due, bitter as it was to have to do so. She would even make

111

herself submit to lying in his arms again. Perhaps, if she shut her eyes to keep out the sight of his taut, elated face, his strangeness and his hard violent body would be just endurable.

If ever, of course, they were to reach the end of this journey.

As they bumped out of the little town Jemima turned to take a long last look at the sea. She tucked the baby more closely against her, and her sad face grew calm.

"Now I'll be able to sleep again," she said. "The sea used to keep me awake at nights. I hope I never have to look at it any more."

"There are other things ahead," Fred said uneasily.

"Such as what?"

"You ought to know, Jem. You'll have to cook in a camp oven outside, and the house is only one room, really, with an attic. The roof leaks, and there isn't much furniture." (And the forest is all around. The tree ferns make wonderful cover for anyone stalking. If the birds start screeching and flying out, you've got to grab your gun and be ready . . .). He didn't add those things. The very thought of them made a light sweat break out on his forehead. He was not brave, he told himself sadly. He could only pretend to be, for the sake of Mr. Whitmore, whom already he revered, and for Jem and the children, and for that patch of ground he was preparing for its first crop of potatoes.

Jemima was laughing. Her thin face, so prematurely worn for her twenty-six years, was full of optimism.

"You think I care about a little thing like a roof leaking, Fred Potter!"

She cast one more furtive glance over her shoulder at the grey line of the sea receding into the horizon as a nightmare receded, and she said sharply to the two children bouncing in the back of the dray, "Jimmy! Lucy! You're never to forget your brothers."

For the first ten miles of the journey the little convoy had the company of a dozen or so militiamen on horseback. They rode ahead across the scrubland that was mostly the tawny tussock grass, sprinkled with stunted manuka bushes, and added greatly to the excitement of Katie and the two children. But when the road forked, one fork going on over the plain and the other towards the forest, they waved their farewells.

Katie sighed audibly, and Saul said it was time to stop for lunch and some musket practice. While Fred lit a fire and brewed tea, the women should have their first lesson in firing a gun.

This was not a particularly successful experiment. Jemima was quite hopeless and also terrified. She would be of more danger to her friends than to any possible enemy, Saul decided, and told her bluntly that she had better attend to the children, and leave the fighting to Briar and Katie. Katie was fearless enough, but erratic, and screamed with excitement each time the gun exploded. Briar loathed the cold, heavy feel of the weapon in her hands. But she was the only one of three who knew this was not a game. Some time, tonight perhaps, during the long dark hours, she might, in deadly seriousness, have to be able to use this weapon. So she gave all her concentration to the lesson, and at the end had the dubious satisfaction of hearing Saul say that for a beginner she was not too bad, she might even be able to hit a haystack in the dusk.

When he came up to take the gun from her she whispered, "How far are we from that place?"

"The militia have gone that way. We won't pass it. Now come and eat."

Fred had milked the cow and Jemima had warmed milk for the baby. There was plenty of milk for Jimmy and Lucy, too, and hot tea for the rest. Suddenly it was a picnic. The sun shone, the tea tasted smoky and fragrant, the baby fell asleep, and the women, already tired from the jolting of the waggons, would have liked to do the same.

But Saul was urging them on. "We've got to do another fifteen miles before we camp for the night. Let's get moving."

Now the country changed from the scrub-covered dunes where the sea-winds swept to partly cleared bush, the track running between tree-stumps and the ever-springing ferns, into patches of dense green. The going was rough and exhausting. The drays creaked and squelched through patches of mud and crushed bracken, birds fluttered and darted in the branches, giving alarmed cries, and, Lucy frightened, began to sob.

Saul turned. "Stop that child crying!" he rapped. Briar was aware of Katie's startled gaze. "Is someone listening?" she asked.

"If there's anyone listening, they can hear us a mile away," Saul said grimly. "But there's no need to advertise our presence more than can be helped."

Then he added encouragingly, "I've done this trip more

times than I've kept count of, and nothing's ever happened to me. Don't be alarmed."

But the gaiety had vanished from the little party, and tension had taken its place. They were all getting tired, too. Briar felt jolted in every bone. Her bonnet had been whipped off by an overhanging branch and her hair loosened. She began to feel in a dream. Presently she would awake to find herself back in Aunt Charity's house in Wellington, listening to Sophie's prattle about gowns and husbands and parties. If only she were there . . .

An uncontrollable tear slipped down her cheek, and Saul said in his curt voice, "Not you, too, my love. It's enough that the children cry."

Briar hastily wiped her cheek "I am not crying!"

"No, and you won't do so."

She hated his hard autocratic voice.

"Perhaps you should have married Sophie."

"Perhaps I should."

"She would just as easily have had you as Peter."

"And you?"

Her eyes blazed beneath his keen regard. "You know that I didn't fall into your arms!"

He suddenly gave his great laugh. "Let's talk about this tomorrow when we're safely through the night. One requires some certainty of a future to make quarrelling worth while. We'll come into open ground soon and we can find a camping place."

Katie, who had been dozing at the back of the waggon, her head resting on the piled-up baggage, suddenly awoke and gave a stifled scream as a brown kaka swooped overhead, giving its harsh cry.

"O-oh! I didn't know it would be like this."

"Don't be such a baby!" said Briar sharply. "One strange bird, and you scream."

She was aware of Saul's sidelong glance. She tilted her chin and sat more erect. Let her back break, she would not show another sign of weakness.

At last the bush thinned out, and they came into open country again, dominated by the great snow-covered peak of Mount Edmont, and with actually a thin plume of smoke from a farmhouse in the distance. Everyone's spirits rose at this sign of other white habitation, and after a brief rest from the jolting of the waggons they continued their slow monotonous journey until dark.

Saul chose their camping spot near a stream, and well in the open so that although they were painfully visible, especially if it were bright moonlight, any marauders would also be visible before they could attack.

He did not state these reasons, and the women were tired enough not to start fretting about danger. After supper Jemima wrapped herself and the children in blankets beneath the waggon. Katie, whose eyes grew a little rounder and wilder at each strange bird call or rustle of the wind in the bracken, presently crept in to join Jemima. Saul handed Briar a blanket and told her to do the same beneath the other waggon.

Stiff with weariness, Briar sat upright beside the flickering fire. "I prefer to stay here," she said.

"As you wish. But you must sleep some time."

The edge of the forest, and the lower level of the bush was black against the sky. The sturdy bullocks, tethered to tree-stumps, were moony white and startlingly visible. If the lurking enemy could see nothing else in this little camp, he could see the undisguisable forms of these animals, and know that white men were near. It was useless for Saul to be casual and easy, as if no danger existed, for he had his rifle within reach.

"You'd better give me a gun," Briar said briefly. "But load it first. I'm not expert enough to load it in the dark."

"Very well," Saul agreed. "But there's no sense in us all keeping watch. Fred, you'd better get some sleep. I'll wake you at midnight."

"Yes, sir." Fred looked uncertainly at Briar's erect figure. Saul, who missed nothing, added crisply, "My wife will sleep later. Try not to disturb the others when I call you."

Then they were alone as they never had been, not even last night in the bedroom at the Ship Inn. They might have been the only people in the world, Briar thought, this strange dark man lounging easily on the other side of the fire, and herself.

She was too tired to think much about it. Had it been Peter Fanshawe, she thought wistfully, she would have moved over to him and leaned her head against his shoulder. As it was, she had to preserve her dignity and her semblance of courage. For Saul's nature was not made for gentleness. He was swift and violent, and expected her to match her mood to his. Last night . . . How Sophie would have screamed, she thought, and gave the merest ghost of a giggle. This, to her horror, threatened to turn into a sob. She stiffened herself abruptly. If she was sitting in the middle of the wilderness with a man whom she didn't love it was entirely her own fault.

"Well," came his voice across the fire, "do you like these southern stars?"

"At the moment they're singularly unattractive."

"Who taught you to speak so well?"

Her voice came sharply, "My father." She added, as reluctantly, "He was a schoolmaster."

"Was?"

"He's too old now."

"You've a great deal to tell me about yourself. But there's all the winter to do that."

She shivered, drawing her cape about her. "It feels like winter now. Couldn't the fire be bigger?"

"I don't want to show a light over the whole of Taranaki. I told you to wrap yourself in that blanket and sleep."

For the first time her voice wavered. "I couldn't sleep." She gazed towards the dark line of the forest. Trees, stiff and straight, seemed to move out of it towards them, silently. No, there was nothing coming. It was her tired eyes giving her double vision, making even the stars swing in the sky.

"Tell me some more about your family, Briar."

But she was too weary to improvise. She could think of nothing but that she hated those two imposters who had looked at her from the mantelpiece last night. Solid, humourless, dull. Her parents had not been dull or unloving, she knew.

"Why did they let you come to New Zealand?" Saul's voice prodded.

"They thought it for my good."

"Have you any brothers or sisters?"

"No."

"Yet they let you come?"

"I'm here, aren't I?" she said impatiently. "Do you mind— I can't answer questions—I'm listening."

"Don't listen. There's only the wind, or a morepork calling."

"What's the time?"

Saul held his watch to the firelight. "Almost time to wake Fred."

"Have you done this often before?"

"Often, in the early days."

"And you've been—attacked?"

116

He nodded briefly. He would have moved over to sit beside her, because her erect stubborn little figure looked so forlorn. But it would relax his watchfulness too much. Tonight he had others besides his wife to think of. And he was in no mood to cope with the hostility which his proximity seemed to arouse in her.

The moon swung higher in the sky. The bullocks had folded their legs beneath them to sleep at last, looming in the darkness like gigantic mushrooms. Jemima's baby whimpered a little, and Jemima stirred, comforting it. The wind had risen and sounded like the sea. Saul threw more of the dry scrubby manuka branches on the fire and sparks flew up. The little scene was illuminated fragmentarily, then sank into gloom. Briar had slumped a little as if she might be asleep, still sitting stubbornly upright.

Then, with the abruptness of night creatures, a kiwi gave its harsh squawk, and Briar leapt to her feet and stumbled blindly towards Saul.

"The guns! Quick!"

He was laughing quietly. "It's only a kiwi."

"My God, what a country!"

"You're worn out. Lie down."

"I can't—" her resistance was drugged with sleep—"in a crinoline."

"Then take the damned thing off."

"Saul Whitmore!" Her outraged voice was sharply awake. "This isn't a bedroom."

"More's the pity." But he desisted from his intention, for this was no time to lose his wits. "I'm going to wake Fred now. For goodness' sake take off that preposterous gown and lie down, or you'll be of no use to anyone tomorrow."

"I had meant to stay awake all night. My responsibility— as mistress—" Her voice was slurring again. Before Fred had crept, grunting and yawning, from his cover, she had stumbled on to the blanket and closed her eyes.

The moonlight, the flickering fire, the moving shadows disappeared into a dream, the wind stopped rustling in the long grass. She was stiff and sore with cold and exhaustion, but later warmth crept into her body, and she had an illusion of being wrapped in comfort. She awoke in the first daylight to find Saul lying beside her, his body keeping her warm. The sun was rising, the birds calling, they were all still alive, and the day was somehow miraculous.

CHAPTER 15

Late that afternoon they came into the little settlement not far from Lucknow. The sight of smoke on the horizon had cheered them immensely, and even the baby who had been restless and irritable all day stopped whimpering and sucked her fist with a semblance of content.

But when they bumped into the narrow lane, already sticky with mud, that was obviously the village street, Briar and Jemima had to conceal their dismay.

For the thriving settlement Saul had told them of was merely a dozen or so wattle and daub huts with thatched roofs and tin chimneys. Tree ferns and bracken and the untidy *raupo* bushes grew everywhere. At the end of the street was the church, a wooden building scarcely the size, Briar thought, of Aunt Charity's dining-room, but with a stout kauri door and even a tiny steeple.

There was a public house, a tin shanty-like structure, with a horse hitched to the verandah post, and next to it a shop which ambitiously claimed on its sign that Elisha Trott stocked merchandise of every discription.

A handful of people had appeared in the muddy street. These were headed by a large white-haired woman in a brilliant red calico dress. She came up to them, and without ceremony held out her hand to Briar. Her large face was shining.

"I'm so glad to see you, my dear. I'm Martha Peabody, the minister's wife. I've baked a plum cake and I've got the kettle on. So step down and have tea with me. Have you had a good journey? Saul, it's good to see you."

Saul sprang down. "If you'll give me a chance, Martha, I'll introduce my wife. How did you know we would arrive today?"

"I watched the weather. Oh, and there's a baby! Oh, my dear."

She had plunged forward to take the baby from Jemima and fold it to her immense maternal bosom.

"Now, this little one needs rest. Come in, all of you. There's plenty for all. The children, too. My, we need you children. We're starting a school, and so far we've only got four pupils. Saul, you said rightly. You have got yourself a pretty wife. But she looks worn out. Are you going on to Lucknow tonight?"

"Of course. It's only four miles." He sensed something in her face and lowered his voice. "Where's the Reverend?"

"He's off doing a burying. He'll be back before long."

"You mean—"

Martha nodded briskly. She turned to take Briar's hand. "It does us all good to see new faces. We're a very small community, as you can see."

"Mrs. Peabody," said Briar urgently, "has your husband gone to bury those poor people who were murdered by the Hauhaus?"

"Yes, my dear. But don't be alarmed. *Thou shalt not be afraid for the terror by night, nor for the arrow that flieth by day.*" She gave her serene smile. "That's my weapon, rather than carrying a gun. Though I can do that, too, if necessary. My husband thinks this is just an isolated incident, and there's no need to be afraid. But Saul told us you were not the kind to be afraid."

Briar's voice was stiff. "I don't see how he could have known."

"He's no fool. Now let's all come in and sample my plum cake."

Somehow they all crowded into the tiny book-filled parlour, and ate the cake and drank the hot strong tea. Then Martha took the women into the back yard to explain the workings of a camp oven.

"Look," she said, displaying the small brick edifice, "you stoke it with bundles of bushy manuka tied up with flax—see, the bundles must be the right length. Then, when the bricks are white hot draw out the embers with a scraper like this, and brush out the oven with a manuka broom dipped in water. Then in goes your bread and meat at the back, and scones and cakes in front. When the bread's baked there's still heat enough to bake apples or quinces or potatoes. Mrs. Whitmore, of course, will have a real stove at Lucknow, but you, Mrs. Potter, will have to do with this kind. It's perfectly simple. Except when it rains, of course, and water drips down your back." She gave her broad humorous smile. "But we're all pioneers, aren't we? Can't have roses all the way."

This was sound wisdom, but Briar had a moment of deep

misgiving when she left Jemima in the tiny hut that was to be her home.

It was built in the familiar wattle and daub pattern, which consisted of a row of saplings stuck in the earth, and then crossed horizontally with other saplings. The spaces were filled with clay, and the roof was merely thatched with the strong native grass. Inside, there was one room with an earth floor, and a ladder leading to a loft.

Fred had obviously been trying to brighten the place. There was furniture made from packing cases, a dressing-table covered with chintz, with a small mirror propped on top, an iron bed in the corner and a rag rug on the floor.

Jimmy and Lucy thought it was the greatest fun. They longed to climb the ladder and sleep in the tiny loft. Jemima, after a moment of suppressed panic, brightened and said, "With the things I've brought I'll be able to make it nice. Some curtains for the window, and my pots and pans hanging here."

Fred gave her a look of gratitude. "Come and see my potato patch," he said eagerly.

"Jemima, wouldn't you come and live at Lucknow? There's plenty of room, Saul says."

Jemima looked at Briar affectionately, her old-young face full of resolution.

"This is where Fred's to grow his potatoes. It wouldn't be the same on someone else's land, would it? And we'll have a cow, and the sheep. No, we'll be fine, Miss Briar. You get along and see your own home. We'll come over to visit later."

Briar was overcome with desolation at the thought of leaving Jemima and the children, and of continuing the journey with only Saul and Katie.

"Lucy's too small to walk four miles," she protested.

"She'll have to learn to," said Fred phlegmatically. "She's got sturdy legs and good stout boots. Don't you worry, Miss Briar. Jem will be over to help you settle in."

So this, too, was being the mistress, Briar thought. Jemima, thin, white-faced, tired, with three small children, could walk four miles to help her, a healthy young woman of nineteen, settle into a house which one assumed was six times as palatial as this hovel of Jemima's.

But last night, she remembered reluctantly, she and Saul had borne the knowledge of danger and the responsibility while Jemima and the children had slept.

It was giving and taking after all. Besides, Briar planned

to teach Jimmy and Lucy to read. She could give according to her ability, just as Jemima could. Life was full of dangers and difficult situations, but also challenging. Perhaps already, she thought with a slight shiver, she had conceived a child to be born in this green wilderness.

As Briar got back into the waggon for the last stage of the journey the whole village assembled to wave goodbye. One woman, clasping a small child in her arms, kept pointing at Briar in a strange way and Briar could not help remarking, "I suppose they've forgotten good manners, so far from civilisation."

"She's not pointing at you, but at your bonnet," said Saul. "She probably hasn't had a new one for five or six years."

"Oh, is that all!" On an impulse Briar untied the ribbons and tossed the bonnet down to the woman. "Please have it," she said.

"Oh, may I! Oh, thank you, ma'am! It's beautiful! Chipped straw and green velvet ribbons. Oh, my!"

Her face was radiant. So it was on a note of laughter that they resumed their journey.

"The poor thing!" said Briar. "Not a new bonnet for five years! Why, even—" She bit her tongue. She had been going to say that even when in service her mistress had occasionally given her a discarded bonnet or at least new ribbons.

"Well, she has no place to wear it except church," said Saul practically. "And a shawl serves just as well for that."

"My goodness!" Briar exclaimed. "I can tell you it's just as well you didn't marry Sophie. She'd have starved quicker from lack of finery than lack of food."

"And you?"

"Oh, I—" she dropped her eyes. "I haven't been used to a great deal."

"Then you must write to your mother and ask her to send you the latest fashions. I can arrange to pay for them in English currency."

"Thank you, Saul," she replied stiffly. She hadn't realised that accepting his kindness would be as difficult as enduring his domination. "But I shall wear out what I have first. If each bonnet is to last five years then I have plenty until I am forty years old."

"That's splendid, but I don't intend Wellington society to see my wife in a bonnet twenty years behind the fashion. Or even one year, for that matter. As soon as we're settled I expect you to entertain guests."

"Me!" she whispered, thinking of the trays she had carried, the hair she had brushed and arranged, the gowns she had mended, the young ladies she had fetched and carried for.

"Yes, you, my dear. And, if I'm not mistaken, you're more than able to. You have the ability of an actress."

"You mean, I can imitate?"

He had not noticed, or chose to ignore, the icy offence in her voice. "With excellence. And we're not entirely in the wilderness. You'll be surprised at what women can produce in the way of ball gowns, even here. Not people like Amy Perkins, of course, whom you gave your bonnet to. Her husband is a drifter. But there are other houses like Lucknow not too far away. We have week-end parties. You're not at the end of civilisation."

"Why didn't you tell me this sooner? Sophie wanted me to take another ball gown, but I said it was taking up valuable space needlessly."

"Sophie can bring it when she comes to visit, as no doubt she will."

And so, perhaps deliberately, though one would not have suspected him of such thoughtfulness, Saul had conjured up a picture of light-hearted pleasure. The menace that had hung over them yesterday and during the long night receded.

The house was too new. It had no character. It was raw and young and as yet unloved. Like a human face, it required lines of living stamped on it. But compared with the hut in which Jemima was to live, it was a palace. Secretly, to Briar, it was a palace anyway, for she had never possessed more territory than a share in a servant's bedroom in the attics, or, as in Wellington, a narrow, austere little room to herself.

But here there was a drawing-room, a dining-room, a wide hall, a study, and an immense kitchen, and upstairs there were no less than six bedrooms, and most wonderful of all, a bathroom with a huge flowered porcelain tub which had been a source of wonder and perplexity to the Maoris who had helped transport it.

The furniture was sparse as yet, but there was the piano in the drawing-room, a good oak dining-table and chairs, opossum and sheepskin rugs on the floors, and in the drawing-room a very good carpet. A white Minton vase containing

122

ferns stood in the hall, there was a well-filled bookcase, and various trophies, spears and swords, and a fine antlered deer's head, decorated the walls.

The double bed in the big bedroom had brass knobs, and a snowy cotton quilt. The windows, as Saul had promised, looked over the tree-tops to the soaring cone of Mount Egmont. Even the dressing-table was not unadorned, for from somewhere had been found a pincushion, a china tray and an old silver mirror. A small vase held some sprigs of fuchsia obviously freshly picked.

Briar had walked through the house in almost complete silence. She had not been able to express her feelings, for they were quite dreamlike. This could not be real, she could not be the mistress of a place like this. Why, even Sophie had only two bedrooms and a narrow dark parlour. Nothing so grand as a drawing-room with a piano, nor a window that held within its frame the towering peak of a mountain.

Excitement and pride made her heart swell and her eyes glitter.

Then she turned and saw the tall figure of her husband in the doorway. For one chilly moment it seemed to her that he was sinister, the shadow hanging over this brilliant new life, the owner not only of the house but of herself.

He was waiting for her to say something. What was there to say, except that she wished he were not there?

"Who picked the flowers?" she asked at random.

"Mabel Kingi, I expect. But you'll have to train her as a servant. She's lazy and ignorant."

He crossed the room towards her. "Well, what do you think of our house?"

My house! she longed to say. She had come so far and been so determined. She deserved a reward all for herself, not one to be shared.

"It's very fine," she murmured, not looking up into his face which she knew would be full of pride for something he had created. She didn't want it to be his creation, but hers.

Then she backed away. "No, Saul. Not now!"

"I shall kiss you if I wish," he declared calmly, and then his lips were suffocating her again. She had to submit. It was, after all, the price. Nothing could be obtained without a price.

Later, when she lay in the wide bed, it was no use to say, "What about the Hauhaus? Aren't you afraid of them tonight? Shouldn't you be watching?"

For he answered, "The dogs will bark. And my men sleep

with their ear to the ground. Come, love! You have your reward. Now I have mine."

"My reward!" she gasped.

"The position you married me for. Don't imagine you ever deceived me."

His triumphant face, full of mockery and without tenderness, was intolerable. So if he made no pretence as to his feelings, neither would she. Stiff with distaste, she submitted to him. There was no danger that she would display the weakness of tears again, for now she was too full of anger and resentment. And also not a little panic as to whether her new exalted position in life would ever compensate for this.

From sheer weariness she drifted into sleep to the calling of the little brown owls, the moreporks. The fragile forlorn sound followed her into her dreams. It seemed to be the symbol of the strangeness not only of her life, but of this new country.

Moonlight shone in the window, and the peak of the mountain had a ghostly brilliance against the pale sky. The full moon rode over the forests and rivers and lakes, shining impartially on farmhouse and *pa*. Far away, across the Rimutaka mountains, the smoke from the great bonfire outside the forest *pa* of Titokowaru had died down, and the fuel that had fed it lay blackened and unrecognisable. Farther away, in the lonely and savage hills of the Urewera, the fiery Te Kooti was holding a war council. Fires were lit, and round the tall *niu* pole adorned with its ghastly emblems of severed heads, the naked, magnificent figures of his recruits from the Urewera, the Waikato and the Taranaki tribes revolved in a fanatic dance.

Much closer to Lucknow, not more than thirty miles away, the moon shone with its impersonal white light on four new graves, and in the wreckage of the ravaged home were strewn relics that had been brought lovingly and sentimentally across thirteen thousand miles of ocean—a copper kettle, a pot pourri jar with its faint clinging fragrance of English roses, a silver hand mirror, the severed china head of a doll, and the damp and blackened wreckage of a treasured best gown of green silk with velvet trimming.

At this moment, in other forest *pas,* tribal chiefs were adorning themselves with their mark of high rank, the white-tipped huia feather, sign of a *rangatira,* and holding councils as to whether or not they would remain peaceful towards the white man, or take up arms and follow the great Te Kooti.

For now *Manu Rau*, that wily white soldier, was dead, this could be the time to revenge themselves on the *pakeha* for taking their land and killing their young men, leaving them like broken canoes on the battlefield.

Just before dawn a dog barked, the staccato sound as fraught with terror as had the peaceful cone of Mount Edmont suddenly erupted smoke and fire.

Saul leapt out of bed and was at the window in a flash. Then he picked up his rifle, which had been propped against the wall within reach, and went downstairs.

He seemed to be gone for hours. Briar sat rigidly upright, wondering whether to choose to be attacked in her nightgown in the false security of the big bed, or to scramble into some petticoats and at least leave a decently clothed body to lie headless on the ground.

But there were no more sounds and at last Saul returned.

"Is it all right?" she gasped.

"I think so. The dog was probably barking at a wild pig, or an opossum."

In the just growing light she could see him towering over her, to her tired and bewildered mind still haunted by her strange desolate dreams almost as terrifying a figure as the lurking enemy.

"Do we have to be afraid every time a dog barks?"

"Just careful. But don't worry. It won't be forever. Perhaps another year or two."

Had that poor woman who two nights ago had died sprung up in terror every time she heard a tree rustle or a bird cry out?

"Two years!" she repeated, aghast. For even this one night had seemed to be forever.

"Are you wishing yourself back in Wellington?"

She couldn't see this large, well-built, high-ceilinged room in the dark. But she remembered everything about it, also the rooms downstairs, the piano, the bath tub with its pink flowers, the staircase and the Persian carpet.

Deliberately she shut her mind to the other more distasteful aspects of her life. Besides, she would not give her husband that ironic satisfaction.

"I'm not wishing myself anywhere else," she said composedly.

In the full light of morning her spirits came surging back.

She had slept again when Saul had left her, and awoke to Katie's cheerful voice.

"It's eight o'clock, ma'am. I've brought your tea. I've made it myself because that black heathen in the kitchen doesn't know the first thing about making tea. You could stand a spoon up in what the men drink. Did you sleep well, ma'am?"

"Yes, thank you, Katie. It looks a beautiful morning."

"It is, ma'am. And I've never heard such birds. Gurgling and whistling and making more noise than Mabel Kingi. She sings all the time, those sad heathen songs. I don't know how I'm going to get along with her, ma'am."

"You'll have to," Briar said crisply. "We're here in this isolated place, so it's most important that we all live peacefully. Remember that. I want no quarrelling."

Mabel Kingi was the daughter of a chief and a white woman; she had been seduced by and then married to a white man, Thomas King, who had subsequently been drowned while trying to cross a flooded river. By then Mabel had learned enough of the strange ways of the *pakeha* to remain with white people.

While he had lived, she had loved her husband and had tried to please him by learning to cook and keep house in the European way. But it was not a natural accomplishment to her, and she preferred to grow fat and indolent, sitting on her haunches smoking her clay pipe and singing the haunting songs of her race, rather than doing anything so strange and unnecessary as polishing floors or using a duster.

Eating, yes. She could boil potatoes and the sweet kumaras, and turn immense sides of mutton on the spit, and even produce solid lumps of over-baked bread. But to pick flowers to stick in jars, and make the wide high beds standing on four iron legs, and keep the linen white—no, that was not suitable employment for a chief's daughter.

Didn't these white people know that the great towering mountain, Mount Edmont, was her ancestor? Once he had used to speak in roars and rumbles and immense clouds of smoke, and although for many years now he had been silent, one never knew what day his angry, awe-inspiring voice would be heard.

If the new white mistress, for instance, demanded too many duties of her, giving her no time to sit singing her songs, it was very possible the mountain would tremble and smoke and the great voice come forth. Or if that *pakeha* girl, Katie, with the strange red hair and the cheeky grin, got too sure of herself and ordered her, Mabel Kingi, a chief's daughter, to do this and that, then certainly the watching ancestor would speak.

So the middle-aged Maori woman, fat and slovenly in the cast-off cotton dress of some previous mistress, gave her flashing smile and rolled her enormous dark eyes, and sang, in her high pure voice, the ancient songs of her people. But if her dignity were assaulted she drew herself up in royal affront and even slightly daunted her mistress.

Indeed, in that first week, Briar found herself constantly making peace between Mabel and Katie.

Katie would come flying upstairs. "That black bi—begging your pardon, ma'am, that Maori is deliberately making dirty footprints with her great bare feet on my clean floor."

And then Mabel, stalking upstairs, arms folded, head held high, brown eyes flashing, black hair streaming down her back, every inch a *rangatira*, would appear exclaiming, *"Pi korry!* Mabel Kingi will not be talked to like a servant. I will call to my ancestor who dwells in the mountain. He will cover you with fire and smoke!"

And Briar, desperately borrowing Aunt Charity's hauteur, would say firmly, "If you two are going to fight, one of you will have to leave. That's final."

Katie, at least, did not intend to leave. For although the country was deadly quiet, except for the chattering birds, there were a great many more men about than she had thought there would be, and already the shepherds were showing interest in her impudent red head.

Mabel did not intend to leave, either. She loathed and abominated work of any kind, but it was better to do a little of this than be cast out to survive by weaving and selling rush baskets, and wandering from place to place. Although the white people had this necessity to scrub floors and wash many petticoats, at least one approved of the comfort of their houses. Mabel's indolent air hid a good deal of shrewdness. She meant to stay the possessor of the little room next to the washhouse, where she slept on a woven rush mat and hung up her two cotton dresses.

So there was an uneasy peace, and Briar, exercising a firm determination that hid her own nervousness and lack of experience, was able to get the house in order.

She hung the two portraits one on either side of the fireplace in the drawing-room, and spent a morning resolutely admiring them. She had an impetuous wish that old Mrs. Whitmore could materialise beside her, so that she could say, "See! Now are you ashamed for me to be your son's wife?"

But before Mrs. Whitmore was invited to visit she had to learn to do a great many things: make candles and bake puddings and cakes, give dinner parties with the right air of assurance, learn to ride and shoot more accurately, and conceal her hostility towards her husband from the servants.

Even had she been able to, she did not see any reason to hide it from Saul himself. For he had a similar and almost devilish disregard for her feelings.

CHAPTER 16

Leaving the baby with Martha Peabody, Jemima trudged over to offer her services in the big house, and to gape and admire. Delighted to see her, Briar chattered almost as hard as Sophie.

"I'm learning to bake bread. Already I can do it better than Mabel. Saul says we're to have a dinner party soon, so I'll be able to use my wedding silver, and Saul has a Meissen dinner service that belonged to his grandmother."

"It's yours now," Jemima said softly.

So it was. A dinner service as fine as any a duchess would use. One of her rewards . . .

"Oh, Saul has various family things," she said airily. "Most of the good families here have. But, of course, one has to take great care of them because they can't be replaced. I shall trust no one but myself to wash and dry them."

Jemima clasped her hands. "I'm so glad for you. You've done so well. And you haven't forgotten your friends."

"Not you and Fred, anyway." Briar's voice softened. "And little Rose. Are you all right in that tiny cottage?"

"We're fine. The roof leaked a bit until Fred fixed it. And the baby caught a cold, but she'll be all right now the place is dry. Jimmy and Lucy love it. They think it's a game. They didn't even mind when everything I cooked at first was either burnt or raw."

She was so thin and pale. The bones showed delicately beneath her skin, bird bones, framing eyes too large and sunken. She hadn't entirely recovered from her ordeal on the ship. But her eyes met Briar's indomitably.

"When Rose gets rid of her cough and the potatoes are up and the winter's over," she said cheerfully, "we'll be grand. Fred says it rains a lot in the winter, but he's fixing it so we can have a fire inside."

"Jemima, I wish you'd come and live here for the winter."

"Oh, no, I can't. Fred's so proud of the first place that's really his own. He stays awake half the night listening to see that no wild pigs come rooting up his potato patch."

"Saul listens, too," Briar said involuntarily.

Jemima's eyes flickered with alarm. "Is it really for wild pigs? Or is it for the Hauhaus? We heard about those poor people murdered."

"I know," said Briar. "But Saul says that was an isolated incident. He's talked with the militia, and they say they've searched the forest for miles round. Everything is quiet, and they think any outbreak or war will be in the Waikato or Poverty Bay area. Of course we have to be watchful all the time, but if there are any of those marauding bands they'll attack lonely farmhouses, not villages. So you're really quite safe, Jemima. But I must come and see the baby. She's not really ill, is she?"

"Doctor MacTavish says not. I suppose I've got nervous, losing—" Jemima's lip suddenly trembled. She groped for Briar's hand. "Oh, Briar dear, I'm to have another baby."

"So soon!" Briar exclaimed.

"I know. It's always been like this. One beginning to walk, and the next arriving. Usually I've been pleased, but this time—" she lifted haggard eyes. "This time I'm scared.' Here, in the wilds, with Doctor MacTavish probably miles away. He sometimes drives his horse and buggy twenty miles in a day."

"Now look," said Briar, recovering from her first shock, "it can't be as bad as it was on board the *Mary Louise*. Nothing can be as bad as that. If Doctor MacTavish is away you've got Martha and me, and other women who all know what to do. Saul's mother told me I'd have to know what to do," she added, "so that's another thing I can prove to her."

Jemima noticed her belligerence, and gave a shaky laugh. "If it's going to help your mother-in-law to like you, then I'm glad. But she'd like you, anyway."

"No better than I like her," Briar retorted.

"Perhaps when *you* have a baby—" Jemima suggested.

But Briar shivered. It was all very well to tell Jemima to be brave. How would she herself behave in these circumstances? Jemima, after all, had already had five children, and at least knew what to expect. But supposing Doctor MacTavish were away, or ambushed on some lonely road, supposing the Hauhaus were threatening to attack, supposing there were only Saul's dark face to bend over her . . .

"It's much too soon to talk of my having a baby," she said firmly. "We'll get yours first. You must take care of yourself, Jemima. No more walking over here. I'll come to see you."

But after Jemima had gone, trudging across the fields, a child on either side, Briar had a moment of deep depression and disillusion. She had so envied Fred's tenderness towards his wife, and their happiness together. But where did that sort of thing get a woman? Six children before she was twenty-seven, two dead and one ailing, and a dreadful hovel in the dangerous wilderness because her husband had a fancy to plant a potato patch and own a cow. Must a woman make so many sacrifices to gain that tenderness in a man's eyes? She, at least, Briar decided, would not do so. Or would she, supposing it were Peter Fanshawe's eyes which held the tenderness?

She hoped that, even to please old Mrs. Whitmore, she would not have a baby for a long time. But how did she know, she thought bitterly, that there was not one beginning to grow within her already?

She put on boots and walked the four miles to the village the next day to see Jemima's baby. The visit to the village was pleasant. She met the Reverend Peabody, with his shock of fine white hair and lively blue eyes. He held her hand firmly and said, "Ah, my wife's been telling me about you. Come and see my school."

He took her into the tiny church where the forms for worshippers on Sundays had been pushed back, and a schoolmaster's table and blackboard set up. On one of the long forms sat seven children, one of them a brown-faced, curly-headed Maori boy, grinning enchantingly, and two of the others Jimmy and Lucy Potter.

"There," he said expansively. "The whole class. Ages five to eleven, so one needs to cover a lot of ground. I'm relying on you to help me, Mrs. Whitmore. If you read and write as charmingly as you speak you will be invaluable."

Once, so long ago now, Andrew Gaunt had looked at her,

an ignorant waif, and decided briskly that whether she had a brain or not it was his duty to teach her to read and write. He had discovered that she had a rewarding intelligence, but that had been beside the point. She had been material to be shaped. Now she had the opportunity to follow in his footsteps. The knowledge was curiously moving and satisfying.

"But don't other people here read and write?"

"My wife is too busy, and Elisha Trott only knows how to add up figures. The others—yes, they can spell their names, not much more. Though through no fault of their own. They've had no opportunity."

Briar suddenly knew that she could not lie to this man.

"I have only been a servant all my life," she said.

"My dear child, it's not your position in life but what's in yourself that counts." He twinkled, suddenly. "And not only that. Children like a pretty face. You'll be immensely popular."

A quick glance at the children confirmed that. Jimmy and Lucy were beaming, the Maori child's face was split from ear to ear with his grin, and the others were eyeing her with the candid appreciation of the young.

Abruptly her eyes filled with tears. The Reverend did not appear to notice. He said in his gentle absent voice, "Twice a week in the afternoons. We have school primers arrived from England. I can see you looking at Honi. His mother works in the public house. It keeps him out of mischief coming to school. You'll find him a charming scamp. We hope to have more of his kind before long. That's the best way to end the war."

Today Jemima was happier about Rose, and about herself. She apologised for being so weak and cowardly yesterday, and said that now she was beginning to look forward to the new baby. And Rose was much better.

Briar, looking down at the baby in her wooden cradle, was not very reassured. For although the little creature smiled and waved her tiny hands, she looked almost transparent.

"Is she really better, Jemima?"

"Oh, yes, her breathing's a lot easier. And she's taking her food again. Doctor says that with some sunshine you won't know her in a week. And see how nice I've made the house."

It was true that the dark little room was much more cheerful. Jemima had hung cretonne curtains at the window, and pinned colourful pictures cut out of a child's picture book on the walls. The patchwork quilt that covered the bed was a gay spot of colour. The earth floor had been covered with dry rushes, and Jemima's precious pots and pans hung round the crude fireplace Fred had built. There was even a rocking chair that Martha Peabody had given her.

"We're as cosy as can be for the winter," said Jemima cheerfully. "The next time you come you'll see baby much better."

It had been a pleasant visit, and there would be things to talk to Saul about over the dinner table this evening. For they had not found it easy to converse, and did so only to keep up appearances in front of the servants. The worst of it was that every sentence they uttered seemed to have undercurrents. Even the simple announcement that she was to teach the children would make suspicion flare in Saul's face. Why was she doing it? To escape his company? Could she endure him as little as that?

He would have liked to explore her mind as well as her body, but that at least was a part of herself she intended to keep secret. So uneasy trivial remarks were exchanged across the dinner table, and each longed for the meal to end.

However, this evening they had an unexpected guest, Tom Galloway who owned an adjoining farm, and had ridden in with mail. He had just returned from a trip to Wellington, and had been entrusted not only with letters from Sophia and Aunt Charity, but also with mail newly arrived from England by the ship *Dauntless*.

He stayed to dinner, and talked late about local affairs, chiefly as to what significance the death of Major von Tempsky would have. He predicted a redoubled attack on the part of the enemy; they were superstitious beggars, and since von Tempsky was not, as they had thought, immortal, others of the white men could be killed even more easily.

Suddenly remembering Briar's presence, Tom apologised and attempted to reassure her. "They're not likely to come this way, Mrs. Whitmore. But your husband might be called off to join the militia at some time. We local settlers have to do a spot of fighting now and then. You must come and visit us, Mrs. Whitmore. My wife will go crazy seeing a new face. And a very charming one," he added gallantly. "Where did you find her, Saul?"

Before Saul could reply, Briar said flippantly, "He discovered me on an emigrant ship. He's convinced I sailed all the way from England to fall into his arms."

Saul bowed slightly, his eyes smouldering. "The advantages

132

on both sides were equal. A happy coincidence, don't you agree, Tom?"

Tom's open face was bewildered. He had always been a little over-awed by Saul Whitmore, and now there was a wife to match him. This must be some joke they were having, to deride one another publicly, but in private—well, one had only to look at them . . . Tom sighed a little, thinking of his own marriage from which hardship and drudgery had long taken the romantic edge. He said his farewells, planning to wake his wife when he arrived home to tell her about this new woman with the diamond-bright eyes who was more than a match for Saul Whitmore.

Saul himself, when Tom had gone, said in a controlled voice, "Let's not air our differences in front of the neighbours, my love."

Briar, who could not have explained the reason for her sudden perversity, looked up from Sophie's letter which she had seized greedily as soon as Tom had gone, "Are you afraid of scandal, Saul?" she asked coolly. "You should have thought of that before you married so impulsively. You do not even begin to know me yet."

"On the contrary! I can read every thought in that calculating little head. And think again. You can afford scandal less than me. But don't worry. Tom Galloway is going home to tell his wife how charming you are, and I'm sure you'll never give him reason to think anything else." His knowledgeable eyes, boring into her, left her infuriatingly without an answer.

She pointedly turned her attention back to Sophie's letter, though she could not, just then, take in its contents. She *would* not always come off worst in an encounter with Saul. She would get her revenge.

Sophie's letter was as garrulous as her chatter.

Peter is mad to get a farm. He thinks Saul is making a fortune while he is slaving in Uncle Hubert's bank. He wants us to come to visit you while he looks about and has Saul advise him. What fun if we can come, only I don't know how I shall survive the journey, as I am to have a baby. Isn't it exciting! And I should not be at all surprised if you are in like case. You have no idea how we have all missed you, particularly, if you can believe it, Aunt Charity. She has been so despondent and dolorous and says she is bored to death with Wellington society. Prue still frets for Edmund,

133

who I don't believe will be faithful to her. If Peter and I come to Lucknow, perhaps we may bring Prue with us to cheer her up . . . Do write and tell me if you have any balls in Taranaki and what clothes I should bring. Though soon enough I won't look decent in anything . . .

"Well, are your letters so absorbing?"

She had forgotten for a moment that Saul was still there. She looked up to meet his narrowed gaze, and suddenly, for a reason she could not name, she didn't want to talk about Sophie's letter and the news it contained.

She resisted an impulse to tear it into pieces and throw it on the fire, as if by doing so she could deny its news.

Sophie to have Peter's child! And to come to this house swelling with it, looking smug and complacent and languishing.

"My mother is coming to visit us," Saul announced.

"Oh, no!"

His eyebrows rose. "Are you alarmed at the thought?"

"Of course I'm not alarmed. But Sophie and Peter want to come, and probably Prudence. Peter wishes to become a farmer."

"Does he?" commented Saul, with a note of scepticism that put her instantly on the defensive.

"And why shouldn't he, if you and others can?"

"This country needs workers, not dilettantes."

"You would call Sophie's husband a dilettante?"

He looked interestedly at her heightened colour. But all he said was, "Oh, I realise well enough he's the type of man women like. Then it seems as if we're to have a house party. You'll be glad to see Sophie again, won't you? You'll be able to show off your housekeeping."

He was talking politely as if the servants, or the neighbours, perhaps, were listening. Briar tried to answer in the same way.

"On the contrary, it will be Sophie showing off." And then, to her horror, her voice trembled and her eyes filled with tears.

Saul looked at her in surprise. "What is it? Was there bad news in your letters? Does the thought of guests coming worry you? And why will Sophie be showing off. Oh, I believe I can guess easily enough. She's to have a baby. Is that it?"

He had come to take her face in his hands and tilt it to-

134

wards the light. She blinked angrily at her revealing tears. What was he reading into them?

To her amazement, it was entirely the wrong thing.

"My love, I believe you're jealous. Then we must do something to remedy that. At once."

His eyes were so close, so bright, so mistakenly knowing. She began to laugh softly, in derision. "Why, I believe you think *I* want a baby! Oh, no. That's the last thing I want. Quite the last thing. And don't look at me like that. I'm not jealous of Sophie. I'm merely rather tired—perhaps a little homesick for Wellington. That's all."

He drew back. His voice came, distant and cold. "My mother will be extremely disappointed to know how you feel."

He should not have mentioned his mother. "What has it to do with her?" Briar flared. "This isn't her life. It's mine."

"And mine." He continued to regard her with critical appraisal. His eyes were stone. "I had hoped for children. But not immediately. There's plenty of time. If you're tired, why don't you go to bed?"

He spoke as if the bed and the bedroom were entirely hers, as if she could close the door and be alone.

But she couldn't. She was married. It was her duty to have her husband with her every night for the rest of her life. The moonlit darkness seemed to stretch ahead forever.

In any case, she refused to be dismissed like a disobedient child. She met his gaze challengingly. "Then I may write and ask Sophie and Peter to come?"

"They will be very welcome."

"You think I will make an efficient hostess?"

"There's no need to speak so meekly. You know that you are capable of doing that excellently."

"Meaning there are other things I do less well?" The same perverse impulse was driving her to speak.

"Need you ask?"

"I am asking."

"Then why do you deliberately hold yourself from me? Or do you deny that, too?"

"I do my duty," she flashed.

"Oh, God! That deadly word. I thought—I hoped—I was marrying a woman with blood in her veins. Instead, I find myself with a lump of tallow, an unlit candle, to hold in my arms all night."

She had gone very pale. "If you can talk in riddles, so can I. Perhaps you do not have the match to strike."

135

"No!" he declared savagely. "I don't believe that. I believe you're hiding yourself from me. Where are you, Briar? Tell me about yourself. Those are your parents—" he pointed to the pink and white faces of the two strangers hanging over the fireplace—"you came from England as a lady's maid to get a passage out. For some reason you wanted to leave home. But you've never told me why. And why, incidentally, were there no English letters for you today? Didn't your parents write? I had letters from London and Devonshire. Why weren't there any for you?"

For the first time her voice faltered. "They—must have missed the ship."

"Are you telling me the truth? Have you run away from home? Is that why you've refused to write to your parents? Then why do you insist on them hanging there? Why did they have to share our wedding night?"

His voice was hammering at her. She might have known he would guess soon enough. She couldn't keep up the pretence forever. Anyway, it had been only meant to impress him at the time, and to give herself courage. Now she cared no longer. She let her strange mood of perversity possess her completely.

"I got no letters from England because I have no one to write to me." Now that it was made, it seemed so bald, so sad, an admission to make. The tears ached in her throat. But if it cost her her life she would not weep while his incredulous gaze was on her. Her chin went up. She would match his arrogance. She was not like him the kin of an earl, she was a waif, a nameless orphan. But she would not be despised.

"You mean those are not your parents?"

Briar looked up at the smug stupid faces and realised how she disliked them. "I haven't the slightest idea who they are. I bought them for a guinea from an immigrant. If you don't care for them you may put them on the fire. And if you are angry that I lied to you you may beat me if you wish. I am your wife, and as I have reminded you, I do my duty."

"I shall not beat you," he said slowly. "I don't believe you're worth it. You seem to be nothing but a little cheat. You schemed to get a husband—I don't blame you for that. In your position I'd probably have done the same. But at least, having done so, having thrown yourself at me in that infernal marriage dance, you might put your heart into the rest of the game and play fair."

136

"I didn't throw myself at you," she flared. "You tripped me. You ruined the whole thing."

"I did, too. Because I thought you were Sophie. You were wearing her dress. If it comes to that, I didn't mean to get you." Suddenly he saw the ironic humour of it and threw back his head, roaring with laughter.

Briar flushed with anger. "And what do you find so funny about it?"

"Why, you must admit, my love, it's an amusing situation."

"So that's the word you would use. Amusing. I am nineteen. I may live to be seventy or even eighty. I confess I don't understand you, Saul. I simply cannot find anything to laugh at in the contemplation of the next fifty years."

His face was abruptly still, his laughter gone. "Why, that's a tragedy, isn't it?" he said, very quietly.

Then, without touching her, he turned and went out of the room. If he had touched her, with his arrogance gone and his face curiously poignant, she might have responded, if only from pity and remorse. She had felt a sudden painful impulse to do so.

But he had gone. So there was nothing for her to do but blow out the lamp and go upstairs to bed. When he came, and the candle was out, she would try to swallow her pride and admit that she had not been entirely fair, but that she was very young, she was not yet very good at marriage, if he would have patience . . .

There was not, however, an opportunity to make this self-sacrificing speech, for Saul did not come to bed. After all she had the big bedroom to herself, as if she were a girl again and entitled to privacy.

By the morning she hadn't the least intention or desire to apologise.

CHAPTER 17

Saul was already having breakfast when she went down. In a bright conversational voice she said, "Good morning. Were you alarmed about a Hauhau attack last night that you did not come to bed?"

He met her gaze with a hard, indifferent one. "No, I had a sick colt. I stayed with him."

"Nothing serious, I hope?"

"No. He seems better this morning. Been eating something to upset him, probably. We don't know a lot about some of the plants here. The *tutu* plant, for instance, will kill cattle in a few hours."

"How terrible!"

"But that grows chiefly in the South Island, luckily for us." Katie had come in with a fresh pot of tea. Briar said good morning to her, and sat down opposite her husband. They surely, she reflected ironically, gave every appearance of being a well-bred, happily married couple, conversing politely at breakfast. It was not apparent that she had suddenly become so distasteful to her husband that he did not wish to share her bed.

"Briar, as soon as you have finished your breakfast will you write letters to Sophie and to my mother inviting them here as soon as they care to come. Can you have them done in an hour?"

"Yes. But why this urgent hurry?"

"I'm leaving for New Plymouth immediately. I'll take them with me and they can be sent on the return journey of the *Seagull*."

Now she was startled. "You're going away?"

"Only for the night. I should be back before midnight tomorrow. There are stores which have arrived for me that I must arrange to transport, and other business to attend to."

"You didn't tell me this last night?"

"We were talking of other things." His voice was aloof and unemotional. Suddenly she was in a panic. Had they quarrelled so seriously? And what was to happen if they had? Although she could not view the next fifty years with equanimity, it was disastrous to view them with no marriage.

"Must you go yourself?"

"I could send Fred Potter."

"No, he mustn't be away from Jemima just now, with the baby sick, and everything."

"I imagined you would say that." Did his gaze hold a little approval? She couldn't be sure.

He went on, "When you have written the letters I want you and Katie to get ready to come as far as the village with me. You can stay with the Peabodys, and I expect Jemima can manage a bed for Katie."

"Why can't we stay here?"

"I don't wish you to."

"But I'm an excellent shot now with a rifle, and there have been no alarms. Surely for one night—"

"I don't wish you to stay here," he repeated impatiently. "I know it's been safe so far, but it will be safer in the village. So make haste, will you."

"Very well," said Briar slowly. "I'll go and write the letters. But there's no need for you to wait for Katie and me. Fred can take us later in the day. You can be miles on your way by then."

He considered. "Perhaps that would be a good idea. But I wish you to go as soon as possible, you understand. Before midday."

An hour later he said goodbye to her. Once, even as short a time ago as yesterday, his arms would have crushed her, he would have commanded in his fierce way, "Kiss me!"

But now his embrace was perfunctory, and for the benefit of the servants only. There was just a brief moment when he seemed to search her face with a look of angry hostility. Then he leapt on his horse and was gone.

Briar turned abruptly from the sight of his tall figure riding off. She gave her shoulders a slight shake and went back indoors. Now that he had gone she no longer felt guilt for her behaviour, and relief flooded over her. For the first time the house was entirely hers. She wanted to run over it from top to bottom, revelling in its superiority, planning further decorations and improvements which she could show off to visitors, pretending, indeed, that there was no tall arrogant figure to come striding through asserting his ownership. All this day and the coming night and tomorrow were hers. She intended to enjoy them to the full.

"Katie," she said, "go and tell Fred to unharness the horses. I've decided not to go to the village after all."

"But, ma'am, I thought the master said—"

"What the master said is none of your business. I just haven't time to be away for twenty-four hours. Soon guests will be coming to stay and the house is not nearly ready for them. Today, we're going to spend making soap and candles and preserves, and later we have to measure and hem curtains."

"But, ma'am, supposing—"

Briar looked at Katie's wide eyes and said impatiently, "We're going to be much too busy to be nervous. And any-

139

way, there's no reason to be nervous. Nothing has happened while the master was here, has it? So why should something happen immediately he goes away? Now tell Mabel we shall need her help. She can begin by scouring the preserving pan. No, you'd better do that, Katie. Mabel hasn't the faintest idea of the use of soap. She can start gathering apples for preserves. I have a recipe that Mrs. Carruthers gave me."

Aunt Charity had written in her letter yesterday, "Are you being firm with your servants? The first lesson they must learn is to obey without question. And do not tolerate any kind of laziness. Give them an inch and they'll take a mile . . ."

With a fire crackling in the stove, and a pleasant smell of burnt sugar and peeled apples, the kitchen was a cosy place when Fred put his head round the door.

"Ma'am, is it right what Katie told me? You're not going to the village?"

"That's quite right, Fred. We're much too busy, as you can see. Put the horses out and get on with your work."

"But Mr. Whitmore said particularly I was to take you."

He was being as difficult as Katie. Indeed, he even looked afraid. His face was pasty, and creased with worry. He was probably always afraid, Briar realised, and her voice was kind as she said, "I take all the responsibility for this change of plan. You will not be blamed."

He went away reluctantly, and Mabel, sitting squarely at the table, a carving knife in her hand, her huge eyes rolling fiercely, said, "Ho! If any of those bad Maoris come here, I call to my ancestor. He fix them, plenty smoke and fire." She rocked backwards and forwards with laughter. She was not being a haughty *rangatira* today, but merely a fat brown woman who was enjoying the excitement of these strange pursuits in the kitchen, boiling down fat until it was so hot it bit if one stuck one's finger in it, then pouring it carefully into moulds to make the long yellow candles that gave light mysteriously, as if a small flame had been stolen from her ancestor in the burning mountain. And peeling the green skins off a pile of apples, and tossing them into the great copper pan for their fragrant cooking. Today she was enjoying herself, and was even prepared to temporarily forget her antagonism for the red-headed Katie.

Indeed, the three of them were not mistress and servants, not white-skinned or brown, but merely three women following the pleasant domestic pursuits of centuries.

It was not until dusk that Briar began to feel nervous. She had sent Fred home to Jemima, and now there were only the three women in the house, and the two shepherds who slept in huts near the stables.

All at once the big house seemed full of stealthy sounds. The wind blew a curtain inwards, a bird, a bush parrot perhaps, or a pigeon, scrabbled on the roof, the stairs creaked. Briar would have stayed with Katie and Mabel in the kitchen, but they were busy getting the evening meal, and she wanted to measure and hem the lace curtains for the room in which Saul's mother would sleep. It was foolish to be nervous, for other evenings had been exactly the same as this, when Saul had been outdoors clearing the bush or riding round his sheep. He never came in until after dark, when the lamps were lit and the curtains drawn.

Everything tonight was as usual, except that she had taken the precaution of bolting the front door and having a loaded rifle leaning against the wall near to her. This she looked at with distaste, for although practising with it had been entertaining enough, the thought of actually aiming and firing it at a human being filled her with horror.

The sunset lasted a particularly long time, then the sky was suffused with a delicate gold long after the sun had disappeared. Briar had delayed lighting the lamp, but at last had to do so in order to see to thread her needle.

She had just sat down to her work again when one of the dogs barked. She started violently, then forced herself to think reasonably. The dogs barked at a number of things, as she had discovered during the last weeks, when every sound had to be interpreted. Now it was probably because the shepherds were coming home, or a wild pig was rooting in the undergrowth. She picked up her skirts and went to peer out of the window into the growing dusk. Everything was normal. There was no movement but the swaying branches of trees in the wind, and now the only sound was the rattle of flax bushes. She didn't want to disturb the women in the kitchen because she was nervous that a dog had barked.

She went out there and said casually, "Are the men in yet?"

"No, ma'am. It's only six. They don't come in for another half hour."

Katie, busy ironing pillow cases with the heavy flat iron heated on the stove, was not disturbed and had apparently paid no attention to the barking of the dog. Briar looked out of the window towards the sheds. Again there was no movement, and the dog was now silent.

Mabel Kingi gave her deep rumbling laugh. "He'll be all right, missus. He halfway to town now."

Her brilliant brown eyes were knowing, her smile full of warm sympathy. Aunt Charity would have said she was being much too familiar and impertinent, but how did one teach a simple Maori these finer distinctions of behaviour. Briar found her beaming face comforting, and mentally decided to overlook some of her laziness and ignorant ways. She was warm-hearted, and in trouble would be an immense help.

She returned to the lamplit drawing-room and picked up her sewing.

It was five minutes later that she raised her eyes to the window and saw the brown face looking in.

She did not know why she did not scream. She rose slowly, her work falling to the floor. The rifle was leaning against the wall on the other side of the room. By the time she had reached it that figure outside could have smashed the window with his tomahawk and leapt in.

She must do nothing to antagonise him. She must stand her ground, giving him stare for stare, and hope that Katie would not come in and begin to scream, hope that this was a single prowler and that the shepherds, coming home, would come up behind him and seize him.

Indeed, she could not have moved to do anything, for the stare of that dark face, almost black with tattooing, with the white-tipped huia feather stuck in the long hair, the arrogant straight nose, and the lips drawn back in a snarl, hypnotised her as a leopard crouched to spring might have done.

It seemed to be hours that she stood there, transfixed. Then, as abruptly as it had appeared, the dark face was gone. A moment later there came the pounding at the front door.

Katie screamed and came flying into the hall. "Who is it, ma'am?"

Briar had seized the rifle, but now she did not know what to do. If the door fell in to the pounding she would fire. But she could kill only one, and by the sound she knew that the figure at the window had not been alone.

It was Mabel who, trembling and rolling her eyes, made sense.

"You open the door, missus. They not fight. If they fight they break windows and chop down door. They want something. You go see. But you drop that gun, missus."

142

She couldn't open the door to a group of savages who would cut off her head and gouge out her eyes and then cook her body, like that of a wild pig, on a spit, Briar reflected in horror. She remembered the ferocious face at the window and thought that she would faint.

"Oh, ma'am!" whispered Katie, clinging to her as the pounding was redoubled, and wild voices shouted unintelligibly. "What shall we do?"

Strangely enough it was Katie clinging to her that dismissed her own panic and forced her to think clearly. She was the mistress. She was responsible. It was because of her that they were still at Lucknow and not safely in the village. So if anyone were to die, it must be she.

"Go into the kitchen, Katie," she ordered crisply. "You stay here, Mabel. If they want something I shall need you to interpret. Now I'm going to open the door."

She went steadily forward, fumbled with the bolts, and swung open the door.

There must have been eight of them standing there in the dusk. They were a war party for their bodies were oiled, their faces daubed with red paint, and they carried muskets and tomahawks. Their leader, the one whose face had peered in at the window (Briar recognised him by the feather in his hair), wore a fine cloak of kiwi feathers, and, she noticed with sudden excitement, a greenstone *tiki* hung round his neck.

He began to talk rapidly and unintelligibly. He beckoned to one of his party, and the man stepped forward and put a rolled up cloth in his hand. This the young chief shook out, and Briar looked uncomprehendingly at the long narrow length of red silk with strange symbols embroidered on it. Then she saw that the chief was pointing at a part that was torn. It was a bad rent, and seemed to distress him very much. He shook his head and pointed from the rent to her.

"What does he want, Mabel?" Briar asked quite calmly.

"He wants you to mend the flag, missus."

So that was it. He had looked through the window and seen her sewing. But was that all that such a fierce-looking party had come for? To have a bit of silk mended?

"Ask him what the flag is, Mabel?"

The chief talked excitedly at great length, and when Mabel interpreted her eyes rolled frenziedly and she seemed both afraid and impressed. "It's *Te Wepu*, missus. Te Kooti's war flag. He never goes into battle without it. It was hurt in the

143

last battle. He thinks he lose fight if it not mended. He must find white lady to sew."

The chief spoke again, and Mabel went on to explain, "The flag was made by missionaries, lady missionaries living in church. White ladies, missus. So only white lady can sew."

The length of the flag was rapidly unrolled, and a dark brown finger pointed to the symbols embroidered on the red silk, a crescent moon, a cross, a mountain, a star and a bleeding heart. It was an enormous length, about fifty feet Briar estimated, and she suddenly realised why that proud flying pennant would stir superstition in the hearts of the brown warriors. The 'white ladies in church' must have been nuns, and the flag made in days of peace and embroidered with motifs suitable to the people and the country.

"Ask them where Te Kooti is," said Briar.

At this question there was a muttering and a fearsome scowling and shaking of heads. The leader spoke again and Mabel interpreted, "He say you sew *Te Wepu*, missus. Te Kooti not here. He far away."

Briar looked at the menacing figures. If she wanted to live, she realised, she must do as they asked. She prayed that her hands would not tremble too much to thread her needle.

"Bring me my workbox, Mabel. And the lamp. I will do it here. I don't intend to have these heathens in my house."

She sat on the carved wooden hall seat. It had come, Saul had told her, from his English home in Norfolk. It was sixteenth century and had been used by generations of Whitmores in their manor house. With the lamplight shining on her bent head, and her hands stitching unhurriedly, Briar herself might have been sitting in that sheltered English home. It was incredible that she was in the wilds, with a half-dozen armed and ferocious savages standing at the doorway, and the cold night wind sweeping in.

If Andrew Gaunt had taught her well, so had his wife. She had had to do a great deal of sewing and mending, and every stitch had had to be neat and precise. Habit stayed with her now, and her stitching was quite as fine as that done by the nuns in the convent when they had wished to please the peaceful and friendly natives of New Zealand by making them a flag. No one could have known it would fly over such terrible battlefields, nor that one terrorised woman would one day be called on to repair it.

Suddenly, as she worked, she heard a peculiar rasping sound from the back of the house, and Katie came creeping in to say that two of the Maori warriors were sharpening their axes on the grindstone at the back door. "They mean to kill us when you have done this!" she whispered.

Briar lifted her eyes to meet, unflinchingly, the hard inimical stare of the chief. With a casual movement she felt at her neck and flipped out the greenstone *tiki* which she always wore. It was almost identical with that worn by the chief himself.

The merest flicker passed over his face. After a moment he said something to his men, and one of them disappeared. Presently the grinding noise stopped. Briar noticed that two of the others replaced their tomahawks under their flax mats. She bent her head to her sewing again. Her hands did not tremble. Her fierce will would not allow them to. To show herself afraid in the eyes of these savages would be humiliating indeed.

At last the work was done. She handed the flag to Mabel. "Give it to them."

Mabel waddled across and suddenly, with a gesture of disdain, threw it at them.

One of them made a sharp angry sound. The chief held up a detaining hand. His face was quite impassive. He was very handsome, Briar noticed now, with curly dark hair, a fine forehead and a magnificent nose. He could have been at the court of Caesar, or followed the armies of Hector or Agamemnon on a field in Greece. The sun had darkened his skin and he wore different raiment. That was all. The royal air remained.

He made a short sharp utterance, turned, and all at once they were all gone. The doorway was empty. Only the cold wind swept in.

Katie promptly began to have hysterics. She laughed and sobbed and declared that she was nearly dead from fright. Briar told her sharply to be quiet, and herself went and closed the door and bolted it. She was trying desperately not to have hysterics herself. The palms of her hands were wet, her head spinning.

"Why didn't they kill us, Mabel? They meant to when I had mended their flag. Didn't they?"

Mabel touched the greenstone *tiki* on Briar's breast. "They said you were *tapu*, missus."

"*Tapu?*"

"Not to be touched. Magic. That was lucky for you, missus. They were very bad men from the Waikato tribe."

"And now I've mended their flag so they can fight again," Briar said ruefully. But her fear was leaving her. An enormous feeling of relief that she was still alive, that no one was harmed, and that her lovely house still stood was filling her.

She said briskly, "Pull yourself together, Katie. You're not hurt. I think we'll all have a little of the master's brandy, kept for emergencies like this. Oh dear! What about the shepherds? Have they got ambushed and killed?"

"I'll soon see," said Mabel. "But I don't think they're dead. I think they're hiding in the bush. Oh yes, I think so."

Her assumption was apparently correct, for shortly afterwards the night was rent with wild war whoops, and presently the two men, pursued by Mabel, brandishing a stick and shouting ferociously, "I kill you, you cowards! You hid in the ferns! *Pi korry,* I kill you!" burst into the kitchen.

They were overcome with shame, but they had no guns, and they had thought the house was surrounded by hostile natives. At any moment they had expected it to go up in flames. They were not as cowardly as Mabel had supposed, but helpless to do anything.

"You will go into the village for the night now, Mrs. Whitmore?"

"Now? When the danger is over? Oh no, I'll stay here. If Katie wishes to go, one of you can take her. And I want a message taken immediately to someone responsible reporting this. It may mean Te Kooti is near. So the alarm must be given. But I shall stay here in my own house."

Katie, after a moment of indecision, went to stand beside her. "I shall stay, too," she declared. "I was scared to death, but now I don't mind so much. I never really thought I'd see Hauhaus so close." The unaccustomed brandy had gone to her head. She had forgotten how afraid she had been, and was remembering only the muscles rippling under the shining brown skins, the flashing eyes and proud curling lips.

Those brown men, they made her feel queer.

CHAPTER 18

The invaders disappeared like mist before the wind. Although all the available men were collected and a search party formed, no trace was found of the little force. Even their footprints were concealed.

They had the ability to disappear into thin air, and like Mabel Kingi's ancestor dwelling in Mount Egmont could almost have gone up in a plume of smoke, or flown on the wings of mountain birds.

Only Doctor MacTavish, returning late from an outlying farm where he had been attending a sick child, thought he saw a movement in the bush and took a pot shot from his buggy. Then, not stopping to investigate, for the shadowy form may have had many companions, he had whipped up his horse and hurried home.

Briar went to the village the next day to take her first reading class. Although she still jumped at her own shadow, she tried to maintain an air of calm. It was the duty of pioneer women not to get into a state of panic. She would not admit that her proud air was also to cover her feeling of guilt for not having obeyed Saul, and for placing other people besides herself in danger.

In the village the story of her coolness and presence of mind had preceded her and become greatly exaggerated. The women gathered round her, exclaiming and asking questions. The fear and tension was easily detectable beneath their vivacity.

"Oh, Mrs. Whitmore, how could you sit and sew? I'd have fainted from fright—"

"Of course, if you'd had young children to think of—"

"Did they really hold tomahawks over your head?"

"Do you know that was *Te Wepu* you mended. The Whip. They say Te Kooti won't go into battle without it. Couldn't you have put it on the fire?"

"And have her head cut off? Don't be so daft, Amy Perkins! If I could have even threaded a needle in those conditions I'd have been mighty proud of myself."

But one person who was not full of admiration was Martha Peabody. When the others had gone back to their cottages she spoke severely to Briar.

"I thought Saul told you to come to the village as soon as he'd gone. How'd he feel if he came home to find you tomahawked or shot?"

Briar had enjoyed the admiration of the other women. She didn't care for Martha's direct gaze. She was being chided like a servant, and no one had any right to do that.

147

She lifted her chin. "But I'm not either of those things, Martha. I'm not even hurt."

"You might have been, and then Saul would spend the rest of his life blaming himself."

Briar's eyes flashed. "Oh, you're just thinking of Saul!"

"I'm thinking of you both, my dear. You're young and you have so much ahead. None of us can afford to take risks, but some can be spared more than others. And that's a fact. But at least you kept your head when you had to," she added fairly. "Saul will be proud of that."

Unaccountably tears sprang to Briar's eyes. She was suffering from reaction, she told herself. She had had very little sleep for two nights, and her head seemed to be permanently tilted in a listening position. Saul would not be proud of her. He would be even more angry than he had been when he went away. He would have no sympathy for the fact that when it came to the point she had behaved coolly and well, but would only be conscious that she had disobeyed him. Perhaps he would be sorry that she had not died at the hands of the Maoris, and thus rid himself of a difficult and troublesome wife. It was a chilling thought to realise that he might wish her dead . . .

Saul, riding home by starlight, heard the news long before he reached Lucknow. He encountered a straggle of tired searchers who had been on the move for twenty-four hours, and they told him of his wife's ordeal, and with what flying colours she had emerged from it.

At that moment Saul was in no mood to appreciate Briar's courage. He was, as she had anticipated, furious that she had disobeyed him. He was also suffering some remorse for his own behaviour. He had known he should not leave Lucknow, even for a night. Business had to be attended to in New Plymouth, but he could have sent someone else to do that. One of the shepherds would have been reliable enough. But the discovery of his wife's feelings about the prospect of bearing a child had deeply shocked and dismayed him. He had thought every woman naturally desired a child, even if she did not necessarily love its father. But not Briar, apparently. Not his infuriating unpredictable wife.

He had felt caught in a trap. Why had he been taken in by a girl's sparkling eyes and a promise of spirit and warmth that was not there? His mother was right. He had been fooled, and he was to pay the price for his blindness for the rest of his life. Every morning he was to awake beside the cool remote form of his wife, and every evening crush his resentment about her damned untouchable quality, her air of suffering his embraces only because it was her duty.

Soon, he knew, he would not be able to bring himself to touch her at all, and then what lay ahead? A desert, a wilderness of nights when each lay on his own side of the bed, afraid to move lest the movement be misinterpreted. What sort of a cage was that to live in? And who, in heaven's name, had invented the sacredness of double beds? Scandal or not, he would move to another room and, when the Maori menace died down, he would make more and more frequent journeys to New Plymouth and Wellington. He did not intend to be shackled.

But it was galling to admit that his mother had been right about Briar. She was nothing but a scheming servant girl seeking security and importance. In spite of her brilliant eyes that could so unnervingly fill with tears, and her soft quivering lips. She was a clever actress. Even her modesty and alarm on her wedding night must have been assumed to conceal her distaste for him, for he would warrant she would not behave like that with all men.

Nevertheless, she did have courage. It was easy enough to visualise the cool proud tilt of her head as she obeyed the command of the savages. But that did not excuse her from her deliberate evasion of his own instructions. He would never have gone away had he known she intended to stay at Lucknow. What sort of a man did he look, leaving his wife unprotected while he rode off for thirty-six hours?

That was the canker that bit at him and drew his brows down in anger. Also he had been riding ceaselessly for twelve hours. He was too tired to cope with this new happening. He was also bedevilled by a crazy dream that he would arrive home to find his wife waiting to fly into his arms.

She did not run to meet him, of course. She did not even get up from her chair, but sat over her sewing, as calm as she must have been the previous evening when watched by far more savage and hostile eyes. He could not know that, for all her composure, she had been sitting with her ears alert to the slightest sound, controlling her trembling and starting at the rattle of a window or the sudden cry of a bird, as she had done ever since the previous night.

"Well, Saul, you're back," she said quietly.

He towered over her, spattered with mud, weary, puzzled

149

and angry. He wanted to tell her that he was thankful she was still alive, but her remote face made him become as stiff as she was.

"You didn't do as I told you."

She broke a thread, and shook her head slightly. "I was not afraid to stay here."

"Do you realise you might have died? Katie, too."

A rueful expression crossed her face. "Yes, I do, Saul. I'm sorry about Katie. I should have made her go."

"But not yourself?"

"I preferred to stay in my home."

So that *was* it, as his mother had predicted. She was mercenary and acquisitive and ambitious. She wanted merely to own a house that was, by this country's standards, very superior. As to being Mrs. Saul Whitmore and waiting anxiously and impatiently for her husband to return, such emotions seemed to be beyond her understanding.

"I'm sorry if you are angry I disobeyed you," she went on.

"That's the least of it! Don't you realise how near you came to death? Weren't you afraid?"

"Of course I was afraid. But if there had been no one here they'd most likely have burnt down the house. As it was, I did what they asked and it was all right."

He caught a glimpse of her eyes, enormous and dilated, before she dropped them over her work again. He realised that she had been very frightened, and still was, and a reluctant admiration stirred in him.

"I shouldn't have left you," he admitted grudgingly.

"But everything's well, Saul. I wouldn't be surprised if Te Kooti or his men never come near this house again. It might be *tapu* now. So that will be something I have achieved, won't it? And I declare that silly Katie hasn't been the same since. Mooning about forgetting all her tasks as if she's in love! But you'll want some food. Here I am sitting and chattering. Did you have a good journey?"

"Fair enough."

"You're back very quickly."

He nodded. He would not admit to this strange woman, suddenly as talkative as the simpering girls in Wellington, that he had made haste back. Her garrulity had temporarily puzzled him and put him off his guard.

"And your business was satisfactorily accomplished?"

He nodded again, then added briefly, "I've brought some

material, chintz and lace. You'll want to pretty up the house for guests."

"That's wonderful! Can I see the things now?"

At the mention of presents her face had lit up like a child's, and Saul's cold reason came back. He must always remind himself in future that her pleasure and that bright-eyed look he had so misinterpreted could be bought.

But it seemed that she also had notions about payment. For when at last, dog-tired and postponing it until the last minute so that she might be asleep, he went upstairs, he found the candles still burning, and Briar not in bed, but sitting in front of the dressing-table brushing her hair.

The soft dark cloud fell over her shoulders and round her face, which looked small and fine-featured and very young. She had on her high-necked long-sleeved nightgown, but the sleeves fell back over her slender wrists, and her breasts were outlined gently against the fine tucking and hemming.

That small still face, burnished with the candlelight, was going to haunt him all his life, he thought irrelevantly, before anger and contempt swept over him.

So she was turning into a coquette, was she? Not only the visit of the Maoris, but his abrupt leaving her had frightened her. She had seen the respectable façade of her marriage collapsing. But did she think he was simple enough to be seduced by this coquettish display of the loving wife? He had given her credit for more intelligence. After her previous display of restrained shivering dislike, did she imagine he could be deceived by her tumbling into his arms?

But this game was one that he as well could play. He threw off his clothes and yawned prodigiously. "I haven't slept for thirty-six hours. Hurry and put out the light."

He was not unaware of her quick sideways glance, although he appeared to be occupied with getting into bed.

"I must first tie back my hair," she said composedly, and for the next few minutes her shadow moved tantalisingly across the wall. Little slut! thought Saul furiously.

He shut his eyes and was to all outward appearances sound asleep when at last she had blown out the candles and slipped into bed.

His contempt for her deviousness kept him immobile. The picture imprinted on his eyes of a beautiful seductive woman at her mirror was a dream. She would vanish at his touch.

He was not to know how bewildered and deeply humiliated

151

she was by the rejection of her advances. Her instinct had told her so surely that this was the only way to make amends for their quarrel, and although she had felt like a harlot sitting there in the candlelight, brushing her hair, she had made herself do so.

But he had not wanted her. Either from genuine tiredness, or because his passion for her was not so strong after all, or because he had still not forgiven her, he had turned away.

And now they lay side by side in their prison . . .

CHAPTER 19

It was true that Katie had suddenly become dreamy and unreliable, dropping what she was doing to stop and listen, or to go to the window and gaze across the green fields to the edge of the bush. Briar spoke sharply to her several times, asking what had bewitched her wits, and wondering privately if the fright of the visit from the Maoris had affected her brain. Mabel Kingi was openly scornful of her forgetfulness, and as for the two shepherds who had been competing for her attentions, they now received critical and almost contemptuous glances, as if they were beneath her regard.

But it was only a strange dream she was living in. The reality did not come until two days later.

It was mid-afternoon, and she had taken the billy can of hot tea to the men clearing the bush, scything and chopping at the tough fern and flax and bracken to bring into the sunlight more good grazing land. On her way home, a good quarter mile from where the men were working, she had seen, shining in the shadowy forest, a branch of brilliant rata blossom.

The bright colour pleased her, and she decided to take some home to decorate the house. Without a thought of danger she plunged into the forest, out of sight from the fields or the house. Then abruptly something closed like fingers round her ankle and she fell. It was one of those tough twisted fern roots, she told herself, and began to scramble to her feet. For a moment she had had a fright. It was just as if she had been grabbed, she thought, giggling shakily. And then she fell again as the same thing tightened its grip on her ankle.

It was a snake, she thought wildly. She was panic-stricken as she caught a glimpse of something brown in the undergrowth. She gave a scream, and there came a sharp grunt from somewhere, and then, paralysingly, a deep voice, "No noise, please!"

Katie sat down abruptly, kicking the ferns away, and saw the brown face and the great brown eyes staring at her. The naked sinewy arm that stretched out gripping her ankle was indeed like a snake, but a human one, supple and warm.

"What—what do you want?" she gasped.

"Food!"

Katie's eyes dilated. Did he mean to eat *her?* "Why—don't you get some, then?" she asked, with all the boldness she could muster.

The Maori dragged himself a little towards her. He pointed to his leg. "Hurt," he said in his terse voice. "Hungry. Get food."

So he was wounded and unable to move! Katie's first reaction was one of intense relief. She was not to provide a cannibal feast at this moment.

"I can't do much while you hold my ankle like that."

The Maori made another painful movement, raising himself on his elbow. His face, only lightly tattooed so that it was not really frightening, was turned up to her. The muscles over the broad naked shoulders and chest rippled.

Katie felt a piercing excitement that made her breathless. "I'll get you food if you let me go, but how do you know I'll come back alone? How do you know I won't bring Mr. Whitmore and guns? You're one of those who came to the house the other day, aren't you? You should really be shot."

"No one was hurt," the man said defensively. "And I say, if you don't come back alone all my people will come to this place. They will burn and kill. No one escapes this time. *Te Wepu* will fly. Te Kooti will come."

Katie shrank back, awed by the sudden transforming ferocity of his face. She believed every word he said. Te Kooti would come. They would all die. Unless she brought this wounded man food, attended to his wound, set him on his way.

"Then let go of my leg," she said sharply.

"You come back alone?"

"If I can. I'll have to steal food. It might take me a while. Is your leg bad?"

"It will heal."

"I'd better bring bandages. You stay there." She began to giggle breathlessly. "But you have to, don't you? Unless you crawl away."

The man's head had sunk into the ferns. Katie sensed his weakness. He was nearly dead, not from the wound, but from starvation.

"Oh, dear!" she whispered. "I'm going to cover you with ferns so no one will see you. I'll be as quick as I can coming back."

She flew home across the fields, but in sight of the house restrained her pace and crossed the yard to enter the kitchen nonchalantly. With luck Mrs. Whitmore would be in the drawing-room sewing, and Mabel sleeping, squatting on the floor on her sturdy haunches, in the kitchen. She knew there was a cooked leg of lamb in the safe hanging outside, but she wanted bread, too, and material for bandages.

After that first threat to the imprisoned Maori, she did not for a moment intend to give him up. She had found him. She would care for him as one would an animal caught in a trap. Though no animal had those enormous liquid eyes, or burnished body, the very sight of which filled her with an inward trembling.

Mabel was sleeping, as she had hoped, but Mrs. Whitmore heard her and called, "Katie, is that you?"

"Yes, ma'am."

"What time are the men stopping work?"

"At dark, I guess."

"Then there's time to hang these curtains. Come and help me."

"Oh, ma'am, I was supposed to—to dig a root of potatoes."

"Mabel can do that. Since when has she left you to dig potatoes? Come along. What are you staring at?"

She had been looking helplessly out of the window at the line of the forest. When she didn't come back he would think she had forsaken him. Or else broken her promise and gone to get men and guns.

"Really, Katie, the cat's got your wits these days. Come along upstairs and let us do this work. Mr. Whitmore's mother will be here almost any time now, and what's she going to say if her room isn't properly furnished?"

154

"Yes, ma'am," said Katie docilely, following her mistress up the stairs.

This meant she would have to make her trip to the forest after dark. She didn't think she would be brave enough. And how was she to find her way back to that spot? The whole thing seemed desperately impossible.

But if she put some candle ends and matches in her pocket, or better still borrowed the carriage lamp from the stables, she could manage. She could make the journey while the men were having their supper with Mabel in the kitchen. She usually had hers there, too, when the master and mistress had been attended to in the dining-room.

But tonight she would say she didn't feel like eating, and was going to bed early. Her room was behind the kitchen, and a door led on to the verandah. It would be perfectly simple, so long as she could find her way in the dark.

It did require a great deal of courage, after all, but she kept thinking of that poor brown man with his great appealing eyes lying helplessly in the ferns. Besides, he hadn't seemed entirely native. He spoke English too well, and his skin was a lighter brown than was usual for a Maori.

Loaded with provisions, bandages, a leg of lamb, a pocketful of candle ends, and the heavy stable lamp, Katie somehow made her difficult journey. When she reached the dark edge of the forest it took her quite half an hour, even with the light of the lamp to aid her, to find the track where the rata blossom had shone. Owls were calling and a wind stirred. It was horribly eerie.

"Here, you!" she kept calling in a low voice. "Where are you?"

At last there was an answer. She stumbled forward in the gloom.

"Begorra, I thought I'd never find you!" Her cheerful Irish voice challenged the alien stirring of the forest, and the dark shadows.

"Here," said the voice again, and the circle of light from the lamp shone on his dark face where he sat propped against a tree.

She produced the food and he pounced on it like a famished wolf. It gave her a queer satisfaction to see him at last growing satisfied and leaning back, replete.

"Now for that leg," she said. "I've brought some ointment and bandages. I know a bit about nursing, because I did it on the ship coming out. What sort of wound have you got?"

155

"Bullet."

"How is it you speak English so well?" Katie asked. She had glanced at the raw wound and didn't like what she saw. If this was the man Doctor MacTavish had taken a pot shot at, she wished the doctor were here to repair his damage. But she was not squeamish where illness was concerned. She set down the lantern and began to work.

"My mother was a white woman," he explained.

"So you're a half-caste, too. What's your name?"

"Rangi."

"What does that mean?"

"It means the sun."

Katie looked up at him. The light caught his face and shone on its dark sculptured features. He looked like some heathen god, she thought. That long broad-tipped nose, and the curling black hair knotted at the top of his head. And he was called after the sun. She felt half bewitched.

"You don't hate white people, do you, Rangi?"

"No. We were good friends till the war started."

"You—don't eat them?"

His eyes brooded on her. He answered in a sad voice, "That is a bad custom. It should not have been brought back."

"But yet you follow Te Kooti?"

"My people have many wrongs. We must fight to end them. It is weak not to fight. *Ka whawhai tonu! Ake! Ake! Ake!*"

"What on earth does that gibberish mean?"

"We will fight on for ever and ever and ever."

Katie looked up practically. "Well, you won't with this leg, that's certain. But I don't think the bullet's in it. It looks clean enough. If you can hide for another few days you might get away. I'll bring you more food if I can."

"You are good."

"Oh, that!" said Katie, her voice scornful because she couldn't bear the thought of his superb almost naked body, his great shoulders, his liquid eyes. "Why do people want to fight? They're mad. Let's all be friends, I say."

"Your hair is like the rata flower."

Katie burst out laughing. "Oh, not as red as that. Well, there you are, Rangi. If you keep still that swelling ought to go down. But you'll have to keep out of sight. I'll bring you more food tomorrow."

"There's a hollow in this tree. I creep inside."

"Oh, that's fun. Like playing bears. And I'll know where

156

to find you. I'll have to go now, or someone might be wanting the stable lamp and get worried. But I'll come back. There aren't any of your friends about, are there?"

"No. I was alone when I fell."

"What were you doing around here, anyway?"

"Getting new followers for Te Kooti."

"And then you mean to fight?"

"Not here, perhaps. Perhaps far away."

"It had better be far away!" Katie cried. "If you come back here brandishing a tomahawk I'll shoot you myself, Mr. Rangi the Sun!"

She knew she ought to tell someone about him, especially about the information he had given her. But she couldn't bear for him to be killed. And after all he had said the fighting would be far away. He had practically promised. That was if Te Kooti or any of his fierce warriors listened to a half-caste. If they didn't, nothing could be done about it, anyway. No harm could be done by letting Rangi live and escape.

On the third day Katie obeyed her clamouring instinct and crept into the hollow of the tree beside him.

And on the fourth day he was gone.

Which was just as well, perhaps, for Saul had had a lock put on the outdoor safe to protect it from opossums or whatever other marauders had been stealing meat, and it would have been difficult to continue taking provisions into the forest.

But Katie stubbornly continued to look for Rangi until the winter rains set in, and she could no longer cross the fields without being bogged. She had to hide her desolation and the way her newly discovered body ached for him. He would come back, she told herself fiercely . . .

CHAPTER 20

After a week of almost constant rain the track to the village became impassable unless one wanted to sink into mud over one's ankles. Briar was condemned to a dreary week in the house, not improved either by Katie's strange broodiness or Saul's complete aloofness. About Saul, she was becoming very clever. Outwardly she behaved with a polite formality, but inwardly she refused to let him have any effect on her at all. She could not, after that humiliating night when he had scorned her. She would never forgive him for that. Never! It had been all she could do to lie by his side, and only her firm intention to remain the mistress of Lucknow had kept her there. If Saul could be obstinate, so could she.

Now she fretted about what was happening in the village, knowing most of the cottages would be leaking, and at last urged Saul to go and remove the Potter family, at least, to the comfort of Lucknow.

It was shortly after he had gone that Mabel appeared to suddenly go mad. She began screeching and bumping about in the kitchen, and when Briar rushed out, could scarcely speak. Her eyes were bulging, her lips blanched. She pointed a trembling brown finger at the window.

"Oh, missus! A bad omen! Someone will die."

All that Briar could see was one of the pretty little fantails that, almost as tame as kittens, would occasionally fly indoors and take an inquisitive look around.

"Mabel, don't be silly! It's only a fantail. I'll open the window and let it out."

Mabel was crouched against the wall, ready to take wing herself.

"It means death, missus, when it comes inside."

"What nonsense, Mabel! Nobody is going to die."

Nevertheless she watched with some anxiety for Saul's return, and when he arrived alone premonition seized her. But it appeared that Jemima and the children had nothing worse than bad colds.

"Martha and Doc MacTavish are looking after them," he reassured Briar. "They'll be all right as soon as the sun shines."

"But what about the baby? She's so frail already. She can't fight another cold. I should never have let them come to this province. They'd have been much better in Wellington. Oh, this horrible rain! Is it never going to stop?"

"At least it's making things comparatively safe for us," Saul pointed out. "I've reliable reports that Te Kooti's on the other side of the mountains, and the snow will lie all winter. So we can relax in that respect."

"Only Maoris," Briar said, with contempt. "I'm much more worried about little Rose."

"Let's hope you can go on speaking of the Maoris in that

tone of voice," Saul said ironically. "I assure you he deserves a great deal more respect."

But Briar wasn't listening. She suddenly said, "I'm going to see Jemima if I have to swim."

Saul looked at her, then didn't bother to argue. "No need to swim. We'll take the horses. But it's late. It will be dark in an hour."

"I'll stay the night. I'll pack a bag. And tomorrow I'll insist on their coming back here. They can be well wrapped up. The journey won't hurt them any more than that damp cottage."

She was thankful that she had gone, for although Jemima and the two older children were progressing well enough, the baby seemed very ill. Her face was a disturbing bluish colour, and she breathed with difficulty.

She was going to die, Briar realised at once.

The damp smoky cottage was hastening her death, but there was nothing she could do about it except be cheerful for the sake of the others.

She put down her bag and said, "I'm staying. Come back for me tomorrow, Saul. Jemima, get back into bed at once. What are those children doing in the loft?"

"Oh, they get restless, staying in bed. Jimmy gets out, and of course Lucy has to follow."

"I'll go up to them presently. I'll tell them a story. How long have you had these colds?"

"Only two days. The baby's worse. The doctor says it' croup."

"Well, we'll get her right. And you, too."

Briar's voice must have carried more conviction than she felt, for Jemima sank back with a contented sigh.

"Everyone's so kind, but you share my troubles best, Miss Briar. Don't laugh at the umbrella. We put it up where a drip keeps falling on the end of the bed."

What a place, Briar thought angrily. Cold, damp, choked with smoke from the stubborn fire, water running down the walls and curling up the carefully hung pictures, fungus growing on the floor. This, for the sake of his wretched potato patch and his cow and his sliver of independence was where Fred Potter would make his wife and children live.

Indignation made Briar hurry about, coaxing the fire to burn, climbing the ladder into the low-ceilinged loft to visit the delighted children, hanging the kettle over the fire to boil, and tidying the cluttered room as best she could.

But when Fred came in she could no longer be angry. He looked so forlorn and so anxious. She had to do her best to comfort him, too. And later, after tea, she got Jimmy and Lucy down from the attic, and with the baby in her lap where she seemed more contented, told stories to them all.

The lamp burned yellow and the manuka wood had a tangy smell. Jemima's precious copper saucepans gleamed, the chintz curtains were drawn against the dark, wet night. Only an occasional drip fell heavily on the opened umbrella. It seemed as if, for a little while, they were all children, not living in a wet wilderness but in the palace of the fairy queen. Jimmy's round face was lost in enchantment, and Lucy nodded against her shoulder.

"And they all lived happily ever after," Briar finished, and wondered why there were tears in her eyes.

She made bread and milk for the children, and tucked them back into their bed in the loft.

Jemima wanted to take the baby into her bed, but Briar firmly refused. Jemima was to sleep tonight, and Fred also. When Doctor MacTavish knocked softly at ten o'clock everyone was asleep except Briar, who still sat with the baby in her lap.

"Is she very bad?" she whispered, with a wary glance towards the curtains drawn across Jemima's and Fred's bed.

"Aye. She's no stamina, poor little lass. Keep her warm and comforted. Send Fred if you want me in the night, otherwise I'll be in first thing in the morning. And you might mind Mrs. Potter, too. She's not in the best of health herself. Bless you, lassie. Goodnight."

It was a long night, and early in the morning, just after she had stirred and looked a little better, as if she would give her tremulous smile, the baby died.

There was not even time to rouse Fred. Briar sat perfectly still. The little form in her lap, with its snowflake face, was as quiet as time.

Faint daylight was beginning to show through the windows. It had stopped raining and the birds were beginning to sing. Suddenly she hated their alien calls. She wanted to scream to them to be quiet lest they woke the baby.

And when there was a thump and some hushed giggling overhead, she wanted to hush the children sharply, "You'll wake your little sister!"

But their two heads had appeared at the loft, and they were looking down with round inquisitive eyes. Briar had a

160

sudden sad knowledge that all their lives they would remember this scene, the dim room, and herself sitting so still
in the rocking chair, the dead baby in her lap.

A little of her felt dead, too. But there was no time in
the hours that followed to think of that. For Jemima's grief
brought a new disaster, and by evening it was apparent that
there was not going to be a sixth Potter baby at the present
time.

"All for the best," Doctor MacTavish said briskly. "She
was in no condition to have another sickly child at this
stage."

Be not afraid for the arrow that flieth by day . . . came
Martha Peabody's calm voice. "I'll take care of Jemima now,
Briar, if you and Saul will have Jimmy and Lucy for a few
days. They'll think that's a party."

"It's Rose who was mine," Briar said numbly. "She was
always mine."

"And the Lord's," added Martha gently. "Now go home
with Saul. He'll take care of you."

She wanted to weep, but could not. When Saul took her,
with uncharacteristic gentleness, in his arms, she strained
away, crying tensely, "I want to go home."

"We're going home, my love."

"No, I don't mean to Lucknow. I mean to England. I hate
this country. I hate the rain and the forest and the danger
and loneliness!" Her face was twisted with pain. "It's where
children die."

"Your child won't die, Briar."

"Rose was my child. She was named for me. I don't want
any other. I've told you so."

He took her hand, but she snatched it away fiercely. "Don't
touch me! I'm telling you the truth! I don't want any other
child!"

"You're tired, my dear. Come home and get some sleep."

"But I mean that, Saul."

Her strange tension and unhappiness were driving her on.
How she hated the grey sky and the rain and the mud and
the green dripping trees. But most of all she hated his dark
face, always watching her, leaving her no privacy even in
her thoughts. She should have been able to run to him for
comfort, but instead she hated him. For he would do to her
willingly and thoughtlessly and at his own pleasure what Fred
had done to Jemima, making her eventually suffer pain and
death.

"We'll talk of this another time," Saul said at last.

"I want to go home," she muttered again.

"And where, in England, is your home?"

She looked into his implacable face. "In a ditch," she wanted to say, mockingly. Her eyes fell. There was nothing to do, after all, but go back to Lucknow.

CHAPTER 21

The ten boxes, strapped and fastened, were standing in the hall. Aunt Charity counted them again.

"I thought I was right. There's one missing. Hubert! Is there a wicker basket on the stair landing?"

"There is, my dear."

"There you are, you see, it might have got left. Really, servants nowadays! One has to keep them under one's eye all the time. Polly!"

"I'll bring it down," called Uncle Hubert. "It won't break my arm. Are its contents, in any case, indispensable?"

"They certainly are. Every one of them."

Uncle Hubert came down the stairs to place the wicker basket beside the array of boxes. "And these?"

"Three of them are Prudence's. The rest contain absolutely necessary things. I do not intend to go into the country unsuitably equipped."

"Let me make a note to order elephants in future," Uncle Hubert murmured.

Aunt Charity, resplendent in brown silk liberally trimmed with black velvet, said snappily, "This is no time to be funny, Hubert. We must leave in five minutes, and the carriage isn't at the door. Where is Tom? And what's Prudence doing upstairs? Really, the way that girl mopes and moans! If the country doesn't cure her, I'll pack her off home to her mother. Has the wind gone down at all?"

"Blowing great guns," her husband observed with relish.

"Then I can resign myself to a night of suffering."

Aunt Charity shrugged her plump shoulders fatalistically. She was not too perturbed, however. She was much too excited about the project in hand. It was a large and ambitious one, and she was in her element.

"Now, Hubert, while we're gone you're not to pamper the servants. And if you plan having people to dinner—though I can't imagine who you will care to ask now Government House is shut up—please do *not* use the best dinner service. I trust no one to handle that but myself. And be sure to write whenever possible. If any important new people arrive from England it is understood I come home immediately."

"But you may be in the process of organising a large country ball," her husband pointed out.

She glanced at him suspiciously to see whether his gentle lugubrious face held malice. "The two things are unlikely to coincide," she said frostily. "But it's true I must do something about social life for Briar. The dear child sounded quite in the wilderness, in her letter."

"That's where she is, of course."

"Nonsense! Something can be contrived, no matter what the circumstances. Sophia and Peter and I, at least, will do our best, even if Prudence and Oriane Whitmore are not the brightest company. But we shall manage very well."

"If you are not all thrown into the cooking pot," Uncle Hubert observed.

"Oh, don't start that nonsense again. There's very little danger. At the time of writing Briar hadn't set eyes on a hostile Maori." Nevertheless, a lurking memory of that horrble description Hubert had once read to her, of the ceremonial cooking of a white person, troubled her a little. She resolutely tossed her head and said, "Anyway, Sophie and Peter are going, no matter what happens. Very wisely, too, as no doubt the best opportunities for young men lie in the land. And Prudence will mope to death if she loses her sister as well. So this is the better of two evils. And I trust we will behave like well-bred Englishwomen in an emergency."

After the excitement and bustle of Sophie's and Briar's weddings were over, it was seldom that Aunt Charity had found life so dull.

Nothing was happening in the town, no new people of any importance had arrived, the Governor and his household had returned to their Auckland residence, and social life was dead. Moreover, with both Briar and Sophie out of the house, Prudence began to mope. She spent most of the day at her window watching for a ship coming in, and when the last ship from England had failed to bring a letter from Edmund she had gone down with a brief but nasty attack of fever that left her more mopey and white-faced than ever.

Aunt Charity had been driven to distraction. Even the news of Sophie's pregnancy had not excited her greatly, for it was obvious that Peter was planning a move to the country any day, and that meant she would be barred from the fuss and excitement of the baby's birth. Unless, of course, she accompanied them . . .

That was when the idea began. She sat up in bed one night with such vigour that her husband, startled awake, exclaimed, "Te Kooti!"

"Don't be absurd, Hubert. We're in Wellington. But I've just had the most wonderful idea."

Uncle Hubert settled down grumpily. "Not another charity ball!"

"Perhaps, but not here. In the country. At Saul's home. He and Briar shall give a house warming. And we," she finished dramatically, "will all be there."

The wind was blowing against the house in sharp gusts, with a sound of approaching winter. Uncle Hubert buried his face in the pillow and hunched the blankets defensively over his chilly shoulders. He was tired of routs and balls, of tea parties and dinner parties, weddings and picnics. There was far more serious business to be done, and his wife had a mind full of nothing but frivolous feminine ambition. She was occupied only with fashion and social triumphs, and the bending of other people to her will.

"Speak for yourself," he said tartly. "I, for one, won't be there."

It was futile to think that that might end the conversation. Aunt Charity was just beginning. She sat up in bed, her wavering shadow enormous across the wall, her plump hands gesturing dramatically. Wellington, it appeared, had bored her to distraction lately. If it hadn't been for the girls' arrival in the late spring she would have expired. But that distraction had been only temporary, and short of a trip to England, the only thing that would save her would be to visit dear Briar and Saul in Taranaki and do what she could to make their lives more gay. One simply could not stagnate, as they were in danger of doing. Besides, Briar was a pretty little thing, and deserved showing off. Having so recently been a servant, she wouldn't have any idea about organising a satisfactory social life.

Oriane Whitmore had mentioned only yesterday that she

was travelling to New Plymouth by the *Seagull* on its next voyage, and Peter intended taking Sophie, so why shouldn't they all go? And if Hubert was so unenterprising as to refuse, then they would go without him!

By this time Uncle Hubert was so uncomfortable, with the draughts creeping into the bed, and the energetic bouncing of his wife, that he murmured, "Do what you like, my dear. The field is yours—and Te Kooti's. Only leave me in peace."

So the ten trunks were in the hall, and Prudence was coming slowly down the stairs, and the carriage was at the door. A new epoch, thought Uncle Hubert ironically as he assisted the rotund form of his wife to mount the carriage steps, was being made in New Zealand history.

Hampered by adverse winds, the *Seagull* took seven days to make the voyage. Battered and seasick, flung like sacks of grain into the bobbing surf-boat, drenched with sea spray and rain, the travellers at last reached shore.

That tough old woman, Oriane Whitmore, had withstood the journey the best. It took more than a little seasickness to defeat her, and it amused her to see Charity Carruthers reduced to a green-faced shadow of herself. This descent on Saul and Briar was an imposition. But apparently the long-faced Prudence could not be left behind if her sister went, and Charity Carruthers would not be left out of the excitement. The young man, Peter Fanshawe, was coping as well as could be expected with such a clutch of women on his hands, though once or twice one caught a look of desperation in his eyes. All in all, the journey had not been without its diversions, and the visitation in such numbers would test Briar's ability as a hostess. Though if she failed lamentably, what could one do about it?

Mrs. Whitmore prayed that Saul was not too disappointed and disillusioned. She also prayed that Briar was, by this time, the same interesting shape as Sophia.

Safely on land Aunt Charity quickly recovered. She swept aside the astonished protests about transport so far into the country at this time of year, and said, "I don't care how long it takes, nor how many vehicles we require, we must get there."

There were five of them, and luggage. The luggage was certainly formidable. Aunt Charity did not intend to explain to these ignorant yokels what space a ball dress made to the crinoline pattern occupied in a trunk, nor how many bonnets it was necessary for a fashion-conscious woman to have. She waved an imperious hand.

"We require all this transported safely, and kept dry. We will pay a reasonable sum, and if you say it's impossible to do this, then you should be ashamed to be pioneers!"

An arrangement for three bullock drays and two drivers—Peter would drive the third—was at last made. It was pointed out that the roads might be impassable in places, that streams could be flooded into rivers, and that the danger from wandering Hauhaus was by no means over. Aunt Charity's mind was on her destination. She refused to admit any obstacles.

"Well," she said, as at last they sat over tea in the Ship Inn, "what would you all have done without me?"

"You didn't give anyone else a chance," Sophie retorted, rather bad-temperedly. She was still feeling ill from the dreadful voyage, and she resented the slight to her husband.

"We, at least, will have available a change of clothing," Mrs. Whitmore observed dryly, her mind on the array of baggage. She herself had travelled with one small carpet bag which contained a silk afternoon dress, night things and underclothing. She had long ago refused to turn herself, a civilised human being, into a beast of burden, always struggling with too many possessions.

"Oh, I shall hold up my umbrella all the way," Aunt Charity stated cheerfully. "I warrant I shall arrive perfectly dry."

This optimistic statement was finally completely disproved on the second day when after wallowing at a dangerous tilt in deep mud, the dray in which Aunt Charity and Mrs. Whitmore were riding overturned and the two ladies were deposited very thoroughly in the mud.

Sophie, who had been near hysteria from tiredness and discomfort, dissolved into uncontrollable giggles. Peter, after an alarmed moment while he thought the ladies might have been seriously hurt, joined her, and even the wan Prudence managed a nervous titter.

Nobody was hurt, and the vehicle was soon righted and set on its way. But the nightmare journey on which they had so rashly embarked had turned into comedy, and Aunt Charity who had intended to teach the poor benighted settlers in the bush something of social life and the latest fashions was in a deplorable state.

"Now it only needs the Hauhaus!" she declared grimly,

re-erecting her umbrella over her mud-spattered but in-
domitable figure.

"They wouldn't dare!" giggled Sophie.

"Told you this journey was crazy, ma'am," ventured the
driver.

"You shut your mouth and get on. I don't intend to spend
another night under these waggons. Mrs. Whitmore, I don't
know how you stand all this."

Mrs. Whitmore calmly wiped mud from her face, and gave
her faint smile.

"It's not as bad as India, Mrs. Carruthers. There we had
heat, and no water."

Aunt Charity looked at the dripping trees and drenched
grass.

"If only there were more moderation in things. Peter, as
soon as we're within reach of Lucknow you're to go on
ahead and prepare Briar and Saul for our arrival. Tell them
our most urgent need is for baths."

So it happened that Peter took Briar completely by surprise. She thought it was an apparition standing on the doorstep, except that no apparition would look so travel-stained.
His eyes were as blue as she had remembered them. Used by
now to only Saul's black brows, she temporarily forgot her
resentment against him for her thwarted plans, and felt
nothing but pleasure.

"Peter! Peter Fanshawe!"

"Yes, it's me. We're all on the way. We've had a ghastly
journey, to say the least. Can you possibly put us all up?"

"All?" Briar repeated blankly.

"Mrs. Whitmore and Aunt Charity and Prudence and
Sophia."

"All of them!"

"Isn't it crazy?"

He stood there laughing in that light-hearted careless
manner that she hadn't known since the days in Wellington
when everybody laughed. In the fortnight since the baby
Rose's death she hadn't even smiled. But now, all in a moment, it was as if clouds were lifting and she was alive again.
It was miraculous.

"Oh, Peter, it's wonderful to see you. We knew you and
Sophie were coming one day, but you hadn't written—"

"There wasn't a ship sailing to take a letter, and then Aunt

167

Charity got this crazy idea to come, too. And Mrs. Whitmore was coming, anyway. And we couldn't leave Prue—"

"Of course you couldn't. I'm so happy to see you!"

She stood with her face lifted to him, her cheeks bright, her eyes sparkling. She was grown-up, he was thinking. And yet he had caught a glimpse of this desirable young woman just after her wedding, when he had kissed her. He hadn't really noticed her before. She had been just a servant girl.

But now . . . And Sophie had grown plump and languid and petulant in her pregnancy . . .

He was aware that Saul had come into the hall, and said, "My God, Saul, you don't know how good it is to see you after that journey. We thought you must live at the end of the world. I'm afraid you have a visitation arriving."

"Splendid!" said Saul heartily. "Just what we were needing. Isn't it, Briar?"

"Oh, yes, indeed. I can't believe it. It's so wonderful. I must go and tell Mabel to put plenty of hot water on. Saul, will you go and meet the waggons? Oh, isn't this exciting!"

He had never thought to see her again, Saul reflected wryly, this brilliant-cheeked girl full of life and vitality. Since the baby Rose's death she hadn't let him touch her. He had thought it was because of shock (he would not admit it had anything to do with his own humiliation of her), and had been forced to decide that there was nothing to do but give her time to get over it. But now, all in a minute, there she was, that person he so rarely saw, laughing and gay and surely full of warmth and passion. It was as if one had to know the trick of finding her—perhaps this good-looking young Fanshawe had it. Or more likely her pleasure was for the arrival of old friends. After all, it had been lonely and strange and full of tension here. What else could he have expected?

But would that laughing bright-eyed person come to their bedroom that night? It was so unlikely that his lips curled bitterly at the thought.

All at once the house was in a tremendous bustle. Kettles of water were put on the stove to heat, fires lit, beds made. It was like a ship arriving, Briar thought, with people and news from another world.

She had come out of her queer frozen state and was on fire with excitement. She felt that at last a dream had come true. She was a child, and it was her birthday and there were people who loved her and brought her gifts.

But she did not feel a child when the rest of the party had arrived and she saw Sophie's swelling figure. The colour heightened in her cheeks. She flung herself from Aunt Charity's muddy embrace to Sophie and then to Prue. Last, she welcomed old Mrs. Whitmore politely, and felt the sharp eyes on her slim waist, seeking.

"Well, *I'm* not having a baby!" she wanted to say pertly.

But she bit her lips and made all the polite welcoming remarks. Had it been a terrible journey? How brave they all were. There were fires lit, and Katie would help them to change and unpack.

"We've a real bathroom," she said, with enormous pride. Then she remembered that she was the hostess and must be poised and adult.

"You may all like to have trays in bed this evening. You must be quite worn out. I'll show you your rooms."

"I must go to bed," said Sophie. "My back is breaking."

She would, of course, draw attention to herself and her condition. She was never one to be in the background. If she were to stay here to have her baby Briar would have to overcome her strong resentment.

But there was old Mrs. Whitmore eyeing her again. She pinched in her waist ostentatiously, and said, "Of course, Sophie dear, you must rest immediately. Come upstairs."

Sophie lay in bed, her hands clasped smugly on the bulge of her stomach.

"Briar do stay and talk. We've thousands of things to discuss."

"I know, but—"

"Oh, pretend you're my maid again and I command you to stay." Sophie's eyes went round the spacious room, and were honest enough to show appreciation and envy. "This is like a fairy-tale come true for you, isn't it? Aunt Charity always felt like a fairy godmother, and she hated it when that stopped. So she was determined to come and visit you and try to go on feeling that way. She's much more proud of you than she is of Prue and me."

Briar was glad to seize on another topic of conversation. "Is Prue still fretting for Edmund?"

"Yes, the little fool. We all know now he's forgotten her or he would have written. There have been two ships in that could have brought letters. We hoped a visit to you would do her good. She knows how happy Peter and I are, and if she sees you and Saul happy, too—you are happy, aren't you, Briar?"

"Of course I am. What do you think? With all this."

"I know it's an awfully grand house for the country, but houses aren't everything. Aren't you having a baby yet?"

"I'm not in a hurry," Briar said primly.

"It's not a matter of whether you're in a hurry or not. It just happens. Briar, you do *love* Saul, don't you?"

"What's love got to do with it?"

Sophie's eyes widened, shocked. "Why, everything! If I didn't love Peter I couldn't let him touch me."

"Oh, don't be such a hypocrite, Sophie. You'd have fallen into the arms of the first man who'd have you."

Sophie looked a little affronted, and agreed reluctantly, "Well, perhaps I would have. Love comes afterwards. Haven't you found that out? Haven't you really, Briar?"

Briar stared at her angrily. Here Sophie was, supposed to be envying her her big house, her servants, all the superior furniture and comforts. And instead she was pitying her! With those round pale blue eyes, that smug plump face, that swelling stomach lifting the bedclothes.

"Of course I love my husband."

But Sophie continued to look at her sceptically. "I don't believe you do. I believe you're afraid of him."

"Afraid of him!"

"Well, I would be, I admit it."

"I'm not afraid of anybody," Briar said crossly. "When those Hauhaus came—"

"Hauhaus! Heavens! Tell me!" Sophie gave a little shriek and settled down to listen.

When Briar had finished she said satisfyingly, "How brave you were! I'd have died. I never believed those things really happened in spite of what Uncle Hubert said. Oh, Briar, you're not leaving me! Not in this room alone!"

Briar laughed, pleasantly superior again.

"Don't be a silly. We're all close at hand. Besides, if you could make that long journey in your condition you needn't be afraid of a Maori or two."

Sophie sighed. "But that's what a pioneer woman is expected to do. Peter told me. He's so crazy to get land and make his fortune. I don't suppose fortunes are made that quickly. So I have to have my baby in the wilds. But if we can have a house like this—"

"It took Saul four years to build this one."

"Oh, yes, I know I'll have to be patient. We'll just have a cottage at first, which won't be any worse than the house we had in Wellington. How that chimney smoked! I was never so glad to leave a place. And the Governor had gone to Auckland, so social life had simply stopped. Oh, and Miss Matthews has made me two new gowns. I'll show them to you tomorrow. They say the crinoline is going out, which is a pity because it's wonderfully convenient for concealing one's condition. And I don't doubt I'll be this way often enough."

In the next room which Aunt Charity was to share with Prudence, that lady prepared for bed, putting on almost as many clothes as she had discarded. But she was clean and pink-cheeked again, and none the worse for her experience. Indeed, she radiated cheerfulness.

"Well, Prudence, you can see what Briar has done for herself by being sensible. You can do just as well, or better, if you'll only put that ne'er-do-well sailor out of your mind."

"Yes, Aunt Charity."

"Don't be so meek, child! Show some spirit. Wouldn't you like a house like this?"

At the window, Prudence said in a low voice, "It's lonely and dark. I was frightened all the way. I kept thinking of things Uncle Hubert said the Hauhaus do. They really do do them, don't they?"

"So it's rumoured. I've yet to see such things with my own eyes." Aunt Charity dismissed that subject, refusing to be deflected. "You see how well and happy Briar is. Though I don't believe—"

"You don't believe what, Aunt Charity?"

Aunt Charity's mouth was tightly pursed. "Never mind, dear. Though Oriane Whitmore is going to be very disappointed if I'm not mistaken. Now, hand me my smelling salts. Oh, what a journey that was! Your Uncle Hubert will never believe it. But we're pioneer women now, Prudence. That's something to be proud of. And I believe that drawing-room is large enough to hold a very adequate ball. We must get Katie to unpack our bags tomorrow. An idle piece, if ever there was, that girl. I'll have to take her in hand."

Prudence at last climbed into bed beside the large mound of her aunt.

"Shall I blow the candles out, Aunt Charity?"

"Yes, please. We must get some rest. This bed is very

comfortable." Aunt Charity suddenly bounced upright, almost ejecting the slight form of her niece from the bed. "Do you know, Prudence, this is the first time I've ever slept apart from your Uncle Hubert since we were married. And I intend to enjoy every minute of it!"

Of the guests, only Peter and Mrs. Whitmore, who seemed made of iron, stayed up to supper. Conversation was general until Peter excused himself to go up to see how his wife was, and Briar followed to say goodnight. As she came back she heard Mrs. Whitmore saying, "Well, Saul, you've built a fine house."

"I'm glad you like it, mother. I looked forward to showing it to you."

"Who are those people?" She was pointing to the portraits over the mantelpiece. Briar, at the door, stood rigid.

"They're Briar's parents."

"Oh! I didn't know she had pictures of them. She was very secretive when I talked to her."

"She wanted to surprise you with them."

"Well—they look respectable enough. I'd hoped you'd have some news for me by now."

"Give us time, mother."

"Yes, I know. I'm impatient. If anything should go wrong —nothing is wrong, is there?"

"What should be wrong?"

Briar heard the harsh impatience in Saul's voice. Suddenly she pressed her hands to her face and crept away. She should not have been listening. She hadn't wanted to hear his loyalty to her, either about those two horrible portraits which she had neglected to remove, or about the fact that she had not conceived a child.

She hadn't tried not to, had she, she asked herself indignantly. Not until the last fortnight, anyway, after Jemima's baby had died, and the little snowflake face, so still, so lost, had haunted her. Then she had cried out when Saul had put his hands on her, and he had drawn back, his head high, his face dark and stony. He hadn't touched her again.

But now he had lied for her. She wished she hadn't heard.

Saul came to bed very late, as he had been doing for the last fortnight, coming in quietly when he had imagined her asleep, and hoping not to disturb her.

But tonight, although he was late, she had not put the candles out. She was uneasily conscious of an obligation.

"Not asleep?"

"No."

"There's been too much excitement for you." His voice was faintly indulgent, as if he spoke to a child. "My mother thinks you are managing very well."

"What's it to do with her?" Briar asked sulkily.

"Naturally she's interested."

"Why did you lie to her about those portraits?"

"A small courtesy to my wife."

She would have thanked him, but for his airy voice, as if the lie had meant little to him. Through half closed eyes she watched him undress. He had a lean hard body, she noticed. Tall and taut and hard, with that proud head. Not a gentle man. Not like Peter with his summer blue gaze.

"Well," he said, "if the Hauhaus attack tonight I wonder who'll scream the loudest. I suppose you women will be planning some festivities. You'll enjoy that, won't you?"

"Of course," Briar replied, in a similar polite voice.

He threw back the blankets. Instinctively she shrank into a smaller space. She hadn't meant to. She didn't think he had noticed. He lifted the candle to blow it out. Then on an impulse he held it where it illumined her face, "What are you looking for?"

"The girl I saw this afternoon." His face, heavy with shadows hung over her. "She's not often with me. Well! Too much to hope for after this long day, I expect."

"Saul, don't be whimsical!"

"But you don't like the other things I can be, either. Do you?"

He looked a moment longer. His eyes seemed heavy with sleep. With deliberation he blew the candle out. It thudded on to the bedside table in the dark. Then with a swift neat movement he turned over and apparently went instantly to sleep.

Briar lay stiff and unmoving, illogically furious with him for his look of disappointment.

CHAPTER 22

In the morning Aunt Charity, fully restored by a night's rest, took charge in the kitchen. Within an hour Mabel Kingi, after vainly calling on her ancestor in the mountains, said she was taking her things and leaving.

She waddled, with an air of alarming dignity, to her room, took her two faded cotton dresses off their hooks, bundled them into an old potato sack and was ready.

Aunt Charity explained to Briar. "That abominably lazy, dirty and impertinent Maori woman is leaving. And good riddance to bad rubbish. Now you can get some decent help."

Briar controlled her anger. "And where from, pray?"

"Why, the village, of course. I know it's a pitiful place. We came through it yesterday. But there must be some decent white girls—"

Aunt Charity's voice became less certain beneath Briar's flashing regard.

"We'll go into the village later, Aunt Charity. You shall meet everybody and see how many young girls are clamouring for jobs. In the meantime, excuse me while I calm Mabel down."

"You mean you're going to apologise to a native!"

But Briar did not stop to witness Aunt Charity's horror. She hurried to Mabel's room, and found the stout Maori woman sitting on the floor clasping her possessions, tears running down her cheeks.

"I don't want to leave you, missus. But that fat *pakeha* I will not have in my kitchen. She has too much of the mouth. And she picks up rugs. Why does she pick up rugs? Does she think a devil hides under them?"

"She's looking for dust, I expect," said Briar, wondering if she should have looked beneath the rag mats, too.

"Dust! Is she afraid of that?" Mabel asked, her brown eyes bulging with interest.

"She's not used to seeing it in a house," Briar explained. "Now, Mabel, please hang up your dresses and come back to work. It's time to get the vegetables ready for lunch. Besides, it's a long wet walk to the village, and no one there is likely

174

to give you a job or a bed. And you can't possibly walk to New Plymouth in this weather. Besides, there are still those bad warlike Maoris roaming about. So you'd really better stay."

The fat dark woman was wavering. She clasped her hands round the loose top of the potato sack and considered.

"Where else would you get a beautiful room like this?" Briar said persuasively. The walls were not papered and the floor was bare, but Mabel, she knew, had been immensely proud of her warm dry room in a *pakeha's* house. "And don't you like working for me?"

Mabel nodded violently. "Oh, yes, missus. I have great love for you. I call on my ancestor to protect you. You are kind, and brave. But that other big one—he will pour smoke and fire on her!"

"Then you'd better stay to see it happen, hadn't you? Now, no more nonsense. Hang up your dresses and get back to work."

Mabel fumbled in the bag. "Yes, missus. I obey." Then her head lifted, her eyes flashed, her face grew full of her impressive hauteur.

"But no more lifting of rugs off the floor! You make her understand that, missus."

Briar returned from that encounter to find Aunt Charity upstairs giving Katie a demonstration on making beds. Katie, however, was shrewdly taking the instruction in good part, for Aunt Charity, in her enthusiasm, was doing the lion's share of the work.

"That girl," she said to Briar afterwards, "is a slut."

"Oh, no, not Katie!"

"She's too bold. And she skimps her work. Her mind is on other things, and I could make a guess what those things are. I hope you don't allow her too much freedom."

"She may do as she likes when her work is finished."

"Tut, tut! Then we must keep her very busy."

Briar swallowed her irritation. But later, when Aunt Charity began enthusiastically to make plans for a ball, she calmly asserted herself. Had Aunt Charity forgotten who was mistress of the house?

"Now who is there to ask?" Aunt Charity said brightly. "Saul, you must help me to make a list. What people are suitable in this district?"

"You mean, supposing it were for a Government House ball?" Briar put in smoothly.

"Well, perhaps. Though one has to be a little more flexible, Briar dear, in these isolated parts. One would ask the minister and his wife, for instance, and the doctor and his wife. Also the gentlemen farmers. There must be several in this district."

Saul, looking bored, said he expected the Galloways would come, and the Masefields, if they could put their baby to sleep upstairs, and the Cranby-Smiths. Though it was bad weather, and everyone was still a little uneasy about the possibility of a surprise attack by the Hauhaus.

"I believe there was a large ball on the Eve of Waterloo," Aunt Charity said imperturbably. "A much more major war, if I may say so. Now don't let us worry about things that may never happen. My husband has that pessimistic turn of mind, too. Give me some names for my list."

"I'll give you some," said Briar, with deceptive calm.

"Splendid, dear. Whom?"

"To begin with, Fred and Jemima Potter. I shouldn't think Jemima's ever been to a ball in her life, and if ever anyone deserved to, she does. She's just lost her youngest child, and also had a miscarriage."

"Briar!"

"It will cheer her up," said Briar, thinking that if Aunt Charity had had to watch Jemima suffering she would not have been afraid of using that word, nor bothered as to whether it were an indelicate one to use in mixed company.

"Then there's Amy Perkins," she continued. "I gave her one of my bonnets. She hadn't had a new one for five years. She'd just adore to see some of the latest ball gowns."

"But, Briar—"

Briar's cheeks were flushed. She was aware of them all watching her. So Aunt Charity could quarrel with her servants, and be snobbish about her friends, could she? She would show her who was in command of this situation.

"And Elisha Trott who has the village store. He's nearly sixty, and he's a bachelor. He'll make a very suitable partner for you, Aunt Charity. I'm sure he dances a very energetic polka." She ignored Aunt Charity's popping eyes, and went on, "Then there's Tom and Joe Brown who grind the flour, and their wives, and Rima Ludlow who is a full-blooded Maori. I teach her little boy Honi to read. And Amos O'Brien from the public house. Have you got them all down, Aunt Charity?"

"My dear Briar, I can only imagine that you're joking!"

Briar was acutely aware of old Mrs. Whitmore's eyes on

her. What was she thinking? Did she care what the old lady was thinking?

"I'm not joking, Aunt Charity. These people are my friends. I see them whenever I go to the village."

"That's quite another thing. There are limits to one's social obligations, even in this country. Isn't that so, Saul? Mrs. Whitmore?"

Saul's eyes were narrowed with what seemed to be amusement. His mother said cryptically, "This, I imagine, will be my daughter-in-law's ball."

Aunt Charity's eyes glinted angrily. "Briar, this really is quite nonsensical. What would all these people have to wear to a ball?"

"It wouldn't matter what they wore. They'd find it fun enough to see our fashionable clothes." She had been enjoying herself enormously—she felt revenged for Aunt Charity's interference in her housekeeping affairs—but now she was deeply serious.

"Don't you realise, Aunt Charity, that some of these women haven't been to a town for years? They haven't had a new dress for years. They have no fun except what they can make for themselves, and little enough of that. They live in extreme discomfort, and always, lately, in a state of tension in case the Maoris attack. This ball would be a wonderful happening for them. And you'll be surprised how clever they can be at making themselves look festive."

"But, my dear child—" Aunt Charity, without supporters, was making a last despairing stand—"you don't realise how important it is for cultured people like ourselves to form some kind of society in this country. We must have standards. We mustn't all become a lot of barbarians."

"I think you're saying all this to the wrong person, Aunt Charity. I can't think that associating with Jemima Potter and Elisha Trott will turn me into a barbarian. Anyway, these people are my friends, and if we give a ball they come. If they are not asked, there will be no ball."

"Saul—"

Saul shrugged his shoulders. "Sorry, Mrs. Carruthers. That seems to be my wife's decision."

He didn't say whether he agreed with it or not. But Briar imagined a little of the frosty disappointment of last night had gone out of his face. Did it matter if it hadn't? She had enjoyed herself a great deal, she had proved she was mistress of her house, she had cared little what went on behind Mrs.

Whitmore's enigmatical gaze, and she had seen a look of warm admiration on Peter Fanshawe's face.

Sophie, of course, shared Aunt Charity's consternation, and Prudence's pale withdrawn face showed no feelings at all.

But the important thing was the tremendous pleasure Jemima and Amy Perkins and Hannah Brown would get from seeing attractive ball dresses, and listening to dance music. Everyone, she decided, must wear her very grandest gown.

"Saul!" she demanded imperiously, when they were alone, "you don't say whether you approve of my asking all those people."

His face was unreadable. "You will be making social history in the colonies."

"You think this is easy for me to do because I was so recently a servant myself!"

"On the contrary, great ladies also behave in this way."

So she didn't know what he was thinking.

During the two weeks preceding the ball she was happy. She loved having the house full of people, even interfering irrepressible Aunt Charity, and the silent, tall, black and bird-like figure of Mrs. Whitmore, speaking seldom but missing nothing, giving no indication as yet whether she approved or disapproved.

It was wonderful to have Sophie and Prudence to whom to chatter, and her confused anger towards Peter had resolved itself into satisfaction that she could show off to him how well she had done for herself. And indeed allow herself the pleasure of flirting with him a little, making him aware of what he might have had, had his eyes been wider open. Foolish Peter. She could have made much more of him than Sophie ever would.

Saul took Peter out most of the time. If he was going to be a farmer he had to find out what sort of a life it was. Also, if he wished to buy land in this province, he must seek for the most desirable and suitable property and stake his claim. A great deal of the bushland was to be sold by the Government, which had acquired it at a shamefully low price from the Taranaki Maoris. One knew the natives had been badly treated, Saul said, but no wrongs would be righted by white settlers failing to take up and put the land into useful production. At least that was one thing the ignorant and lazy Maori would not have done, and eventually he would find that the country under the white man flourished, and that there would be room for all.

Sophie, uncharacteristically, was the one who lost her spirits. She agreed with Aunt Charity that it was idiotic inviting all those village people to the ball. Briar was belittling herself—or was she showing off? She was certainly very full of herself, darting here and there, her cheeks bright, her great eyes sparkling, as if she had never been to a ball in her life.

But then she probably never had. Except that fiasco in Wellington when she had slipped in and cleverly snared Saul, and then run away. It must be a great excitement to her not only to be going to a ball, but to be giving it. And naturally enough she was friendly with the villagers. They were her kind, one had to remember, even if she were a good enough actress to make one forget it.

Sophie was not usually so malicious. But it irritated her to see Briar hurrying lightly about the house, sliding down the banisters (oh, yes, she had caught her doing that one day, petticoats in the air!) lacing in her infuriatingly slim waist and really looking quite enchanting.

She herself had grown slow and heavy, and although that in itself was satisfying enough when one thought of the eventual result, it was maddening to be in that condition just now when she would like to have been having fun, too. Besides, she had grown too large to wear her prettiest ball gown.

And also one had to admit secretly to oneself that a great deal of the zest and excitement had gone out of social functions when one had successfully caught a husband. Now one could flirt only with the greatest discretion, and indeed there was no opportunity even for that when one's waist had suddenly swelled by six inches.

So Sophie gloomed and complained. "I shall wear my grey silk."

"Oh, Sophie, that's elderly. We decided to make a grande toilette, for Jemima and Amy Perkins and the rest. Don't you remember?"

"It's all very well for you," Sophie snapped. "What would I look like in pale blue brocade?"

"Magnificent," said Briar. "Please, Sophie! I want you to wear it."

If she ever spoke to Saul like that, Sophie reflected, looking at Briar's dazzling melting eyes, he must be foolish with devotion. Even that dark arrogant man! Though one had to admit no tender glances ever passed between them. Indeed, they behaved almost like polite strangers.

"I shall never do my brocade up," she grumbled. "And the doctor says I mustn't lace myself tightly until after baby is born. You wait until you're in this condition."

"When I'm like that I shall dance until the very last moment. Sophie, please be gay. Do you know, this is my very first ball?"

Reluctantly Sophie smiled. "You funny little thing! And I wondered at first if you and Saul were happy. Now you look as if it's Christmas and all your birthdays rolled into one."

"That's exactly what it is," Briar said, with sudden sobriety. Then her face sparkled aagin. "Do come downstairs, Sophie. You rest too much. Doctor MacTavish says if you do that your baby will be too large and that will make the birth difficult."

"Briar!"

"Do you think that's indelicate, too? It's just practical. You have to be practical to stay alive in this country."

"Briar, how oddly you talk!"

"Do I? Perhaps I've grown up. Now do come downstairs. Peter and I are going to practise the polka."

The house glowed like a Chinese lantern on the night of the ball. It must be visible for miles, Saul grumbled. But even he did not protest too much, for gaiety was in the air. The pianist and the fiddler had arrived, and in the distance, down the rutted road, the carriage lights of the first arrivals twinkled. It was a still, frosty night, with scarcely room to set a lighted candle between the stars in the sky. Smoke from blazing wood fires hung fragrantly in the air. Already far-off voices echoed, and there was the thud of hooves as carts and buggies and sledges approached.

In the kitchen, Mabel, in the better of her two cotton dresses, stood beaming over the piled plates of food. She didn't understand white people's ways. Food cooked in an oven and put on plates to be eaten cold was not the Maori way. Nor was the lively music played by the fiddler in the fern-hung drawing-room at all like the sad and haunting melodies of her race. But this was still a *tangi*, sure enough, and she was going to enjoy her part of it.

Katie, too, had a hectic time getting all the ladies dressed, lacing Aunt Charity until that lady was purple in the face, but resolute, re-doing Sophie's hair three times because she had decided that if her figure had lost its elegance at least she could make the most of her hair, helping old Mrs. Whitmore into her sober black silk and cooing with pleasure over her mistress's toilette. Never had she seen her look so vivid and glowing, and it was not just the best rose pink silk with the low neckline, for even in her petticoats she had seemed to palpitate with eager life.

After these duties, Katie was not too tired to put on her own best gown, though she had to tie over it a freshly starched apron. But that she might be able to discard later. When all the guests had been relieved of their wraps, and such children as had to be put to sleep upstairs were safely asleep, she would peep into the ballroom and tap her feet to the music.

But it was Briar whose evening it was. As the first guests came up the drive she stood in the lighted doorway and her heart swelled with uncontainable excitement.

This was the unimportant servant girl, the waif without a name, standing here in her beautiful dress in the doorway of her fine home waiting to welcome guests to her very own ball.

It wasn't true!

But it was true. The fiddler was playing an Irish jig, the candles were blooming like crocuses, footsteps were crunching on the gravel, voices laughed and called to her.

Surely this was happiness!

Sophie was the last to go down. Peter, waiting impatiently, said, "Do come along, dearest. You look very well indeed."

"I look like an elephant. And it's no use your telling me I don't."

He came to kiss her on the forehead. "I like you to look like an elephant at the present time. At least, a very small elephant."

"Oh, you're so kind, my darling, and it must be terrible for you. I shan't be able to dance, of course."

"One short waltz won't hurt you."

"Aunt Charity would be scandalised."

"Never mind about that. Briar doesn't mind scandalising her, and see how she gets away with it."

"Oh, Briar! If we had been in England, none of this would have happened to her."

"We're not in England, my love. And don't grudge Briar her triumph."

"I'm not grudging her anything. But don't dance with her too often tonight, Peter."

"Why not?"

"It would be more courteous to look after other guests," Sophie said evasively. "Some of those terrible village people. Darling Peter, don't hate it too much."

"I shall enjoy it enormously," Peter assured her, "if ever we get downstairs."

"Oh, dear! My hair! It's coming down! I declare, no one could do hair as Briar could. But she's been too busy this evening for me to ask her. Peter, don't wait for me, but please send Katie up immediately."

When Katie came Sophie was at the window looking out. Her window faced to the side of the house, with a view over the wild garden, and beyond it the dark line of the encroaching bush.

She started violently as Katie came in. "Oh, Katie! You frightened me."

"Is something wrong, ma'am?"

"I thought I saw something move in the garden. Beyond that bush. Can you see?"

Katie peered out nervously. "I can't see anything, ma'am."

"No, I can't either now. I must have imagined it. Or it might have been one of the guests taking a short cut." She shivered slightly. "Draw the curtains, Katie. And then do pin up my hair more securely. Hurry, please. I must go down. Is everyone arriving?"

"Lots of people, ma'am." Katie giggled. "There's one baby already."

"Then you'll be kept too busy to get into mischief. There, that's better. Now I can go."

After she had gone, Katie went to the window again and stared out. After a moment she blew out the candles, so as to accustom her eyes to the dark. But she could see nothing beyond the gloom of the bushes and trees. For a moment, when Sophie had mentioned her suspicion, a wild hope and fear had leapt in her.

But there was nothing out there. She lit the candles, and pausing a moment, looked in the mirror at her own pert face with its crown of untidy red hair. Really, with all those people to dress there was no time to look tidy herself. She stuck in a hairpin or two, hastily. It didn't matter how she looked, for no one would pay any particular attention to her. She didn't want anyone to, anyway. She wasn't in the mood to laugh at he feeble jokes of the shepherds or return their suggestive glances. She hadn't been in that sort of mood for a long time. White men! They were so dull!

The drawing-room no longer looked spacious. With chairs round the wall, the piano at one end, space for dancing in the centre, and thirty or so people either dancing or standing about, it was crowded.

The party was going with an immense swing. Somehow the women, even the ones from isolated farms who obviously had on their only best dress, and that several years behind the fashion, managed to look festive, with new ribbons, or a treasured ivory fan, or hair done in a tortuous array of ringlets. They talked harder than they danced, for company was rare and parties even more rare. The unaccustomed proximity of numbers of people was intoxicating.

Jemima Potter sat beside her husband, her thin face full of its optimistic light, and crouched on the stairs peeping through the banisters, Lucy and Jimmy were overcome with wonder. Amy Perkins had obviously borrowed the green velvet ribbons from Briar's bonnet to trim her pathetically shabby dress, but they would be restored to the cherished bonnet for church in the morning. Martha Peabody, immensely stately in her best black silk, chatted in the same easy sociable manner to everybody, and the Reverend, gallantly doing his duty, danced a measured waltz with Aunt Charity.

Peter begged Briar, when she could spare time from welcoming her guests, to dance with him. She agreed sedately, and revolved in his arms, seeing with secret satisfaction the admiration in his eyes at last. She would like to have shaken him and said, "Why couldn't you see that I'd have made you a much better wife than Sophie?"

"Briar, why didn't I notice sooner how beautiful you are?"

"Didn't you?"

"But you were in disguise, weren't you? Waiting to come out and dazzle everybody." His hand tightened on hers. "You're so soft and sweet—even with that thorny name."

This sort of thing was intoxicating. She had had little enough admiration not to find it flattering. It also eased the galling memory of her earlier failure with Peter.

The music sounded beguilingly and she gave herself up to it, dipping and swaying, smiling, lifting brilliant glances to Peter, chattering about nothing, feeling, at last, successful and irresistible.

183

Saul was dancing with Prudence. Briar caught a glimpse of Prue's long gentle face, unusually animated, as they went by. Sophie sat on the couch at the other end of the room, and, in spite of the opportunity to play the great lady to Jemima and others, her face wore a heavy sulky look.

The music stopped. The fiddler grinned and wiped his brow. In ordinary life he was Harry Jones, the handyman and roustabout at Tom Galloway's. The bearded gentleman who played the piano with admirable dash and fortissimo was a travelling salesman who plodded about the countryside with an aged horse and a cartful of miscellaneous wares: bolts of material, ribbons, sewing cottons, large glass jars of sugar candy, tea and spices, tobacco and pots and pans. He offered his services as a musician en route, and would, for a meal and a bed, enliven a lonely household with a rousing evening at the piano, were the owners so fortunate as to possess such an instrument.

The room was suddenly a buzz of talk.

"Let's get some air," said Peter to Briar.

The moon was shining, she knew. It would have been pleasant to walk outdoors with Peter, feeling the frosty air on her face and savouring more of this intoxicating feeling of being admired and desired.

She was aware of Saul's eyes on her.

It was not because of that, but because she hadn't the slightest intention of doing anything so rash as disappearing outdoors that she said lightly, "I must look after my guests. Peter, please be an angel and dance with Amy Perkins. She'll remember it forever."

The music was beginning again. There were hard fingers on her arm.

"Perhaps I may dance with my wife?"

She smiled the gracious acquiescence she would have given a stranger.

"I haven't seen that dress before."

"Naturally. There hasn't been an opportunity." Saul's voice had a strange note, curiously quiet, that made her nervous. She began to chatter. "It was some material Sophie gave me. Miss Matthews made it. She's clever with her needle, isn't she?"

"People have been kind to you, haven't they?"

"Oh, very kind. When I was to be married—" She stopped, knowing very well that most of the kindness she had received was because of her impressive marriage.

"Why did you marry me, Briar?"

She looked at him sharply. "Saul! What a thing to discuss now! We have guests. It's a very successful party, isn't it? I'm sure everyone's enjoying it enormously. It's the first party I've ever given, you know. Am I doing all right?"

"Must you be coquettish? You know that you're excelling yourself." His ironic voice disturbed her, as did his quietly smiling face, and his intense black eyes that saw, she was certain, into her very heart. But she could say no more, for he had stopped dancing and was saying easily, "There's Sophie, all alone. Go and look after her. As for that other question—we'll talk about that later."

Katie was in the kitchen alone when the tap came at the window. She spun round and saw the dark face pressed against the glass. Suppressing a scream, she stood petrified. Who was it?

Then white teeth gleamed in a broad smile. A hand beckoned. She flew to the door.

"Rangi!"

"I come for you, little Rata Flower."

"You can't come for me now! We're in the middle of a ball."

There were footsteps in the passage. Mabel, who was carrying trays of food into the dining-room, was coming back.

"Quick!" hissed Katie. "Round to the other side of the house. I'll meet you."

He vanished like a shadow. She had shut the door, and stood breathing quickly, hoping Mabel had noticed nothing. Mabel, however, was too interested in the events inside the house to care what happened without.

"All that food, he disappear," she said in astonishment. "Missus said bring more."

"I can hear the baby upstairs crying," Katie improvised. "I can't stay to help you, Mabel."

She skimmed down the passage and into her own room. There she shut the door and went to the windows that opened so conveniently on to the verandah. This part of the house was hidden from the ball-room. Tiptoeing across the verandah she watched.

A dark form detached itself from behind the ngaio tree and came swiftly towards her. In the moonlight she saw the broad naked shoulders, the supple waist, the long lithe legs beneath the flax mat. There was something hard at his waist, too, she noticed as he dragged her towards him. A toma-hawk! Oh, well. A Maori warrior was always armed, wasn't he? And she couldn't think coherently because that familiar intoxicating dizziness had swept over her. She smelt the rank odour of oil from his skin, and because that odour was already associated inextricably in her mind with the other piercing sweetness she had experienced in the hollow tree, she was lost.

She let him take her away through the long wet grass, down the slope out of sight of the house, and, in a little grove of gum trees, lying on the crackling resin-scented leaves, the same irresistible sweetness surged over her.

She was lost, she knew. But she didn't care. There was nothing in the world but this hard body and the sure search-ing hands. And afterwards, his dark face in her loosened hair, as if it fascinated him, although in the dark he could not see its colour.

"What are you doing back here, Rangi?" she managed to ask at last.

"I came to look for you."

"All by yourself? Aren't any of your friends with you?"

"Not here. I came alone."

His face in the dim light was alien, dark, terrifying. Yet as his body moved against her she was deeply deeply sunk in her intoxication.

Then abruptly he sprang up. He seemed to listen. He lifted his hand in a half salute.

"I come again one day."

"Rangi! You can't just go like that!"

"I have to go. But you will be all right, little Rata Flower. Your house will be all right."

Then, leaping swiftly across the long grass towards the bush, he was gone.

Her dress was ruined, of course. And her apron. Both crushed and smeared with grass stains and damp. And her hair was tumbling down. In a daze she reached her room, and lighting the candle with trembling fingers sat re-living her intoxication.

After a little while the sound of music penetrated her hearing. Goodness, she thought vaguely, the party was still going on. It had seemed a whole lifetime away. What should she do? She couldn't present herself in this dishevelled state. But in a moment Mabel or somebody would be looking for her. What should she do? Climb into bed and say she was

186

suddenly sick? Or change into her working dress and pretend something had been spilt on her good one.

Yes, that was the better idea, though how she could manage to pass plates of food with steady hands she did not know.

Yet somehow she managed. Somehow, with her hair still inclined to fall down, and a vacant smile on her lips, she got through the rest of the evening. There were two plates broken, but Mrs. Whitmore had expected some accidents and was not angry. And her clumsiness in helping the departing guests into their wraps was put down to the fact that, poor child, she had been working like a slave all the evening, and looked worn out.

At last, without any worse mishap, she reached the haven of her bed. But then in the silence her thinking powers began to return. What had Rangi been doing in these parts? Why had he said that she and this house would be all right? Was it because other houses would not? Was he with a war party? He had had a tomahawk, but no gun. Why had he slipped away so quickly and secretly? Were dreadful things being planned for this night? Should she have told Mr. Whitmore and the other settlers, so that they could be prepared?

Should she? The remorseless question pounded at her tired brain.

But if they got up a search party and went off with guns Rangi would be killed. She couldn't bear him to be killed. She had saved him once, and now she could not destroy him. Besides, she loved him. He filled her with that terrifying irresistible excitement. She couldn't bear never to see him again.

She couldn't tell anybody about his visit. How could she explain it, anyway? Everything would be all right. Anyway, suddenly, she was just too tired to worry . . .

CHAPTER 23

Briar was tired, too. At least the moment she entered her bedroom she knew that she was. Before that she had been full of energy, not wanting the dancing to stop or anyone to go home. But the fun had to be over some time, and now it was over. She was in her bedroom, and Saul unexpectedly was

187

there before her. He looked as if he were waiting for her.

Uneasily she remembered that unanswered question when they had been dancing. But surely he wasn't going to start cross-examining her now. It was late, nearly three o'clock, and she really was very tired. Exhausted.

She yawned experimentally. "Oh, dear! I'm nearly dead."

He made no answer. All at once he was a very vital presence in the room, although he made no sound or movement.

"Did you enjoy our first party, Saul?"

He did not answer her question. Instead he repeated his former one. "Why did you marry me, Briar?"

It was as if they were still dancing in the crowded room, and nothing had happened since except his impatient waiting for her reply.

"Really, Saul! At this time of night. To start being so intense."

"Stop acting! If you can. Stop borrowing fine phrases and be yourself."

Briar's eyes flashed. "Myself? Well, that's simply a servant girl. I didn't think you would want your wife to behave like a servant."

"I'm not asking you to behave like your profession, but like yourself. The woman in your heart. There is one there. I catch a glimpse of her sometimes. Not often. She shows herself more to certain other people."

"Saul, really—" There was no humour in his face, no tenderness. It was hard and tense. It was even a little frightening. "I don't understand what you're trying to say," she finished lamely.

"Why did you marry me, Briar? Go on, tell me. I want to hear you say it yourself. Tell me that you married me for this house, for instance, for the pleasure of giving a party as you did tonight—"

"I hadn't seen this house when I promised to marry you," she interrupted.

"But you knew it was here. And the other things."

The colour rose in her cheeks. She was beginning to grow angry, too. Frightened of him? As Sophie would be? She would never never allow herself to be frightened of any man.

"What else did I know of you?" she flared. "You were a complete stranger. You were, after all, prepared to marry me on those terms."

"I was not aware I was making any terms. I was marrying

188

a woman I thought was there. Someone warm and loving and full of spirit. I was sure I was right, even though my mother said I was wrong. She said you were just a little nobody seeking your fortune. I guessed that, but I still believed I would find a real person beneath the mercenary one.'"

"You should have believed your mother, shouldn't you? Since now you've discovered it's true."

He had come towards her to stare at her intently. His face in the candlelight was craggy, deeply lined, full of shadows.

"Is it true, Briar? Is it true?"

"Sophie says love comes after marriage," she faltered.

"But it hasn't for you. Has it?" He put his hands on her shoulders. "Oh, yes, you can sparkle for other men. Peter Fanshawe was the man you wanted to marry, wasn't he? The one you meant to trap instead of me. Well, if you'd got him, I'd have wished him joy. And you, too. Because he's a namby pamby, and in a week you'd have despised him."

"So you don't think I despise you?" Briar asked icily.

"No, you might hate me, but that's very different. That can come close to love."

"You flatter yourself!" she exclaimed, with intense scorn.

"Oh, I know all your pretence to ladylike ways. But I'll stop you bringing them into bed with you!"

"Saul! Don't speak to me like that!"

His eyes glinted dangerously. "I'll speak to you exactly as I please. You're my wife. You belong to me. And my God, I'll make you love me!"

"Saul, you're tearing my dress!"

She was as angry as he, her cheeks flaming, her eyes shining with hate. She tried to escape his grip. "I ask you not to touch me, if you're a gentleman."

"No ladies or gentlemen tonight," Saul muttered, pulling at the fastenings of her dress, and when they evaded his impatient fingers, giving a sharp tug that ripped the material. "Just a man and a woman. And no false modesty. You're not shocked. You're not that kind. You're made of flesh and blood and fire and passion, and I'll prove that to you this very moment."

"Saul, I warn you I'll scream!"

"Scream if you like." He had picked her up, and flung her on to the bed. The movement set the candles flickering madly, and almost putting them out. His face above her swung crazily.

"I've been too patient with you, that's the trouble. God

189

dammit it, how many petticoats does a woman wear! Now scream! But after I've kissed you."

And then, of course, it was too late. And she didn't want to any longer, even had she had the breath. For she had no breath. It had been swept away on a hurricane. She lay, small, spent, wondering confusedly what had been pain and what pleasure. And knowing that she never, never wanted to raise herself to get up out of this bed again . .

CHAPTER 24

Morning seemed to come before she had closed her eyes. At least, Saul was out of bed to watch the rising sun, so it must be after seven o'clock.

She couldn't face the day nor her husband's face yet, and turning over buried herself deeply beneath the warm blankets.

"Get up!" came his voice.

She heard in astonishment. Was he going to continue to speak to her as he had last night?

"Briar, get up!"

She emerged indignantly from the bedclothes. "Is the sun up already?"

"It's scarcely five o'clock. That isn't the sun. It's a fire."

"A fire! Where?" She was wide awake now. She leapt from bed to rush to the window.

Yes, it was still night. The trees were black against the sky, the ground a vast shadow. But the sinister pink and orange glow on the horizon grew brighter.

"Hauhaus!" she whispered.

"I don't know. Get dressed. I'm going to rouse everyone. Go down to the hall. See that everyone's there within ten minutes. I'll scout around."

He was already half dressed and pulling on his boots.

"But there hasn't been any noise! I thought they shouted and barked—" Her voice faltered. When the terror had burst on her that other time she had not had time to be afraid. But now, if there was to be waiting and listening for hours, she did not know how she would behave.

"They yell in an attack," Saul told her briefly. "If they're going about in small hands looting and burning they creep up silently. Only the birds or the dogs tell you. Hurry and get dressed."

He had picked up his rifle which she had grown accustomed to seeing at his bedside.

"Don't be too alarmed," he paused to say with belated reassurance. "This may not be the Hauhaus. It may be a completely accidental fire."

Then he had gone, and she heard him walk down the passage to knock on other doors.

Instantly the house was full of noise, thumps and excited voices and a high pitched scream that could only be Sophie's. Heavens! Sophie's baby! The next thing would be its premature appearance.

She was surprised that she could think even as coherently as that. Her hands trembled so violently that she could not cope with buttons or laces. She dragged on a warm petticoat and woollen dress, then flew to the window again to watch that ominous glow in the sky.

Could she hear wild yelling far far off in the still dawn?

The glow seemed to have spread, as if the fire grew larger. No, it was another fire. Probably about a mile from the first one. The sky flickered orange and red.

Briar clutched at the windowsill. It was the Hauhaus! They had come at last, just as Uncle Hubert and Saul had always predicted they would. The false security was over. She was cold and shivering with fear.

"Briar!"

That was Saul's urgent voice at the door. She turned, wanting for the first time to rush into his arms, not for love but for protection, because he was strong and brave and the only one who knew how to fight these devils.

"Aren't you dressed yet? Go and help my mother. She's stiff with rheumatism. Hurry!"

"Saul, it is the Hauhaus. There's another fire. I'm frightened to death!"

By the light of the single candle that he held she could see his face, set in grim lines, despising her.

"You've no time to be frightened. My mother is an old woman and needs help. So does Sophie who's in no condition for this sort of thing."

There had been no word of comfort or reassurance for her. He had gone leaping down the stairs, shouting through the opened door to rouse the shepherds.

But he had spoken the truth. There was no time to be frightened, for the other women, bundling into their clothes, did not need looking after. Sophie was a trembling jelly, swearing that she was shaking too much to put any clothes on, that she felt ill and was certainly going to have her baby at any moment. Aunt Charity had struggled into the elaborate dark red velvet gown trimmed with lace and flounces that she had worn for the ball, and was standing, dazed and bewildered, a large incongruous figure, as if prepared for macabre festivities. Prudence, white and trembling, was trying to protest effectively, "That gown isn't suitable, Aunt Charity!"

"Why not? Why shouldn't I wear my best gown to die?"

"But you're not going to die. We're just going to the stockade."

"I've no doubt that will be the same thing, if all your uncle has told me is true."

"Don't be silly, Aunt Charity," Briar said with a calm of which she had thought she was incapable. "We're merely to go downstairs until Saul comes back. He's been through this sort of thing before. He knows what to do. Get her downstairs, Prue. Take warm cloaks. It will be cold outdoors."

Old Mrs. Whitmore was another matter. There was no panic or hysteria. But the night set her rheumatic bones into a stiffness that made quick movement impossible. Briar had not known this, and silently paid tribute to the old lady's fortitude.

"I'll help you with your dress, Mrs. Whitmore."

The deep dark eyes stared at her. "Why aren't you screaming, too?"

Involuntarily Briar answered, "Saul wouldn't let me." And wondered dazedly if she were thinking of the Hauhaus, or of Saul's extraordinary behaviour last night.

And was that only two hours ago?

"I'd like to," she said shakily. "Is this your warmest cloak, Mrs. Whitmore? We might have to hide in the forest."

"Give me my stick. There, that's better. Now, don't worry about me. I've seen howling dervishes before today. Look after Sophie. She's the one who'll need care. Go along, then."

Her autocratic voice was like her son's. The pair of them, Briar thought bitterly, behaved as if she were their despised slave. Very well, then, she'd let the old woman fend for herself, and go down to rouse Katie and Mabel.

She met Peter Fanshawe on the stairs. He, too, carried a lighted candle, for the hour before dawn was very dark. She noticed absently that it trembled violently in his hands.

"Is this really a Hauhau attack?"

His face was pale, but his eyes were dilated with excitement. The shaking of his hands may have been from cold and anticipation, not from fear.

"Saul will tell you what to do," she said briefly. "Bring Sophie down and see that she's well wrapped up."

When Saul came back they were all huddled in the hall, and there was a horseman galloping down the track to the house.

In the very early dawn they could not distinguish who he was until he reined in his horse at the door.

It was Tom Galloway.

"Hauhaus!" he shouted. "They've burnt the Masefield homestead, and there's another fire starting. Arthur Masefield and his wife are dead. They were ambushed going home from here last night. The devils tomahawked—" He stopped, realising that most of his listeners were women. His face was haggard and hectically flushed. "I'm trying to warn everyone. Get the women to the stockade, Saul. We're all heading there."

"Has anyone gone for the militia?" Saul asked curtly.

"There's been no time—"

"I'll send a man on my fastest horse. They may have seen the fires by now, anyway. Have you any idea how many of the enemy there are?"

"About fifty, I think. Bring all the guns and ammunition you've got."

Briar pressed forward. "Tom, are your wife and baby all right?"

"On their way to the stockade. You'll probably catch up with them. Good luck!"

He was gone, a feverish figure galloping into the paling sky, and one of the shepherds was coming round the house leading the horse and dray.

Instantly Sophie began to scream. "I must have some luggage. I can't leave all my clothes here. They'll be burnt."

"Get into the dray!" ordered Saul curtly.

"But they're my best gowns! I'll never replace them. And what will I wrap the baby in?"

"Your petticoat! Mother, give me your arm. Aunt Charity." Saul's eyes did linger a moment on Aunt Charity's magnificent preposterous figure. "Well, there's a good soul. The only one to turn this into a party."

Aunt Charity gave a wan smile. "That's what I said. Prudence didn't agree."

"Saul!" cried Briar, clinging suddenly to his arm, "will our house be burnt down?"

"Perhaps." His gaze was inscrutable. "Will it matter, if we're still alive?"

Everyone else was in the dray. Briar hesitated, ignoring the orange splendour in the sky, but turning to look at the house which last night had been so full of light and gaiety, and of which she had been so proud. Her eyes filled with tears. If the house were lost she had lost her new-found identity, she thought incoherently. She would rather stay here and defend it . . .

With a quick movement Saul lifted her in his arms and flung her, not gently, into the cart.

"Be sentimental at some other time," he said briefly.

The front door was left swinging open as they moved off. It was as if the house had been discarded like a piece of unwanted clothing.

But Saul, who had gone back to mount his horse, paused to shut the door, and Briar felt vaguely happier.

Then there was no time to think any more about it, for Katie began to have hysterics.

"Make that girl be quiet!" snapped Mrs. Whitmore, and Briar had a sudden memory of the tiny Rose wailing as they rode through the forest, and Saul commanding silence. Now the baby occupied her minute plot in the new churchyard, lying beneath the encroaching ferns and *toe toe* grass, and it didn't matter much about the noise Katie made, for wherever the enemy was, he was no longer silent.

Nevertheless, Katie's loud sobbing was infinitely distressing, and Briar spoke sharply to her.

"Be quiet, Katie. Pull yourself together."

"Oh, ma'am. This is all my fault. If only I'd told you!"

"Told us what?"

But at that blunt question Katie broke into a fresh noisy burst of sobbing, and it was Mabel who made a laconic answer.

"The spirits must have talked to her, missus."

"Spirits!" echoed Aunt Charity incredulously. "To Katie! What would a spirit have to say to that empty little head? And what spirits?"

194

"In the owls, missus. The moreporks. That's where they live."

Briar repressed a shiver, remembering the forlorn, interminable cry of the moreporks in the night, and almost believing that the dead could speak through those little feathered bodies and enormous soulless eyes. But as Aunt Charity had said, why should they talk to Katie?

Katie hiccupped and mumbled, "Those poor people might not have died if only I'd told."

But she could not be persuaded to explain further, and rested on her unexpected and mysterious laurels of being a little psychic, and the recipient of special warnings.

The stockade had been built on the highest piece of ground overlooking the village. It was constructed, as in the manner of a Maori *pa,* with a double palisading of *totara* timber hauled from the forest, round which a three-foot-wide trench had been dug. Within the palisade were low huts thatched with tree fern, and earthed up at the sides to provide the maximum protection from flying bullets.

Tom Galloway had been ahead of them, and already most of the villagers were inside the stockade, huddled in little groups, cold and shivering in the growing light. The glow on the horizon was brighter, and it seemed to the listeners' strained ears that the horrifying outlandish yelling of the Hauhaus was audible in the clear air.

Jemima Potter was there, with Jimmy and Lucy clinging to her skirts. Her thin face was incredibly sharpened with a fear that was all too easy to read. Was she to lose these two remaining children?

In her anguish for her friend, Briar forgot her own fear and went down on her knees to wrap her arms round the children.

"Don't be frightened, little loves. Soon we're going to light a fire and have breakfast outdoors. And you won't have to go to school today. Isn't that fun?"

Jimmy smiled reluctantly. He was a sturdy little boy who approached things in a phlegmatic manner that was pathetically adult. But Lucy was too quiet. Her eyes were too large. She stood in her long woollen dress, her bonnet tipped askew, her little boots muddied and worn, and silently searched Briar's face for reassurance. She had seen too much for a five-year-old. And now the ultimate horror was to come.

Briar blinked back her tears. She was aware, gratefully, of Martha Peabody's approach.

"Well, here we all are, and Lucy, too. Dancing all night and up at dawn! What a splendid pioneer woman she's going to make. Come, Briar. Help me to make some tea. That's what we all need. My husband said we shouldn't light a fire, but what's one more trickle of smoke? *Thou shalt not be afraid of the terror by night, nor for the arrow that flieth by day . . .*"

"Martha, have you been through this before?"

"Not in such a grand stockade, dear. The last time, we crawled on our bellies in the forest, hiding among the ferns. Not a comfortable exercise!"

The large calm woman had an astonishing effect on the huddled listeners. They began to stop trembling and complaining. They got wood for the fire, and set out cups (brought by the far-seeing Martha, along with milk and sugar and tea, and such bread and biscuits as she had on hand), and comforted their children.

Mabel Kingi took over the stoking of the fire, squatting on her ample haunches, her clay pipe hanging from her lips. She had never approved of the bad ways of the Hauhaus, and regarded them as evils to be exterminated. She would fight with ferocity if need be. As the morning mists cleared, and the cone of Mount Egmont, brilliantly white and pure, shone clear above the forest, she fixed her dark liquid eyes on it, and her thick lips moved in a silent prayer. After that, whether the courage of her ancestors entered her or not, her calm equalled that of Martha's, and it was obvious that the women at least, in this little lost fort in the forest, would not be allowed to panic.

Saul was organising the men. The plan was to stay in the stockade and resist any attack until the militia arrived. That, if they had seen the fires, or if a company of forest rangers should be luckily encountered in this vicinity, should be before evening. But if they were many miles away it might be necessary to hold out until the following morning.

The strength of the enemy was unknown, but one did know one's own pathetically slender strength. There were, at the most, ten able men to man the loopholes. That included the Reverend Peabody, whose floating white hair would present a target visible from a long distance. Since he was a reckless fighter, Saul would have liked to keep him out of the firing line, but this, he knew, was impossible. So one would have to rely on the possible wild shooting of the Hau-haus, and the efficacy of Martha's prayers. The women, such of them as could be relied on, and he could count those on less than the fingers of his two hands, would have to crouch behind the men and reload the guns. If a man fell the woman would have to take his place.

Martha Peabody would do this admirably. He had seen her fight on a previous occasion. So would Rima, the full-blooded Awara Maori from the public house, and Mabel Kingi. So would his mother, if one could allow a woman of seventy to stand in the firing line—or if one could prevent her. His own wife? Yes, he told himself without hesitation. She might seem small and fragile, but she had a steely core. She would not fail him, whether it was for him, or her own life, or her house that she fought.

As for the rest, there was Tom Galloway's wife, Mary, who was an unknown quantity and who had a baby to care for; Jemima Potter who would have been resolute enough if she had been able to master even slightly the handling of a gun, but this she had not been able to do. She had better stay in the huts with the children, and Sophie and Aunt Charity and Prudence, all of whom Saul decided would be of little value in the actual fighting.

There was also Amy Perkins, a silly feckless creature, made more so by her weak drunkard husband, but still enough of a pioneer woman not to panic too badly. Besides her, there were one or two other wives who were untested in battle, and lastly Katie, who apart from proving herself a completely erratic shot, had been hiccuping and sobbing all morning, and seemed to have gone completely to pieces. She would be as little value as Sophie, handicapped by her pregnancy.

This was the total of his slender resources, this handful of human beings, and an inadequate supply of ammunition. But he himself, the Reverend, Elisha Trott, Fred Potter, Peter Fanshawe (there was another unknown quantity, though the fellow seemed keen enough, his face burning with excite-ment), Doctor MacTavish and the others would fight to the death. One prayed the women would not be required to do similarly.

The sun rose tardily, and warmth crept into the stockade. Steaming mugs of tea, and a ration of biscuit all round, cheered the little group of besieged. Saul had posted look-outs, and instructed everyone thoroughly in his or her duties. He had also cheered them by telling them that, with luck, all of this would be over in a few hours. The militia would be here, and the enemy pursued and defeated. There may indeed be no attack at all. But they must be watchful every moment. The men must stay at their posts, and the women care for the children, and keep their spirits up.

The Reverend, the wind in his hair, his face cheerful and benign, stood in their midst and said a short prayer.

"Oh God, have mercy on us in this lonely spot. If we are to suffer, let us suffer with fortitude, let us think for the other and not for ourselves. Grant us to live, and not to sleep in these woods, unless that be Thy will. If we must die, let us do so bravely, and trusting in Thee. Amen."

The birds were singing riotously. A tui perched on the palisade and gave its breathtakingly pure call before swooping away. Magpies warbled and pigeons cooed. Two fantails flirted and screeched among the fronds of a tall tree fern, spreading their tails with delicate grace. In the corner of the stockade the horses stamped and fidgeted restlessly. The children, cheered by the sun and the atmosphere of calm, began timidly to play. The women threw off their cloaks and relaxed a little. Aunt Charity sat on a fallen log, her magnificent burgundy-coloured skirts spread about her. As the calm continued she had recovered a good deal of her aplomb, and was obviously convincing herself that all this had been a tremendous scare about nothing. And now, for no good reason, she had ruined her gown. The skirts were bedraggled with mud and damp.

With some contempt she watched Oriane Whitmore roaming like a restless crow about the stockade, a gun tucked under her arm with a great show of belligerence and bravery. She, Aunt Charity, did not intend to try to fire a gun. She sat resplendent on her log, a strange uneasy queen reigning over a strange domain, ready to do what she could if danger arose, but determined not to make a fool of herself by holding a gun the wrong way and shooting herself in the stomach.

And Sophie had better not make a fool of herself by having her baby today. There was nothing immediately wrong with her, in spite of her incessant moaning and sighing.

But if anyone were to ask Aunt Charity, there *was* something wrong with Katie O'Toole. And that was the usual thing, if her acute observation told her accurately. Briar would have to get rid of that little slut, that was certain. She

198

would speak to her when they went home—if they ever did go home, of course . . .

What a day! And all that gaiety last night only a few hours past.

Briar was thinking the same thing. She was living in a dream. It could not be that all the people who had laughed and danced last night were now crouching here, miserable, cold and afraid. It would not be that the Masefields lay dead on the road home, perhaps decapitated, with their blood-drained heads stuck on some dreadful pole . . .

Neither was it true that at any moment, perhaps even now, she no longer had a fine house full of possessions which everyone admired, but only a curt-voiced husband with no spark of tenderness or feeling—except that last night some wild feeling from him had caught her like a flame, and her body had no longer allowed her to think . . .

Ironically, the Hauhaus had saved her from having to converse with Saul this morning. For what would she have said? Or what would he have said to her?

By noon the sun was high, and the ground steamed. That creeping mist was the only sign of smoke, and the day, apart from the birds, was silent and completely peaceful.

Boredom, following tension and overwrought nerves, made everyone jumpy and irritable. Aunt Charity snapped at Prudence to put her bonnet on, didn't she know she had to preserve what looks she had if ever she were to find a husband. Prudence answered meekly enough that she hadn't brought a bonnet. Indeed, in the early dawn, no one had thought of sunshine and boredom. But Prudence's gentle face had a new resoluteness, and Briar suddenly knew that she was not going to crack. The faithless Edmund had provided her with her first lesson in adversity. Now she was stronger than one would have supposed.

Sophie, lying in one of the dark cool huts, said she had a shocking headache and her back was aching, and if Peter wanted to live in these parts he would have to do so without her. She was taking her baby, if ever it were safely born, back to Wellington. Anyway, she hated the country. She would die of boredom if she stayed here, for she did not intend to spend her time making preserves and rag mats and teaching children to read. There were far more important things in life than that. She wished they had never come here. Now, apart from probably losing her baby, she had lost all her wardrobe . . .

It was that last remark that made Amy Perkins suddenly

sit up exclaiming, "My bonnet! My best bonnet that Mrs. Whitmore gave me! I've left it at home."

"It will be all right," said Briar, with some impatience. "It will still be there tomorrow."

"But it won't. The Hauhaus will come and burn everything."

"Then I'll give you another."

"You won't have one to give her," Sophie put in sourly. "Yours will be gone, too."

"And it was so beautiful," Amy sighed. "It was the first one I'd had for years. I used to hang it on the end of the bed at night to look at it." She sprang up. "I don't think I can bear to lose it."

"Amy, what are you planning to do?" asked Martha Peabody.

"Just go home and get my bonnet. It won't take more than a few minutes."

"You'll stay right here, Amy Perkins. The Lord might call on you to die today, but not for a bit of frippery."

Amy looked abashed. "Well—perhaps you're right. But everything seems so quiet. I don't think there's a Hauhau within miles. And I did set a store by that bonnet."

She wandered off slowly, apparently to see what her three children were doing.

It was half an hour later that a shout came from the palisade. It was from Elisha Trott, the wizened little man who looked far more at home in his dark shop behind his counter piled high with a fantastic miscellany of goods than he did shouldering a gun.

"Look! Who's that?"

It was Amy Perkins. Somehow, when one of the look-outs had been inattentive, lulled by the false security into having a quiet smoke, she had managed to climb the palisade, scramble across the trench, and run down the track towards the village.

"She's gone to get that wretched bonnet!" cried Briar.

"My God!" Saul exclaimed. "Where does she think she's going? To church?"

Briar clambered up behind him. "Oh, Saul! Will she be all right? She said there wasn't a sign of a Hauhau. She values that bonnet so much."

"You women and your finery!" said Saul disgustedly. He sprang down. "I'm going after her."

But the Reverend had come up to put a detaining hand on his arm.

"No, Saul. Leave her. If there's no enemy about she'll come back. If there is, you'll both die, unnecessarily. And the fact is, we can't spare you, Saul. If anyone's to go after her it must be her husband."

But Joshua Perkins, a little grey in the face, more than a little hang-dog, had no intention of risking his life for his wife's vanity.

"Reverend's right, Mr. Whitmore. Either one'll die, or two. Look, she's almost there. And it's as quiet as a Sunday."

"It is a Sunday," said the Reverend ironically.

The slim figure of Amy Perkins, petticoats held up out of the mud, feet nimble, had disappeared round the bend leading into the village. There was not a sound within the stockade as everyone watched and waited.

Would she appear again, blithely wearing her bonnet? Or would there be a sudden shocking scream, a yelling and whooping as of mad dogs?

The next five minutes were interminable. Then there was a gasp and a stifled cheer as the little figure appeared again. She waved cheekily to the watchers at the top of the hill. The bonnet was in her hand.

"Run!" shouted her husband hoarsely. "Run, you blasted little fool!"

Amy picked up her petticoats and began to run. At the same moment the shot rang out.

One moment she had been running blithely, the next she had spun round, as if her petticoats had been sharply twirled, and then she was lying in an awkward bundle on the ground. The bonnet had rolled away from her, down the hillside. Her eager fingers had not been able to hold it, after all . . .

"To your posts!" roared Saul. "Hold your fire! Wait till you see them!"

There was no more than a moment to wait before the brown bodies, gleaming with oil, faces contorted in a frenzy, yelling their strange blood-chilling staccato cry, were flinging themselves at the palisade.

Then the quiet sunny afternoon was transformed into bedlam. Each sound was co-ordinated into a savage orchestration, the squawking of birds startled from trees and flung into the air in wild flight, the crash of guns, the continuous yelling of the Hauhaus, and the screams of the women and children.

Briar, crouched behind Saul, rapidly reloading his gun as he handed it back to her, found herself in a state of complete cold calm. Her hands no longer trembled. She worked quickly and efficiently, not looking up, not thinking of anything in the world but the immediate task.

"Poor Amy!" she was repeating over and over in a tuneless chant. She saw rather than was aware of Rima, the handsome Arawa, falling behind Fred Potter, and while she was thinking mindlessly that now Fred had no one to reload, Aunt Charity suddenly appeared, and, crouching like an overblown peony on the ground, took over from the wounded Maori woman. When Fred was hit in the shoulder, and swayed, then toppled from his perch, she caught him dexterously, and laid him beside Rima. She did not stop to attend to him, however, but took his gun and holding it clumsily mounted the step.

Her first shot knocked her backwards on to the ground. In a flurry of petticoats and bad temper she scrambled up, reloaded the gun and climbed back on to the step. She did not fall again. She stood there, magnificent and seemingly indestructible, and above the crazy noise Briar heard a cheer go up from the watching women.

No one could have been less aware that she was being cheered. Aunt Charity took erratic aim and fired once more.

Then all at once the wild yelling died away, and the shots came only from the defenders of the stockade.

Aunt Charity leaned forward shaking her fist. "You cowards! Come and fight! You murdering cowards!"

"Get down!" shouted Saul. "Do you want a bullet through your head?"

Aunt Charity turned dazedly. Her face was as deep a red as her dress, her eyes blazing.

"They wouldn't fight! They've run away!"

"They'll fight all right. They've merely withdrawn to make another attack. Briar, can you take my place for a minute while I look at Fred, and Rima. Who else is wounded?"

The bullet which had struck Fred's shoulder, knocking him out, fortunately proved to have inflicted only a minor wound. But Rima, the big Maori woman, was dead. And Elisha Trott had had a bullet skim through his hair and lift the skin from his scalp. So far the little garrison had escaped remarkably lightly. Briar did not care to look over the palisade into the trench where several of those magnificent wildly leaping bodies, clad in nothing but a brief flax mat, now lay still.

Nor could she bear to look down the track to the huddled bundle that was Amy Perkins.

She stared rigidly towards the green of the bush, seeing, she imagined, a brown face, a white-tipped huia feather behind every fern frond, every flax bush.

Fred, his shoulder roughly bandaged, was back at his post. His face was yellowish-white, and his stocky figure had the rigidity of extreme fear. But he would stay there until he fell again.

Peter Fanshawe, also, was determined to stay where he was, for how could he do otherwise, even though his hands were so wet he could scarcely hold the slippery gun, and it was quite impossible, because of their trembling, for him to take aim. He tried to call out to Briar, with her smoke-blackened face, but she was not taking her eyes off the menacing bush, and anyway his voice had been merely an almost inaudible croak. Perhaps, now that first baptism of fire was over, he would be less afraid . . .

Then suddenly Briar shouted, "Te Wepu! The Whip!"

Surely enough, there it floated, that long crimson pennant, over the tree ferns and *raupo* bushes. Te Kooti's emblem of battle. Te Kooti was here!

Saul leapt back to his post, pushing her out of the way.

"Keep down! Don't fire, anybody, until they're on us!" But the attack did not come. Instead, the silence was sinister, oppressive. One of the brown forms in the ditch groaned and writhed. Sophie, in the hut, suddenly began to scream and was as suddenly silent, as if someone had placed a hand over her mouth. The serene crimson pennant floated over the green bush.

"Come on!" muttered Aunt Charity restlessly. "Come on, you devils!"

"It's going," said Saul suddenly, in a low voice, as if unable to believe his eyes.

"What?" demanded Briar.

"The Whip! It's moving away. They're retreating. Now why the devil—"

His question was answered less than five minutes later, when a wild flurry of shots sounded beyond the village. There were yells, and the sound of galloping horses.

Saul sagged momentarily against the palisade. He had not realised how tired he was, nor how empty of feeling.

"The militia's here," he said flatly. "It's all over."

CHAPTER 25

Saul was already in the saddle, and his horse fidgeting. He leaned down to Briar.

"I've told you—Lucknow still stands. Captain Maltby passed that way. I wonder," he reflected, "why the Hauhaus left it untouched?"

"Perhaps because I mended their flag," Briar suggested.

"Perhaps, who knows? Now do as I have said. Remain here until all danger is past."

"Must you go?"

"Of course I must." His tone was tinged with impatience. "This is our chance to capture Te Kooti. He's taken to the forest, but Captain Maltby has an Arawa guide who knows all the native tricks about disguising a trail. And most of his men have been trained by von Tempsky himself. But there may be a big battle at the end, and we'll need all the men we can get. It's my duty to go and help to end this war, once and for all."

"Yes, I know."

"You must look after the others. Don't let my mother or Aunt Charity become too overbearing. See that Sophie is well while Peter is away."

"Must he go, too?" Briar asked in a low voice.

"He's insisted on it. But we shouldn't be away too long, with luck."

"How long?"

"Three or four weeks, perhaps. Perhaps longer."

"Sophie's baby will be born by then, most likely."

"Well, that's a woman's affair, isn't it? There'll be plenty of you."

He was glad he was going, she thought resentfully. Already, now the dreadful day was over, he was full of energy again, and eager to be off.

"You haven't washed your face." His eyes held an unexpected gleam of amusement.

She must look a sorry figure, standing there exhaustedly with her aching eyes and her powder-smudged face.

She tried to smile, then thought of Amy Perkins and her face stiffened. "I have no more vanity."

He slid off his horse. "And I don't mind your black face."

He had already kissed her goodbye, a quick perfunctory kiss that indicated his impatience to be off. But now he did so again, and this was not the polite kiss of farewell. In spite of her dulled exhaustion, a flame coursed through her veins.

"Saul—take care—"

But he did not hear her whisper. He was on his horse again and riding off, not looking back. She stared at his straight shoulders, his high dark head, until she could see them no longer in the dusk. Then she began to cry, and forgot she had not said goodbye to Peter who had ridden off a little earlier with the jingling troops.

The tears made a poor effort to wash her grimy face. She was still crouching there when Martha Peabody found her.

"Come, love. We're all going home."

"Home?"

"Not to Lucknow. Not tonight. But we'll find beds for everyone. What we all need most is a good square meal."

"Food!"

"You'd be surprised," said Martha serenely. "And my husband will say a special grace. We prayed to stay alive, so those of us who are must be thankful."

"Yes. I'm sorry, Martha."

"Not at all. It's natural that you hated to see Saul go."

"Yes, I did." Her voice was low and full of a private surprise. "Do you think he knew?"

"Why, he'd be a fool if he didn't. Come then, my lamb. I need help, and you're to be my right hand, if not my left one, too."

It was all over, the headlong flight, the tension, the waiting and the boredom, and then the sudden horrifying striking of death in the sunny afternoon.

Now it was safe to return to their homes, those whose homes still stood. And those who were alive to go.

Only now could Briar begin to realise the horror of the Masefields, dead on their way home from dancing, and Amy Perkins wastefully giving her life for a piece of finery. Though no man should judge her, for a man did not understand the hunger in a woman's heart for pretty things which she was forever denied.

As for the rest, Fred Potter's wound was painful but not serious, and Elisha Trott, a bandage round his head, had

205

already re-opened his store, as business might be profitable with so many people about.

Sophie, although blotched with tears after her farewell to her husband, and still complaining endlessly that she was on the verge of collapse, had come through the ordeal remarkably well. So had Aunt Charity, who walked about restlessly in her grand dishevelled dress, her cheeks flushed and her hair tumbling down, an actress not recognising that the curtain was down and the play over.

It was discovered, however, that Mrs. Whitmore had sustained a bullet wound in her upper arm. This she had wrapped up herself and concealed from Saul, but after his departure had nonchalantly asked Doctor MacTavish to look at it, and had sat stiffly upright, refusing his customary sedative of a neat brandy. She had behaved as everyone would have expected her to behave, veteran of much bloodier battles than this one had been, but afterwards her face had a grey tinge which the doctor found disturbing. He advised that she be got to bed as soon as possible.

But of all the defenders of the little fort, perhaps Katie O'Toole had behaved in the strangest manner. For she showed a morbid interest in the fallen enemy. Five Hauhau warriors in full war paint had died in the trench. Their companions had not been able to carry off their bodies, for the arrival of Captain Maltby and his troops had sent them fleeing silently through the forest.

Wishing to spare the women distress, Saul had ordered that their bodies be decently covered with fern branches until dark, when they would be removed for burial.

But Katie, wild-eyed and white-faced, had thrust her way among the men and stared painfully at each stiff and silent body. Then she had fainted.

She, too, had had to be carried from the field of battle. But when she regained consciousness she could not be persuaded to explain her behaviour. She seemed to have lost her tongue. Her little, white miserable face, on which the freckles stood out like dark stains, was dumb and secretive. She only wanted to go home, she said at last.

"To Lucknow?" asked Briar.

Katie nodded, her tumbling hair a fiery pillow for her three-cornered, woefully plain face.

"Then you shall, Katie dear. Tomorrow will be safe."

"It was safe today," said Katie stubbornly.

But she could not say why. The secret had to stay locked

in her heart, together with that awful nightmare of staring at the twisted brown bodies, each one, with its gleaming shoulders and long muscular legs, Rangi. Until the faces were turned to the sky and she saw that none was Rangi. And in her vast relief the sky had tipped upside down and she had fainted.

Beds were arranged for the night as best could be. The tin-roofed public house, scarcely more than a shack, was filled to overflowing. Sophie and Aunt Charity were to share one room, and Briar and Prudence another.

It was an uneasy night. Prudence sought her bed early. She was still shaky and on the point of tears after the dreadful day, and did not know where to turn for comfort. Sophie was too wrapped up in her own importance of having survived such a day in her condition, Briar seemed temporarily to have lost her keen wits and become vague and inattentive, and Aunt Charity, Prudence knew, had always despised her. After today there would be even more cause for Aunt Charity to scorn her, for she had been petrified with terror. She had crouched in the hut with Sophie, and had not been able to bring herself to venture out, even when the hideous howling of the savages and the noise of battle had died away.

It was useless to wonder why she could not be like Briar or Aunt Charity or Mrs. Whitmore, firing a gun and stimulated enough by danger to be almost unaware of it. She was not like that, and could never be. She was timid and shy and not even pretty, and it was small wonder that even Edmund had decided to forget her.

So, desperately tired and shocked and unhappy, she crept off early to the tiny makeshift room which she was to share with Briar. It was merely a lean-to at the back of the public house. When she set the candle down on the dressing-table, that was an upturned packing case covered with a rather grubby piece of printed cotton, she saw that there was only one bed, and that a narrow iron one with bedding that did not look particularly clean. However, this was no time for finicky behaviour and, as long as she could loosen her petti-coats and lie down and rest, she would not be too critical.

She had scarcely done this, leaving the candle burning because she could not bear to be in the dark alone, when she heard a faint scrabbling beneath the bed.

She lay, frozen into rigidity, listening. Had she imagined it? No, there it was again, followed by a low moan.

207

Heavens, had one of those savages, wounded, sought refuge beneath her bed!

Prudence sprang out and then stood shivering, unable to bring herself to look beneath the bed.

It was a pathetic hiccupping sob that brought her to her knees at last. Peering into the darkness she could see nothing but a minute, even darker form. Its size gave her courage. She thrust her arm underneath and dragged out the child.

A very dark Maori boy stood blinking enormous eyes in the candlelight. He had been crying a great deal, as his woeful little face showed. Now he hiccupped again and said something in his own language.

"Who are you?" Prudence asked.

"Honi," the boy whispered, his eyes downcast, immensely long beautiful lashes resting on his tear-stained cheeks.

Honi! The big Maori woman Rima's child! A sensation of horror possessed Prudence. Rima was dead, she had seen her still body lying in that nightmare stockade this afternoon. But since Honi had taken refuge here, this must be Rima's room. She and Briar were to sleep in a dead woman's room! Prudence shivered, feeling sick with revulsion.

Then she realised that enormous tears were rolling down Honi's cheeks, and all at once something happened inside her. She lost her fear, and her inclination to faint. Instead, anger and indignation swept through her, making her heart beat fast, and bringing colour to her cheeks. She hurriedly put on her gown, buttoning it awry, then gathering the child into her arms went into the passage and along to the door marked BAR.

There was a great deal of noise coming from within. All the brave white men were no doubt celebrating the fact that they were still alive. They had forgotten that everyone was not so fortunate.

Prudence had never been into a bar parlour in her life. She momentarily winced at the thought, then boldly pushed open the door.

There were perhaps half a dozen men there, lounging over the counter, and behind the counter her host, Amos O'Brien.

He looked startled at her entrance, and said, "Has that little devil Honi been worrying you, miss?"

"He hasn't been worrying me," Prudence said clearly, in tones remarkably like Aunt Charity's. "It just happens he's lost his mother and no one seems to have given it a moment's thought."

Amos twisted his long moustache and shrugged. "Well, what can I do besides feed him? But they're tough, these little brown devils—begging your pardon, miss."

"He needs more than food!" Prudence declared indignantly. "He has feelings the same as us, I imagine."

A limp, untidy-looking man with sad eyes, bleared from liquor, or weeping, one could not tell which, moved away from the bar to stand in front of Prudence.

"Honi's not the only one to lose his mother today. My own kids have, too."

Prudence looked at the man's sad defeated face. This must be Joshua Perkins, Amy Perkins' husband. He was more than half drunk already, she realised incredulously. And yet his wife lay dead and his children must be left to fend for themselves.

"More shame to you!" she declared hotly. "Standing there drowning your sorrows."

The man nodded. "Aye. I suppose it looks bad. But the kids are all right. Jemima Potter put them to bed. They're all asleep. And I couldn't stand it there alone, thinking of Amy. Seeing her die like that. Yes, I guess it looks bad, me being here drinking."

"A man has to drown his sorrows sometimes, miss," Amos put in. "Josh doesn't know how he's to manage now. Three kids and no woman. And you standing there hugging that Maori brat!" he finished with sudden anger.

Prudence could feel Honi's arms twined round her neck. He was sketchily dressed and did not smell too sweet, but his little body had a warmth and trust that was strangely moving. She thought of Briar teaching the children to read and write and remembered how she had admired her. Here was a much greater crisis than learning letters. Was she equal to it?

A great determination and excitement suddenly possessed her. She felt oddly as if she were emerging from a cramping shell.

"This Maori brat has nothing to do with any war we're fighting," she said, with spirit. "And neither have your children." She looked at the lugubrious face of Joshua Perkins. "So someone must make up to them for what they're suffering. If you'll allow me, Mr. Perkins, I'd be very glad to look after your children until you can make some better arrangements."

She was aware of all the men watching her with startled eyes. Was she, she wondered with indignation, such an unlikely person? She knew she looked as if she had never washed a dish or a child's face in her life. But she would show them she could do it as well as the next woman, and certainly better than that whining Amy Perkins, who had no doubt been responsible for a great deal of her husband's fecklessness.

Her head went up resolutely. "Don't be afraid I can't manage, Mr. Perkins, because I can. I'm one of five sisters, and my mother taught us all to cook and housekeep. But I'll only do it on condition that Honi comes, too."

"By God!" said Joshua Perkins slowly. "By God, I believe you mean it!"

"I certainly don't waste my time making offers I don't intend to carry out."

"But you're a lady!"

Prudence's usually pale cheeks had a flush, her eyes a sparkle. "Will that do your children any harm?"

"No, ma'am. Not at all." Joshua's eyes were fixed on her face almost hypnotically. "Nor me neither. Seeing as you seem to mean the offer, I'll be glad to accept. I'm grateful to you, ma'am. And so would my poor Amy be."

Prudence nodded. "Then let's go, shall we?"

"I'll take you there, but I'll come back here to sleep. It'd hardly be the thing, a young lady—"

"As to that," Prudence interrupted calmly, "do as you wish. But today's been strange. I believe I'd be happier to forget the conventions and have a man close at hand."

"The young lady's right, Josh," said Amos. "In these times, the main thing's staying alive, isn't it?"

Joshua Perkins straightened his shoulders, and looked almost sober already. "You're quite right, ma'am. Here, let me carry the kid."

Sophie, the next morning, did not want to go back to Lucknow. She said that never, after that dreadful time in the early morning, could she stay in that house again.

"And what do you propose to do?" asked Aunt Charity, with deceptive softness.

"Go back to Wellington, of course."

"And how, without your husband?"

"Oh, I expect I shall have to wait until he comes back," Sophie admitted fretfully. "Why he needed to go off on this campaign, I can't imagine. Only seasoned soldiers are expected to do such a thing."

"Well," said Aunt Charity thoughtfully, "Amos might put us up here, or Jemima might let you share her loft with the children. But it wouldn't be suitable for your baby to be born either in a public house or a loft."

"Oh, Aunt Charity, you're talking exactly like Uncle Hubert. Stop teasing me. I know I'll have to go back to Lucknow for a time. But I warn you, my baby will be born much too soon."

"If you could go through a day like yesterday and not miscarry, you can face anything, my dear. I won't waste sympathy on you. You're as strong as a horse. It's your sister who's worrying me. I believe she's out of her mind."

"Prue! What's she been doing?"

"I've just found out that she's not only spent the night in Perkins' cottage, but that she intends to stay there and take care of the children, and that ne'er-do-well, Perkins."

"Prue!" screeched Sophie.

"Yes, your sister. She must have lost her wits after the stresses and strains of yesterday. And because of that wretched faithless sailor, of course. The next thing we know, she'll be marrying Perkins and living in utter squalor."

Unexpectedly and maddeningly, Sophie began to giggle. "But you wanted to find her a husband, Aunt Charity. You've been complaining she would look at nobody."

Aunt Charity turned a scandalised face. "Really, Sophia! To joke about this! I declare, those yelling Hauhaus alarm me less than the behaviour of young women nowadays."

It was true that Prudence had stuck to her decision to care for the three motherless children, and Honi. Jemima and Martha would help her, she said. Later, other arrangements could be made, but in the meantime Joshua Perkins was humbly grateful, and seemed overnight to be a changed man. This change, Briar thought sceptically, was not likely to last, for Joshua was a weak character. But the gentle serenity that had come into Prudence's face would last. She was sure of that.

So there was a depleted and downcast party to go back to Lucknow. Only Aunt Charity, still managing to look impressive and queenly in her velvet gown, Mrs. Whitmore with her arm in a sling, her brilliant sunken eyes as watchful as ever, Sophie, cumbersome and irritable, the silent Katie, Mabel, puffing imperturbably at her clay pipe and Briar herself. A party of women, but a battle-tested party nevertheless, and not now so likely to panic at the slightest sound.

A party full of memories, Briar thought, the last one the sad little scene at the graveside of Amy Perkins, and the two Masefields who had been brought for burial to the churchyard, whatever mutilations they had suffered a secret of the men who had found them.

"Now the storm of battle is over," the Reverend said in his grave gentle voice, and Briar reflected that had they remained in England, and not crossed so many thousand miles of ocean with hope and ambition in their hearts, they might still have died at this early age, of smallpox, perhaps, or childbirth, or some other ill.

One had to have some philosophy. One could not think that the crazy spinning round of Amy Perkins in the sunlight, the cherished bonnet escaping her at last, was entirely haphazard. She had been meant to die at that moment, in that year of her life, whether she were to have formal cypresses or the plumy *toe toe* grass waving over her grave . . .

Life, for the next few days, was exceedingly humdrum. Quiet as Prudence had been, they missed her in the house. But most of all they missed the men. Sophie said she could not endure to sleep alone, and moved in with Aunt Charity, who complained that the bed was too small for two such large women, but who nevertheless seemed dourly pleased. Briar kept silent about her own solitary bedroom, and how she sometimes woke thinking she heard Saul coming in, dropping his boots with a clatter, turning to survey her with his gleaming eyes, saying abruptly, "Put the candles out!" Or once long ago, "I shall make you love me, I promise."

But Saul did not come in. She woke in the mornings to her own solitary figure in the big bed, and to her gnawing anxiety and loneliness.

Te Kooti was a wily and ferocious fighter. He would lay an ambush. The white men would be leapt on in the dark tangle of the forest, and slain. Then an immense funeral pyre would be lighted. Or worse still—but that last nightmare her mind turned away from. She could not even begin to face it.

She tried to fill in the long days. Although it still rained a great deal, as the lush growth in the bush and fields indicated, she began to plan her garden. She would have a shrubbery of rhododendrons, and native trees, such as the *kowhai* with its pale hanging blossoms, like yellow moths, and the native mistletoe and fuchsia. Then a wide stretch of lawn, and a rose garden, and a herbaceous border with all the English flowers, michaelmas daisies, peonies, chrysanthemums, thrift and mignonette. It would take patience and skill. One did not make a garden, as one did not find happiness, overnight. But in ten years, fifteen years, people would begin to talk about the garden at Lucknow.

She discussed with Fred Potter the plants that would thrive best in this particular soil, for Fred was full of surprising knowledge, and already dedicated to his own small patch of garden.

Sophie said rather meanly, "I believe so long as you have your house and garden you don't care whether Saul comes back or not. I feel very differently about my husband, I can tell you. I think of him every minute."

To this, Briar was silent. She did not intend to speak of her private feelings to Sophie. She could not have put them into words, anyway. For the vision of Peter with his laughing summer blue eyes, so long cherished, seemed mysteriously to escape her now. Or if it came his eyes were dark—black, impatient, scornful. Which was a very queer, disturbing thing.

Mrs. Whitmore had refused to stay in bed. But the wound in her arm did not heal as quickly as it should have, and the grey tinge remained in her face. Nevertheless, she remained active, and it seemed to Briar that the burning dark eyes were on her all the time, silently assessing, criticising, making secret judgment. She hated and despised the old woman. No, not despised. One could not despise someone of her character and fortitude. But how could one live up to it? And did one want to? Having her about was rather like giving houseroom to an untamed elderly crow, who had to be treated with respect if one did not want a sharp and vicious peck.

Nevertheless, the test came a few days later, and it was brought about by Aunt Charity, or more indirectly by Katie.

Katie had not seemed to recover from the shock of the Hauhau attack. She had remained wan and listless and half-dazed, bursting into tears frequently, and nearly jumping out of her skin at the slightest noise.

At last Mabel Kingi pronounced, "That Katie no good any more, missus. The spirits talk to her and she gone queer."

"It's been the shock," Briar said. "Be patient with her for a while, Mabel. She'll recover. She'd never seen fighting before."

Mabel shook her head, and said it would take more than

213

bad Maoris to have such a devastating effect. It was the spirits, there was no doubt about that.

But Aunt Charity, coming in at the end of the conversation, said firmly, "Spirits, indeed! There's a simpler answer than that to Katie's trouble. Briar, I've been wanting to talk to you about this. You'll have to get rid of Katie. If I'm not mistaken, she's—" Aunt Charity hesitated, looking at Mabel and searching for suitable delicate words—"in a certain condition."

"The spirits have flown off with her wits," said Mabel stubbornly.

"Very well, Mabel. Go and attend to your work." Briar turned to Aunt Charity. "Come into the drawing-room and explain exactly what you mean."

"There's nothing to explain," said Aunt Charity, "except that my eyes do not deceive me in these matters. And if you ask me, it's entirely what might have been expected. I noticed from the very beginning that she was a loose type and had eyes for nothing but men."

"I didn't ask you, Aunt Charity," said Briar politely, "and I still hope you're wrong. But before we discuss this further, I'll see Katie herself."

It was not an easy interview, and Briar came away from it feeling very young and uncertain. How did one handle this kind of situation? She was too newly mistress of a house to know what to do. All she could think of was Katie lying sobbing on her bed, and admitting that if certain symptoms were correct then what Briar told her must be true. She must be having a baby. She had wondered why she felt so sick and tired, but she hadn't known what those things meant. No one had ever told her. But if she was having a baby and was to be turned out, she would be better dead, wouldn't she?

Then, seeing that Briar's distressed face bending over her was little older than her own, and just as perplexed, she burst out with the whole story.

"I couldn't help it!" she sobbed. "Rangi was so sweet while I looked after his wounded leg. He was so gentle, like a little boy. And then afterwards—I know it was wrong—I just couldn't help it. And I'm not sorry because it was so wonderful."

Her defiant eyes challenged Briar. "I don't mind if I have a brown baby. I'll love it just as much. But if you turn me out, ma'am—and Rangi probably dead by now—"

"But, Katie, a Hauhau!" Briar exclaimed incredulously. "Weren't you terrified?"

"Not of Rangi," Katie said stubbornly. "He was just a man. Oh, I know they go mad when they're in battle. That's their way. And their priests, those horrible old *tohungas,* make them take awful oaths round the *niu* pole. Rangi told me. But when the war's over he'll come back. If he isn't dead . . ."

Helplessly Briar squeezed the girl's damp hand. "Perhaps he'll come back. If he doesn't—you'll have the little brown baby. Like Honi, in the village. Honi's sweet. Oh, dear, Katie! What are we to do?"

For a moment they were just two girls, innocent, bewildered, caught up in the inevitable pattern of their lives.

But when Briar returned to the drawing-room, where not only Aunt Charity but Mrs. Whitmore waited, she was no longer a girl. She was old, old.

"Well?" said Aunt Charity uncompromisingly.

Briar nodded. "It's true, Aunt Charity."

"And who is the man? One of the shepherds, I'll be bound."

Mrs. Whitmore did not speak, but Briar was overwhelmingly conscious of her sitting there watching, withholding her judgment.

"No, not one of the shepherds, Aunt Charity. A half-caste Maori, called Rangi. Rangi, Katie explained, means the sun, and for a little while I believe he was the sun to her. Her baby will be a quarter-caste. Usually they're quite beautiful, as you've probably noticed yourself."

Aunt Charity was opening and shutting her mouth in scandalised speechlessness. At last she managed to say, "You speak of this calmly, Briar, as if it were a perfectly ordinary happening."

"I should think it isn't too uncommon. Mabel herself is a half-caste. After all, there were very few white women here for some years after the first settlers came. It's only natural."

"Briar! We're not speaking of the country's morals as a whole, but of your servant's. You've given her notice, of course."

Briar's chin lifted. "No, Aunt Charity."

"Then for goodness' sake do so at once, or I will do it for you. She must be sent packing."

It was clear that Aunt Charity had not yet encountered the dangerous tilt of Briar's chin, nor realised its import.

"Not from my house, Aunt Charity."

"What! You mean—but good heavens, child, don't you realise—condoning this kind of thing—setting this sort of

215

example—" Aunt Charity, beginning to purple, was rapidly growing incoherent. "The neighbours—"

"None of the neighbours here will care in the least that my maid is to have an illegitimate child," Briar said serenely. "Martha and Jemima and the others will stand by her, and when the baby is born the Reverend will christen it in his church. Along with Sophia's," she couldn't resist adding wickedly.

Aunt Charity puffed her cheeks and exhaled loudly. "Of all the—Mrs. Whitmore! Can you tolerate such a thing? In your son's house, in his absence!"

The old lady spoke slowly, "It is Briar's house, too. In fact, she is the mistress of it."

Silly old fool, in her dotage! Aunt Charity thought furiously.

"But Briar is quite inexperienced. She needs the guidance of older women like ourselves. She mustn't be allowed to make such a serious mistake. After all—"

"After all," Briar interrupted, in her high clear voice, flags of colour flying in her cheeks, "I was a servant like Katie, too. I did not, to be exact, have this thing happen to myself, but my own mother did. Neither of you know that I also am illegitimate. I know neither my mother nor my father. My mother, indeed, was found dying in a ditch, and I was rescued from her arms by a passing labourer who took me home and gave me his name. Johnson. Briar Rose Johnson. But who I am really, no one knows. I'm a waif and stray. I wish I had at least known my mother before she died, but I didn't. And therefore I don't intend that that shall happen to Katie's baby, brown, black or white, fatherless or not. So you can talk to me as much as you please—" Tears were in her eyes, but her chin had not descended the fraction of an inch, her voice did not tremble. "You can tell Saul this story if you wish—he knows a little of it, but not all. You can tell the whole world. But Katie stays."

"Well!" gasped Aunt Charity. She turned helplessly to the silent old woman in the corner. "Oriane!" She had never called Mrs. Whitmore by her first name to her face before, but this situation demanded some closer intimacy. "What are we to do about this?"

The old lady gave her shoulders a shrug, as if she were shaking out her feathers. "I can't see what you are worrying about, Charity Carruthers. Briar has made her decision. It will stand. If I know my daughter-in-law, as indeed I am just beginning to. But if all this about yourself is true, Briar, what on earth are you doing with those preposterous portraits? Take them down and burn them. That's the best place for them."

So Katie stayed. And although Aunt Charity made no secret of her shocked disapproval, Briar could not tell what Saul's mother was thinking. Indeed, the old lady's enigmatic silence was becoming aggravating to a point beyond endurance. Briar realised that her ardent championship of Katie had been mixed with a desire to sting Mrs. Whitmore into some kind of admission, but none except that sardonic remark about the portraits had been forthcoming. She kept her lips severely closed, but one felt that she was a little like Mabel Kingi's ancestor dwelling in the mountain, and that at some time there would be a devastating eruption.

CHAPTER 26

Prudence sent Joshua Perkins over to Lucknow for a trunk of her clothes. She had no time to come herself, the children more than occupied her time, but would Briar put in only her two plainest gowns and underclothing, and would she also send her recipe for making hot batter biscuits which she could cook over the open fire, and which the children would enjoy.

Aunt Charity could not be left out of this interview. She put Joshua Perkins through an acid questioning, but unexpectedly the man stood it with some dignity.

"How long do you imagine you are keeping my niece in this most unsuitable position?"

"I'm not keeping her, ma'am. She says she wants to stay."

"Oh, she says it, of course. She's got her head full of ideas about duties as a pioneer woman. But I imagine you will make other arrangements as soon as possible?"

"If I can, ma'am. It isn't easy—"

"I shouldn't think it is, the way you've been living," Aunt Charity said in her outspoken manner. "Not many women would take on that sort of position."

"I have a regular job now, ma'am, working for Mr. Galloway. And I've stopped drinking."

"Ha! It's a pity you didn't do that while your wife was alive."

Joshua bent his head, saying nothing.

"Well, then, man," Aunt Charity's voice was gruff with belated sympathy, "find a reliable woman to look after your family, and let my niece come home, since she seems too stubborn to come until then."

"She's a wonderful young woman, ma'am."

Aunt Charity shot him a suspicious glance. Surely this creature was not getting ideas! She'd very soon put a stop to that. What could he possibly see that was wonderful about Prudence, with her long meek face, except that she was a gentlewoman? Although that last, no doubt, was an irresistible qualification to a man of this kind.

Really, it was too bad of Prudence, first a foolish love-affair and now this ridiculous self-sacrificing behaviour. It was all extraordinarily unsuitable, and would have to be hushed up when they went back to Wellington, or what faint chance she had left of getting a husband would vanish. Aunt Charity was beginning to wish she had never set eyes on the girl.

"Did you get the things?" Prudence asked, when Joshua returned. She was bending over the open fire cooking something on a skillet, and only half turned to see Joshua's arrival. It was dark in the little earth-floored room, and he could not see her face.

"Yes, ma'am. Where shall I put them?"

"In the attic. Where else? If you can find room."

Her voice was sharp. Really, he was so slow and stupid. Where else would he put her things, but in the tiny cramped room she shared with the two girls, Amelia and Mary. Joshua and his three-year-old son, and Honi, slept in this room downstairs. And that was another thing, she could not stir in the morning until he was up, for she couldn't come down the ladder while he was in bed.

It was so difficult to dress in the attic, with her head bumping the sloping ceiling, and nowhere to hang her clothes. And then they had to come down to wash in the back yard, only once a week heating sufficient water to wash all over by the fire inside, and then doing so in nervous haste, afraid that the latch on the door would not be sufficient to keep out a sudden intruder.

Prudence had never imagined living like this. At first she had thought that for all her noble feelings of sacrifice, and for all the pleasure it gave her to see the children timidly turning to her, she could not stand it. But if she ran away it would be just one more failure and she would despise herself forever. She would make herself stay, even though the roof leaked, and the children caught colds, and were constantly damp and dirty, and everything she cooked was either burnt or half raw. Besides, Joshua was behaving very well. He had not been inside the public house since the night he had carried Honi home with them, and he was being gentle and quiet, not complaining when the food she prepared was badly cooked, or when she couldn't manage the children.

"You let me catch him complaining, seeing what you're doing for him!" Jemima Potter said fiercely.

"He has a right," said Prudence, but she was too tired to argue. It seemed that she never sat down, and that had she wanted to there was no comfortable place to sit.

When Joshua came in with her clothes, the room was full of smoke and the smell of scorched mutton, her eyes were smarting and her back aching. She did not care what he had brought or where he put the things. All she could do, in that moment, was think of the comfort of Lucknow, and the inestimable pleasure of time to sit with needlework or a book. Amelia was getting another cold, and Honi had eaten something that had made him sick. It was going to rain again, one could tell by the way smoke billowed down the tin chimney, and she would have given a great deal for a real bath or a meal she had not cooked, or tried to cook, herself.

"What did my aunt have to say?" she called after Joshua, as he climbed the ladder to the loft, dragging the small trunk after him.

"She says you must go home."

"She would say that. But I can't go at present."

Joshua pushed the trunk into the loft, and turned. "I've promised your aunt to find another woman as soon as I can."

"And where do you think you're going to find one?" Prudence asked tartly. She rubbed her smarting eyes, and bent over the cooking pot.

"I thought of asking Mr. Galloway to let me go into New Plymouth. I might find someone there, a half-caste Maori perhaps, or someone arrived from England looking for a job."

"Someone just arrived would be even worse than me," said Prudence. "At least I knew what to expect when I came

219

here. But I do it all so badly." She sighed. "I thought I could do it so much better."

"The children like you, ma'am."

Prudence's lip trembled. She hadn't meant that to happen, but she was so tired, she had caught a chill, she thought, bending over the wash tub in the rain yesterday. It would be heaven to go back to Lucknow, to Aunt Charity . . .

"The smoke's hurting your eyes." Joshua's voice was gentle. Who, seeing him a week ago, bleared with drink, ineffectual, a failure, would have suspected his kindness and perception?

"Yes—it's bad today. I—perhaps I have a cold, too. Amelia had one this morning. I should have kept her in bed. I'm not a very good mother yet."

"You're fine." She realised that he had taken her hand. His own was work-scarred, the skin rough against hers. No one, she thought, had taken her hand in that way before, not with love or passion but with that inarticulate sympathy and gratitude.

"I *could* be a good mother!" she heard herself saying fiercely. "If you'd be patient— It's what I want to do." She looked at his startled and grateful face. "It makes me a real person," she said. "I don't think I've ever been a real person before."

CHAPTER 27

Two weeks later Peter came back to Lucknow. He arrived one evening, almost falling off his horse at the door, and having to be helped inside.

"Peter, are you wounded?" cried Sophie in the greatest alarm.

"Where's Saul?" asked Briar tensely.

"Did you get Te Kooti?" demanded Mrs. Whitmore.

"Don't ask the poor boy so many questions," Aunt Charity ordered, taking charge as usual. "Can't you see he's worn out?"

Indeed, Peter looked completely exhausted. He was unshaven, red-eyed and covered with mud. Also, he had developed a slight twitch to the side of his mouth which Briar found extremely distressing. But he said he was not wounded. He had some sort of fever, through being constantly wet and chilled, and eventually had been ordered to make his own way back from the trail.

"Then the rest of the troops are not far away?" Briar asked.

"Far enough," said Peter obscurely. "That awful forest!"

"And Saul is well?"

Briar had to persist with her question, for Peter did not seem to want to answer.

"Oh, Saul! He's indestructible."

Whatever envy or dislike may have made him speak in that voice of Saul, it was obvious that Peter, with his dulled eyes and twitching mouth, was far from indestructible himself.

When he began haltingly to relate something of his experiences his fear was in every sentence, his horror of the perpetual twilight of the forest, the dripping rain, the undergrowth cleared with painful slowness, and always the possibility of an ambush.

"The track disappeared completely after three days," he said. "The natives could follow it, but we couldn't. We had to cut our way with hatchets and billhooks through supple jack and flax and those everlasting ferns. Finally we were moving at the rate of about a quarter mile an hour, working from dawn to dusk. And then it rained for three days without stopping. That was when I developed this fever. It was always half dark in the forest, even at midday. We couldn't even light fires, everything was too sodden, and we didn't dare show any smoke. We'd run out of food, so we had to eat horseflesh raw. And fern roots pounded up."

"How terrible!" Sophie gasped.

"But didn't you ever catch up with the enemy?" Briar asked.

Peter's face twitched. He rubbed his hands together. "Oh, yes. We attacked a *pa* but it wasn't defended for long. The enemy slipped away into the forest and left only their dead. After that all we could do was kill any stragglers we could find and decapitate them."

"Decapitate!" whispered Sophie.

"We had the Arawas and some Wanganuis on our side. They thought there was a price given for every head produced. So they gathered their ghastly trophies and tipped them out at Captain Maltby's feet. Head after head!"

He began to laugh breathlessly.

"Peter dear!" remonstrated Aunt Charity, "I know you've had a terrible time, but do you think Sophie should listen to these things?"

"But I must hear them," said Sophie, in dreadful fascination. "You didn't see—anyone eaten—did you, Peter?"

"Thank God, no! We weren't close enough to their camps for that. But we heard the chanting round the *niu* pole. That's their sacred pole they stick up in the middle of the *pa*. Usually it has a human head on it, a white man's. It would make your blood curdle when they dance the *haka* and scream. And Te Kooti has the nerve to quote from the book of Joshua, so a captive told us. *And the Lord your God He shall expel them from before you and drive them from your sight; and ye shall possess their land, as the Lord your God hath promised unto you.* What with listening to the early missionaries, and mixing Christian teaching with their own superstitions, they've mixed a fine potent brew, haven't they? The land Te Kooti speaks of is of this land," he added slowly. "You know, it's made me lost my taste for it."

Later he suddenly remembered that he had a letter for Briar.

"From Saul. He told me what he said in it. We're all to go back to Wellington at the earliest possible moment. I, for one, can't go quickly enough."

Briar hardly knew what she had wanted Saul to write to her. She only knew that she could scarcely believe the brief emotionless letter he did write.

My dear Briar,

I have asked Peter to carry this letter for me. He is in bad shape, and must get back to Wellington as soon as possible. He hasn't the temperament for the country in its present state. If Sophie has had her baby and is able to travel, there should be no delay. I want you, as well as Mrs. Carruthers and my mother, to accompany them. You also, I am sure, will be happier in a town. Circumstances permitting I will be down at some time before the summer is over.

I am sorry things have happened in this way, but Te Kooti as well as other factors have combined to make it so. We are steadily getting the upper hand of the enemy, but there is still a struggle ahead.

Forgive this hasty note. It is written in difficult conditions with rain dripping down my neck, and the captain is impatient to be moving on. I trust it reaches you safely, and I expect you to obey my wishes. Leave as early as possible. That is important.

Your obedient husband, Saul.

Sophie was the one who was overjoyed. She had decided she could not abide the country, and would have expired from loneliness and boredom had she had to remain there.

"No one has asked you to prolong your journey in the country," Briar said with some coolness. "The weather is better now, and the journey back to New Plymouth should not be too difficult."

"Now don't be hoity toity, Briar," said Aunt Charity sharply. "You know that Sophie can't travel in her condition. I don't intend to see her having her baby under a tussock bush. She will have to remain here until the child is born."

"And when will that be?" asked Peter impatiently.

Sophie blushed with a semblance of modesty. "It will take its own time. I don't believe it will ever be here."

"Can't you hurry it?" he asked uneasily. "We have to get away. It's important to hurry. Saul said so. I'd hoped the baby would be here by now. But at least we can have our transport arranged, and our packing done to leave at the earliest moment."

When Briar could swallow her pride sufficiently, she asked Peter if Saul had discussed with him the urgent reason for their all leaving Lucknow.

"Is it because he's afraid of another Hauhau attack?"

"No, I don't think so. They've got the enemy pinned down in the north. The country here is clear."

"Then why—" Briar dropped her eyes. She could not let him see the unhappiness in her own. "Why must I go? My place is here."

"I imagine Saul thought you'd fret when we'd gone," Peter said uncomfortably. "Some life and gaiety would do you good. He said he hadn't been fair to you, expecting you to live in the wilderness like this."

"Does he say that I, too, haven't the temperament?" Briar flashed.

"Just that it's an unnatural life for a woman."

"Others stay. No one suggests that Martha Peabody or Mary Galloway or Jemima Potter should go back to the town for gaiety. Why should I want gaiety, anyway? I've never been accustomed to it."

223

Peter looked away uneasily from her indignant regard. "I'm only telling you what your husband said."

"I don't care to take orders. Even from my husband." Briar's voice, by the greatest self-control, was calm. "This is my place. I shall stay here."

He thought he could get rid of her that easily, she was thinking, anger seething within her. He might be down in the summer, or perhaps in the autumn, if the farm and his duties as a volunteer in the army permitted. And what was she, the discarded and unwanted wife, to do in the meantime? Live on the generosity of Aunt Charity, or, worse still, that of her contemptuous and righteous mother-in-law?

So Saul had decided he did not want her as a wife, after all. The last night they had spent together when he had taken her so violently—that had not been from love, as some perverse instinct had made her hope. It had been from hate. Hate and anger and disappointment. Whatever he had hoped from her as a wife, and he must have hoped for something to have married her at all, she had failed to give him.

Indeed, she had failed deliberately, for she had been too obsessed with her antagonism for him to think that there might have been other ways of looking at her marriage, and that being a wife was not just running a house and making one's body available, reluctantly, when required.

And now, whether she wanted to look at marriage in another way or not, it was too late. Saul had politely finished with her.

Or no doubt he was congratulating himself that he had.

But he was wrong. She was not to be got rid of so easily. She was Mrs. Saul Whitmore, the mistress of Lucknow, and there, no matter what her husband ordered, she would stay. She was quite determined.

She spoke to Katie, putting the position to her. "Everyone else is to go back to Wellington, and you may do so, too, if you wish. Mr. Whitmore has sent instructions that we are to go, but I intend to stay here, and I'd be happy to have you with me, if you would prefer that."

Katie did not hesitate. She nodded her untidy red head. "I'll stay, ma'am. What could I do in Wellington, in my state? And besides Rangi might come back. I always watch for him."

"Then let's hope he comes without his war paint," Briar said earnestly. "If we're to be here alone we don't want any Hauhau attacks."

224

"Rangi wouldn't let them attack Lucknow, ma'am. He told me so."

"I don't know how much one can trust a Hauhau," said Briar. "But I'm glad you're staying, Katie. Now I want you to help everybody with their packing. Mrs. Fanshawe wasn't feeling well this morning. I don't think her baby will be long in coming, and we'll all be busy enough then, without trunks to pack."

It was later that day that Katie came to Briar to report that Mrs. Whitmore would not permit her things to be touched.

"Oh, she likes to do her own packing," Briar said easily.

"No, ma'am, it isn't that. She says she isn't going."

Briar found Mrs. Whitmore in her room, sitting at the window.

"Katie tells me you refuse to leave," she said bluntly.

"I do." The old lady turned her deep dark eyes on Briar. "I intend to wait here for my son's return. I shall be perfectly all right. Mabel will look after me."

Briar heard, or sensed, the triumph in the old woman's voice, and understood the workings of her mind. She was delighted about this turn of events. She was planning to witness the ignominious departure of Saul's despised wife, the ambitious little upstart whom he should never have married, and to install herself in the house instead.

Well—she had never deceived herself that Saul's marriage had been popular with his mother, and this evidence of failure should not distress her too much. Nevertheless, Briar was conscious of a cold anger and determination.

She said politely, "If anyone is to stay and welcome Saul home, it is to be me. I am, after all, his wife. And there is no need for two of us to be here. So please, Mrs. Whitmore, will you be prepared to leave within the next two or three weeks. Saul would be worried to know you hadn't obeyed his wishes."

The old woman's lips twitched slightly. Her eyes did not waver from Briar's face. Once the intense regard would have flustered and alarmed Briar. Now she cared no longer. This was just an old woman fighting a losing battle, and one should be sorry for her.

"And what about his feelings if you disobey him?"

"Oh, that." Briar shrugged. "He's used by now to my flouting him. He may ask me to go, for my own good, but he will hope I stay."

"Are you so sure of that?"

The pain struck unfairly at her. She had thought she had it in control.

"Whatever he may think, that's a personal matter between Saul and myself." She looked at the rigid face, and added hotly, "I know you have always been against me. You judged me without giving me a chance. You thought I couldn't run a house or manage servants or talk like a lady. But I've proved to you that I can do all those things. I can even make other women—women, mind you, not men—look at me in admiration. You know that yourself. You can't deny it. You know that Saul has no need to be ashamed of me. I may not know who my parents were, but I was born with a certain amount of ability, and surely that counts most in a new country. Even having been a servant all my life has distinct advantages. So why do you sit there condemning me? You've been doing it ever since you arrived here. I won't endure it any longer. You shall go, with Aunt Charity and Sophie. I insist. This is my house. I refuse to ask you to stay!"

The old lady waited until she had finished, then, looking at her flushed cheeks, she said calmly, "Anger becomes you. I noticed that when you were defending your friends in the village, and your servant girl expecting her quarter-caste baby."

"Never mind my looks, Mrs. Whitmore. Just stop criticising me in my own house."

"You are quite wrong, my dear. I have never opened my mouth to criticise, and if it comes to that I think you do very well as far as being a good housekeeper is concerned."

"But not as a wife!" The words, half guilty, half indignant, were out before Briar could stop them. This horrible old woman made her lose her temper and her prided dignity. "Oh, I know what it is, of course. You are only waiting to see me looking as Sophie is. That's all I am to you, the means of having a grandchild. Well, you may have to wait a long time—" Infuriatingly, her voice trembled. Saul had ordered her to go back to Wellington. Obviously he did not want her any more. It was one thing to resent him in her bed, but quite another to be resented herself. How she hated these Whitmores, mother and son, with their single-minded selfish desire that gave no consideration to her feelings. "You may have to wait forever!" she declared.

"A great pity." The brief remark, spoken little above a

whisper, got beneath her skin in the way that Saul, with a sudden unguarded glance, could do.

She looked up reluctantly, and saw that Mrs. Whitmore's face seemed even more gaunt than usual, and her lips had a bluish tinge.

"Mrs. Whitmore, are you all right? Is your arm paining you?"

"My arm has recovered. Thank you for your courtesy."

"The doctor said you should rest more. You will be able to do that when you get back to Wellington. One is inclined to listen too much here. It becomes a habit. If a dog barks—"

"But I am not going back to Wellington."

Their eyes met, stare for stare. Ruefully, Briar knew she had met her match. She could not, after all, turn the old woman out into the bush.

"It seems that Saul will have to be angry with us both," Mrs. Whitmore said in her harsh voice. "For I can see that you are as determined as me to stay. I am staying because I love my son. Yours must be another reason."

Before Briar could make any answer to that outrageous statement, the old woman went on calmly, "You'd better go and see to Sophie. If I'm right, the baby will arrive within the next twenty-four hours."

CHAPTER 28

They stormed the *pa* just before dark, having lain hidden in the wet ferns, with the rain steadily soaking them into almost the same sodden state as the earth, until this moment of unguardedness of the enemy, when he had his cooking pots out and fires lit.

The surprise was so complete that the initial resistance was over almost at once, and the surviving warriors were flying for their lives by the time Captain Maltby's men poured over the palisades.

But after all they were wrong in their suppositions that Te Kooti was hiding there. The disappointment was overwhelming. They had thought they had trapped him, but he had been gone for some days, the survivors said. He was far north, they said evasively. It was obvious that if they knew anything

227

more definite than that they were not going to divulge it.

There was a prize, however, and it had fallen to Saul. He stood over the body of one of the dead, and picked up the long crimson pennant that lay muddied on the ground.

He swore softly in surprise. "The Whip!"

Captain Maltby was at his side, and bending over the sprawled figure. He turned it slightly to see the face with its elaborate tattooing, the calm, wide-open eyes, and the rich greenstone ornaments decorating neck and ears.

"Shot through the heart," he said. "Neat work, Saul. You realise who it is?"

"Te Kooti's personal standard-bearer, I imagine."

"Te Kooti's best friend, Hine Te Mataia. He's not going to like this."

"He's not intended to."

The tired captain laughed suddenly, with humourless triumph.

"His luck will change now we've got the flag. He was superstitious about that, just as he is about his devilish _niu_ pole."

Saul pulled the stained silk through his fingers. "My wife mended this once."

"Yes, I heard about that. Under fire, so to speak. Jolly good show."

"Perhaps. But I've a notion that's why my place was spared in the last attack. There's not much chance of mercy next time."

"Don't worry. We'll have Te Kooti before he can get down south again."

Saul's face was grim. "He's wilier than a fox."

"Even the wiliest fox can't escape the hounds when they close in. Come and see what's in these pots. It smells like pork and I'm damned hungry."

But after they had buried the dead, the sodden earth turning easily to their spades, Saul took a few minutes to scribble another note to Briar.

"If you have not been able to leave yet, do so at once. Don't wait for Sophie's baby. It is better to risk it being born on the way . . ."

He would give it to the first man riding south. He wished the death of Te Mataia and the capture of this symbolic strip of material, _Te Wepu_, had taken place before Peter Fanshawe had returned. He could have impressed on him the urgency of the women getting out. But surely they would have gone by now. Briar had disobeyed him once, and consequently had been forced to sit and make these neat stitches —his fingers found the place—in the now muddied and blood-stained silk. Surely after that risk to her life she would not disobey him again.

But remembering her sparkling eyes and her too frequent moods of perversity, his face darkened. He couldn't trust her. She had no predictability, and the warmth in her blood seemed to be saved only for defiance of him. Thinking of her tantalising soft-skinned hostile body in his arms, he began to wonder whether it would not have been better if he had never set eyes on her. But when he thought of the possibility of that body being mutilated by savages he was in torment.

CHAPTER 29

Being Sophia, with a hankering for plenty of fuss and attention, she would decide to have her baby at midnight on the wettest night of the year. As soon as she felt her first pains the house was in an uproar, Aunt Charity padding about in dressing-gown, nightcap and slippers, Peter half dressed and trying to conceal his panic, Katie roused to boil water, looking round-eyed and apprehensive, and Mrs. Whitmore saying, "Go back to bed, all of you. Nothing will happen before morning."

"But the doctor must be fetched," exclaimed Aunt Charity.

Mrs. Whitmore shrugged. "It's a wet night to turn out unnecessarily. I'd make a guess that midday tomorrow would be time enough."

Sophie groaned loudly. "I must have a doctor at once."

Mrs. Whitmore said, gently enough, "You'll be all right, my dear. Relax and try to rest. There's plenty of time ahead to scream." But outside the room she said in her dry contemptuous voice, "Nothing would kill that young woman. She will demand all her life and, unfortunately, I fear, get her demands. Well, then, who is going for the doctor?"

"Peter has gone out to saddle a horse," Briar said. "Mrs. Whitmore, you should be in bed. I'm going to send Katie

229

back to bed, too. There's no need to frighten her in advance, since Sophie won't be a silent sufferer."

"And what about you?" the old lady demanded.

"Oh, I have no need to be alarmed," Briar said lightly. "As I told you this afternoon."

Peter had brought the horse to the door and had come back inside. Briar heard him moving about downstairs, and went down to find him in the drawing-room helping himself to rum. He looked up guiltily as she came in. She noticed that his hand was trembling badly.

"It's raining infernally hard," he said. "I can feel that fever coming back in my bones."

"You must wrap up well. You're wet already. Didn't you put a coat on to go out?"

"I didn't realise it was raining so hard. I guess I got in a bit of a panic. Sophie suffering like that—"

"She's not suffering much yet," Briar said shortly.

He peered at her. His eyelids were a bit swollen, as if he were only half awake.

"You women—not much sympathy—for one another."

But he didn't mean that, Briar realised. He meant that she had not much sympathy for him. Going out in the dark wet night, afraid. He was not afraid for his wife, who after all was only going through what all women went through year after year, but for himself, because his tortured imagination saw a Hauhau in every wind-blown bush, behind every dripping tree.

He could not admit to this dreadful fear, of course. So he drank rum, instead, and tried to hide his trembling.

Abruptly, pity filled Briar. Poor Peter, he could not help this. It was the way he was made. For sunshine and an easy life, for all the pleasant things which could be acquired without payment in hard work and loneliness and bloodshed.

He should never have tried to be a pioneer. His imagination and ambition had allowed him to see only the advantages of a new country, and none of its hardships. So he was going to be one of the failures, or at best a mediocre, unmemorable citizen.

But it was not his own fault, for everyone could not be full of courage.

"Is the horse ready?" she asked.

"Yes, it's outside. I just slipped in for a drink, to keep out the cold." His uneasy blue eyes sought hers.

Briar made a sudden decision. "I think it would be better

f I go for Doctor MacTavish. I'm more used to the track han you. I know all its peculiarities in the dark. I'll be much uicker, probably. And Sophie would rather have you close t hand."

His frank relief was mixed with shame. "But, Briar, a voman abroad at night—"

"We have to do that in this country. It's one of the azards. I shall be back as soon as I can. Tell Aunt Charity ou have your fever again."

"Briar, you're quite wonderful!"

Once that effusive compliment would have meant a great eal to her, because it would have meant she could have had 'eter Fanshawe as her husband, her slave, whatever she de- ired. Now she was only thankful for the fate which she had scaped. One could be ambitious enough to marry without ove, but not without respect. At least she had found no eason not to respect her own husband . . .

She carried a carriage lamp because of the extreme darkness f the night, and rode astride since there was no one to see er with her skirts hitched up. She had never been out so late lone, in spite of her careless assurance to Peter, but she vas not nervous. At least, not until the dark shape of a wild ig blundered across her path and the horse shied violently. he was almost over its head, but managed to save herself t the expense of the carriage lamp, which went flying into he darkness, its light instantly extinguished.

Her horse was surefooted and knew his way. She could till progress without the aid of a light. But now the muddy nd water-logged track seemed endless, and the black bush rowded too close on either side. Rain fell with a persistent atter, and the wind crashed through the forest. The never- easing wind in this country had an eerie quality, because of he unfamiliar trees and bushes it disturbed. The *toe toe* rass with its feathery plumes swished, the *raupo* bushes rackled and the bigger trees creaked and sighed. It formed . pattern of sound that effectively shut out the approach either f prowling night animals or the stealthy scouting of a Hau- au brave.

Though now, Briar told herself steadily, there were no Iauhaus in these parts. Growing more accustomed to the lark she urged her horse on. The sudden cry of a bird made er start again, it had sounded so close, almost as if it had ome from that clump of flax by the roadside. It was not a all she could identify, for it had neither the melancholy of

the little owls nor the harshness of the kiwi or weka. In fac
wasn't it strange to hear a bird call at all on such a wet nigh

As she rode on, digging in her stirrups, the call came agai
and she still could not identify it, but it had seemed to ha
a secret urgency . . .

When at last she stumbled off her horse at Doctor Ma
Tavish's door she could scarcely speak. Soaked to the ski
breathless and afraid, she got out her message.

"It's Sophie, doctor. Mrs. Whitmore says there's no hurr
but Sophie is in a state, as you can imagine. And so
Peter."

"It seems he must be, seeing he let you make this journey
Doctor MacTavish said dryly.

"He has his fever back—he couldn't have come out in t
rain. Let's hurry, doctor. But we must go carefully past
certain point. I heard something."

"You did, eh? What sort of noise?"

"The kind of bird that doesn't call at night. At least,
don't think it does, but I'm still ignorant about birds her

"I'll get my gun," said the little doctor in his unperturb
voice. "We'll go back in the buggy. Your horse can lead l
hind. But come in and get a drop of brandy. You look as
you could do with it. Perhaps you'd like to spend the nig
here, and I'll go on alone."

Briar pushed the wet hair out of her eyes. "Don't be sil
doctor. I have to help Sophie."

The trip back was uneventful. There was no sound but t
splash of the horse's hooves in the soggy mud, and the w
wind in the forest. Briar had not realised her tension until,
the front door of the house, she tried to climb out of t
buggy and found that she was too stiff and cold to do
Doctor MacTavish swung her out easily and set her down.

"Run and change into dry clothes, lassie." And, as Au
Charity opened the door, "Good evening to you, ma'a
Where's the patient?"

Sophie's baby was born in the early morning, with tolera
little trouble, although Sophie might well have been imitat
a Hauhau attack from the noise she made. But afterwa
she was infuriatingly smug, cradling her plump pink-fac
son in her arms as if she had performed some highly origi
act. She did not notice that her husband was more than th
parts drunk, nor that Briar was white-faced and exhaus
after her midnight ride to the village, and then assisting at l
first birth.

232

"We must make a list of names," she said. "A name, particularly for a first son, is so important. And I can't wait to get back to Wellington to show him off. Doctor says we should be able to travel quite soon as both baby and I are so well."

Briar, stumbling to her room to rest, told herself that everything old Mrs. Whitmore had predicted had come true. She had had to cook and clean, and fight the enemy and assist at childbirth. Somehow she had done it. She had even done it without anyone noticing her sickening qualms and apprehension.

So now there was no need to cry, especially since she had no idea why she was crying. Because she was lonely? Because it was Sophie who cradled a baby in her arms?

After she had slept, however, she felt better. Indeed, since it had stopped raining she decided to ride a little way along the track and try to identify the part of the bush from which she had heard the bird's cry last night.

She told no one where she was going, and afterwards she was thankful for this, for although there was no sign of life in the dripping forest, lying on the rain-flattened grass beneath a flax bush she found a black feather with a white tip. A huia feather such as a *rangatira* wore in his hair to show his rank. The huia bird did not live in these parts. It was found only in the higher mountains. So the feather must have been dropped by a human agent.

Briar sprang on her horse and rode hard into the village to report what she had discovered. A scouting party, led by Amos O'Brien, was formed at once. Most of the young able-bodied men were away with the troops, so if an attack were to come it would be a sorry thing for the defenders left here. But late that evening Fred Potter came to report that no sign of the enemy had been found. The rain-sodden huia feather must have lain beneath the flax bushes since the original attack a month ago.

Briar's anxiety was lessened, but not completely dismissed. She had begun to listen again in that strained uneasy way. She was impatient to get all her guests away, particularly Sophie and the baby. How dreadful if something should happen to the baby. She wished, too, that she could prevail on old Mrs. Whitmore to change her mind. But one had only to look at the old lady's implacable face to know it was useless to try.

Within a fortnight Doctor MacTavish pronounced that

Sophie, who was a remarkably strong young woman, was fit to travel, and Aunt Charity, Sophie and the baby, and Peter, prepared to set out on their journey to New Plymouth, there to await the *Seagull*.

Peter was obsessed with his desire to get away, and Sophie, too, was happy to depart, her baby wrapped in an enormous quantity of shawls and blankets. It was left to Aunt Charity to shed tears.

This she did copiously, for not only was she leaving that stubborn and stupid Prudence behind, in her most unsuitable role of mother to the Perkins children, but she had developed a genuine affection for Briar.

Being Aunt Charity, however, she could not show this in any way but by criticism.

"Briar, you should be obeying Saul and coming with us. It's very unwise of a young bride to defy her husband. It will lead to trouble. And Saul, I am sure, is not one to put up with this sort of behaviour. Another thing, I'm most unhappy about your keeping Katie. You'll regret that, I can tell you. It's up to people like us to set a moral standard in this country. Young women like Katie don't slip only once. Most likely you'll have this happening all over again in a year's time, and then what are you to do?"

She surveyed Briar's face fretfully.

"I can see you're not taking notice of anything I'm saying. But just remember, I warned you. And Briar, do try to persuade Prudence to leave that squalid household. Oh, I know she's doing what must be considered a worth-while job, but who is going to marry her after this? Except that poor creature, Perkins himself. Oh dear, now Peter wants to be off, and there's so much I still have to say to you. You're such a difficult, unbendable person! So strange for one so young! But nevertheless I love you—" Aunt Charity sniffed tremendously. Her large face was scarlet with emotion. "Almost as if you had been my own," was her parting cry.

The little group stood in the road watching the waggons out of sight. Sophie's handkerchief was fluttering, and Aunt Charity every now and then turned to lift her arm in a vigorous wave. She was already, no doubt, in her own mind back in Wellington talking volubly and endlessly to Uncle Hubert about her hazardous trip, her encounter with the Hauhaus, and her strenuous efforts to put Briar's and Prudence's lives in order.

Watching the bumping waggons grow smaller in the distance, Briar silently prayed that the travellers would reach New Plymouth safely. The shepherd who had volunteered to drive one waggon, and Peter driving the other, were armed and on the alert, but the danger, everyone said, was negligible.

Yet Briar could not rid herself of her feeling of premonition. The sparkling day, the quiet forest, the slow spirals of smoke from chimneys, all seemed too peaceful. But perhaps her low state of mind was caused only by the sadness of saying goodbye to friends, and the constant knowledge that Saul had wanted her to go with them. It was so terrible to feel unwelcomed and unwanted in one's own home.

She had a right to stay, she told herself fiercely. She would not be intimidated by a domineering and impatient husband. How dare he try to turn her out! She would not be ruled by him.

Everyone had come to say goodbye to the travellers, but now Prudence had dried her tears and was saying that she must go back to prepare the children's dinner. She had Honi by one hand and the youngest Perkins child by the other. Jemima was there, too, and Fred Potter was waiting in the dray to take them all back to the village.

"Do you wish you had gone, Prue?" Briar asked.

Prudence shook her head. "Aunt Charity's very difficult to oppose. But I'm glad I didn't give in to her. I like it here. The children are sweet now they've got to know me, and Mr. Perkins is so kind. Everyone says how he has changed."

"Let's hope it lasts," Briar said sceptically. She had never recovered from her feeling of guilt that it was her bonnet that had brought about Amy Perkins' death, and that this obscurely was the fault of Amy's husband for not having been a better provider.

"I think it will last," said Prudence seriously. "You know, I think his wife, poor thing, nagged him too much, and complained all the time. A man has to escape from that, hasn't he?"

She hadn't nagged Saul, Briar thought privately, but in other ways she had failed. Didn't even old Mrs. Whitmore say so?

"What about you, Briar?" Jemima was saying. "Aren't you sorry you didn't go with them?"

"No! Of course I'm not sorry!" Her voice was too emphatic, giving away her inner turmoil. "My home is here, just as yours is. But perhaps you wish you could have gone?"

Jemima shook her head. She was not so thin and meagre as she had been at the time of the baby's death. Her face had plumped out a little, and her eyes were bright.

"Oh, no, Briar. Didn't the children tell you? One of the ewes Mr. Whitmore gave Fred had twin lambs this morning. We've practically got a farm!"

"Potatoes will be up soon," called Fred from his seat in the dray. "Everything's fine."

Somehow it all seemed too good to be true. Watching that waggon also jolt away, Briar told herself that there was no need to worry. Prudence was emerging from her crushed lifeless state and becoming a contented and self-respecting young woman, Jemima was better in health, and would almost certainly be producing a strong and healthy baby to take the place of fragile little Rose within the next year. Katie was looking forward with unashamed pleasure to the birth of her coffee-coloured baby, and Sophie had gone home as the proud matron with her first child.

So why did she feel this cloud hanging over her, Briar wondered? Was she the only one who had made a dreadful mistake with her life?

CHAPTER 30

The two women sat alone at dinner. Katie served the meal as Briar had taught her to, carefully and quietly. The table was laid with a sparkling white linen cloth, and the well-polished silver that had been Uncle Hubert's wedding present. Briar wore her buff-coloured gown, and had her hair done in a careful arrangement of curls. She had obviously taken pains with her toilette in spite of the fact that they were just two women sitting down to dinner in the wilds.

She was so determined, thought old Mrs. Whitmore ironically, to play the lady. The perplexing thing was that her appearance and manner did not seem assumed. They were perfectly natural. So either she was a brilliant actress, or there was, as one began to think, good blood in her ancestry. Katie, from a similar situation in life, could never have acquired that cool poise. With her tumbling red hair and her pert grin she was forever a maidservant.

But this daughter-in-law, with her polite conversation about politics or the classics, was a permanent puzzle. Those downcast eyes beneath the beautifully marked brows hid a world of secrets.

"Tell me," she said abruptly, interrupting Briar's remark about the sad lack of books in this country as yet, "What do you really want out of life?"

"Why—something more than my poor mother had."

"Your mother might have had love, brief though it was."

Briar's eyelids lifted to disclose a sudden unwary look, almost like pain. Then they fell again and she said composedly. "Then you think I do not have love?"

"You must give it, to receive it. Or did you think your face and figure was sufficient? Perhaps you really thought that was enough to trade for this house and your position."

"Isn't that for my husband to judge, Mrs. Whitmore?"

"From his point of view, yes. But you surely have a point of view yourself. Of course, you might think this emptiness sufficient."

"Emptiness?"

Mrs. Whitmore waved her narrow yellow hand. "Don't these rooms seem empty to you? Hollow? Well, love them if you must, but I always thought one required human beings to love. I'm afraid you'll come to learn that Saul thinks the same way."

Briar's head was bent over her plate. "If this is an oblique way of reminding me once more that I must have children, that also is mine and my husband's business. I thought we had agreed not to speak of it again."

The cool voice seemed more insolent and hurtful than a blow, especially when one had even begun to have serious doubts about the accuracy of one's early judgment of this girl. But now, in a gust of anger and disappointment, Mrs. Whitmore lifted herself from her chair. The sudden movement made the candles flicker, and her face was all shadows, gaunt and ravaged.

"You selfish little adventuress!" she cried. "If that's how you feel, you have no right in this house! Why don't you go back to where you belong?"

She should not have sprung up so quickly. The pain struck in her chest again and she could scarcely breathe. She must get to her room and be alone, away from this cool disdainful girl . . .

"Where do I belong, Mrs. Whitmore?"

If the pain had not blurred her senses she might have noticed a note of lostness and perplexity in the girl's voice. As it was, she could only think it was one more act of defiance.

"How do I know? With your pots and pans, perhaps. If you will excuse me—I am not hungry—rather tired . . ."

Briar was at her side, one strong young arm round her shoulders. "Mrs. Whitmore, you're ill. I had thought for some time that you were. Sit down. Let me get you some brandy."

"No, no. I'll go to my room. Just get me a light."

In a moment the candle, snatched from the dining-table, was held out to her, but her trembling hands refused to hold it steady. Grease spilt, and Briar took it back from her.

"I'll carry it. Come." At the door she paused to call, "Katie! Fill a hot water bottle quickly. Bring it up to Mrs. Whitmore's room. Now—can you climb the stairs?"

"Of course I can climb the stairs!"

"I believe you are as stubborn as I." The voice seemed merely a whisper in her ear. Foolish to think it was like a little frost melting, and that secretly one had longed for that frost to melt. Foolish to think at all, for it required all her strength and will to climb the fine staircase that Saul had so ambitiously built in his house.

When she reached her room she was speechless, her eyes black caverns in her face.

"Just lie down," said Briar. "Later I'll help you undress. Then I shall go for Doctor MacTavish."

In a little while, propped by pillows, and with the hot water bottle at her feet, Mrs. Whitmore recovered.

She said quite strongly, and with all her old decisiveness, "There's no need for the doctor. I know exactly what is the matter with me, and it's nothing he can cure. Rest is all that is necessary. Just leave me."

Katie, white-faced and alarmed, obeyed automatically. She was the genuine maidservant, trained to obey. But this other one, this slim figure so poised and elegant in her silk gown, said, "I shall sit beside you until you fall asleep."

"I prefer to be alone."

"You prefer to be arrogant and critical, just like your son. But I expect you have a heart, too—if one can find it . . ."

Mrs. Whitmore opened her eyes to the face bending over her. In the candlelight it looked soft and vulnerable. Almost pleading. But that must be an illusion of the flickering light.

"Then sit!" she said in her dry harsh voice. "If you must stay. How can I sleep with you hanging over me?"

When at last Mrs. Whitmore seemed to be asleep Briar left her. She tiptoed out to find Katie lurking at the door in tears.

"What's wrong with you?"

"Oh, ma'am, is she going to die?"

"Of course not. She's only tired. She's asleep now. Don't be such a baby, Katie. Dry your tears and go down and help Mabel with the dishes."

"They're done, and Mabel's got the willies."

"Mabel, too!" said Briar impatiently. "I'd better come down."

In the big kitchen, lit by the oil lamp on the table, Mabel squatted on the floor in her favourite position, her clay pipe unlit hanging between her broad lips. Her loose fitting cotton dress seemed suddenly too big for her, and her eyes were huge, and showing their whites.

"Now what's this nonsense, Mabel?" Briar demanded sharply. "Are you going to behave like this every time someone is ill?"

Mabel rolled her eyes. "Bad things are coming, missus. I feel them."

"What sort of bad things? If you, too, think Mrs. Whitmore is going to die—"

"It's not the old one, missus. She's ready to die, anyway. It's other things." She puffed deeply on her unlit pipe and said obscurely, "The owls are calling."

Briar's heart missed a beat. "The owls always call."

"Not so loud, missus."

"That's only because the house is quiet, now our guests have gone. You're not used to this strange quiet." Instinctively Briar looked at the dark window pane. Then she said decisively, "Get my shawl, Katie. I'll just go and have a word with the shepherds. They'll have noticed if there's anything unusual."

She took a lantern and stepped out into the cool dark night. The owls were not calling now. It was very quiet. The lantern light made a moony patch on the gravel. Nothing stirred about the stables or in the cleared fields beyond. Although did that tree stump move? Was it a tree stump?

Briar covered the reminder of the yard rather quickly, holding up her skirts from the mud and rapped on the door of the shepherds' hut.

One of the men opened the door at once. "Something wrong, Mrs. Whitmore?"

"My mother-in-law is ill. Later someone may have to go for the doctor, but I think she'll be all right until morning."

"We'll be here, ma'am. Just give us a call."

One of the men was elderly, grizzled and stooped, but with the toughness of the wanderer. The other was a mere boy.

"Have you heard anything strange tonight, Jed?"

"No, ma'am. Can't say I have."

"Mabel says the owls have been calling a lot."

"Always do, don't they? There can't be anything wrong or the dogs would bark. That's one animal the Hauhaus can't fool. Anyway, they're not likely to get down this way at present. The rivers are too high and the fords are guarded."

"Yes, I expect that's true," said Briar with relief.

"Give us a call, ma'am, if you're worried. We'll be off at dawn to go round the sheep. There are some early lambs. But we'll be over to the house first. So if you're still uneasy we'll decide what's to be done."

"Thank you, Jed. I'm sure there's nothing to worry about."

She went back to the house and turned roundly on the two wide-eyed and apprehensive women. "There's nothing to be shivering and trembling about. I don't know what's come over you. Everything's quite peaceful, and no different from any other night. Now get off to bed, both of you, and prepare to be in a more cheerful state of mind in the morning."

Before going to bed herself she took another look at Mrs. Whitmore. The old lady did not seemed to have stirred. She lay in the guttering candlelight, her high bony nose pointing to the ceiling, her breathing quiet. With some vague instinct about shutting out noise, Briar crossed to the window and softly closed it. Then she wondered why she had done so. Because if the dogs barked at something worse than a creeping night beast, soon enough no closed window would keep out the ensuing sounds.

When she reached her own room she was trembling as much as Katie and Mabel had been. It was utterly foolish to let herself become affected by Mabel's superstitions, but the fact remained that before she had discovered Mabel's state of mind, her own had been similar. She, too, was filled with an apprehension of something worse than the illness of Mrs. Whitmore.

Why were they all so jittery tonight? Why could she not bring herself to undress lest that be unwise? It must be only that the house seemed so quiet and empty since the departure of Aunt Charity and Sophie and the little squalling baby, and Peter who had grown into a much louder, more voluble person since he had taken such a fancy to the rum bottle.

Nevertheless, she could see no prospect of sleep if she did undress and get into bed. She drew the curtains, and lit extra candles, and sat down at the little table on which stood the fat family Bible of the Whitmores. She opened it at random, searching for Martha Peabody's favorite text. But another one caught her eye . . . *And they shall dwell safely in the wilderness, and sleep in the woods* . . .

She read it again, with a strange sense of tranquillity. Sleep in the woods. That was what she was doing, whether it were meant literally or not. For her life with Saul promised to be a long bewildered groping through dark places. Always supposing, of course, that he would allow her any more life with him.

She turned to the inscription page and began reading the entries. The Bible must have been a wedding present to old Mrs. Whitmore and her husband, for the first entry recorded their marriage.

27th January 1815 Capt. Reginald Whitmore to Oriane Marley, daughter of Robert Curtis Marley and Beatrice Marley.

The next entry, of course, was:

21st June 1830 Born to Reginald and Oriane Whitmore a son, baptised Saul.

And the last, one she had not known was there, it must have been written in the last few days. It made her heart give a curious leap, as if seeing the statement in black and white made it more real than the days and nights she had spent with Saul.

3rd October 1860 Married—Saul Whitmore to Briar Rose Johnson of England.

That was all. Just the meagre fact that she had come from England, the one fact in her life of which she was sure. Oriane Whitmore, the proud daughter of Robert and Beatrice Marley, must have found it bitter to make that entry.

But supposing there were an entry to follow this one, the facts of it could be put down fully. To Saul and Briar Whitmore . . .

Briar held up her fingers, and counted the days again, as she had done so often lately. How many now since that night which she still could not begin to forget . . .

An owl called suddenly, very close, and Briar lept to the window to draw back the curtain a cautious inch. She thought she caught a glimpse of a bird swooping towards the ngaio trees, but she could not be sure, and now all was still again.

Not entirely still, however, for footsteps shuffled along the passage outside her bedroom.

"Who's there?" she cried.

The door opened a timid inch. "It's me, ma'am," said Katie. "I can't sleep. I'm so scared, I don't know why."

"Come in here," Briar ordered, and the girl, in her high-necked flannel nightgown, with her red hair tumbling child-ishly stood shamefaced and forlorn.

"Aren't you feeling well?" Briar asked.

The freckles stood out on Katie's pale face. "A bit squeam-ish, ma'am, but only because I'm scared. I keep thinking I hear things. Creeping in bushes, and whispers."

Briar licked her dry lips and managed to say, "You weren't scared when it was Rangi coming to your window."

"I know. But it isn't Rangi tonight."

The ready tears were slipping down her cheeks again. She looked no more than twelve years old, and it seemed im-possible that her body was already swelling with a child.

"Now look, Katie, you've just caught Mabel's supersti-tions. I'm going to be very angry with her tomorrow for up-setting everyone."

"But aren't you scared, ma'am? You're not undressed and in bed, and it's after midnight."

"I wasn't tired. But now you're here you might as well help me to undress. Unbutton my gown. Ugh! Good gracious, child, your fingers are as cold as ice."

"I'm sorry, ma'am. Don't be angry with me."

"I'm not angry with you. No one can help, in this wilder-ness, being a little afraid." She was trembling herself as she stood in her petticoats, the air like cold water on her bare arms. "When Mr. Whitmore comes back—" Involuntarily her gaze strayed to the big bed, so smooth and empty. It was after midnight, certainly, but there were still seven hours till daylight. Seven hours to lie alone, thinking and listening.

"You'll catch your death of cold, running about in your nightgown like that," she said crisply to the shivering Katie. "You'd better get into bed. We'll keep each other company."

Katie's eyes widened. "In your bed! Do you mean it?"

"You heard me. I can't afford to have you ill, too. Besides —" Her eyelids drooped tiredly. What were they after all but

242

two girls, both frightened and unhappy, one having no more defences than the other in time of danger? "Besides, I confess I'd like your company," she added simply.

In the morning Katie awoke and sat up with a little shriek. She had forgotten where she was, and in full daylight was over-awed to find herself in the mistress's bed. Then irrepressibly she began to giggle.

Briar straightened her own mouth severely. "There's no need to sit there giggling. Go back to your own room and dress. I imagine that now it's daylight you won't be too afraid."

"Oh, no, ma'am. I feel fine now." Katie scrambled out of bed and drew back the curtains to disclose a clear sky with the first pale sunlight brightening the trees. "Look, the sun's shining!"

Briar stretched lazily, relief filling her. The night was over, and nothing had happened. All their strange fears had been unjustified. It was after seven-thirty, she saw, so the shepherds must have had breakfast and gone on their rounds of the sheep and the first early lambs. They had promised to let her know if anything alarmed them, so all must be well. Just wait until she got downstairs and told that lazy superstitious Mabel what she thought of her for frightening them all.

"As soon as you're dressed, Katie, bring my tea. I'm going to see how Mrs. Whitmore is. She will have tea in bed, too."

Hitherto Mrs. Whitmore had refused such luxuries, but she would not be allowed to do so this morning. As soon as Katie had scampered off, all her carefully learned dignity lost while she remained with bare feet and in her nightgown, Briar dressed and went to Mrs. Whitmore's room.

At the door she had a sudden fright, for the old lady lay so still. But as she went up to the bed she saw the dark hollowed eyes watching her.

"How are you this morning, Mrs. Whitmore? Did you sleep well?"

"Well enough. The night was quiet."

So she, too, must have caught this strange apprehension, and lain listening.

"Are you feeling better?"

"A little weak, perhaps. I may stay in bed for an hour or two."

Again Briar felt premonition. This was the first time she old lady had admitted to any feeling of illness, or indeed had been willing to remain in bed. Was she very ill? Doctor Mac-Tavish must be sent for, secretly if necessary.

"Katie's going to bring you some tea. That silly Mabel gave us all a fright last night, saying she was nervous about the owls calling, but you see it's a beautiful morning, and all's—"

Before she could finish the reassuring words, a flock of birds, small green parakeets, flew from the bush and circled round emitting sharp cries.

They would settle in a moment, Briar thought, watching them hypnotically. If they did, it would mean they had only been disturbed by a wild pig rooting or some other innocent cause.

They did not settle. They swept in another vociferous circle. Then one of the dogs barked.

Mrs. Whitmore started up in bed. "What are you looking at?"

"Nothing. Just the fine morning—"

"Why is that dog barking?"

"I suppose there's a wild pig—" Her voice broke off. It was too far off to see clearly, but she thought she had caught a glimpse of a tall black feather rising above the low screen of bush. The dog was now barking furiously, and had been joined by others. Surely wherever the shepherds were, they would hear . . .

"Don't worry, Mrs. Whitmore. I'll just go downstairs and make sure all's well."

"Where's your gun?" Vigour had come back into the old lady's voice. It was crisp and authoritative.

"In the hall."

"See that it's loaded. Bring it up here."

Briar was at the door. "I'll just have the doors bolted, in case—" She didn't finish the sentence, but flew downstairs and called to Mabel and Katie.

"Have you been watching the bush? Have you seen anything?"

Katie's face was ashen white, and she was clutching the table. Mabel was staring out of the window. "Something's scared those dogs, missus. And it isn't owls this time."

"Katie! Pull yourself together. Help me bolt all the doors and windows. Mabel, see that the guns are loaded. Quickly I depend on you."

The last window has just been bolted when Mrs. Whitmore called from upstairs, "Briar! Bring me a gun!"

Briar grabbed the gun Mabel handed her and flew upstairs. "What is it, Mrs. Whitmore? Have you seen something?"

"I may be old and sick, but my eyesight has never failed me. There are at least three natives moving about on the edge of the bush. They may be friendly, but I don't think so."

The old lady, with a wrap pulled round her, was at the window staring out. She put her hand out for the gun, and opened the window a little to aim it.

"Are you—going to shoot?" Briar whispered.

"Not yet. Hold your fire, my husband always said. Let's make sure these are the infidels."

She looked so gaunt and strange, with her burning eyes and dishevelled appearance, that Briar wondered momentarily whether her illness had affected her mentally and she thought she was back in India being attacked by the mutinous sepoys.

"Briar! If this is an attack—Ha! There's another of the devils! See! Beyond that flax bush."

Briar clutched the window frame. "Then they are Hauhaus."

"Now, listen!" Mrs. Whitmore's voice was as curt and emotionless as Saul's in similar circumstances. "As soon as they get near enough I'll try to pick them off. At least, my fire will attract their attention. And while that's happening you and Katie are to be ready to slip out and make for the forest."

"*Leave* you!" Briar exclaimed.

The fierce eyes held her. "You'll do exactly as I say. I'm an old woman about to die any moment. Oh, yes, that's true enough. My heart has been troublesome for some time, and last night—But don't let's waste time talking. I may be sacrificing a few weeks, perhaps only a few days of my life. You and Katie have everything ahead of you. *So do as I say!*"

It was impossible to defy that intense formidable voice.

"Will it be safe in the forest?"

"Safer than here. Creep under the bracken and lie still. I'll hold off the devils. If I can't—" she shrugged with superb indifference. "I'll save my last shot."

"Mrs. Whitmore! I want to tell you—" Tears were running down Briar's face, and she could scarcely see the gaunt yellowed face propped against the window, that gaunt, unloved face that was yet, in some strange way, loved because it held so much that was now painfully familiar. "Mrs.

245

Whitmore, I lied to you last night. I am to have a baby I want you to know—"

Swiftly the dishevelled grey head turned. "You are just saying that!"

"No, it's true. I've been sure for seven whole days, and before that—in myself—I knew, although I was too stubborn to tell you."

She was not prepared for the blazing joy in the old woman's face. For a moment both of them had forgotten the imminent danger. They were facing each other at last. Then, in an impulsive gesture, Mrs. Whitmore put out her hand.

But before Briar could grasp it the terrible barking cry rent the still morning. The brown forms came leaping out of the bush, hatchets and spears waving. Six, eight, ten . . . Briar had her hands pressed tightly to her ears to shut out the dreadful whooping.

"Quickly!" screamed Mrs. Whitmore behind her. "Run! Run, I tell you. Out of Katie's window. Keep low in the grass."

"I can't."

"Not for yourself. For my grandson! Go!"

Then, with careful unhurried aim, Mrs. Whitmore fired. The shock of the noise brought Briar to her senses. She was flying down the stairs, the yelling of the Hauhaus, the crash of the gun, and Mrs. Whitmore's voice in her ears. "This is not my country, nor yours. It's his. Give it to him!"

She hadn't said those last words. Yet they were in Briar's head as surely as if they had been shouted after her. She found Katie huddled in the hall, and grabbing her hand dragged her towards her room.

"We have to get to the forest. Hurry. Mabel! Come!"

But Mabel's panic once again had vanished when danger was on her, and with true Maori ferocity she was making terrible grimaces while she crouched at the window with gun, ready to take aim.

The sun struck on their heads as they scrambled through the window into the long soaking grass. It was a hundred yards down the slope to the nearest screen of trees, and then another hundred to the bush.

Another shot rang out from the other side of the house and the yelling increased. Running for their lives, their long skirts tangling in thorn bushes, their hair tumbling down the two girls panted and stumbled to the protection of the trees. Briar could scarcely believe that they had not been

246

pursued. The thudding of footsteps must have been nothing but the beating of her heart.

Katie was collapsing already, gasping for breath and clutching at her stomach. The next thing, thought Briar in a moment of clarity, was that she would be coping with a miscarriage in the middle of the forest.

"Come on, Katie! Come on!"

"Oh, ma'am! I can't!"

"You can, and you will. Mrs. Whitmore isn't going to die in vain."

There was another shot, and the sudden explosion galvanised Katie into movement. It was she who led the way now, skimming across the field, her skirts held up above her knees.

"*Hau! hau!*" rang the whooping cry. "*Hau! hau!*"

But it was farther off, and when next Briar ventured to look over her shoulder even the house looked small, and the brown forms dancing around it no more than shadows.

"They haven't followed us," she gasped. "But we mustn't stop yet. We've got to hide."

Katie's hand was on her arm. "Look!" she whispered hoarsely. "Look!"

Briar stared again, and saw the wisp of smoke. "Oh, *no!*"

"They're—setting fire to the house!"

Briar pressed her hands to her eyes. The yelling sounded across the green fields, wet and shining in the early sunlight. The plume of smoke thickened. Another shot came—Briar knew instinctively which one that was. The one Mrs. Whitmore had kept for herself. Abruptly the earth tilted and the wet grass caressed her cheeks.

Katie was shaking her violently and dragging her upright. "Ma'am! We've got to hide. They'll soon be looking for us."

The yellow flames were leaping now, and their heat seemed to touch her icy cold face.

"I shouldn't have left Mrs. Whitmore! I shouldn't have!"

"And be burnt to a cinder yourself? Much sense that would be. The old lady was right. She was dying, you could see that. And you and me—" A look of adult wisdom crossed Katie's grubby sweat-stained face. "I'm right, aren't I, ma'am? We have to save our babies."

"If we can," said Briar grimly, not enquiring how Katie had divined her secret.

"Oh, look!" screeched Katie. "They've seen us. They're

pointing. Quick! Run, run!"

With one panic-stricken look at the suddenly advancing savages who were gesticulating and waving their tomahawks, Briar turned and fled after Katie into the cool wet tangle of the forest.

CHAPTER 31

At that precise moment, as Briar and Katie fled from their pursuers, Sophie, Aunt Charity and Peter, continuing their journey to New Plymouth, suddenly saw three horsemen approaching, riding hard.

"Hauhaus!" screamed Sophie, clutching her baby to her breast.

Peter had his gun raised to fire. Aunt Charity snapped, "Put that down, you fool! Can't you tell a Maori from a white man?"

"The second one is a Maori," Peter flung back. His face was already wet with perspiration. Had there been any cover he would automatically have fled for it, but there was nothing in this damned plain but tussocks no more than knee high. All the same, he could probably pick off the horsemen, one by one, if his hands were steady enough to fire and reload. The second one was undoubtedly a Maori. Even at this distance his black oiled hair gleamed in the sun.

"There are some friendly Maoris," Aunt Charity declared and with superb aplomb stood up in the jolting wagon and waved.

The leading horseman waved back. The little group rapidly drew nearer, and suddenly Peter shouted, "It's Saul!"

"And you'd have murdered him," exclaimed Aunt Charity in disgust, before she composed her face into a welcoming smile for the mud-splattered horsemen.

Saul slid off his horse and in a moment his eyes had taken in the occupants of the two wagons. "Where's my wife and my mother?"

"They refused to come, Saul. Nothing would persuade them."

Sophie, uncovering her baby's face, thrust him forward with a proud smile.

"How lucky meeting you, Saul. Now you can see my baby. He's just over two weeks old. You'd hardly think it, would you? Doctor MacTavish said he's as big as a month old baby already."

Saul, giving no more than a glance at the pink face of the infant, interrupted curtly, "Was all well when you left?"

"Oh, perfectly." Aunt Charity looked at the other two horsemen, standing a little way off. Heavens, one of them was surely a Hauhau, with the curling tattoo marks on his face, and his air of proud disdain.

"When did you leave?"

"Early yesterday," Peter answered. "We've made good time. The road's not in bad condition. We thought it wise to push on as fast as we could."

"More than wise," said Saul. "You'll have no trouble now you're clear of the forest."

"Was there likely to be trouble?"

"To Lucknow, yes. Rangi—" Saul indicated the silent Maori, "told me of it. I had the bad luck to kill Te Kooti's best friend and capture the whip. So a personal revenge as a face-saver has been planned. Lucknow isn't going to escape this time, unless we can get there quickly enough." He paused to say in utter exasperation, "My God, why didn't my wife do as I told her?"

Then he was on his horse again and shouting, "You've only ten miles to go, but don't waste time. Good luck!"

As the horses thundered off, Sophie exclaimed in tones of deep offence, "He scarcely looked at baby. He wasn't the slightest bit interested. Poor Briar! I pity her, married to such a hard-hearted creature."

"At least he's concerned for her safety," said Peter, and muttered to himself, "Thank God we got out. Thank God!"

"That Maori, Rangi," said Aunt Charity thoughtfully. Isn't that name familiar? Where have I heard it before?"

"How could you possibly have heard it, Aunt Charity? A heathen like that. I wonder how ever Saul can trust him!"

Saul not only trusted Rangi, but was deeply grateful to him for his warning. For it was Rangi who had discovered the plan of eight or nine young hotheads to please their great leader, Te Kooti, by riding into Taranaki to take revenge on the hated and feared white man, Saul Whitmore, by destroying his home and family.

His upbringing in Maori *pas* and villages had never given his white blood a chance. But recently the memory of that slim pale-skinned woman with hair like fire had stirred strange feelings in him, and he had a great longing to return to her. With this longing had come a sickening of Hauhau brutality. It was wrong and it was bad.

He spent a long night communing with the spirits, not Te Kooti's fierce and terrible God who demanded human sacrifice, but the gentle Maori spirits dwelling in forest and mountain. Then he deserted his *pa*, and at great personal danger sought out Saul Whitmore in the enemy camp.

But when Saul had been given leave by Captain Maltby to ride south and to take with him Tom Galloway and the Hauhau deserter, Rangi, it was only to find that rivers were in flood and impassable, and they had to travel down the longer coast route through New Plymouth. So they were a day later than they had meant to be, and now perhaps it was too late.

Saul had hoped against hope that everyone, as he had instructed, would have left Lucknow, and when he saw the waggons in the distance he had sighed with relief. Surely Briar and his mother would be there, with the rest.

But he might have known Briar, from pure perversity, would disobey him. This time it looked as if her perversity were going to be her doom.

The horses were tired. The men had been riding almost non-stop, getting fresh horses where they could, for three days. Rangi's dark face with its innumerable scoring of whorls and circles showed no sign of fatigue, but Saul and Tom were red-eyed and tight-lipped.

Fifteen miles from Lucknow Saul's weary horse stumbled into a hole and lamed itself. There was only one thing to do, and that was to leave Tom behind with the lame horse and ride on with Rangi. Although the track was reasonably firm and dry, it was dusk before they came in sight of Lucknow—or where Lucknow had stood. For the smoking ruins were unrecognisable.

Furiously Saul spurred his tired horse and covered the remaining distance.

The enemy had gone, for the figures he could see were occupied only with throwing buckets of water on the fragment of the house still standing. He recognized Doctor

MacTavish, and Amos O'Brien, and the square form of Mabel Kingi. Mabel was the only woman there.

Saul leaped off his horse as Doctor MacTavish came running towards him.

"Saul! Thank God you're here!"

"Where's my wife and my mother?"

Doctor MacTavish indicated a form, covered with a tarpaulin, a little way off. "There's your mother, Saul."

"Burnt!" Saul exclaimed grimly.

"No. It was more merciful than that. Mabel tells us she kept her last shot for herself."

"Briar?" Saul demanded.

"She and Katie made for the forest. We haven't been able to find them yet. The men are still searching."

"You're sure they weren't caught?"

"No sign of it, Saul. Mabel says the devils gave chase, but unless they've kidnapped the girls—"

"This enemy doesn't kidnap," Saul said briefly. "He doesn't waste time. We've got to go on searching."

Rangi who had been sitting silently on his horse in the background suddenly rode forward. "I find them, Mr. Whitmore. I know where. Little Rata Flower—" There was a secret look in his glowing brown eyes. Then he spurred his horse and rode towards the forest.

"Come back!" shouted Saul. "You'll be shot."

But the Maori, leaning low on his horse, the feathered cloak flying out from him so that he looked like an enormous bird, continued his wild ride.

"Who's that?" asked Doctor MacTavish. "What's he up to? If he goes crashing into the forest the men will think he's a Hauhau."

"He is a Hauhau," said Saul. "But it seems my wife's red-haired maid has cast a spell over him." He picked up his reins. "Come on, let's follow."

It seemed as if they had been lying in the dark mould-smelling hollow of the tree forever. At intervals they had heard distant crashing and unintelligible shouted words, and once Briar had thought she had heard her own name called. She would have ventured out then, but Katie clung to her in a panic.

"No, not yet. We must wait till dark."

"But the men may be searching for us."

"The Hauhaus might be! Let's wait."

Briar was so tired and shocked that she let Katie persuade her. Presently the forest grew quiet, except for the birds, and in the cool darkness her tension lessened and she almost slept. She must relax because of her baby, she told herself. If only for Saul's mother's sake, she must have this baby safely.

But the old lady was dead. She must be dead by now.

Then all the more reason to guard this life within herself . . .

She tried to realise that Lucknow was no more, that all her treasured possessions, the six airy bedrooms, the piano, the Persian carpet, the silver Uncle Hubert had given her, the portraits of the two impostor parents, all her clothes, were nothing but blackened wreckage, that in her torn and muddied gown she was a waif once more.

But the events of the day must have turned her brain, for none of that seemed to matter very much. "This emptiness," Mrs. Whitmore had said. And now the emptiness was there no longer. Strangely, it was a relief.

Hours later, when both hunger and cramp were making the girls restless, and Briar was determined to venture out, there was suddenly a renewed crashing in the forest. It came nearer and nearer, and then stopped directly outside the hollow tree.

Katie whimpered with fright, and clung to Briar. She hid her face as the ferns screening the entrance were roughly pulled aside.

Briar herself suppressed a shriek as she saw the dark face peering in. It was impossible to identify it in the gloom, but she knew it was that of a Hauhau because of the long powerful naked arm, and the sudden rank smell of oil.

The faintness of extreme fear swept over her. Then a deep musical voice said softly, questioningly, "Little Rata Flower?"

Katie sprang up, crying incredulously, "Rangi! It's Rangi, Briar! It's all right."

Stiff, dirty and dishevelled, the girls tumbled out of the sheltering hollow. Briar still stood back warily, for this might be a trick. Rangi, for all Katie's trust in him, was a Hauhau.

But he was saying, "Come. It's safe now." And as Briar looked at him she suddenly saw the green *tiki* hanging round his neck. Automatically her fingers went to her own hidden beneath her dress, and as she wondered if once more the strange little god had brought her luck, she raised her

252

eyes and saw a tall figure beneath the trees on the other side of the clearing.

She stared. She must be dreaming. It couldn't be Saul! Then he stepped out into the light and she saw that it was.

"Saul!" she cried. Miraculously her stiff tired limbs came to life. Picking up her draggled skirts she flew towards him. She saw that his arms were held out, and she hurled herself into them, feeling herself crushed against his hard chest, and dizzy with the exquisite pain.

His cheek was against hers. There seemed to be dampness on it. Or was it her own tears? Neither of them spoke. Words were unnecessary and impossible. But life had come flaming back into her, and when Saul suddenly swung her light body into his arms she buried her face against his shoulder, knowing that this was where she had always longed to be.

Reality had to be faced. Riding on the front of Saul's horse out of the forest, Briar said bleakly, "Your mother is dead, Saul. At least she must be because she was in the house when it was set on fire."

"Yes, I know she's dead."

"She saved my life, and Katie's. She made us escape. She fired until she had once one shot left, and she promised that would be for herself." Her small dry voice made the recital almost prosaic. "She was very brave."

Saul was silent a few moments. Then he said quietly, "She was dying, anyway. MacTavish told me that just now. He gave her only a few weeks. So let her have her moment of glory. She'd have liked it that way. After all, she had to come to admire you very much."

Briar's head shot up. "Me!"

"Yes. She told me not so long ago, just when I was ready to agree with her that I'd made a fearful mistake in marrying you. When we really thought we hated each other. But my mother admired your spirit and the way you stood by your friends. She said you were the woman to have my children, if ever I could persuade you to."

"And—what did you say?" Briar's voice was almost inaudible.

"I said if I could only persuade you to love me, I'd be happy."

They had emerged from the forest, and Saul abruptly drew rein. Briar realised that he had stopped deliberately to look down over the smoking ruins of the house. The harshness had come back into his voice.

"But you married me for a fine house, didn't you? Now I have none. So what about it?"

"We'll build another. There's plenty of time."

"In the meantime you'll be content to live in a tiny cottage like Jemima's?" he asked sceptically.

Briar rubbed her dirty weary face. She knew he would not believe her, but it was true that she did not mind having no possessions. She had been born to it, it was nothing new to her, and now at last she could accept the fact. Also, she had been wrong in thinking that this fertile, exciting country was hers. For it was going to belong truly only to those bred in it. And that was the heritage that she, the waif and stray, who had travelled so far with such high ambitions, was going to be able to give her son.

The knowledge was strange and wonderful.

"I don't mind if our baby is born in a cottage," she said dreamily, then, as Saul's arm tightened round her in an imprisoning grip, she realised that he did not yet know this news. She looked up into his face, seeing in it all her future.

"It's true, Saul. We are to have a baby." Secretly she hoped the child would inherit that proud arrogant look. "I told your mother this morning, just before—" her voice trembled. "I'm so glad I told her. Though one can't know whether it matters to her now."

"It will matter," said Saul.

"And you?"

"If you are happy about it, so am I."

She met the dazzling tenderness in his eyes. She had never heard humility in his voice before.

But her composure deserted her when they reached the village and she saw the little cluster of people waiting for them.

"Here's Briar!" she heard voices calling thankfully. "Here's Briar safe."

The words were an echo out of her lonely, day-dreaming past. She had never thought to hear them really spoken with such love and gratitude. And there were the familiar faces lifted to her, Jemima's, Prudence's, the wide-eyed children's, Martha Peabody's. The faces of her friends. She slipped off Saul's horse to be gathered into their arms.

Later that evening, tucked up with heart-warming care, in

Martha Peabody's own bed, the nightmare part of the day receded from Briar's mind, and she began to think practically once more.

She asked that Saul should come in, partly because she wanted to discuss matters with him, but more because the sight of his lean, hard body filled her with such wild, secret delight that she could not bear him out of her sight—though this she had no intention of letting him know at the moment, or there would be no conversation at all.

"Sit down, my love. There are things to discuss."

Saul raised his brows slightly at her imperiousness, but sat down meekly enough.

"First, a home and work must be found for Mabel while our new house is being built. She fought very bravely for us this morning, and she tells me she only escaped by hiding in one of the dog kennels which, I gather, left her rather bruised. Not being the shape entirely suited to dog kennels." Briar repressed a small giggle. "And also she lost both of her dresses, which we must replace as soon as possible because they seem to represent her status in life. And then there's Katie. I think now Rangi's such a reformed character he'll probably marry her in a church, but if he doesn't we must protect her and her baby. That's important. I've promised her."

"I'm not arguing it, my love."

"Then why are you scowling?"

"Because you sound remarkably like Aunt Charity."

Briar sat up indignantly. Then she realised that he was laughing, and reluctantly her lips twitched, for it was the first time they had ever laughed together.

"You do not still wish to send me back to Wellington?" she asked involuntarily.

"On the contrary, I shall never trust you out of my sight again."

He observed her incipient tears, and because Martha Peabody's bedroom was not the place to take satisfactory measures about checking them, he went on, with forced calmness, "I picked up mail on the way today."

Briar moved her head indifferently. "There'll be nothing for me. I have no family, you know, and no one to write to me except you. And your letters, my dearest, must improve and show some affection or I shall leave you."

"You're wrong, there is a letter for you."

With childish eagerness she sat up to receive the strange letter. Who could be writing to her?

"Saul!" Her voice was an awed whisper. "It's from Government House. It's addressed to us both."

"I know. Open it."

Briar tore the thick envelope open, and pulled out the gilt-edged invitation card. *Mr. and Mrs. Saul Whitmore are requested* . . .

"Saul! We're invited to curtsey to the Governor and his wife."

Saul looked at her widened eyes. "You can do the curtseying, my love. Allow me merely to bow."

Briar gave a small gurgle of laughter. "Me!" she whispered. "To meet the Governor." Then she lay back with a deep sigh. "But it's really rather unimportant, isn't it? I shall do it only for the sake of our children."